T0356036

EMBER

LAURENCE LIGON
EMBER

A NOVEL

EMBER
A NOVEL

iUniverse books may be ordered through booksellers or by contacting:

iUniverse
1663 Liberty Drive
Bloomington, IN 47403
www.iuniverse.com
844-349-9409

Because of the dynamic nature of the Internet, any web addresses or links contained in this book may have changed since publication and may no longer be valid. The views expressed in this work are solely those of the author and do not necessarily reflect the views of the publisher, and the publisher hereby disclaims any responsibility for them.

Any people depicted in stock imagery provided by Getty Images are models, and such images are being used for illustrative purposes only. Certain stock imagery © Getty Images.

ISBN: 978-1-5320-6941-3 (sc)
ISBN: 978-1-5320-6940-6 (e)

Library of Congress Control Number: 2019906144

Print information available on the last page.

iUniverse rev. date: 11/18/2021

The Atkins Family Tree

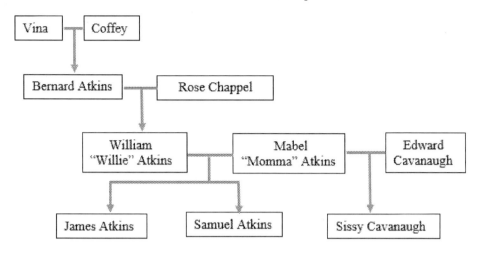

The Knight Family Tree

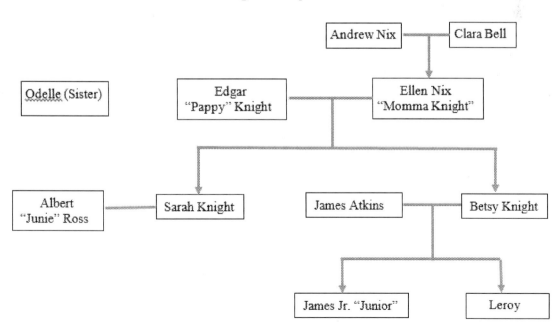

DEDICATION

To my ancestors. I tell their story.

PROLOGUE

Secrets and Lies – Brawley, California 1972

July was a time of torment in the Imperial Valley. The desert heat combined with irrigation made for an unbearable combination of triple-digit temperatures and high humidity. The towns in the valley were eerily quiet during the day when most of the residents stayed indoors. Within an hour or two of sunset, people ventured outside to water their lawns or spend the cooler part of the evening on the patios watching their children play. The fragrance of lemon blossoms and freshly cut grass floated along on a peaceful breeze. As night approached, the quiet returned, except for the random barking dog, or the rustling of leaves and branches.

This night, on a dimly lit street, a man hidden by tall stalks of sweet corn stared across the narrow road at a vacant, wood-framed dwelling. The way ran the length of the long block and dead-ended at a canal bordering the many farms in this unincorporated part of Brawley.

A few moments later, he hurriedly crossed over to the metal gate at the front of the abandoned house. He paused, rechecking the roadway, then continued down a brick pathway that led to the front door. Stapled to that door was a notice with the word "CONDEMNED" in bold letters. He mumbled a few words as he went inside. He took slow and deliberate steps, drawing a deep breath of the thick, musty air.

As the clandestine figure made his way around in the darkness, avoiding the many items strewn about the floor, he grabbed a handful of old newspaper from the floor and twisted it into a long roll. With his outline illuminated by the flicker of a burning match, he turned the paper toward the flame. His hands shook as it caught fire. In the windows, a bright light radiated as the blaze spread quickly.

A short time later, he made his way outside, returning to the field across the road into the shadows and waited. Blood pulsed in the man's neck and wrists as beads of sweat ran down his face. Soon burning embers floated peacefully upward into the night's canopy, resembling a hoard of fireflies.

Inside the house, the fire swept across the floorboards, consuming everything in its path. It spewed a putrid scent of burning plastic, wood, and metal into the air.

As the fire roared higher, the man's heart pumped faster. He retreated from the road when the smoke drifted into the field and burned his eyes. People ran about frantically as he whispered calmly.

"Thine iniquity is taken away."

A fire truck's swirling red lights grew closer. The wailing sirens wound down as if they were out of breath. The man caught glimpses of silhouettes rushing about as the flashing light emblazoned random pockets of darkness. The man watched for a moment longer, his hands shaking nervously. He then moved even further from the road as it filled with curious onlookers.

"And thy sin is purged."

The inner frame of the house collapsed, causing a loud explosion as more panes of glass shattered onto the seared ground in a thundering succession. Thick, blue smoke billowed into large clouds.

The firefighters worked quickly to keep the swiftly spreading blaze away from adjacent homes and the wild brush in the nearby fields. The house that James Atkins built fell mortally wounded. The man paused, glancing back one last time, not realizing that there were eyes upon him as well. He was not alone with his secret.

Five hours later, the raging fire was finally under control. All that remained were smoldering embers and an eerie stillness permeating the air. The morning breeze carried the scent of charred remnants across the whole town.

PART ONE

1925 — 1960

HOMESTEADING

HONDO, TEXAS – 1925

James Atkins was born on a cold, fall day in October 1919 in Hondo, Texas. He was the first-born son of William "Willie" Atkins and his wife, Mabel "Momma" Atkins. When the census taker came by their farm, he marked the column for Race with the letter "M" signifying mulatto. Like her mother, Mabel's skin was the color of wheat, and she had the same moles on her face and neck, passed down the generations. No one spoke of how these attributes got into their blood, but the truth of her pedigree was not a cheerful one. The slavemaster's son raped Mabel's black grandmother when she was only fifteen, and Mabel's mother was born from it.

James grew up fast on his grandfather Bernard's farm after the family moved there in 1925. His parents put him to work as soon as he could carry a sack of seed. James bonded with his grandfather during many days in the hot sun, drinking the cool creek water, and hunting rabbits in the brush beyond their home. Grandpa Bernard and James wandered many trails together.

Bernard's small plot on the western edge of Hondo was not a prime location, but it supported crops and grazing for a few heads of cattle. The soil was a decent sandy loam good for cotton, corn, and okra. A small offshoot of the Medina River ran adjacent to the property and supplied a steady flow for both the field and home.

The family lived in a single-room hut. In a corner, next to Grandpa Bernard's cot, was a bed made from straw and wood planks where the children slept. On the other end was a large stone hearth and wooden pantry with Mabel's spices and dishes.

Against the opposite wall was Willie and Mabel's bed. It, too, was made from straw. The many windows in the home allowed fresh, cooling breezes to flow. A side door led to a small pen that sheltered the mules and hogs.

As a young man, Bernard worked many odd jobs to provide for his family. One was treating sick animals, though he had no formal training. He had what he called "the spirits" and told his Grandson James that the animals spoke to him.

"What's that bull saying, Grandpa?" James asked one day as they passed the pen.

"Oh, he ain't thinking 'bout nothing but eating, boy," Grandpa Bernard answered.

"How do you know, Grandpa?"

"See how he standing there, shaking his head?"

"Yeah," the boy nodded.

"That's how I know."

Bernard had a keen sense of ailments and remedies he had learned over the years when he worked the Atkins Plantation, just outside of Uvalde, TX. A bloated belly meant the animal ate too much clover and a little turpentine or linseed oil relieved the pressure. The knowledge served him well. He made friends with some of the local ranchers and earned enough money to buy the land he now farmed with his son Willie, Willie's wife Mabel, her daughter Sissy, and two sons – James and Samuel.

Mabel was from Natchez, Mississippi. Her skin was a milky shade of caramel that complemented her deep-set amber-colored eyes. A resourceful woman, she would barter with their Mexican neighbors for peppers and squash with the berries and wild onions they gathered.

Sissy, Mabel's daughter from her first marriage to Edward Cavanaugh, an Irishman, was a tomboyish girl of eleven. She had the same long auburn hair like her mother, but her freckled face was more the color of a pinto bean. Sissy was three years older and several inches taller than James was. She was never without her red scarf, no matter the time of year. A woman at church gave it to her one day for her birthday, saying a young lady needed nice things. Sissy loved how well the color went with her ruddy cheeks. She'd prance around the farm, repeating what the woman told her in the same pitch and tone. That scarf made her feel fancy and beautiful. She wore it so much the ends began to fray.

It didn't matter that Sissy wasn't Willie's child, she was his favorite, and this created quite the rivalry between her and the younger James. She was rough with him most times and bested him at whatever game they played. She was bigger, stronger, and faster, and Sissy let him know it every chance she got, teasing him for giving up the chase or outrunning him even when he had a sizable head start.

Samuel was Willie and Mabel's second son, born two years after James. He shared some of his mother's mixed parentage – the light-colored eyes and hair. Samuel had a calm demeanor and was not as rambunctious as his older brother. He enjoyed being around his mother and half-sister. He was always willing to help around the farm, but there wasn't much for a six-year-old to do.

One morning, Grandpa Bernard and Willie set out to clear the land of the briar patches and grasses. In some places, mesquite and prickly pear trees formed a thicket that the men had to cut through with axes and machetes. Grandpa set controlled fires around the property, burning the chopped bushes and shrubs. He used a small can of oil to set the blaze, saving the tall, fountain grass for last. Bernard loved the sound the wind made as it blew through the grass. The thick, top blades braiding against each other sounded like maracas.

A blue haze rose into the sky as James and Samuel played not far from Grandpa's fire line. The bright, orange tinder crackled through the bush, and a breeze caught the smoke, pushing it back toward the children. The sweet, peppery-scented plumes burned their eyes and nostrils.

"Grandpa said you best get away from around there," Sissy called as the fire approached. She stood a few feet away with a machete in hand, her armpits sweaty with perspiration. Grandpa Bernard had her pruning back some weeds.

"I ain't gotta listen to you," James shouted back at her. It angered him that Grandpa wouldn't let him do this work. Bernard told him he was too small to handle the ax. Sissy laughed at him, throwing more salt on his hurt feelings. She then stepped closer, towering over him, but James stood his ground.

"You better do as I say." She bumped him with her chest.

"Ain't gonna," he replied, returning a shoulder bump of his own.

She dropped the machete and grabbed his shirt with both hands, then pushed him to the ground. Samuel stood by, silently watching. He was rarely the target of these incidents, but he often tired of their battles.

"Stop all that!" Grandpa yelled, his hulking figure appearing through the haze.

He yanked down the handkerchief he had tied over his nose and mouth. "Sissy, go on and help your momma with supper. And you boys get away from that fire!"

Sissy turned on one foot and walked away in a huff as Grandpa Bernard covered his face again and disappeared back into the smoke.

The family worked all day, and as dusk approached, the sky shimmered with touches of red and yellow at the edge of the western horizon. A few clouds captured the last rays of sunshine. The still-burning coals hissed and crackled as Willie added some more shrubs and chopped limbs. To James, they looked like eyes. He watched in amazement as his father ran his hand slowly through the flames.

"Magic," Willie smiled at the boys; their eyes were wide with bewilderment.

"Daddy, ain't you scared of gettin' burned?" James asked.

"Iffin, you know the magic, you won't get nair a burn," he said, running his hand back and forth through the flames.

James crept closer to the fire and mimicked his father while Samuel watched.

"That's it. You got the magic too." Willie grinned as James moved his hand through the flame, barely feeling the heat on his palm.

Samuel finally gathered up enough courage, but only poked his finger in and out, giggling, but James was mesmerized. He ran both hands across the fire, making circles and semi-circles above it as the flames flickered, burning blue and orange.

"Supper's ready. James, Samuel. Come on now!" Mabel called from the shack.

Samuel and his father brushed off their hands. Their clothes smelled of smoke, as they started home.

"Come on, boy. Time for supper," Willie called to James, who was still staring intensely into the embers.

James stepped back from the diminishing fire, but not before it spat one last time, startling him. He looked into the pit of smoldering remains and whispered, "I'm not afraid of you." He then ran off toward home.

Sissy stood by the door; arms folded when he got there. James tried to walk past her, but she leaned into him with her shoulder, pinning him against the frame.

"That's for talking back to me earlier," she scolded.

James tried to push past her, but she wouldn't budge.

"Momma! Sissy won't let me pass!"

She then punched him hard in the chest, laughing out loud as she ran away. James thought better of giving chase.

After dinner, Willie ate the last piece of the pie that Sissy made from berries she and her brothers had gathered from a tree near the stream while the children played a game of Miss-Mary-Mac. Mabel enjoyed the laughter. Their voices warmed her heart. For all the animosity between Sissy and James and the hardships on the farm, they had more moments of togetherness and family that they wouldn't trade for anything.

Before coming to Texas, Grandpa Bernard was the property of Colonel Lewis Wilson, who owned a plantation near Chinquapin, Mississippi, a small hamlet, not far from the Pearl River. Though the colonel was not an overly cruel man, his overseers did most of the disciplining; he gambled and did so poorly. A year before the start of the Civil War, when Bernard was just a boy of maybe six or seven years old, his life changed forever. On a muggy night, there came a pounding on the door of his family's hovel. They stumbled outside half-dressed in a frightened, sleepy confusion, clutching at their clothes and each other. The colonel stood outside, surrounded by several men.

"Well, go on," the colonel shouted angrily. "Let's settle this quickly."

The family stared at each other in terror. They had no idea what the colonel had laid upon them.

When Bernard's mother, Vina, realized what was happening, she screamed and clung to the children. She relived the horror of the auction block in New Orleans, where each of her siblings was sold off one by one.

"Please, no….no!" she sobbed.

One of the men, dressed in a dark evening jacket and trousers, walked back and forth, boldly inspecting them from top to bottom while ignoring their pleas.

"What about the wench?" he asked his partner.

"No. I need a strong back."

At that, he walked to Bernard and tapped him on the shoulder. Vina turned her face into her husband's chest, unable to look on.

"Step forward," the man commanded. The child complied though his eyes were wild with fear.

He grabbed the boy's face and stuck his thumb into his mouth to examine his teeth.

"Don't you dare bite me!" he warned when Bernard clenched his jaw. "I'll whip you good."

Bernard relaxed, allowing him to touch his teeth and tongue. The man then grabbed Bernard's arms and shoulders and squeezed them.

He then turned to the colonel and announced, "He'll do."

Vina screamed. "Not my baby! Please, Massa Wilson. Please!" She begged the colonel, falling to her knees.

The colonel paid her no heed. "Be gone." He waved the men away.

The young Bernard walked with them into the night until he was out of sight. Vina cried until she had no tears left. She cursed herself for having children. Futility replaced the tiny bit of happiness Vina had mustered on the plantation. Here, she could at least offer her son a small measure of protection and love. Now Bernard would have to bear the pain and cruelties all by himself.

Bernard's father, Coffey, fell into a deep depression after that night. An excellent worker, he languished in the fields, unmoved by the overseers' whip. The events of that night ate away at the colonel's heart. He realized the humiliation Coffey must have experienced and attempted to broker a peace when he came upon him one day, peeling husks from corn.

"How's that barley coming?" The colonel asked warmly.

"Fair sir," he answered, not looking up at him.

"Should fetch a good price at market."

"I reckon so," Coffey replied in a weary voice, tossing another ear into the tub. The colonel lit his pipe, and seeing that forgiveness was not at hand, took a few puffs before moving on.

Bernard's new masters took him to Medina County, Texas, where he endured the lash and the life of a slave for nine more years. He became accustomed to the sound of cracking whip. It startled him when he first arrived in Texas. Master

Wilson's people rarely set it to use, but not here in Medina County. The punishment was given freely, and his overseers were generous men. His new family told him to forget his people in Mississippi as if that life never existed. They were only trying to protect him, and they had no idea a war would break out among the states from which they'd all gain freedom. At the end of the great conflict, Bernard made an effort to find his real family.

But a hopeful reunion was not to be. Colonel Wilson had died a few years after that fateful night. His heirs sold their interest in the plantation, scattering Bernard's people to the wind. Bernard had to swallow that awful bitterness.

In 1874, he married Rose Chapel, a local girl. He was a young man of maybe nineteen or twenty at the time, and his bride was only sixteen. He and Rose had seven children before a cholera outbreak took their lives. He watched them die one by one, including his wife. Only his eldest son, William, survived. With what remained of his family, Bernard moved up the road to Hondo.

Hondo was much like many small, cattle towns in Texas. Most people had lived in these parts for generations. Bernard remembered riding into town on the back of his master's wagon and seeing this little corner of land covered with brush and briar patches. No one seemed to want this ground, and it wasn't far from a Negro cemetery where Bernard had buried his mother and father. Not his blood parents, but the ones who looked after him when he came to Texas as a young boy. Bernard had paced out their graves from an old tree and laid some stones to mark their final resting places.

When Bernard had saved enough money, he purchased twenty acres from a local rancher. He looked out upon this corner of earth and smiled. They'd have to clear it of the Mesquite trees, fountain grass, and cactus, but it was his. Bernard had more than his father could ever have imagined; he had his freedom, some land, and a stake in his destiny. Bernard was born into slavery, and never imagined a time when he'd be a free man, never mind owning land. That was too big a wish. He had memories of chasing butterflies and climbing trees growing up. But he also remembered the master's lash on his flesh, the pain, and the hurt of separation.

Now twenty years later, while working the mule team, Bernard took his shirt off and poured water on top of his head to cool off. It was a scorching hot day, and his grandsons sat under a shady tree and watched. They waved to him as he strapped his arms through the reins and passed them. It was then James saw the twisted flesh on his grandpa's back.

"What happened to you, Grandpa?" he asked, pointing to the disfigured skin.

He chuckled. "You know why I call them white boys crackers?"

"No."

"Cuz of how hard they crack that whip."

"A cracker whipped you, Grandpa?" James asked, frowning.

"Sho did, boy. For spilling some turpentine. Whipped the skin right off my bones. My momma saved my life. She knew how to treat them wounds, or your grandpa wouldn't be here. And neither would you." He smiled at him but turned suddenly serious. "That's why you don't mess with none of them white folks. They are the meanest, angriest people I know."

EXODUS – GEORGIA, 1925

While James and his family were settling in Texas, Ellen and her husband Edgar Knight had decided to move from Georgia to California. She and Edgar took a three-day train ride west, arriving at the junction in Yuma before settling in Brawley. The stifling oppression of Georgia, where they both grew up, was now the past. The year the couple would leave the South, whites banished black families from the town of Jasper in nearby Forsyth County. It seemed the world was closing in around them as violence against the Negro escalated.

Ellen's childhood memories of that part of Georgia were serene and peaceful. Dogwood trees lined the streets where children played. Folks waved to passersby, and people were quick to say hello. However, beyond the manicured hedges and church gatherings was an ugliness that weighed upon their consciousness.

"Look at all these empty pews." Alfred Adams said as he surveyed the nearly unoccupied church. Adams owned a small café in town.

"Henry Evans drove off for Chicago just last week." Added Andrew Nix, Ellen's father.

"Everybody leavin'," Adams continued. "Thomas Jones sold his place too."

"I can't see it being much better up North," Nix interjected.

"Tell that to the folks in Eudora. You hear about ole man Tobias getting lynch?"

"What you say!" Nix shouted.

"Found him strung up along the river there. Both his eyes gouged out."

Andrew stood, his mouth agape. "Lord, have mercy."

The news was more terrible than Adams shared. When they found Tobias, pieces of his body had been cut away–hands, feet, and sections of skin. All of them taken as ghastly souvenirs. And worse yet, no one had seen or heard from his wife and young children for several days. Everyone assumed the worst.

Andrew could not comprehend the depravity in white people's souls to commit such heinous acts. Not even the life of an unborn was sacred as he heard of a few murdered pregnant women. Andrew was not one to drink, but he came home with the smell of alcohol on his breath after hearing this tragic news. Ellen's mother, Clara Bell was upset at his late arrival. She had sat by the window for hours waiting for him.

"I was worried about you."

"I'm fine," he snapped as he closed the door.

"What's gotten into you? Is that liquor on your breath?"

"Leave me be woman!" Andrew yelled. It shocked Ellen and her younger sister Odelle, to hear him speak to their mother this way. The girls knew their father as a gentle, hardworking man. That night, his anger came out to his family stronger than the anguish and hopelessness he felt.

It seemed no matter how the Negroes bent, gave, acquiesced, appeased, or avoided white people, they were continuously subjected to their violent whims. Ellen could not comprehend such hatred. Most white people she knew were polite and friendly, but she wondered if one of them would someday want to lynch her, too.

The impact of the seething hatred in the South revealed itself in the many Sunday sermons devoted to staying strong and finding faith in the Lord. Worry took over their thoughts each time a loved one left home for the smallest of errands. But it was not only Jim Crow that Ellen wanted to escape. She did not want the same life as her mother and grandmother. Though times were good and they had all that they needed--a nice home, friends, love, and clean clothes, Ellen longed to make her way and not only be known as one of Mr. Nix's girls. She did not want to raise other people's children and clean their homes.

Ellen and Edgar were high school sweethearts. He was a man of few words with soft eyes, a thin mustache, and smooth, sepia-colored skin. Edgar was the kind of person everyone wanted to have as a friend. He planned to set up his law practice in Atlanta but got work as a technician while studying for the state bar exam. Ellen would joke that he would become the fifth black lawyer in the whole state if he passed.

Edgar was good with machinery. It seemed to be in his blood, but he struggled to reconcile his fear of white people and his place in the world. He had few problems with the folks in town, and he often wondered if it had something to do with his light complexion and Native features. His great-grandfather was a Creek Indian, and Edgar had his high cheekbones and straight black hair. He didn't particularly threaten white men, but Edgar still feared they'd turn against him as they did their black neighbors across the South. It bothered him that so many Negroes owed their very existence to the generosity of white men. Coming out to California did not calm those fears. He worried more about his family still in Georgia.

The couple decided to move to California after Ellen read about the Imperial Valley and the desert oasis created by the Colorado River. Jobs were plentiful, especially after the railroad was extended from Yuma, Arizona, up the steep mountain grade to San Diego. The bustling city of Mexicali, Mexico, was on the other side of the border. Ellen was hooked, but it took some convincing to get her family to see it her way. Most of their friends and neighbors had left, boarding trains to northbound cities like Baltimore and Philadelphia. The idea of loved ones living so far away did not appeal to her parents, but the real issue was people were leaving. Congregations shrank, pews emptied, and homes went up for sale. The exodus had begun, and it was time for them to leave. For many, it was not a matter of pride but a necessity.

"I see you crying." Her mother, Clara Bell, asked her one day. She found Ellen staring at the hickory tree in the neighbor's yard in the days leading up to their departure. "Don't wipe them away now."

Ellen turned to her mother; her face still wet with tears. "Momma, I never said this was easy."

"I don't blame you for wanting to go. It's a big world out there. I want you to be protected and happy."

"I want that too. I am not looking to change the world, just the view from my front window."

Her mother nodded. "I wish you could do that here and not out in California."

"Me too, Momma. Me too." Ellen was tough, but deep down, the bigotry cut at her, and she fought hard not to become bitter and spiteful. Leaving was, to her, a matter of survival.

The day they departed arrived faster than she wanted. The couple went to the train station with family in tow, bags neatly packed, and tickets in hand. Ellen hugged everyone who had come to see them off. As she turned back to give one final wave goodbye, she noticed a tear falling from her daddy's face, and her heart sank. Ellen did not desire to hurt anyone, especially not her father. She wanted her family to be happy for them, but seeing her father's tears changed all that. Suddenly, she felt it might not be so awful being known around town as Andrew Nix's daughter.

"I love you, Daddy," she cried, her hands trembling as she hugged him.

"I love you too, baby," he replied, his voice cracking. "Come on now. The train's about to leave."

She held his thick, calloused hands, squeezing them once more. Edgar helped her up the steps, and they took seats in the colored car next to the window. As the train pulled away, Ellen wondered if she would ever see her home again.

The changes to the geography were stark over the three-day train ride. The forests and swamplands gave way to the barren deserts in the Southwest. At the rail hub in Yuma, some fifty or so miles from Brawley and their new life, Edgar looked out on the parched landscape and imagined that a trick had been played on them. Dust and sand stretched as far as the eye could see with a few spots of green brush.

"Sure is empty out here," he quipped, surveying the vast stretches of desolate land.

Ellen shrugged. "Not as empty as Georgia."

To which Edgar replied. "I hope that oasis you read about is close by."

"Don't you worry about that, none, my dear." She laughed, planting a kiss on his cheek. "Paradise doesn't always come with a fancy bow."

In the desert wilderness-turned-Eden, Swiss and Germans mingled with East Indians and Mexicans. Filipinos and Japanese worked with Italians, putting their sweat into the earth, and so did Edgar and Ellen.

The couple started out working in the many fields around the valley, packing onions, peas, and string beans. It was hard, backbreaking work, but it put food on the table and a roof over their heads.

A few months later, Edgar got a steady job at Rodger's cotton gin, first repairing the machinery, but the owner recognized his smarts and put him to work as an assistant manager. He did most of the administrative tasks— proofreading documents and filing taxes. Edgar put his degree to good use. Soon people asked him legal advice after they found out he'd gone to law school, and Ellen kept house for a wealthy woman in town.

She saved the money she made, and with Edgar's earnings, they bought two parcels of land where they built their first home. Here, they settled into their new life far away from the pain of Georgia.

The couple welcomed their first child, Sarah, not long after they arrived. Another daughter, Betsy, was born three years later in 1928. Momma Knight, as Ellen was affectionately called, maintained the household and family while Sarah and Betsy worked with their father in the yard and did chores that some believed were man's work. It was Sarah who nicknamed her father "Pappy," and the name stuck.

Momma Knight planted roses in the front yard next to the trellises filled with morning glories. Along the opposite fence-line was her pride and joy—a grapevine sapling given to her by one of the local farmers after the second year the Knights boxed grapes in Coachella. She doted over that vine almost as much as she did her family, nursing it until the roots were strong enough to take hold in the ground. Ellen monitored it daily as it sprouted from the earth, winding its way up and around the stakes Pappy had set. She told her children that the vine was like her third child, needing so much attention, only to wander off on its own. The fruit it bore would be as sweet as the love they put into it. Just like a child, she'd say.

Ellen spent much of her free time out in her garden, tending the plants as well as her girls. She worried about them not having much in the way of kin, but they seemed well adjusted to life in a small town. She wholeheartedly believed they were safer here than in the South.

Firstborn Sarah was a wild seed with a razor-sharp wit that often got her into trouble, and her cinnamon-colored hair, hazel eyes, heart-shaped face, and high cheekbones, made her stand out even more. "You got your grandmother's tongue, child." Momma Knight would say. It was not a compliment, but she admired her spunk. She gave Sarah more leeway to do things on her own.

Momma Knight had had a relatively smooth pregnancy with Sarah, but Betsy was another story. Elna, a woman known about the town as a granny-woman or midwife, told her she'd have a difficult birth. Elna was not a trained nurse, but a practitioner of handed-down remedies and rituals in the healing ways, which some said was black magic. Momma Knight was not much for superstitions, but the old woman's prophesy struck a nerve.

One evening, after being on her feet most of the day, Momma Knight collapsed while working in the garden. Being that it was a typically hot summer, Pappy attributed her symptoms to the heat. He started to worry when she became bedridden for a week and lost consciousness a few times. Pappy was a bundle of nerves, and when Momma Knight's water broke, he summoned the midwife.

Elna arrived a short time later and asked for a small tub of hot water and towels, that Pappy supplied her. She then began to chant softly, calling upon the spirits for guidance. Elna transfixed the young Sarah. She watched closely as the midwife gathered up what she needed from her satchel, including a small iron hook, in case the baby died in the birth canal.

"Don't be afraid, child. Everything's gonna be all right," Elna whispered to Sarah. She then prepared some blackberry tea and had Momma Knight sip it slowly. After nine hours of labor, the delivery came, but Elna realized the baby was breached.

"Mr. Knight!" Elna yelled. "I need you in here."

"Yes, ma'am," he answered, hurrying to her bedside. He looked over at Ellen, his eyes drifting down to the little brown toes protruding from between her legs.

"Set these pillows under her bottom there."

Pappy took a deep breath and did as he was instructed.

"Okay, Mrs. Knight, I need you to push but not too hard," she instructed, holding Ellen's hand gently.

Momma Knight nodded; her face twisted in pain. The midwife let the baby dangle, half-born, for a few moments, and without much effort, the child slowly eased from her mother's womb. Momma Knight struggled to lift her head to see the newborn.

"She ain't breathing!" Elna yelled as she turned the baby over and rubbed her back.

"Oh, Lord..." Momma Knight cried. She feared for the worst every second the child was in distress.

"It's okay, Momma," Pappy offered, but it did little to calm her nerves.

Elna continued to rub her back, chanting rhythmically, her eyes shut tight. Suddenly, there was a little cough, then a gasp.

Elna sighed. "Your daughter's gonna be fine."

Momma Knight fell back to the bed exhausted, her face covered in sweat and tears. The child's breathing was shallow and quick, but she started to cry and squirmed a bit in the midwife's arms. Elna wrapped her up in her petticoat for good luck, then handed the little bundle over to Momma Knight.

"Let me see my baby," Momma Knight gently caressed her head.

Although Betsy's birth was tumultuous, her childhood was marked more by her quiet ways and wandering mind. She lived in her head, brooding and lost in her yearnings, quite the opposite of her boisterous, older sister. She would sit in the tall grass along the canal banks near her home and daydream. She saw herself traveling to places in the stories her father read to her.

Betsy longed to dress in beautiful clothes, fashionable shoes, and to live in some exotic place, none of which she believed was out of her reach. Momma Knight laughed when Betsy told her about her "pie-in-the-sky" ideas. The midwife was only half-right, as Betsy's birth was only the beginning of her difficulties. Momma Knight worried about her children growing up in such a violent world. She feared what kind of people they would encounter once they ventured beyond the tranquil streets of Brawley.

NO RHYME OR REASON – TEXAS 1926

The day Sissy died near the Atkins farm started like any other. That morning Mabel cooked breakfast, and the children did their chores. Storms had passed through the evening before, and Willie had to check on the animals during the night. The next morning, he was out in fields. He could tell from the dark color of the forming clouds and the humid air that another big storm was coming. It rained again at midday, and lightning forced him indoors. In that short period, five to six inches of rain had fallen. It rose so fast that Willie had to abandon the plow for the day and board the oxen. Grandpa Bernard told him as much before he went out. Mabel placed rags in the doorway of the shanty to keep the water out of her kitchen as Willie came up the path.

"Get out them muddy shoes before you come inside!" she shouted.

"It's comin' down!" he remarked. "Where the children?"

"Sissy want to make a pie, so they went down by the creek to pick berries."

"How long ago was that?"

"They should be coming home 'bout now."

"I'mma go fetch 'em," he replied. "Ain't safe."

Willie stayed close to the brush on the muddy trail to keep from slipping. He was halfway to the creek when he heard his boys wailing.

"Where y'all?" he called to them.

"Daddy!" James cried as he and Samuel stepped around the bush. They were shivering and scared.

"Where's Sissy?" He asked over the howling wind, as lightning crackled across the sky.

"Sissy…. Sissy," Samuel stammered.

"Sissy gone!" James screamed.

"Where she go, boy? You not making no sense."

James pointed towards the creek.

He did not wait for an answer; instead, Willie pushed past them, screaming Sissy's name.

When he got to the creek's edge, it was a raging torrent. The ordinarily serene flow was now a surging rapid six to seven feet high. Willie ran along the flooded bank calling for Sissy. Downstream a bit, he found her favorite red scarf caught on a branch. Sissy could not swim, much less navigate the swift current.

He saw where someone had dug into the mud. He prayed Sissy grabbed hold of something. Willie ran for another mile calling for the girl until the pain in his throat and chest became intolerable.

Mabel and Grandpa Bernard joined the search after the boys wandered home weeping and told them what had happened. Mabel directed them to wait there until they came back. The rain continued to fall in sheets, blinding them as they searched. As Willie walked back home he encountered Mabel and Bernard. Mabel rested on a tree stump, her head propped up with one hand covering her eyes. Willie glanced at them, not saying a word, but the forlorn look on his face did not lift their spirits. Bernard held out his hand to her and lifted her up. They returned home at dusk defeated, unable to eat or sleep knowing Sissy was still out in the storm. Mabel wept the rest of the night, and with each rumble of thunder outside, she let out a desperate cry, praying for Jesus to protect her little girl.

The next day the family and some neighbors set out searching again. Through their tears, the boys continued calling Sissy's name as they walked along the muddy path. Hope began to fade as they returned home exhausted, the sun descending into the western horizon.

Not long after, Grandpa Bernard spotted a wagon making its way down the road toward them. He squinted hard to make out who was driving the mule team.

"Someone coming," he said, pointing up the ridge.

As the man rounded the road to their gate and they saw a white blanket on the bed of the wagon.

"You Atkins?" The man muttered, his thick, gray mustache shaking with every word. His eyes were bloodshot.

"Yes, sir," Willie answered cautiously.

"I'm sorry," he replied, stepping down from the wagon.

"What you got to be sorry for, sir?"

The man didn't answer. His hands trembled as he pulled back the blanket slowly. There was Sissy, arms at her sides, her lips blue and cracked; her flowered dress muddy and torn around the thigh.

Mabel covered her face with her hands as she saw her child's lifeless body.

"No, Lord. No!" Mabel wailed, her legs nearly buckling.

"I pulled her from the creek this afternoon. My daughter told me you might be her people," the man imparted.

Willie paused for a moment, "Thank you for bringing her home."

Grandpa Bernard looked at the child and shook his head several times. "I'll be back," he uttered, staring up at the trees that lined the road. He then walked toward the highway. The pain in his heart was too much for him to show.

Willie carefully lifted Sissy's body off the wagon, holding her tight to his body as he walked into the house. Without saying another word, the man tugged at the reins and rode away.

As Willie sat by the fire with the rest of the family, memories of his baby sister Annie flooded his mind. He rubbed his brow and closed his eyes for a moment, picturing the long pigtails she had in her hair. She was only eight when cholera took her and his mother, brothers, and other sisters. He and his father had been away buying cattle, and illness spared them from a horrible death.

Her dying was the hardest for him to bear. She was the last to go. His heart filled with anger when he remembered watching her slip away. She felt so tiny and helpless as she lay in his arms moments from death. Her face wrought with fear and confusion as she struggled to breathe. He had never felt so helpless until now. He stared into her languid eyes as she took her last breath. At least he was there when she died. She wasn't alone, he reasoned.

"James, why? Why didn't you get help?" Willie asked.

"We were coming to get you, Daddy," he answered.

"You telling me the two of you couldn't pull her out that water?"

"We tried." Samuel sobbed.

"Didn't try hard enough!" Willie shouted.

"That's enough, Willie. What more you want them boys to do?" Grandpa Bernard asked.

"More than what they did is all."

It was a bright, clear day when Sissy was buried. There was no hint of the angry storm that had swept her away as friends and family gathered in the yard for her funeral. They laid her in a pine box, her red scarf neatly tied around her neck. Her brothers put a small sack filled with berries in her hand before the pallbearers lowered her coffin into the ground. Willie tried his best to console his wife, but grief overcame her, and she crumbled in his arms.

Samuel placed stones on her grave after Willie shoveled the last bit of earth over her casket. Everyone wept aloud—men, women, and children—except Grandpa Bernard. He stood by, stiff and stoic, without allowing his emotions to betray him. He held James' hand as they walked to the grave and placed some flowers down. As they stood there, James choked up.

"I tried Grandpa. I tried to save her," he agonized, wrapping his arms around Bernard's waist.

"Quit all that fussin'. Life ain't fair, boy. Ain't fair to no one!" he almost shouted. "We all gonna go someday. Now wipe them tears out yo' eyes and stand here like a man."

It hurt James' heart to hear his Grandpa say those things, but he did what was asked of him.

"Ain't no rhyme or reason to this life," Grandpa Bernard continued as Willie fashioned two thin, metal bars into a cross. "Good people dying young, bad people living on. Set your mind on that right now. No rhyme or reason. No, sir."

Willie hammered the cross into the ground. He then looked up to the sky before speaking to the small crowd circled around him. "Lord, it's not for me to question your plan for Sissy, for all of us, but you've taken my only daughter and put a world of hurt in our hearts. I want to believe in heaven. I want to believe I will see her again. Until then, please take good care of my baby."

The last mourner left the homestead as the sun dropped over a row of large trees that ran along the road to the Atkins home. The family sat silently around the table, surrounded by an abundance of food from the repast. There were pies, a roast, and greens, most of it went untouched. No one could think of food when the pain in their hearts overwhelmed any other desire or need.

"Sissy gonna come walking through the door with her big smile, I just know it," Mabel confided, looking at Willie, her eyes filled with tears.

"I want that more than anything, Mabel." He wrapped his arms around her tightly.

"I don't want her buried out there alone." She struggled to get the words out. "When my time comes, I want to be buried next to her. You hear me?"

"Yes, Mabel." He answered. "Same goes for me."

One late night in the weeks that followed Sissy's death, Willie sat alone on a small wooden bench outside the home. He took several deep swigs from a jug of sour mash he'd been drinking that day. The alcohol flowed through his veins, and with each shot, he felt another part of him go numb, but it did little to assuage his hurt.

He staggered to his feet, bracing himself against the wall with one hand and holding the jug with the other, then made his way inside. Willie was angry, had been for several days. He snapped at anyone within shouting distance, and James was his primary target. That morning he'd heard the boy laughing and set in on him.

"What you so happy about?" Willie asked.

"Samuel told me a joke, Pa."

"Look over there," Willie barked, pointing to Sissy's grave. "Happy about that too?"

"No," James mumbled.

"If you'd tried harder, she'd still be here. Smile about that."

Willie now found himself standing over James as he slept. He stared down at him, pausing for a moment. "Should take your ass down to the river and see how you swim," Willie slurred. "You should've tried harder," he continued. "You're her brother…"

"What are you carrying on about?" Grandpa Bernard asked Willie, awakened from his slumber.

"None of your concern, old man," Willie shouted back.

"Then, go to bed!"

"I'mma take this bastard to the creek first."

"And why would you do such a thing?"

"He knew better than to be out in that storm. My little girl is dead because of him. That's right. I said it."

The boys were awake now, lying silently in their bed. Little James covered his head underneath his pillow.

Grandpa Bernard sat up. "Willie, you don't know what the hell you're saying. Put that mash down and get to bed."

"Go to hell, ole man!" he slurred. "Ain't gotta do a damn thing you say."

"What you on about?" Mabel asked, her voice groggy with sleep as she lit a candle near her bedside.

"Both of you shut your damn mouths!" Willie barked.

James turned away from his father, crying into his hands.

"I ain't gonna do no such a thing!" Grandpa Bernard yelled back.

"Stay out of my way Pa," Willie bellowed as he grabbed James' arm. "Come here!" he shouted.

"Papa, please!" James cried. He tried to resist his father, pulling away from him with all his might. Samuel, too, was crying.

"Stop that!" Mabel shouted, but Willie was undeterred.

He yanked James off the bed and to his feet. The boy dug his nails into his father's arms, trying to pry himself from his grip, but Willie was too strong. He twisted his arm and wrenched the boy's shoulder.

"Momma help!" James screamed.

As Willie turned toward the door, Grandpa Bernard stepped from the shadows, shotgun in hand.

"What you gonna do with that?" Willie asked as Grandpa Bernard leveled the gun towards his son.

"You take another step, and I'll blow your goddamn head off," he cautioned, cocking the hammer back.

Willie held his ground, taking another shot from the jug. He smiled at his father, the candlelight dancing off his sweaty brow. He dragged James another step, then released him. James ran into his mother's arms. Willie stared at them and then slowly eased himself into a nearby chair.

"Boy ain't nothing but trouble," Willie grumbled. As his eyes became heavy, he cradled the jug of mash just as he did his baby sister after she passed on. He slept in the same spot and woke the next morning with a monstrous headache and no recollection of the night's events.

Grandpa Bernard told James his father was wrong to say that, but the boy never got an apology from his father.

"We all gonna die someday." He pointed out to his grandson. "And knowing this thing is a curse. See, it was Sissy's time."

Life went on for the Atkins family after Sissy's death. They often passed her grave but did everything they could not relive the pain of that day. It cast a shadow on their happiness.

One morning, while passing the marker, Samuel turned to James. "Sometimes, I can catch the scent of her hair on my pillow," he admitted. "I miss her."

"Yeah," James added, glancing at the cross over her grave. They walked on in silence.

LIFE AFTER DEATH – HONDO, TEXAS

Living in Texas in the early 1930s was difficult. The bottom fell out of the commodity prices, and Bernard almost had to forfeit the farm in the process. All the money they made went to pay taxes and feed for the animals. They only had enough seed to farm a few acres. Everyone had to lend a hand. James and Samuel dropped out of school to help around the farm, and Mabel went down to the highway each day to sell the few valuables they had. The family survived like many others, with luck and prayer.

During the day, the boys strapped themselves to the oxen team and tilled the land, taking turns between plowing and planting. Mabel exchanged some of their harvest with the neighbors for heating oil or beans, whatever the family needed at that time. Their clothes were so worn and ragged that Mabel was afraid to wash them, fearing they'd rip apart at the seams. She spent many days darning socks, anything to save money. They somehow scraped enough together to survive each year.

Amid the Great Depression, Willie's teenaged sons grew strong and sturdy and could now run the plow by themselves. At harvest time, they picked cotton, showing off their cuts and bruises to their hands at dinnertime. They bailed hay and chopped alfalfa with scythes so worn they had to wrap a bandana around where the wooden handles should have been.

James did all he could and more around the farm. He had the animals tended to before anyone had opened a sleepy eye. Whatever his father needed doing, James was quick to volunteer. One day, he came upon his father standing over Sissy's grave. Willie had his head bowed, old cap in hand. James paused for a moment holding the bucket of oats for the mules to eat. Willie caught a glimpse of his son, and their eyes met in the short distance between them. Before James could say or do anything, his father turned away.

Grandpa Bernard was keen on what was going on. Willie's contempt for his eldest son did not go unnoticed.

"Ain't it time you let it go and forgive that boy?"

"What you talkin' 'bout ole man?" Willie asked.

"You know good and damn well what I'm talkin' bout," Bernard snapped. "James is working himself to the bone for you. Don't you see that?"

"Ain't nothing he do gonna bring her back," Willie shouted.

"That's foolish talk. One day you gonna need him. And I ain't talking about running some mule team either!"

Willie shrugged and said no more.

In the passing years, Willie's teenage sons had grown up like weeds, taller than most men had. Samuel was the better looking of the two, or maybe it was his friendly nature drew that people to him. His big smile imparted an easy way about him. James had a bigger frame than Samuel did, and he cut his wavy black hair close on the sides. He was the serious one, the brother people did not fool with, and he was not afraid to take any man on regardless of size or race as two white boys from San Antonio found out when they were passing through town one day.

"Hey Shine, where you off to?" A blond boy called James from the roadside.

James ignored him.

"Boy, don't you hear me talkin' to you?"

James faced them but did not respond.

The boys laughed. "That nigger's hard of hearing!"

"No. I hear fine. Just thinking, you must be from out of town. Most folks around here too embarrassed to drive a piece of junk like you got there."

The boys got out of the truck and began to approach. James calmly laid his sack down.

"Charlie, he ain't afraid," the dark-haired boy stated with a frown.

"He will be after we teach him a lesson," the blond one smirked, slamming his fist into his open palm.

James squared his feet as they came at him. The one named Charlie threw a right cross at James' chin, but he quickly sidestepped it and pushed him to the dirt. Before the other boy could raise his fists, James hit him twice in his face, busting his lip. James then grabbed his shirt and slammed him down on the ground kicking him hard in the ribs. Charlie took one look at his friend writhing in pain and knew he wanted no part of James.

"We're gonna string you up proper when we come back!" He shouted, getting to his feet and backing away.

"I'll be waiting," James taunted.

They jumped in their truck and drove off toward the town of Uvalde. James never saw them again, but when Grandpa Bernard heard about the incident, he was enraged. He'd warned them many times about starting trouble with white folks.

"You old enough to know better," he shouted at James. "And they got the law on their side!"

Bernard stood guard with his shotgun for the next few nights, expecting them to return. James had never seen him so afraid and made a promise to himself that he would stay out of trouble for Grandpa Bernard's sake.

A few months later, a colored man rode up as Samuel happily talked about Joe Louis winning the heavyweight championship while James unstrapped the mule team. The man told them about a local businessman who organized a small league of Negro teams to play baseball on Saturdays. He asked them if they wanted to give it a go.

"We ain't never played," James told the man, squinting out of his right eye.

"Neither have half the boys playing!" The man shouted.

"We don't have anything to practice with neither," Samuel added.

The man shook his head, then opened his trunk and tossed over some old gloves and a ball.

"You think you can catch it if it's thrown to you?"

The boys only shrugged.

Here, let me show you. The man put one of the gloves and had Samuel toss the ball to him. After a few throws, he gave James the glove, and they began to practice among themselves.

"I think we got the hang of this thing!" James laughed.

"Good! Now, you think y'all can get over to practice tomorrow? We gotta game next Saturday."

Samuel nodded, "Yea, we can do that."

The man smiled and got back in his car. "You talk to Charlie Adams when you get there."

The field was not much to look at in terms of aesthetics. Some unsteady hands marked off the lines of the diamond. The groundsmen did their best to get the pitcher's mound to regulation height, but it would have to make due. That first night, a steady stream of locals watched the games, sitting on the trunks of their cars or in folded chairs.

It was early summer in 1938, and Clyde "Shotgun" Edmonds was on the mound for the opposing team, the Del Rio Tornadoes. Shotgun was a big man, six foot three, two hundred and forty pounds, and dark as midnight. He was one hell of a ballplayer, and tonight he was putting on a show. Only one player reached first base on a walk.

"What's got into Shotgun today?" James asked Charlie Adams, their coach, as they sat in the dugout between innings.

Charlie motioned over his right shoulder. There, leaning against the hood of a Plymouth Road King was a white man with gleaming blue eyes and pouty lips locked around a cigarette. He was a slight, soft-looking man, but there was something dangerous about him. He was too calm, the sort of man that was quick to draw a pistol or knife. Any white man not afraid to mingle with black folks was someone to be fearful of in James' book.

"Who is he?"

"There ain't many white folks you gotta concern yo' self with, but that there is one of 'em," Coach Adams answered. "That's Walsh Ney. He out here scouting for his ball team."

"Ney from Castroville?"

"Yep."

The Neys was one of the pioneer families that settled this part of Texas, emigrating from Luxembourg with many of the Alsace French almost a hundred years ago. You couldn't do much in this town before you ran into one of their relatives. After the game was over, Ney walked up to them. His tone was friendly, and he spoke with a slight drawl.

"Shotgun sure gave y'all a run for your money tonight, didn't he boys?"

"He sure did," Coach Adams crowed, stepping forward. The other players had gathered around, shaking their heads and smiling.

"You all did fine, considering."

"Some of them did," Adams declared.

"I have a few positions on a team I'm putting together."

"Well, sir. Got some fine prospects. They need a little work, but …" Coach Adams started.

"I was thinking of James and Sam. It's Sam, right?"

"Samuel, sir. But you can call me Sam," he answered nervously.

"Okay, Sam. You, James, Jasper, and Buckey. Be at Homer's field next Saturday. Four o'clock sharp."

"Yes, sir!" they answered.

As quickly as he appeared, Ney was in his car driving off. Once he was out of sight, the boys hollered as if they had won the World Series.

"I can't wait to tell Grandpa," Samuel announced as they headed home. It was the first time in his seventeen years that he felt like he had accomplished something.

"He don't care about baseball."

"Yeah, but he gonna be proud of us, James. To get a try-out?"

"We gotta make the damn team."

"I'm making the team. Don't know about you," Samuel snickered.

"You so sure of yourself."

"Big brother. I'll get you some tickets to the games if you don't make the team."

"See, that right there is why you won't make it. You got a smart mouth."

"Well, it won't hurt to tell them. Make someone happy in that house. Heck, Daddy ain't smiled once since Sissy died."

James shot him a hard glance.

"Well, it's true," Samuel swallowed hard. No one had mentioned Sissy's name for years around the house. Samuel knew he was picking at an old wound by even bringing it up. James didn't acknowledge the comment, and Samuel was smart enough to leave it alone.

Saturday on Homer's Field, the boys tried out for Ney's lineup and made the cut. Ney was pleased with his recruits and formed a traveling team for tournaments that summer. They were raw but talented. The players would collect their pay after each game. Samuel figured they could make a decent living by doing something they had come to love—playing baseball.

When they broke the news to the family at breakfast the next morning, their father was not pleased. For starters, he feared for their safety traveling around in a still-hostile country. They also needed hands on the farm, and he did not care that Ney paid them a wage or that they might get a note in the local newspaper. Willie looked out of the window to the rows of cotton growing in the field and wondered how they would manage. Cotton picking was hard work, and Grandpa Bernard was up in years; so was Mabel. It was enough that she kept house and made all the meals for the family, now he would have to rely on his elderly family even more. He felt Ney was taking advantage of his boys, and more importantly, endangering his farm and livelihood.

"How the hell you gonna say yes to something without asking me first?" he questioned.

"He only told us last night."

"You didn't answer my question, James."

"What you expect me to say?" James said defiantly.

"That you'd think on it and let him know after you spoke with your family. That's what you should've told 'em."

"He's giving us a chance. We'll make some money too, and it's only for the summer," Samuel added.

Willie trained his ugly glare on Samuel. "Just for the summer? Since when you the boss 'round here? You're only seventeen, and your brother ain't much older than you."

Samuel dropped his spoon onto his plate and shook his head.

"Why you shaking your head? You know something I don't?" Willie wiped his hands on his trousers and pushed his chair back from the table. Everyone present held their breath.

"Who's gonna help me with them twenty-five-pound bags of seed? Y'all not thinking 'bout no one but yourselves," he accused, standing over Samuel.

"Don't talk like that!" Mabel shouted. "These boys have been playing that baseball for a while now. Instead of being proud of what they done, you gonna knock 'em down?"

"Woman, don't raise your voice to me!" Willie glared.

"With the money they make, we can hire on a few hands to help around the farm. Plenty of folks could use a little extra money in their pockets. You can send for your Cousin Billy. I'm sure he'd like a change."

"Now hold on a minute—" Willie stammered.

"I ain't done yet," she spoke over him. "Now, boys. What that man gonna pay you for each game?"

"A dollar ma'am," Samuel beamed with a big, happy smile.

"A dollar? To play some ball? Well, I'll be! I need to get out there!" she laughed.

"Yes, ma'am," James grinned.

"So we can expect two dollars to the house for each game y'all play."

James' smile disappeared as quickly as it came.

Willie chuckled as he sat back down in his chair. "Now, that sounds like a great idea."

"When your first game, James?" Mabel asked.

"This comin' Thursday."

"Yes, we can manage," Willie said, now convinced of his wife's wisdom.

"Anyone want another helpin'?" Momma smiled as she lifted a pan of grits off the stove.

"No," James groaned, staring dejectedly at his plate.

Samuel seemed fine with the idea. It was never about the money. He wanted to show off on the field. But James had plans, maybe buying a car, some new clothes. All that would have to wait.

The Texas Black Spiders debuted that following Thursday night to a good-sized crowd. The team's uniforms were gray with white pinstripes. Their opponent that night was an all-white team from San Antonio nicknamed the Texas Stars. Ney owned that team as well and had big plans for both. If the white boys did well, there was a potential big league contract.

That night Samuel got the start at pitcher and received a loud cheer from a group of young women near the team's dugout as James dusted off his glove and played first base. The Black Spiders played a good game but came up short by a run that evening. Still, Ney was quite pleased with the talent he saw on the field.

Mabel, Willie, and Grandpa Bernard sat in the small living space as the boys came home that night.

"How'd the game go?" Mabel said to Samuel as he came to the door.

"Y'all didn't come out to watch us play?" Samuel replied.

"Grandpa and I did for a bit," she answered, putting her knitting down.

Samuel was disappointed his father had not come to watch their first game.

"What ya think, Momma?" Samuel asked.

"I don't know much about playing ball, but your uniforms looked real nice."

"Those white boys could swing them bats," Grandpa Bernard chortled.

"Funny Grandpa," James whined.

"There are some biscuits on the stove, collards, and beans in the pot," Mabel told them.

As Samuel came back to the table with his plate full of food, Mabel stuck her walking stick out across his waist, blocking him. "You forgettin' something?" she said.

Samuel smiled, reached in his pocket, and pulled out his dollar. James handed his earnings over to Momma's waiting hand as well.

"Now, I shouldn't have to ask y'all no more from here on."

"Yes, Momma," they answered in unison.

James figured that Ney was in it for the money, but wouldn't let that stop him from being the best damn baseball player in Texas. He threw himself into his training twice a day, throwing balls through the opening in an old truck tire or at a scarecrow he'd set up as a batter. Repeatedly, he would cock his arm and throw all his weight behind each pitch as if he were in the game of his life. After that day, James and Samuel focused on baseball, and it would become their way out of Hondo.

The boys worked the farm during the day and set off to practice or played games in the evenings. They set their minds to improve with each outing, and it came to fruition. James pitched a hell of a game after throwing seven good innings the night before, and the team whipped the next four opponents in the coming days.

"You want people to come out and pay to see these games?" Ney asked him one evening after practice.

"Yes, sir, of course," James answered.

"People come out to see good competition, the white man and the colored man in a fair game. The white man can lose a fair game to the Negro."

When James nodded, Ney continued, "But he doesn't want to be shown up. The colored has to know his place. Y'all have to understand that."

James took everything he told him to heart.

Ney laid out several rules when the team got ready to travel up north for games in Oklahoma, Kansas, and Iowa. They were all excited about the chance to play before sizeable crowds, as Ney had promised.

"Ten thousand fans?" Samuel asked. "That's ten times the size of Hondo."

"Yes, it is son," Ney added.

Willie hid his ambivalence from everyone but his wife. She knew he was not happy with the choice their sons had made. He worried, as did Grandpa Bernard, about thirteen young black boys in unfamiliar territory, far from home. Could a couple of white men keep them safe from a mob or crooked sheriffs?

Willie came out to watch their last game before they would leave town. He parked the wagon at the back of the field, and for the first time, he noticed that his children had grown into men. After an inning or two, Willie hitched up the mule team and headed back down the road home. Though he was secretly proud of them, it did little to settle his thoughts. His sons were making a name for themselves, putting their mark on the world. Something he never had the opportunity to do. All he had ever been was another field hand, son of a slave. White people would not know that he was an honest and decent man that he liked hunting rabbits and collecting pebbles. For all his trepidations, Willie did not want to deny his boys that chance to shine in an ugly, unfair world. That's how he saw it, but he had his home, this corner of land, far from town, far from troubles. Now his boys were heading right into the storm.

Another week passed before Willie's sons set out for their first tournament near Dallas, a full day's ride east. Mabel made some cornbread cakes for the long drive. She looked for James to give him the sack and found him outside, throwing rocks at the fence post near the creek.

"What you up to, son?" she asked, walking toward him.

"Just thinking."

"Bout what?"

"Hoping y'all can manage here without us."

Her face turned indignant. "Boy, we managed before you was born. We'll get by now."

"I know you will. Be better if…"

"If Sissy was here?" she finished his sentence.

"Yeah." He looked over to the stream and the place where she had fallen in.

"Well, son, I wish she was here too, but she gone. She gone, James."

"I know Momma!" he cried out, turning away.

"I don't think you do, son." She clutched his arm. "I know you got a crippled heart, James."

"Why you say that, Momma?"

"You won't forgive yourself. It's got to do with Sissy dying, but that wasn't your fault."

"Was my fault, Momma!" he muttered.

His mind replayed the memory as if it happened yesterday. Sissy wore her pink and red-flowered dress. They raced down to the banks of the creek, jockeying as they went. Thundered crackled all around, and the skies were almost black.

"We had a full basket, and the rain was coming down so hard. Samuel begged us to come on home, but I saw them big berries. Big as Daddy's thumb. I wanted you to have them."

"But son—"

"No, Momma." He stopped her cold. "I need you to know what happened." James then let his memory take him back to that painful day.

Samuel yelled at him to hurry as the wind howled and the driving rain pricked them like tiny needles. The rapidly flowing current was rising dangerously close to them. In no time at all, the water rose to James' feet, eroding the banks around him.

"We were laughing, Momma. I rolled my shirt up and started picking them. Then Sissy came over and pushed me away to get to the berries. I got mad and shoved her back." Tears started streaming down his face. "The ground gave way, and the next thing I know, she done fell in."

"Baby, it is not your fault," Mabel pulled him close.

"I tried to save her. I did, Momma. I hear her all the time calling my name. I can't ever get it out of my mind."

Samuel ran along the bank but slipped in the mud and almost tumbled in himself. James had grabbed Samuel's ankles and trousers, pulling him back to safety. He then jumped into the cold, swirling water, but it was too late, she had gone under and out of sight. James was able to grab hold of some bushes on the side of one bank and lift himself out.

"I tried to help her, but she was gone. I'm sorry, Momma! Sissy dead because of me. I killed her."

Mabel grabbed his face with both hands and stared into his eyes. "Don't you ever say that! She in heaven now. What more can you do for her?"

"Nothing, Momma. Nothing."

"That's right. You remember Sissy's smile, baby. Remember the good times. That's how you keep her alive in here." She said, pointing to her heart.

"Why can't Daddy be that way? He still hates me."

"Your father don't hate you, son. He don't know how to place his anger. But you gots to forgive yourself. Forgive yourself," she pleaded.

"I'll try Momma. I'll try," James knew he couldn't keep that promise. As Mabel said, he had a crippled heart.

She opened her arms and held him tightly. Mabel wiped the tears from James' face. "You gonna be alright, son. Believe me?"

James nodded, hugging her once more. The family had gathered outside to see the boys off.

"Listen to Mr. Ney and don't go running off at the mouth. I hear them folks in Oklahoma are a bad bunch," Willie told them, setting their bags down by the door.

"Yes, sir, we will," Samuel agreed.

They waited there for a moment in silence, not knowing what more to say, feeling the weight of leaving the comfort and security that had carried them through their young lives. Willie then shook their hands, gripping them a few seconds longer. It was the best farewell he could muster.

"Strike 'em out, boys!" Grandpa shouted. Momma hugged them each one last time, tears welling up in her eyes, but she never let them see the deep sadness she felt. It was their time. She knew that full well.

James had often dreamed of this moment, of getting off the farm. Now that the day had arrived, his heart began to ache.

By the third game of the trip, the team was on a roll. They beat one of the more experienced teams to capture the tournament title in Oklahoma City. The Black Spiders rode from San Antonio to Dallas to Lawrence, Kansas, then over to Omaha, Nebraska, winning more games along the way. They had been playing together for almost a month and were coming into their own.

Samuel especially had made a big impression. Ney was pleased with his young prospect's pitching and bragged about him to any fan or newspaperman who would listen. It was a part promotion, but also adulation. Samuel had one of the best fastballs he had ever seen, and his curveball was improving all the time. He was getting bolder with his pitching, and it showed in the box score.

After a game in Iowa, a young boy handed Ney a telegram. He read the contents, looked up at the sky, and then over to the bus where thirteen brown faces peered back at him. Ney called James and Samuel off the bus.

"It's your Momma, boys," Ney cautioned when they reached him, his face wrinkled at the brow.

"Momma?" Samuel asked, confused.

"I got this cable here from your father." Ney handed him the folded paper. James opened it carefully and read it.

"Your mother passed away this morning. Funeral's the day after tomorrow."

"What?" Samuel cried and paced in a circle. James tried to settle him down. "How we gonna get back, James?"

"I can put you on a train, but you won't get there till Friday," Ney offered. "I'm sorry, boys. I wish there were more I could do for you."

"We'll be fine, sir," James consoled. They got back on the bus and told the rest of the team about their Momma's passing. Samuel was beside himself, unable to contain his sorrow.

"Why her, James? Why Momma?" he sobbed.

"Ain't no rhyme or reason," James replied, sounding like his grandfather.

The night she died, Mabel had made a tasty stew from a rabbit Willie caught that day. She had a second helping; it was so good. He tried to wake her the next morning after feeding the animals. It was odd because, most times, she was up before him. He called her name a few times before going to shake her. He instantly knew something was wrong when he touched her. She was as stiff as a board. He sat down on the bed, clutching her cold hands, and, after a few moments, he told Grandpa Bernard. Mabel Atkins was laid to rest in a grave next to her daughter.

Her sons arrived home a few days later. The team bus dropped them at the turnoff on the road to their home, and they walked the rest of the way. James took a deep breath before opening the door. Willie was sitting by the fire; his eyes looked worn and tired.

"Hey, Pa," Samuel sniffled.

"How you boys doing?" Willie asked, getting up from his chair.

Samuel opened his billfold and pulled out his money, but Willie waved his hand. "I was going to give this to Momma. I spent two dollars on a nice hat for her to wear to church. She wouldn't mind me spending the money you think?"

"No, son," Willie lamented.

Samuel's hands trembled as he placed the money back in his wallet. Willie looked at James as he came in and set his suitcase on the floor of the shanty. James put his head in his hands, fighting back his emotions. Grandpa Bernard sat down next to him and tapped him on the side.

"I am glad y'all home."

James nodded. "Me too."

For the next three years, the Black Spiders built a strong reputation as a well-oiled team with big hitters, great pitching, and outstanding fielding. Ney raised the pay for his players as other teams tried hard to recruit them, proving he had chosen well, but it was all coming to an end. War was breaking out after the Japanese bombed Pearl Harbor. Grandpa Bernard heard it on the radio while he was in town. Not long after, James was drafted into MacArthur's army, and Samuel volunteered to fight the Nazis.

He was drafted after James had played his best season, becoming the rising star on the team. He was finally growing into his tall frame. At six-foot-two inches, James towered over most people, and his build translated into dominant hitting and pitching. Ney secretly admired James, realizing he was the best player he'd seen in the state of Texas. If the circumstances of his birth had been different, the big leagues would have come beckoning.

"It's just a matter of time, James, before coloreds are in the big leagues. Mark my word," Ney confessed one day after another win.

"Really?" James asked, surprised, "Because I had a dream I was pitching in Yankee Stadium."

Ney laughed. "Why not? A man's gotta have something to hold onto, no matter how improbable."

James looked at him, confused, "What does that mean? Improb? Whatever you said."

"It means…" Ney paused, trying to find a delicate way to explain. "It means when the odds are stacked against you."

"I like that. Improbable huh? You know something, Mr. Ney; I'm used to folks counting me out. I'll take improbable because it ain't half as bad as impossible!"

He shook Ney's hand and boarded his bus. He knew what was in his reach, having read about Jesse Owens breaking more than records in Germany. Owens showed them what a man of color could do when given a chance. Why couldn't

James do the same here? To him, there was not much difference between what the Nazis believed and how white folks in America acted towards the Negro. He had planned to keep sharp by playing winter ball in Mexico, but he quashed that idea. He would be leaving for boot camp in Arizona soon.

THE KNOWING – FEBRUARY 1942

As James prepared to leave for training at Fort Huachuca in the Arizona desert, Grandpa Bernard fell ill. Consumption devastated his body. He had lived a good long life filled with much heartache and happiness, but it would soon be over. The doctor walked through the door and shook his head. Willie dropped his gaze to the floor; then, without a word, he marched to his father's bedside. His sons close behind him.

The family gathered around Grandpa Bernard as he lay on his deathbed. The boys were silent. Grandpa would have scolded them for this display of emotion, but not now. He seemed animated and unafraid, beads of sweat trickling off his brow. He reached out and grabbed Willie's arm, clasping it tightly.

"End of the road, son. I...I cain't run no more."

While Willie struggled to choke back his tears, James took hold of Grandpa Bernard's other hand. Completing the circle, Samuel stood next to him, tears flowing from his eyes.

"I told y'all, one day," Grandpa Bernard pointed out. "One day he gonna call me home. Gonna call you too."

James remembered his grandfather telling him when he was just a boy, that Father Time was unforgiving. Someday they'd all be called home. He called it "the knowing." James struggled to hold in the immense pain rising in his chest. He held it all in just the way his grandfather taught him as a child.

Grandpa's breathing was labored. He struggled to get the words out. "I hope I get to heaven. Be nice to see my Momma and Daddy again."

"You going to heaven, Grandpa," Samuel whispered. "Don't you worry none 'bout that."

Bernard tried hard to smile, but the best he could do was a fevered tremble of his lips when suddenly his body tightened up. He exhaled deeply, his eyes fluttered for a moment, then closed for good, and he was gone.

Willie squeezed his hand. "Goodbye, Papa."

A few months later, James stood near the graves of his mother, sister, and now his grandfather, marked with smooth stones from the creek. He inhaled deeply, trying to capture the scent of the farm, locking it into his memory. Willie was taking his father's passing very hard. James found him many days sitting on the little wooden bench near the kitchen window staring across the field to the horizon.

His father had seemed okay when Samuel left a couple of days prior, but James was worried about him. He appeared older now. Not quite feeble, but indeed not the energetic man he once knew. Willie had the telltale signs of aging - gray at the temples, the blue rings around the irises, and liver spots on his face. He needed a hand up to get out of his rocking chair. Willie was no longer the invincible man James had known as a child. The man so strong he could lift both him and Samuel with one arm. The man who taught him how to shoot a gun and handle a horse and ox. For the first time, he saw his father's frailty and was afraid something would happen to him. He wondered how he would handle being on his own, with only ghosts to keep him company.

The next day James boarded a bus for a two-day ride to Arizona to begin his basic training in the Army.

"Make sure they find you a helmet big enough to fit your head," Willie joked, trying to break the tension. "And come home, son," he implored, clasping James's hand.

"I plan to. You gonna be okay here by yourself?"

"Oh, don't worry 'bout me. I'll be fine."

Before James got on the bus, Ney came walking across the parking lot toward them.

"Mr. Ney, nice of you to see me off."

"I almost missed you," he said, turning to shake Willie's hand. "Mr. Atkins," he greeted him.

Ney handed a red and black shopping bag to James. "I went all the way to San Antonio to get this for you."

"Thank you, Mr. Ney."

"Open it up," he smiled.

James opened the bag, carefully peeled back the paper, and pulled out a Webster's illustrated dictionary. The brown, leather-bound book easily fit in his trouser pocket. James was a little flustered as he held it in his hand.

"You always wanted to know what all the words I used meant. Now you can look 'em up yourself."

"Mr. Ney. I don't know what to say. It's very nice, thank you."

"I figured you'd get all the Bibles you need in the Army!" Ney smiled. "Read it from time to time."

"I'll read it every day."

They shook hands, and a short time later, James was on the short road to San Antonio. From there, he took another bus to Arizona. He settled back in his seat and began thumbing through the pages.

A BAND OF BROTHERS – 1942

Fort Huachuca sat on high ground outside the town of Sierra Vista, not far from the Mexican border. Black cavalrymen had used Huachuca as a base in the last of the Indian Wars. Now it was where Negroes came to train for modern combat.

The blazing hot desert air rocked James back on his heels when he got off the bus. It dried his eyes almost instantly. He loosened his collar and walked into the station house. An Army representative met him there, a no-nonsense, pie-faced white man who mustered up the volunteers and draftees. He put them on a waiting transport to the nearby base.

After a short ride, the buses arrived at the gates of the old fort. There was not much to the place, several rows of aging buildings on both sides of the road serving as barracks, and beyond that, a training ground with obstacles and a testing area for target practice. More hard-looking white men, who opened the gates, met the buses.

Someone growled for the men to form a single line. They then went to the mess hall. After chow, they stood in another line for a physical exam. The army made sure they were fit to fight and die. For most, this was the first time they had been to see a doctor. Afterward, they all lined up for a haircut.

"Why are they cutting our hair so short?" Asked a man in line with James. He was almost as tall as James with skin the color of oatmeal and dark brown eyes. He looked a few years too young to be in the army.

James shrugged. He had no idea what was going on. "Ain't my first haircut."

"Mines too pretty to be laid out all over the floor," the fair-skinned recruit teased.

The men in line burst out laughing, much to the chagrin of the officers around.

"Say goodbye to it," the soldier with the clippers said as James took a seat.

The barber draped a cape around James's neck and started cutting. The metal was hot and burned the back of his neck. A few minutes later, James walked past the remaining men in line with his hair trimmed tight to his scalp.

They laughed as he went by.

The barracks commander was a pleasant-looking man at first glance. He had soft, brown eyes and smiled when he spoke, but the men later found out he was tough as railroad spikes. He let them know it was still the white man's army.

"We start at 0-500 hours tomorrow morning. That's military talk for five in the morning. I suggest you all get a full night's sleep. Are there any questions?"

A sallow man stepped forward with big, lazy eyes and a full nose. He looked like one of the old mules back on James' farm.

"Yes, I have a question. What be a brig?"

"It means jail. Somewhere you do not want to be. Get the picture?"

"Yes… sir." The words ambled out of his mouth.

After the commander had gone, someone shouted. "Why you ask such goddamn dumb questions?"

Another man added, "They already think we're stupid. You tryin' to prove them right on the first day?"

"Well, you don't seem all that smart yourself." The man came back.

"Listen, you ugly bastard," the man growled, getting to his feet. "I don't need to be smart to whoop your country ass!" James recognized him as the youthful-looking recruit from earlier.

"I ain't afraid of you, city boy."

The men faced off, but James stepped between them before anything got started.

"This ain't the time or place."

The young man stared at James for a moment and broke into a smile.

"What's your name, soldier?" he asked, extending his hand.

"James… Atkins." He said, taking the man's hand.

"Eugene Cross." The recruit answered back. James had not seen a black man so many freckles and his shade of cinnamon-colored skin before. Cross spoke fast, and with an accent, James had never heard of before. "I'm from the south side. You know, Chicago."

"Okay," James said, turning to the other man. "What's your name?"

"Antoine DePasse. From Kentucky."

"Antoine? What kinda name is that?" Cross snickered. "Knew he was a country ass nigga!" The men around him laughed.

DePasse stood calm as ever. "Still ain't scared-a you."

Cross quickly retorted. "You should be."

People caught on after a while that Cross was more bluster than bite. He was the youngest volunteer, though you could not tell by his conversation. He was out on the streets by thirteen and picked up a rough crowd and later was caught fencing stolen goods. The judge gave him one of two options either serve your country for four years or go to jail for twelve. The math was simple to him; he joined the military. The men started calling him Chicago for short.

James made a few friends from his unit. They came from all over the country— Roanoke, Virginia; Red Bird, Oklahoma; and as far away as Wisconsin. Some could hold a tune; others were decent craftsmen and artists.

DePasse was from the Troublesome Creek area of Kentucky and seemed slow of mind, but James knew that was not the case. DePasse was devious and slick. He had a way of cursing under his breath. When confronted, he curtly diverted them with a series of "yes sirs" and "if ina pleases you." He played on people's ignorance and bigotry. He also had a keen understanding of the Bible and often quoted it to justify his transgressions.

James wasn't taken in by his antics, and DePasse would smile wide, knowing the jig was up when James called him on his game. He seemed delighted that someone saw through his façade. The troops in the unit nicknamed him Major because he seemed to run the camp, always having extras, whatever a man would want; women, food, whiskey, even hard drugs.

When the other soldiers hazed Major, James didn't defend him but didn't join in either. James believed there was something odd about him, the halting way Major talked and how his yellow teeth were too big to fit in his head. Major did not seem tough enough for soldiering. He looked more like a happy cook or shoeshine boy, but he had a nasty streak and was quick to pull the knife he had hidden on his person. He was one of a few people James had met who was truly not afraid to die.

One night, James found Major standing alone outside the barracks. Major had an old leather flask hidden in his inside pocket and offered James a drink.

"What's got you tonight?" James asked him. Major wasn't his usual upbeat self.

"Just wondering how I got into this shit."

"What do you mean?"

"I wasn't drafted, James. I volunteered," Major remarked.

"Doesn't seem like something you'd do."

Major motioned James closer. "I had to join the Army. It was the only place they wouldn't look for me."

"Who?"

"The law, boy. Who you think I'd be running from?"

"You joined the military to hide out."

"Sho did. The Bible says, 'this hath touched thy lips, and thine iniquity is taken away, and thy sin is purged.' And here, I'll cleanse my soul."

"You ain't making sense, man."

Major leaned in closer to James. "You know what covet mean? It's in the Bible. Means never satisfied and wanting what other folks got. There was this white man, Mr. Shelby, a hateful cracker if there ever was one. The man covets everything. When he saw a black man get something, he wants it. And he had the law and Klan on his side."

Major paused and looked around, worrying about being overheard. He continued when he was sure they were alone. "Well, the white man done got a law passed some which-a-way, and they took my papa's land. That little farm was all he had, and it killed him to lose it. Broke him! He lost himself in a bottle after that. Then he put a bullet in his head one night after drinking all day. So like the angel Gabriel and I came down and smote them motherfuckers. Yes, I did. Burned all they had to the ground, them too."

"You did what?" James asked, confused.

"I smote them," he whispered. "Every last one of them—the momma, the kids, the livestock, and especially Mr. Shelby. Burned they house down while they slept. I hightailed it out of town right after that. I knew they'd come looking for me. He done took everything away from me. He coveted, and that's a sin," Major premised, pointing at James. "And his sin done got him and his family killed. You know, the wages of sin is death. Says so in the good book."

Major took another long swig from the flask and offered it to James, but he waved him off. "The Lord giveth and the Lord taketh away," Major smiled, taking another drink.

James left Major standing alone under the starry night. As James lay in his bunk, he tried to imagine what he'd do if someone had come and taken their land. James believed Major was a yellow-belly to kill women and children, but he wondered though; could he kill a man, take away his life? He would find out soon enough.

Under their sergeant's watchful eye, they matured and turned into fighting men. The training became routine, and some began to relish the stability that the Army offered. Having three square meals a day and clean clothes was a new experience for many of them. They trained to fight as a unit and learned how to shoot and service their weapons. James excelled at the range, especially handling the M1919 Browning Auto machine gun.

A year later, as they completed their training, the men from James' platoon gathered one last time after the graduation parade. They received their service ribbons and first promotion. James earned the rank of E-3, Private First Class. The command orders sent James and his platoon to the Solomon Islands, where they would engage the Japanese. His unit left right away.

The mood was somber when James walked in. The soldiers had gathered around Chicago's bunk.

"What's going on here?" he asked.

"Nothing much. Talking it out. You know," Chicago answered.

"Talking what out?"

"How would you like to go?" One of the soldiers replied.

"What kinda question is that to ask?" James looked at them, astonished.

"Just answer the question!" Chicago growled, "Are you afraid to die?"

"You damn right, I'm afraid to die! So is everyone in here."

"I ain't," Chicago shot back.

"I ain't neither," Major bragged.

"Well, that's foolish talk," James replied. "Being afraid don't make you a coward."

"James, it's just as important to know how a man wants to die as it is how he wants to live." The comment came from Emmitt Haskins, one of the older enlisted men in their platoon.

"What could that possibly tell you?" James asked.

"Would tell me a lot," Emmitt replied.

"Answer the question I asked you, man," Chicago stood up.

"I don't know. I never put that in my mind," James mused.

"Now see, that tells me a lot," Chicago pointed out. "You ain't thinking straight, man. How can you be in a war and never had a thought about gettin' killed?"

"Cause, I ain't planning on getting killed."

Chicago surmised. "Well, I don't want to see it coming. Just take me out quick."

"No, I ain't afraid of the pain," Emmitt claimed.

"You want to suffer?" Another soldier asked.

"I already got myself right with God. You see, I'mma die out there," he answered.

"Stop it!" James shouted.

"No, James!," Chicago commanded. "Speak, brother."

"Well, I know because I see my pa all the time since we got here, and he long dead. So I know."

James sat on the edge of his bunk and listened to them for another half hour. He had not wanted to get to know them for this very reason, aside from where they were born and raised. He secretly believed that this would lessen the pain if any of them were killed, but that was a lie, as he came to find out. These men put on a brave face, but all the people James saw in the clutches of death, each scratched for every ounce of life they had left. When the time came, James admitted to himself that he would too.

IN THE THICK OF IT – BUNA ISLAND

James and the 93rd infantry arrived at Buna Island on February 11, 1944, after three long weeks aboard the USS Lurline. His unit was made up entirely of black soldiers. They settled in for the night after a successful landing and securing of the airfield. Their orders were to clear the area of any remaining Japanese troops, but these weren't the regular army. They were battle-tested and hardened, holed up in dank caves, able to survive on minimal food, water, and ammunition for days, even weeks on end.

James had risen to the rank of staff sergeant, which meant he was foolhardy enough to deal with enlisted men. Though the 93rd was part of the segregated Army, the dying and fighting always seemed to be integrated. The unit had seen action on Gona Island before coming to Guadalcanal or, as James called it, "double-barrel hell."

On top of the dangers of battle, life on Buna was extreme. Hot and sticky did not adequately describe the nightmare they were living. The sudden downpours were a brief respite from the intense jungle heat. Besides fighting a mostly unseen enemy, dysentery and malaria felled many leaving them too weak to fight or control their bowels. Some struggled to breathe. Many wished for death.

Not long after deployment, James and the rest of his platoon came face to face with death. His unit had not experienced any casualties to that point, but that changed. Chicago was hit and hit bad one day on patrol. Gone was all the bravado he displayed in the barracks that day. When his time came, he fought for life.

Dark pools poured out of a hole in his chest, soaking his uniform. James had knelt beside him. Chicago trembled and tried to speak, laboring for breath. He coughed up blood. "I don't wanna….die here…James."

"Hang on," James said.

More blood gurgled from his mouth. His eyes focused on the sky as the last bit of life escaped him. Chicago's head then fell back on the soft earth. James clutched his hand until the corpsmen pushed him out of the way. The camp went silent that night as the reality set in. War was all they said it would be and more.

The Japanese had held the Americans off on the island for almost five months, attacking mostly at night. The enemy called out in the darkness, cursing the men, challenging their bravery, believing these soldiers would not stand and fight. There was a fear amongst the troops that the Japanese could slip past the guards with ease and kill them as they slept.

The jungle was just as frightening and alien, even for the swamp boys in James' unit. Most had been around woods, but this hellish knot of moss and mango groves looked like scraggly fingers digging into the earth. No one could have made up worse conditions. Twisted roots and vines, dingy green, stagnant water, armies of mosquitos and biting bugs was a deprivation the men had never experienced.

The Japanese had dug in tight, waiting in ambush, but after weeks of skirmishes, low on ammunition and food, they changed tactics and made one last charge. A Japanese regiment attacked early one morning, charging down a hillside toward James' platoon and surprising everyone.

The 93rd sprang into action. James grabbed the handles on the Browning and opened fire fifty meters on his flank of the charge. The four-inch bullets ripped men to pieces, splattering blood in all directions. Still, they came forward, their faces wild with rage, screaming as they came closer. The Japanese did not retreat even in the face of heavy fire.

The enemy charge was close enough for James to see the sweat pouring off their faces. Bullets whistled all around him, finding targets on the American side, but he kept tugging at the trigger.

At ten meters, the shimmer of the enemies' bayonets blinded James momentarily. He swung his gun around to his right, firing at a line of troops making up a second wave numbering thirty to forty men, as the first wave of attackers crashed into the American line. James stayed focused despite the hand-to-hand fighting taking place all around him. Neither he nor Emmitt, his gunnery mate, noticed the three enemy troops who had taken positions near some shrubs to his left.

One of the Japanese fighters aimed and fired, hitting James square in the back just above the waist. He fell on his right shoulder, sprawled on the ground while the fighting raged around him. A Japanese soldier stepped over him, stabbing an American before he was shot and killed. He fell over James, his face covered with blood.

Emmitt grabbed the controls and laid fire into the ambushers while James tried to roll to one side. Time seemed to stand still in those moments. James noticed the sun breaking through the cloudy sky. He labored to breathe as the pain tore at his mind. James went in and out of consciousness, but the terror of the Japanese, who were notorious for brutalizing captured soldiers, pushed him to get to his feet. He soon passed out.

When James came to, he was bouncing on a gurney supported by two soldiers. He strained to get a look at who was carrying him. He caught a glimpse of a familiar smirk, and his big, yellow teeth exposed. It was none other than Major.

"We gave it to 'em today, James," he grinned. "We sho did."

They carted James off the battlefield to the triage area then airlifted him and other wounded to a makeshift hospital near the airstrip. After his surgery, a clean-shaven army doctor came in to see him.

"Sergent Atkins," the doctor began, looking over the x-rays through his wire-rimmed glasses.

"Doc," James greeted him cautiously. He knew in the marrow of his bones that it would be bad news. However, he was not prepared to hear what came next.

"You were lucky today, soldier. The bullet missed your spine by about two inches." James sighed.

"I heard you were a fine baseball player. You might not be after today. I'm sorry." James was stunned and held in a scream before it reached his lips.

"You're alive, son," the doctor noted, seeing the look on his face. "That's more than I can say for a lot of these boys."

'Wish they'd killed me,' James whispered to himself. No one in his platoon, no one in his unit, no one in his life understood what baseball meant to him, where it had taken him, and where he could go. James was equal to any man on that diamond. It was the only place he had known where his talents were respected. He had dreams of playing baseball professionally when he returned home. The doctor's words sunk him even further into an abyss of sadness.

That day, James bid goodbye to what remained of his platoon. They had taken on many casualties in the assault. Eleven dead and many more wounded. He spent several months in an Australian rehabilitation hospital. Another year passed before he could walk again.

HER TURN – BRAWLEY, CALIFORNIA 1944

Betsy Knight sat by herself in the soft grass near her mother's grapevine, watching a caterpillar crawl from one leaf to another. She put her finger in its way, and it moved up her hand and arm.

Her sister Sarah blurted. "You let that thing crawl all over you!"

"What are you afraid of?" Betsy answered, pushing the wiggly creature toward Sarah's face. "It's just a bug."

Sarah recoiled. "Ugh, that's nasty!"

Betsy had just turned sixteen and was about to finish her second year of high school. To Pappy, she might as well have been thirty-six. She had spirit and nerve and debated him about anything and everything.

It was an anxious time with full-scale conflicts on two continents. The war effort forced everyone to ration necessities like gas, food, and clothing. They couldn't find a decent pair of stockings since parachutes required rayon and silk. The Knights cut every possible corner. Make do and mend was the mantra of the day, with many families tailoring their clothes or using material from other pieces to make needed items.

Momma Knight collected her ration stamps to buy essentials and traded for others. She pressed clothes for a few tins of corn or sardines. Other days, she donned a pair of heavy work gloves to join the men shoveling mud and debris from irrigation ditches around the network of farmland.

51

Their garden supplemented the family's diet with the beans, squash, and melons. Pappy checked the plants in the morning before he went off to work and again when he returned in the evening. He set up traps to catch rodents and sprayed for bugs. Pappy and Momma Knight did these things from the memory of the Great Depression. The hardships were still fresh in their minds, even if the children could not remember.

Betsy weeded around the vegetables, adding a little fertilizer. Pappy hoped she'd take to the job, care for the garden as he did, but none of this fit into her view of life. Betsy hated the smell of Pappy's homemade mulch and would bathe afterward to scrub the smell off her skin. And when she did find some solace away from him, Momma Knight would fuss at her to do one thing or another.

"Those pennies add up!" she'd shout.

Betsy and her sister Sarah did not mind the hardship, but even small treats were few and far between. It felt like fun was being rationed too. Finally, her mother gave in and let her go to a movie and dinner with a classmate. One afternoon as they prepared lunch for the family, she told her sister.

"Walter asked me out."

"Walter Stockstill? No!" Sarah was incredulous. "And you're going?"

"Momma said I could."

"You asked our mother to go to a movie and dinner with Walter Stockstill, and she said okay? I don't believe you. I need to hear this myself."

"Get back in here!" Betsy screamed, grabbing her arm.

She laughed. "When did Walter get sweet on you?"

"Shut up! He isn't sweet on me."

"Huh? You're not making sense, Betsy."

"He drove by with his father last Saturday. He came back a little later, and we talked."

"And Pappy agreed you could go?"

"Not exactly. I didn't ask him."

Sarah rolled her eyes in disbelief. "Oh, this is going to be fun."

The girls knew how their father felt about dating, no matter how good the family, and they'd planned to keep it quiet as long as possible. But Momma Knight spilled the beans at dinner that day. As predicted, Pappy was not amused. It would not be the last time she held something back from him.

"They should have a little fun. Everyone is sacrificing."

"I don't like it one bit," Pappy fumed, setting his glass down hard on the table. The girls knew he was serious when the tips of his earlobes turned red, and his brow furrowed.

"She'll be fine," Momma Knight affirmed, ignoring Pappy's outburst.

Although Pappy believed she was too young for dating, Momma reminded him that she was only fifteen when he called on her.

"And your father made that ten times harder!" He retorted.

They both paused for a moment then laughed. These were the moments when Momma Knight wished she was back in Georgia. She mused many times of having a home just down the street from her mother so she could speak to her, share some gossip and cold lemonade. Momma Knight closed her eyes to remember her father. He had passed away a few years back, and she was not able to attend his funeral. She had talked to her mother on the telephone a few times since, but it only made her miss them more.

Pappy eventually relented. Maybe it was Momma's peach cobbler, something he could never resist, or that he knew he couldn't change her mind once she'd dug in her heels. And that was that.

BREAKING THE RULES

The day of the date had arrived. Betsy sat alone in the room she shared with her sister. Her clothes spread on the bed. She had never been on a date nor as much as a birthday party without her parents' chaperone. The closer it got to the appointed time, the more nervous she became.

"What you so worried about?" Sarah asked.

"I just know Pappy is gonna say no as I'm walking out the door."

"Don't worry. Let me see what you got out to wear tonight." She pushed past Betsy and inspected what was laid out.

"This is fine, but you better get ready now," Sarah said. "You still have to press your hair."

Betsy did what Sarah told her, and got dressed.

Walter arrived at 6:00 p.m. looking natty in his grey herringbone trousers and a black jacket. He greeted Momma Knight and complimented her home. He took off his gray felt fedora as he entered the living room. Pappy asked him to take a seat, and Walter obliged. Pappy was very calm as they chatted about the weather and Walter's family.

Betsy arrived a short time later. Walter stood, hat in hand, and smiled.

"Hi, Betsy."

Pappy almost did not recognize the woman standing in the doorway while Momma Knight beamed. Betsy was the picture of elegance in a knee-length tan pencil skirt, a white button-down shirt with a broad collar, and a navy blue V-neck sweater. The top buttons opened, revealing a pearl necklace that her mother had given her. She styled her shiny black hair in a simple bun. Betsy felt nervous, but beautiful, all at the same time.

"Hi, Walter."

Pappy stood up, but could not find the words.

"You...ah, ready to go?" Walter asked.

"Yes." Her nerves pushed her to hurry out as quickly as possible.

"Hold on y'all," Pappy cut in. "Wait for Sarah. She's going with you."

"Sir?" Walter asked, confused. Betsy's mouth was jolted open with shock.

"Yes, Sarah's going."

"Pappy, that's not what..."

"Edgar Knight!" Momma scoffed. She never used his full name unless it was something pretty serious. She was embarrassed for her daughter and angry with her husband. Pappy was unswayed. He had kept this small detail in his back pocket the whole time.

"I'm ready to go..." Sarah said, appearing from around the corner in a silk shirt with palm tree prints and a chiffon handkerchief tied around her neck. Her reddish-brown hair was neatly brushed back and tied with a black lace ribbon.

Momma Knight glared at Pappy. "You and I need to talk."

Pappy turned to Walter and mockingly said, "Have a nice time. We'll see you back here by eleven."

"Yes, sir," Walter stammered, clearly unnerved by the proceedings. Betsy was upset and let Sarah know it as they walked to the car.

"You knew this the whole time, didn't you?"

"Listen, Pappy made me promise. Either I go with you, or you don't go at all."

"I can't believe him!"

"Well, this is what we got, so let's just make do," Walter added.

"I couldn't agree more," Sarah consented.

"Of course, you would!" Betsy replied sarcastically.

Walter hurried ahead and opened the door for the ladies. For a moment, Sarah acted as if she would sit in the front seat, but got in the back after Betsy glared at her. They drove away, turning at the corner of South Eastern and K Streets. Betsy tried to get over her anger and not spoil the evening.

Fortunately, the Brawley Theatre was a short drive up Main Street, three blocks over the railroad tracks, and the only one in the north-end towns of the valley. The screen was rolled down by hand, and seats were staggered sets of wooden benches each wide enough for four or five people with more upstairs. During regular movie hours, Blacks and Mexicans had to sit in the balcony, except for Wednesday afternoon when children of any color could sit downstairs and watch a show.

"Looks like a full house tonight," Walter observed.

"I really want to see this film," Betsy fretted.

They purchased their tickets and made their way up to the upper level. Walter surveyed the room for any open seats. All he saw were dark faces staring back at him and not a space between them.

"There's no place to sit."

"What? Let me see," Betsy stepped around him to look for herself. Sarah tugged at his sleeve and pointed down the steps. There were a few open spaces in the back rows on the first floor. Walter shook his head, but Sarah went anyway.

"Where's she going?" Betsy whispered.

Walter pointed to the empty seats in the whites-only section.

"Sarah! Wait!" Betsy cried, but there was no stopping her.

Sarah sat down, and no one seemed to notice. Walter looked back at Betsy as Sarah waved them over. She shrugged her shoulders, and after a brief moment of apprehension, they took seats next to Sarah just as the movie started. Betsy leaned forward and smiled at her sister. She loved how bold and fearless she was. But before they could get comfortable, a short white man with dull, brown eyes and bad teeth tapped Betsy and Walter on the shoulder.

"You niggers get on upstairs where you all belong," the man leered.

"There aren't any more seats," Walter pleaded, ignoring the insult.

"Well, you can stand on the steps like the rest of them. This area here is reserved for white folks. You know that."

"To hell with this! Let's go," Walter stood, towering over the man.

Betsy and Sarah covered their faces and rushed toward the lobby. Betsy was stung by such a hateful word. Race relations in the valley had gotten notably worse since the Dust Bowl migrants from Oklahoma nicknamed "Okies" had come to town. Many of them lived along the canal banks or in small camps until they found temporary housing. They'd lost everything to the drought that ravished the prairie, except their hatred. Trouble began immediately at the local high school, where fistfights became a daily occurrence. Someone would hurl an insult, and a fight ensued. It got so bad that the principal held separate assemblies to suppress any more outbreaks at the school. He asked the Mexican and Negro students to have patience with the newcomers. The school returned to an uneasy sense of order.

Walter was angry as he rushed the girls out the door of the theatre. The nice lady who collected money waved goodnight. Sarah ignored her.

"What do we do now?" Betsy asked, throwing up her arms in despair.

"I'd like to hear him call me a nigger now. I'd whoop that cracker," Walter yelled.

"Let's go to Mexicali," Sarah declared.

"What?" Betsy and Walter asked.

"I said, let's go to Mexicali."

"No, no, no," Betsy replied. "There are plenty of good places to eat right here. We can go to Asia Café. Let's do that, Walter. Come on."

"No. Pappy goes there every Saturday night and brings home leftovers," Sarah pushed. "Let's go to Mexicali."

"Why do you want to go there? You don't even speak a lick of Spanish."

"Bet we won't be called nigger over there. Is that good enough reason to go?"

"How do you know? Mexicans don't like us either."

"Stop being scared," Sarah disagreed. "Mr. Tamayo's family likes us. I have lots of Mexican friends."

"What about Pappy? He's going to ask all kinds of questions about the movie."

"We'll tell him what happened and that we went someplace to eat."

"Someplace? Yeah, that's going to go over well. I don't believe you, Sarah."

"Look, we have four hours. It's an hour drive there and back. That leaves us three. Is that enough time for you to eat?"

"You know you might be on to something, Sarah," Walter smiled.

"You can't be serious, Walter. You're going for this?"

He nodded. "I am. We'll be fine. Let's go."

"Sarah, they'll never let us out again after tonight," Betsy protested.

"Only if you tell them, Betsy," Sarah cautioned.

Sarah was happy; she was able to convince them. She skipped to the car, and they quickly forgot the insult and the movie. After a short drive back to the east side of town, they headed south along Highway 111 to the border.

"Have you ever been there?" Walter asked Sarah.

"No, but supposedly our mom and dad were on their way to dinner the night I was born. Her water broke just before they got to El Centro."

"You were born in El Centro? Our rival?"

"Yes," she professed proudly.

"And you, Betsy? Was your birth as exciting?"

Before she could answer, Sarah cut in, "No! She was born right there in that old house. Momma was in labor all day with her."

"Sarah! How dare you speak of Momma that way?"

"I'm not. I'm speaking of you."

Betsy was surprised with Sarah being so competitive if anything, she defended her, fighting tooth and nail with anyone who dared bother her little sister. Back in fourth grade, their neighbor, Mr. Tamayo's daughter, Isabel, bullied Betsy and Sarah, rushed to her defense.

During recess, Sarah confronted Isabel, throwing her to the ground. Just as a teacher separated them, Sarah swung with all her might, hitting Isabel in the eye.

Later, in the principal's office, the girls' parents were called to the school. Pappy was incensed, as was Isabel's father.

"Look at what she did! Why did she hit my daughter?" Tamayo shouted, pointing to the girl's swollen, bruised eye.

"Your child started this trouble. Not my girls," Pappy retorted.

"My daughter told me that Betsy has been calling her names. She started this—"

"I don't think so, sir," Pappy shouted back. "Your daughter called Betsy 'blackie.'"

The man looked at Pappy confused, then asked his daughter in Spanish if it was true. Isabel nodded after some prodding. Tamayo turned to Pappy and said. "I don't teach my children such foul language. But I have an idea who did, and I am very sorry."

Pappy stammered, not expecting an apology, "Well, so are we. No one wants children fighting and carrying on. Sarah, tell her you're sorry."

Sarah's eyes bulged with surprise.

"Don't make me ask you again!"

"I'm sorry," she replied.

Before she turned away, Pappy shouted. "Now, say it like you mean it."

"I'm sorry for hitting you in the face, Isabel," Sarah said quickly.

"Isabel, *dile que lo sientes*, tell her you are sorry!" Tamayo ordered. His eyes were angry too.

"I am sorry," she answered, barely looking at Sarah.

The principal added, "Okay, young ladies, I never want to see you in my office again. If I do, I'll make sure it's your last day at this school."

The families later became good friends.

So Betsy was rightfully flustered by her sister's antics. She sat with her arms folded in front of her as they drove down the highway to Mexicali. Sarah, of course, couldn't have cared less. She continued to hog the conversation, even as Walter tried to include Betsy.

"What are your chances against Central this year?" Sarah asked.

"Pretty good, as long as you cheer for us," he grinned, poking Betsy with an elbow.

"Fat chance. I see them rolling all over you boys," Sarah leaned in from the back seat.

"Where's your school pride?"

"I have pride, but Central has those Bellamy brothers. They can beat you all by themselves."

"What? Those guys ain't so tough. We busted Sam's nose last game. Teach him to run on my side of the line. Right, Betsy?"

"Yes, I—"

Sarah cut her off. "Your side of the line? Oh, now you own it."

"That's right. I do."

"Betsy, you'll come to watch me play?" He smiled.

"Sure. Why not? There's nothing else going on," she answered dejectedly.

"What is this?" Walter joked. "No school spirit in the Knight's home."

Not long after that, they neared the border crossing into Mexico. Mexicali was a metropolis compared to the sleepy farm communities of the valley. Most didn't even have a traffic signal in the whole town, but here, traffic flowed down the wide boulevards in each direction. The building facades had a Baroque architecture and strategically placed fountains along the route added to their mystical verve of the city.

The air filled with electricity as vendors hawked their wares, people milled about enjoying the company of friends; cars and taxis filled the streets. Betsy's head swirled with the chaos, shouting, and laughter. Women smoking cigarettes in their colorful dresses and chic shoes, laughed with their companions. Handsome men with slicked-back hair and suits escorted them along the crowded sidewalks.

After Walter parked the car, they went into El Sombrero, the first restaurant they saw. The hall had at least twenty tables and two bays of swinging doors. The place bustled with energy and chatter. It seemed that this side of the world was untouched from wartime attrition. Their waiter spoke in heavily accented English, but good enough for the trio to understand. He sounded like many of their neighbor's parents.

"We have a special something for you. Very good. I will order for you?"

"Enough for all of us?" Sarah asked, pointing to her companions.

"Oh, yes. *Mucho! Y muy sabrosa!*" He pointed his index finger to the ceiling.

"Well, I don't know what all that means, but it sounds great," Walter said, handing back his menu.

The waiter returned a short time later with enough food to feed a whole family. There was a seemingly endless supply of warm, flour tortillas to go along with the roasted chicken, breaded fish, rice, beans. Betsy's guilt began to get the best of her as they enjoyed the bounty. Her parents were at home saving the hardened crusts of bread to make meal for the chickens, and here they were eating like gluttons. She wanted to take some of the food back with her so that Momma Knight could enjoy it. She knew that meant lying to her parents, and she had never lied to her mother, at least not that she could remember. The more Betsy deliberated about it, the more it made her heart ached.

"This was a great idea, Sarah," Walter observed as they walked back to his car. "I've never enjoyed food as much as I did tonight."

"Me too!" Sarah exclaimed. "But we better get home soon. Let me drive."

"You crazy?" Before he could finish, Sarah opened the driver's side door and sat down. Walter shook his head for a moment, then handed her the keys.

"You better not wreck my daddy's car!"

"Hush, Walter. Get in."

"Come on, Betsy!" He shouted, opening the door for her. "Can't be late." He and Sarah chatted all the way home as Betsy sat silently in the back. Sarah drove quite well. Walter marveled at her skills and wondered where she had learned. All Betsy could think of was her parents and the sacrifices they were making for them. She could not fully enjoy this small taste of the life she aspired to have. When they arrived, Walter walked them to the door and hugged them goodnight.

Betsy did not go out with Walter again. They greeted each other and made small talk, but there was never another date. She didn't like the way the night had ended. She took some of that out on Sarah.

"Glad you had a nice time on my date."

"What are you getting at, Betsy?"

"Never mind." Betsy was more concerned about the lie they had told, and it began to eat away at her. The guilt she held in bubbled to the surface, and she confessed to her father a few weeks later.

"You did what? Do you know what could have happened to you over there?"

"Pappy, I'm so sorry."

"Oh, you gonna be sorry, all right." He then got up from his seat. "Sarah!" Pappy yelled until she appeared from her bedroom, wondering what all the fuss was about.

"You knew about this and didn't tell me?" He said, almost shouting. "And here I thought you were the responsible one!" His brow furrowed deeper.

Sarah did not respond as he tore into her for another few minutes.

He pointed his finger at them. "No more parties! No more dances. Not 'til you're both thirty years old." Sarah chuckled at that, but it only made him angrier.

"You think this is funny? Don't even dare ask me. You ain't going anywhere, but home and school."

"I knew you'd crack sooner or later," Sarah admitted when they were alone.

"Sorry, I'm not as good at lying as you are," Betsy responded.

"No one asked you to lie, just to keep your mouth shut, Ms. Goodie-Two-Shoes."

"Easy for you to say, you're leaving in a few months."

Sarah would be off to nursing school after graduation. Without her sister around, Betsy's desire to leave would only grow stronger. No matter how badly she felt about that night, how terrible it was lying to her parents, she'd never take back what they had done. Betsy had never before felt so much excitement and freedom. Just thinking about it made her heart flutter. She believed her turn was coming, and coming soon.

A PROMISE – 1946

Sarah packed the last of her belongings into her mother's suitcase, the one she had when she left Georgia. Momma Knight had taken great care of it. The case was still in good condition, which was more than Sarah's confidence. It seemed to wane the closer the time to depart for nursing school came. Betsy sensed it too. Gone was a bit of her cockiness. Sarah had looked forward to this day since she was a little girl. Now, at nineteen, two months out of high school, the weight of her choice became suddenly heavy. She was about to be off on her own. She was leaving for college and had worked odd jobs during that time to pay for her tuition. Pappy saved up the balance to get her through the first year. He promised to send her something each month to help with her expenses.

Her high school diploma hung on the wall above a small chest in the living area. Pappy placed it close to the things dearest to him, the photos of his parents, his children, and his wife. He could now admire her accomplishment while sitting in his favorite chair.

"You 'bout ready to go, darling?" he asked as he grabbed her luggage.

"Yes, Daddy. That is the last one," Sarah said with a smile that belied her sadness. She held down her emotions as best she could. At any moment, she believed she'd burst into tears.

"We gotta leave soon if we are gonna catch that bus. Don't forget, Momma packed you a lunch."

Betsy struggled with her composure, as well. She had retreated in the days leading up to Sarah's departure. There were long stretches where Betsy barely spoke three words. She wondered what life was going to be like in this house, in this town without her rambunctious big sister.

"Enough of this silence, girl," Sarah called from the doorway. Betsy looked to her sister, unfolding her hands from her lap, but did not respond.

"Are you coming to see me off?" Sarah queried as she flopped on the bed next to Betsy.

"No, I'm staying here."

"What? Come on. Get up. I'm leaving now."

"No, Sarah, you'll be okay if I don't come."

"Well, Momma is going too, but if you want to stay." She popped off the bed, pausing at the door, but Betsy didn't move.

Sarah made her way into the kitchen, where her mother was drinking a cup of tea. Sarah had not noticed her aging, but at that moment, she took stock of how dull her skin looked. The streaks of gray hair made her face look even older and tired. She'd slacked off from working in her garden of late, something she had done herself religiously. She smiled when Sarah came into the room.

"My, don't you look snappy!" she quipped, putting down her cup. She labored as she stood up.

"Where are you going all dressed up?"

"Momma, I'm going to Los Angeles. To nursing school. Remember?"

"Oh, yes. Sorry baby. I didn't know it was today."

Sarah heard the engine starting up. The time was growing short.

"Okay, Momma, come on."

"Let me get my shoes."

Pappy opened the door suddenly. "We got to go, Sarah." She could tell he was anxious. "Betsy! Momma!" He called out.

Betsy sighed and moved towards the door.

It was a short ride to the station, and to Sarah's relief, there were no drawn-out goodbyes. Passengers were already boarding when they arrived. The driver was cheerful and placed Sarah's bags in the undercarriage.

"You call when you get in," Pappy stated.

"I will," Sarah answered.

"You got everything you need?" he asked, taking her arm gently.

She nodded. "Pappy, I have to go," Sarah's voice now trembling.

"Remember to call me as soon as you get in." He repeated.

"I will, Pappy." She hugged him. Her hands began to shake even more as she turned to her mother.

"Momma." She felt the tears building in her eyes as she held her tight.

Sarah opened her arms, and Betsy fell into them, tears falling down her face.

"I'm gonna miss you something awful, baby sister," Sarah sobbed. "When I get settled, I want you to come for a visit. Promise me that?"

"I promise," Betsy whispered.

The driver called to Sarah. "Ma'am, we have to leave now."

"Okay," Sarah answered. She hugged Betsy a moment longer. Sarah then climbed the steps and found a seat near a window. She waved to them as the bus pulled away, her hands silhouetted against the dark, green glass.

Betsy's heart ached for days and weeks after Sarah had gone away.

ESCAPE TO LOS ANGELES

Betsy eyed the small clock atop the dresser as she paced back and forth next to her bed for what had seemed like hours. The day had finally come. She gathered her purse and a small suitcase lying on the bed and slipped out the back door. Her mother sat quietly in her rocking chair, reading from her Bible and didn't notice her leaving. Pappy wasn't home, and with him away, time was of the essence.

She sighed heavily, balling her fists with both hands in an attempt to strengthen her resolve. She then pushed open the gate and stepped onto the sidewalk. Betsy was finished with Brawley and Pappy's constant chastising. It might have been tolerable if her actions warranted the criticism, but he was oblivious to the detrimental effect it was having on his daughter.

Pappy believed he was motivating her in his awkward way, challenging her to do better, but if Betsy came home with a B+, Pappy asked why she did not get an A. If she got an A, he asked why she did not get an A+. She began to believe she was falling short. There was no turning back now in her mind, despite not finishing high school.

She knew full well what her leaving meant, the embarrassment her family would endure. People just did not run off without something being very wrong, but Betsy had reached her breaking this point. These ideas and many others went through her mind as she walked past the neat rows of houses on K Street with their well-tended lawns. She knew she had to put some distance between herself and home when she came to the corner store that had been owned by the Nakamoras, a Japanese-American family. It had fallen into disrepair after the internment of the Nakamoras to a camp near Yuma during the war. Some delinquent kids had knocked out the windows as a final insult.

With great sadness, she remembered the family closing the store some four years earlier when President Roosevelt ordered the internment of the Japanese. Betsy recalled standing with her mother as they padlocked the door. It was the last time anyone ever saw them again. And now Betsy was on her way out of town too. She planned to stay with her sister until she figured things out.

She was not completely enamored with the idea, but it was the best one she had. Betsy had spent a few weeks one summer with Sarah in Los Angeles, and it was eye-opening. Sarah had always been independent, but Betsy saw just how much her sister had come into her own. Only six months after leaving Brawley for school, Sarah had taken up with a man from Louisiana named Albert Ross Jr., but everyone called him Junie. He had a stocky build and sleepy eyes. His hands were big as bear claws, but he was gentle and soft-spoken.

Sarah often suspended herself from his curled bicep as long as she could stand it. And he needed every one of those big muscles for his machinist job at a local airplane parts manufacturer. Junie loved his bourbon and showed Betsy how to fix it when she visited. She became the de facto bartender when friends came by. They passed through at all hours to play cards and have a drink or two.

Betsy wondered what Pappy would say if he knew what was going on in Los Angeles, Sarah's smoking, and drinking? Betsy had to admit; she had a great time when she visited. It was not her way of living, but it felt good to be away from her overprotective parents and gossiping neighbors.

She kept her head down, avoiding people driving on the road or sitting outside on their porches. Betsy expected to see Pappy at any moment, feeling breathless each time she surveyed the route.

The station was just a few more blocks now that Betsy crossed the railroad tracks. She saw the flashing taillights of a bus parked in the drive. Her arms burned with fatigue from carrying her suitcase, but there was no time to rest. A whole new beginning was waiting for her just a few blocks away. She'd find a job and save up for an apartment, then get her diploma at another school.

Suddenly, she sensed someone was following her. There was a car trailing behind her. She hadn't noticed, but he had been there for almost a block. He came up alongside, rolling down the passenger window.

"Where you heading?" Pappy asked.

"Away from here," she answered defiantly, keeping her eyes forward.

"I see you done made up your mind, but will you give me a minute to talk?"

"Why, Pappy?" She agonized, taking a short break along the road.

"I just want to say I'm sorry that I made your life so miserable you'd want to leave your mother and me this way."

Betsy glanced into the car at his sad eyes, and then looked away.

"And no matter what you think of me, you have to know how much this is going to hurt your Momma, you running off. She'll think she did something to you."

"That's not why, Pappy," Betsy shook her head, lifting her case and continuing to the bus stop. The burning sensation in her arms became almost unbearable under its weight, but she was determined to get to the station. Pappy eased off the brakes and kept pace with her stride.

"Then what is it?"

"I want more out of life than this town."

"Baby, you may not believe me, but I understand. I came all the way out here for a better life. But you're running away, and that never solves anything."

"I have no choice."

"Yes, you do."

"What would that be?" she asked, tears falling from her eyes.

"Finish high school, and then go your own way. Go to college, or nursing school like Sarah."

"I don't want to be a nurse."

"Okay, but don't leave like this, Betsy. What's your Momma gonna tell her friends at church next Sunday? That her child up and ran away from home? She'll be heartbroken."

"It's not fair, Pappy, to put all this on me."

"Life isn't fair, Betsy. My grandmother raised eleven children and cared for her mother and father all in a little four-room shack. Everyone had to give up a little, but we don't quit on each other."

Betsy stood there, not wanting to be swayed, but feeling compelled nonetheless.

"We're preparing you for your future, whether you know it or not. Isn't that something?"

"What if I don't want that?"

He sighed, "Baby, God gives us our tests. When things go bad, are you going to stand up to them? Make something good from them?"

Betsy started to sob, her shoulders shaking as her lungs heaved for air. Pappy opened the passenger door.

"Come on, sweet pea, let's go home."

She looked down the road toward the bus station, where passengers were now boarding. The driver was out front smiling, taking tickets, and helping the women up the first step. She knew it was her bus, the one for Los Angeles. She paused for another moment, then picked up her suitcase and got into the car. Pappy reached over her and gently closed the door. They drove back to South Eastern Avenue, and Momma Knight was none the wiser.

Although she felt she had done the right thing in going back, she also was convinced that something had died in her that day.

THE ATKINS BOYS –
HONDO, TEXAS 1945

"The war is over, son," Willie announced. It was 1945, and James was back home in Hondo after recuperating in Australia.

"Over?" James asked, confused.

"Heard it on the radio. We dropped another one on 'em Japs, and they done surrendered."

"Another one?"

"Yes, on uh, Nagasaki." He pronounced it (Nag-A-Sack-EE). "That must be some kinda bomb if they only need two to get 'em to quit."

"Yep, must be," James agreed, thinking about the army buddies he'd left on Buna. He smiled. They would be safe.

It had been some time since Willie saw some happiness in his son. He had come home defeated, a different man. Although the war had not taken his life, it had taken the life out of him. His back hurt him so that he was little help around the farm. James needed a cane to walk when he went to the creek to fetch water and had a noticeable hitch in his step.

"Samuel should be home soon now that the Germans done gave up."

"You heard from him?"

"I got a letter last winter. Wrote how he learned some French words. I got it right here somewhere."

"I don't need to read it. That was to you," James uttered.

"He wrote to the family. You're his family, right?"

"I reckon so."

"You *reckon*?" Willie caught himself fussing. He had lost some of his anger towards James in the years he was away. Though Willie would not tell James directly, he was happy James had come home alive. He recognized that his eldest son had grown up in ways he could not comprehend.

But James languished on the farm as he struggled to find something of meaning. Life seemed irrelevant after seeing firsthand how easy it was given and taken away. It shocked him how quickly people mobilized to kill—all the funds, resources, and training put forth without hesitation. *'Nothing like this happens for some peaceful thing.'* He went back to all the men who had lost their lives on the battlefield. *'It was all just a big waste of humanity.'*

James sighed deeply and wondered why he had been spared. The loneliness and isolation of the farm were stifling. James did not know what to do next, but he knew he had to leave Hondo. He kept most of what he felt inside, hidden away from his father. After a few moments of silence, Willie told James, "Son, make sure they bury me out there in the yard, next to Momma."

"Where's this coming from?" James asked.

"It ain't coming from nowhere, just wanted you to know."

"Okay, Pa," he answered.

The sun peered through the thicket of tall trees with the rise in the road. Willie and James stood in the yard, chewing the fat. James was in better spirits today. His recovery was slow but steady. He moved a little better with each day that passed.

"Garcia got some cattle for sale," Willie remarked.

"You see 'em?" James asked.

Willie swatted a bug from his face. "No, not yet, but I'll go by there this week."

Willie paused, focusing on the ridge leading to the farm. James turned to see what had caught his attention and saw the silhouette coming off the rise. "I know that walk," Willie shouted and took off for the road. "That's Samuel."

Samuel met his father halfway and dropped his things. Willie grabbed him in a bear hug, laughing. Samuel had a full beard and was dressed sharply in a plaid duster cap, wool trousers, handmade leather shoes, suspenders, and a paisley silk tie. Willie almost did not recognize his son.

"Ain't he a sight?" Willie asked as James limped over to them.

"What the hell happened to you?" Samuel said, noticing his cane.

"I was in a war. What the hell happened to you?" James hollered, clutching some of the hair on his chin. Samuel pushed his hand aside and threw his arms around him.

"Hope I didn't hurt you!" he laughed.

"You still squeeze like a girl!" James joked.

"Come on in boy," Willie beamed, picking up Samuel's bags.

The three men walked into the house. For Samuel, the rush of familiar smells and scents bought instant relief. Willie stood by admiring his sons. They had survived the war. That Sunday morning, he got up early and went to church for the first time in years, smiling through the whole service.

HYPOCRITES AND LIES – SPRING 1946

Like James, Samuel had a hard time adjusting to civilian life. Samuel also came back a much-changed man, though his scars were not as apparent. It was not long before he got into trouble around Hondo. It was not like him to be so combative, but now Samuel was with everyone. Willie told him he was going to get himself killed. He had already been in a few scrapes down at the Veterans Hall, but one night it got serious.

"Yeah, we fought for six days straight without any sleep, no reinforcements, and man was it cold up in those mountains! It was the coldest winter they'd had in fifty years," Samuel told the vets gathered around the table in the Hall.

A few of the men nodded in agreement, but one of them was heating up. Watkins was a scary-looking white man with eyes as big as egg yolks and a pug nose. He was big too-six feet and itching to test Samuel.

"There weren't no nigras on them front lines," he hissed. "Only men I saw dying was white."

"That's a goddamn lie. I was there in Bastogne." Samuel shouted back.

"Bullshit!" Watkins sneered. "Never saw a spade shoot at anything but squirrels."

Some of the former soldiers agreed with Watkins while others tried to quiet him down, but he was having none of it.

"No! I'm not gonna listen to these nigger lies."

"Nigger lies?" Samuel retorted, standing up. "Bet you cheered when the 761st Tank Division broke the German lines!"

"Well, I'll be goddamned! Nigras won the war, boys!"

"Didn't say we won the war, jackass!"

Samuel and Watkins had a staredown, chests heaving from the alcohol and adrenaline. Watkins then swung his beer bottle at Samuel and missed. Samuel struck him hard in the gut, knocking him over several chairs. Three white men, friends of Watkins, jumped Samuel and held him down. They whooped him good before Sheriff Barnes put an end to it. He knew Samuel was Willie's son and drove him home.

"Why do white people only hear their truth, and no one else's?" Samuel asked on the ride.

"I can't answer that," Barnes ignored his ranting. "Best you stay away from the VA hall."

Samuel nodded angrily. "I don't want to be around them hypocrites no more."

Barnes dropped him in front of the shanty. "You take care of yourself. Tell your Pa hello for me."

Samuel waved to him as he got out of the truck. He heated some water and attended to the cuts on his hands when he went inside. The last time his fists were so bruised was a cold winter night in France. He was on guard duty with two of his fellow troopers, manning a checkpoint when they spotted a German conscript approaching their position waving a white flag. He was young, maybe sixteen or seventeen. After patting the prisoner down, Samuel offered him some water, but before he could take a drink, a shot rang out. One of the men in Samuel's patrol, nicknamed "Red," had killed him in cold blood.

The guilty soldier admitted it was payback for the massacre of black infantrymen at Saint Vith. Samuel stewed for two days before confronting and beating Red with his bare hands. Samuel never reported the incident and served a week in the brig. But he could never forgive the soldier for killing that boy. Samuel clenched his fists again, and as he promised the sheriff, he stayed clear of town.

BEGINNINGS AND ENDINGS – 1947

One day that fall, as Willie returned home from town, he saw his sons tossing around an old baseball in a clearing near the house. It brought joy to his heart to see them smiling and having a good time, but it also gave him a grand idea. That evening at supper, he told them so.

"You boys looked good out there throwing that ball around."

James eyed Samuel incredulously. "I know some girls that throw harder than him!"

"Is that right, Gimpy?" Samuel joked, elbowing James.

"No. Listen to me," Willie insisted, "You should get out there and play again."

James studied his father's face for a moment, realizing he was serious. "Who would we play for around here?"

"I'm saying y'all should get your old team back together. Lots of leagues in San Antonio. Could be good for you both."

"I know you mean well, Pa, but I can't play no more. Almost threw my back out today," James lamented.

"Well, what's wrong with your head?"

"Nothing wrong with my head. It's my back."

"There's still lots you can do. Why not manage the team?"

James looked surprised at the idea, but he didn't dismiss it.

"Just a thought. Do what you like, but you're wasting your talent if you ask me."

The next day after finishing the little work he could around the farm, James hitched a ride into town. He walked a short distance over the railroad tracks, past the businesses that lined the highway, to the neat, tree-lined streets and ranch styled houses. He came up the cement drive and knocked gently on the door at a familiar home. The housekeeper, a young black woman, answered.

"Can I help you?"

"Is Mr. Ney home?"

"He is, but let me see if he wants visitors. Wait here."

"Tell him James Atkins would like to speak with him," James told her. He then waited nervously in the doorway, hat in hand. He had not been over to this part of town in many years, and only then as a laborer.

The housekeeper returned a short time later and asked James to follow her. Pictures of Ney and his baseball players filled the walls and mantles along with the occasional family portrait.

"James!" A rough but a familiar voice came from the doorway.

"Mr. Ney, thank you for seeing me, sir," James was shocked to see the breathing tubes up both nostrils, and his hair was completely white.

"Good to see you, James. I heard you were back in town," Ney said, adjusting himself in his easy chair.

"Sorry I didn't come sooner."

"What brings you here? Can't be to visit an old man in his last days?"

James had a hard time getting out the words. "Well…my pa give me an idea… and I wanted to run it by you."

"I'm flattered someone still values my opinion! My doctor doesn't give a damn what I think!" he joked. "What's this idea?"

"I'd like to organize a baseball team," James acknowledged finally.

"Well, now…" Ney pondered, sitting up in his chair. "Tell me more, James."

"Samuel's back from the war. Don't know if you heard."

"I did," Ney agreed. "I also heard about you getting hurt fighting the Japs."

James held up his cane. "I can't play anymore, but maybe I can manage the team. I know 'em better than anybody else around here."

"I don't get out too much anymore, but I hear scouts are coming to many of the games featuring black talent," Ney pointed out. Then he gave James a long look. "If you're serious, I'll give you the team's old bus to get you started."

James was grateful. "I haven't been more serious about anything in a long time, Mr. Ney. I'd appreciate any advice you could give me."

When Ney told him that there were a few exhibition games played between the Negro League teams and the Big League All-Stars, James knew it was just a matter of time before baseball integrated.

"I'll do whatever I can. You know that, James. But that may not be much." Ney pointed to the oxygen tank. "As you can see, I'm a sick man, and I'm not gonna get better."

They spoke for another hour. As excited James was at the prospect of getting his old team back together, he departed with a heavy heart.

The days after he met with Ney, James and Samuel drove all over the bumpy back roads of Medina County looking for their old teammates. Most were happy to see them and quick to say yes. A couple were already playing on teams but considered switching for the right opportunity. Buckey, one of those few, also volunteered to drive the bus. He couldn't do much more since losing a leg in the war.

James used a little money he had to get the bus repaired, and found a few more players to round out the team. On the first day of practice, Buckey pulled the bus up next to the players and opened the door, "Atkins All-Stars," painted in bold letters on either side.

"Boys, we have a lot of work to do," James admitted as they got on the bus and headed to the field. "The season starts in two weeks, and we haven't had one practice. Now, if we are going to ride around like big shots, we gotta play like 'em."

The team worked their butts off over the next two weeks. There was a new reason to be excited. Just as Ney predicted, the big leagues had their first Negro player. Jackie Robinson started at second base for the Brooklyn Dodgers when the new season kicked off. It made headlines everywhere. Whether you agreed with integrated leagues or not, it was happening. Ministers ended sermons with a prayer for Jackie. School kids all wanted to be number 42, and every colored person's new favorite team became the Dodgers. In no small way did this energize the whole community, the entire country. James was so proud and read the news intently, following every move Robinson made with fascination and pride.

A month later, at their first tournament in San Antonio, the All-Stars beat four straight opponents and took home the first-place trophy and the three hundred dollar prize. The most valuable player went to Samuel to boot. After cashing the check at the local bank, James rushed home to show his father. He placed the money down on the table in front of him and watched his jaw drop. It was all overwhelming to a man, who in his best year, made a hundred dollars. Willie never dreamed they could be this successful. Any trepidation he had about them playing ball faded away.

"It's not all mine. Still, gotta pay the players. Four hundred dollar prize for the next tournament in Dallas next week. Two hundred for coming in second! Can you believe that?" James was brimming with confidence and joy.

"Sky's the limit son," Willie proudly said to James.

James agreed. It was the first time in a long time, he remembered his father smiling at him, and it felt good. "Owe it to you, Pa, for giving me the idea."

Later that afternoon, Willie sat down at his favorite spot on a little wooden bench just outside the kitchen. He waved to the boys as they set off for practice, elated by the prospect of future success. He then leaned against the wall and let the sunshine wash over him. It was hot, but it felt good on his face and arms. He closed his eyes and focusing on the sounds in the garden - the quiet hum of the bees, water flowing across the rocks in the creek, and the breeze blowing through the trees.

Down the road, one of his Mexican neighbors was cooking beans and fresh tortillas. He licked his lips as the delicious smells tempted his nostrils. His stomach growled with hunger, and he contemplated what he'd prepare for dinner. Suddenly, he heard a rustling in the field and opened his eyes. Someone came toward him, a young woman with a colorful bonnet on her head. She smiled at him, and he recognized her.

"Mabel?" he whispered.

Samuel noticed his neighbor's truck parked in the drive as he and James pulled up to the house. Willie still sat on the bench right where the boys had said goodbye to him just a few hours before.

"Hey there, Mr. Garcia," James called out.

Garcia walked over to them. His voice cracked when he spoke. "James, Samuel… your Pa…"

"What about Pa?" James asked as Samuel glanced over at them from the other side of the truck.

"He's gone," he blubbered.

"What do you mean? We just left him a few hours ago," Samuel cried as he ran to his father. Willie's eyes were shut tight, and his lips were curled slightly into a smile. Samuel bent down in front of him and clasped his hands.

"He's gone, James," Samuel sobbed. "Daddy's gone."

James idled as people walked in to pay their respects or to claim some of the tools that were for sale. James acknowledged them, but let Samuel handle the affairs.

He sat on the same bench where they had found his father, wandering through the memories of the people, many of whom were long dead. They came down that road to visit and break bread with his family. What made him quite sad was that his father still had life in him. Though his body was bent, his mind was sharp and his spirit strong. Willie talked about tomorrow as much as he did about yesterday. The pair had much unsettled between them. Now he was in a box buried six feet under the earth.

The brothers had decided to sell the land to a distant cousin. This way, the graves of his mother, father, sister, and grandfather would not be disturbed. But Samuel was having second thoughts. That morning, he and James fought about the decision.

"Why are we selling the land? This ain't right."

"What good is it to be tied to dirt?"

"It's more than dirt, James."

"You can stay if you like," James responded.

Samuel knew he couldn't get through to his brother. James could be as stubborn as a mule when he felt he was in the right. James' decision was influenced by a Ponca Indian friend who told him that no one could ever own land, any more than someone could possess a ripple in the water.

That night, James had a restless sleep, trembling as the spell unfolded. In it, his father had awakened inside the dark coffin alive, buried underground. James could hear his screams as clear as day, and he desperately ripped at the ground until his hands were bloody. When he finally reached the coffin, he found his father resting peacefully, his arms folded across his chest. Then Willie spoke to him.

"Your time will come."

"What do you mean, Pa?"

Suddenly the earth began sliding back into the hole, covering his father's face once again.

"I'm sorry. I didn't mean to hurt Sissy. Can you hear me?" James shouted.

"Sissy's gone. Wasn't your time, son," Willie began before he disappeared under the earth once more.

James woke drenched in sweat, his heart pounding in his chest. He sat up in bed and peered out of the small window near his bed at the black night. He never imagined that this once big, strong man could ever be hurt or taken away. He had a strained relationship with his father, James believed in these last days Willie was trying to make things right between them. Now he was gone, and all that was left were maybes and memories.

A LONG WAY FROM
HOME – APRIL 1949

Despite the sadness of the last year, the Atkins All-Stars won several tournaments and became a barnstorming sensation on the plains. They did so well that they received an invitation to play in the inaugural Indian Head tournament to Saskatoon, Canada. James had no idea where that was. No one on the team did either, but a $2,500 prize was more than enough incentive to head north. The players had been on the road for over a month now. It seemed with each turn off from the highway; they had to deal with bigoted police officers or hostile locals. The unease weighed on every member of the team.

"We're a long way from home and heading to a whole 'nother country," Buckey lamented. "I don't know, James."

"If we don't go, then we'll never know. Can't be worse than what we've seen here."

Buckey nodded and started up the bus. Over the next few days, the All-Stars played in several exhibitions in North Dakota before crossing the border for a game in Weyburn, Saskatchewan. They pulled up to the first hotel that had a vacancy sign in the window. James knocked on the back door. A gentleman answered after a few moments.

"Can I help you?"

James removed his hat, nervously holding it in his hands. "Good day, sir. We are looking for some rooms. Any place in town that serves coloreds?"

The man looked strangely at James and answered. "How many do you need?"

"Uh, six or seven, if you got them."

"Come around to the front, and let's get you set up."

James signaled for Buckey to park in the lot and returned a few moments later to hand out keys.

"What he say?" Buckey asked, excitedly.

"The man just had me fill out some papers. Wanted to know where we were from and what we were doing here."

"Think there's gonna be trouble?" Samuel asked.

"No. It's the darnedest thing. Said he couldn't wait to tell his friends that a team all the way from Texas is staying in his motel."

"Any place we could eat?"

"Told me there's a diner on Main, next to the drugstore."

The players went to their respective rooms to drop off their bags and freshen up before dinner. As Samuel put the key in the lock, he heard someone open the door next to his. A white man and his wife appeared. Samuel stiffened for a moment. The man tipped his hat as the couple walked past him to the stairwell. Samuel wasted no time shutting the door. He later told the boys what had happened to their disbelief.

Thirty minutes later, Buckey had parked the bus in the alleyway behind the diner the motel clerk had mentioned to them. James got off the bus and knocked on the windowpane. A young, blonde woman of sixteen or seventeen opened the door. She gave James the same perplexed look as the man from the motel.

"You're welcome to come inside. We've got plenty of space."

The men shuffled inside the front door of the diner quiet as mice. They looked around nervously at the patrons who paid them no mind. The team sat in a few of the open booths as a curly-haired server gave them menus.

"James! Are you sure about this?" Dean, one of the players, asked.

James nodded. "Act like you got some sense, boy."

For the next few days, the team was astonished by the treatment they received. People smiled and greeted them everywhere they went. Some spoke to them on the streets. The Canadian teams had both black and white players, something they did not see south of the border. It seemed Jim Crow ended at this invisible line called Canada.

During their time around Saskatoon, Samuel developed quite a following. People of all stripes came to watch him pitch. He took the time to speak to the fans and sign autographs. It did not hurt that he spoke a little French and German, which impressed the fans and reporters alike since there were a fair number of immigrants from both countries living in Canada. He always had a big, friendly smile and was humble to a fault.

Between games, he taught a group of youngsters how to throw some of his best pitches. At the final tune-up game before the tournament, Samuel noticed two young women in the stands who were all smiles. He had taken a picture with them the week before. They cheered every time he came onto the field and waved at him between innings as he made his way to the bench. The boys on the team noticed them as well and chided Samuel each time they came to the dugout.

"Concentrate on the game and not the brassieres," James teased.

After the game, the women waited near the bus talking with Buckey while he warmed up the engine. One had straight jet-black hair and an infectious smile. Her olive-colored skin made her brown eyes stand out even more. The other woman was tall, busty, with light blue eyes, and reddish hair.

"Hello, ladies. You enjoyed the game?" James asked, coming towards them.

"Yes, we did. Very much."

"You play a nice brand of baseball," the redhead added.

"Thank you. You familiar with the game?" James asked.

"As a matter of fact, I am," she replied.

"Her father is the coach of the high school team," her friend added.

"Is that right?" James started, but before he uttered another word, Samuel stepped between them and introduced himself.

"I'm Samuel. And this ugly one is my brother James."

The red-haired girl held out her hand. "I'm Gladys Killough. And this is my best friend, Matilde Marten."

"Nice to meet you," Samuel grinned as he shook Matilde's hand and kissed it gently.

Gladys and Matilde joined the team for dinner that night. The evening was very casual, but sparks were flying between Samuel and Matilde. The pair hit it off, and immediately, Samuel seemed smitten with Matilde. As they strolled the streets,

James noticed them holding hands, and it made him very anxious. It did not matter to him that they were in Canada, they were still black men, and these were white women.

James' agitation reached full tilt when they walked in the front door of a fancy restaurant that Matilde knew, and everyone inside stopped and stared. Samuel paid no heed to his brother's concerns or the patrons' glances. He ordered a bottle of champagne before they had even sat down, and then spoke to Matilde in French. James sighed heavily, and Gladys knew something was wrong.

"Are you okay, James?" She asked.

"Yeah. I'm okay," James responded.

"Doesn't seem that way. You look upset."

"Well, a colored man could get in a lot of trouble being out with a white woman. And here we come marching in the front door!"

"You have nothing to worry about here."

James tried his best not to be so self-conscious, but he could never let his guard down that far. That was a luxury only afforded by certain people and not the Negro. Black folks had to have their bearings at all times. James admonished Samuel for flaunting his relationship with Matilde.

"Calm down, James!" Came a chorus from the other players.

"Are y'all crazy? Do you think we're in some Shangrila? These are white folks here."

"They don't seem to mind. Why do you?" Buckey inquired.

'Y'all forgettin' your place. And I'm getting' tired of reminding of you."

The next day after loading up the bus before the game, James turned to the team.

"I'm responsible for you all," he reminded them. "If something happens, I have to tell your family. As the manager, they trust me to keep you safe and get you back home." He looked at each man in turn. "So you don't have to like my rules, but if you want to play on my team, you'll have to follow them."

Over the next few days, the team played well and enjoyed their gracious hosts. Gladys and Matilde even had a small party in their honor. It was the first time many of them had also been in a white person's home, let alone eaten off their plates, and used their utensils. The boys met so many friendly faces on the road, many genuine people, but in the back of James' mind, it could all change in a flash. He kept a watchful eye on everyone.

James felt justified in doing so. He believed, for every decent white person he had met, there would be two or three who would harm him merely over the color of his skin. The players were still amazed by the Canadian hospitality. They had no idea a country full of white folks, just like America, could be so different. Some even contemplated staying behind.

A few days later, tournament day arrived in Saskatoon. Twenty-nine teams were present and loaded with talented players and equally colorful characters. There was Sammie Workman of the San Francisco Sea Lions, who played although he had no hands or feet, and the flamboyant Doc Talley who starred on the House of David, an all-Jewish barnstorming team. From all over Canada and south of the border, squads put their hat in the ring. The St. Louis Black Cardinals were there, along with the Notre Dame Hounds, Moose Jaw Canucks, Weyburn Beavers, and the London Majors. The Prince Albert Bohemians made their first tournament appearance, as did the Chevrolet Cubs.

The weather was never better—puffy clouds and pristine blue sky, with temperatures perfect for both the players and spectators. Fifteen thousand fans jammed into the park over the two days of the tournament and, as one local newspaper put it, "Not even a toothpick thin man could have gotten into the ball game the day of the championship."

The All-Stars were peaking. On the first day, they beat the Wilcox Cardinals 13-0. Samuel was on fire. His pitching was laser-sharp as Matilde blew him kisses during the games. He often touched the top of his cap as a sign that he was thinking about her.

In the final, the All-Stars won the game behind Samuel's pitching to earn the top prize. James greeted the happy team members as they ran into the dugout before the championship presentation. As Samuel strolled in, James gave him a scornful look.

"What now?" Samuel asked.

"We'll talk after the game," James passed on.

The team went out to a local bar after cleaning up and changing. The mood was celebratory, but James was somber and irritated. He watched as the boys drank, smiling gleefully. Gladys tried her best to get him to join the party but to no avail. Samuel and Matilde sat down next to them.

"Okay, James. Let's get this done."

"Now's as good a time as any," James added.

"You want to talk in front of your lady friend?" Samuel asked.

"You talking in front of yours," James snapped.

"Fair enough." Samuel motioned for him to continue.

"I saw what you were doing on the mound today. Moving your hat around before pitches."

"Oh James, he was doing that for me. Don't be angry with him," Matilde offered.

"That's the point. Samuel's not focused on his business. We're in the championship game, and he's fooling around."

"We won. What's your problem, James?"

"It's not that we won. It's how we won. We played a tired team, then you're waving off pitches and all that adjusting your hat was confusing the infielders."

"I took care of my end—"

James cut him off. "And that's your problem. You have to think about the team, not just yourself, or what the newspapers are going to write."

"Is that what this is about? The newspapers and people wanting to talk to me and not to you?"

Matilde sighed, looking sadly at the brothers. "I'm sorry, James. It's my fault."

"No, Matilde. It started long before we met you. My brother has had it too easy."

"You gonna start that shit again?"

"What you do affects everyone on this team. I was shot watching out for my platoon. I know what it means to be a team player."

"I've had all I can take from you. I fought the same as you. Now you're just bitter that you can't play."

Samuel's words stung. "I gave up my life in that war. Do you know what I'd give to be out there? And here you are making a joke of it. All the talent in the world wasted."

"That's your problem. You are always trying to put me in your shoes. I play because I enjoy it. If I can't have fun playing, then there's no reason to do it."

"I expected more of you—"

Samuel stood up before James could finish. "Now is as good a time as any to tell you. I got invited to play against some Big Leaguers in Chicago. I wanted us all to be there, but the more I think about it, the better we go our separate ways."

It felt like a gut punch to James. "I'll be damned. It's settled then," James pushed back angrily from the table and stood up. "You're off the team."

Samuel's jaw dropped. "Why are you doing this?"

"James, please, don't do this," Gladys cried. Both she and Matilde begged him to reconsider.

"Hand your uniform to Buckey. I'll get you your share of the winnings," he demanded.

Samuel looked at his brother for a long time before he spoke. "You think I've always had it easy. You don't know anything about me. Never did." He then got up and walked out.

There was a deep dissatisfaction with James on the drive back to Texas. Most of the guys were not happy when they found out what happened between the brothers. Several of the best players quit on the team soon afterward.

A SURPRISE CELEBRATION
– BRAWLEY, 1950

In the summer of 1950, Betsy got a job as a part-time bookkeeper at Holly Sugar, a sugar beet processing plant outside of town. She enjoyed the work and pay, but she hated the smell during harvest. The scent of stagnant dishwater and rotten potatoes was how she described it. The stink would flood the town when the evening breezes blew in from the south. Betsy had settled in more comfortably after graduating from high school. She enrolled in some evening courses at the junior college the summer after graduation.

Betsy loved being there encouraged by the company of other women who wanted more out of life than being homemakers. Her instructors were equally enthusiastic and gave her lots of praise. Mr. Murray was particularly fond of Betsy, and they often spoke about her going to a university, though he'd make the strangest suggestions to her.

"My sister lives in Los Angeles, and I was thinking of attending UCLA. It's a good school, right?"

"No, no Betsy," Mr. Murray answered. "Those communists have nearly taken over the whole campus. And you'd be so close to Hollywood. It's full of degenerates and even more Reds!"

"Oh my. Well, I've never met any degenerates or Reds on my visits up there."

"You've been to Los Angeles?" he asked.

"Yes, I spent the summer there three years ago."

"Well, count your blessings!" Mr. Murray chuckled.

She wondered, was a degenerate a disheveled drunk with the stench of liquor on his breath? One day on the drive home from work, she asked her father what he felt about it, and he almost jumped out of his seat. Betsy quite enjoyed startling him.

"Where did you learn such talk?" Pappy asked.

"One of my teachers told me—"

Pappy cut her off. "I'll speak to him tomorrow. That is not what I expected you'd learn up there."

"Pappy. Let me finish," she answered, exasperatedly by his moralizing. "He told me I should not go to school in Los Angeles because Hollywood was full of degenerates."

"Well, wait a minute," Pappy stammered. "That might be the case, but I still object to him using that kind of language around you. And why do you want to go to Los Angeles anyhow? Your sister is married. What would you do there?"

"I'd go to school like you did, Pappy. I'd get a good job. I'd go to the beach and do any number of things I can't do here!"

Betsy questioned why her sister's marriage would deter her from living in Los Angeles. Why did that have to limit what she could do? How could anyone forget that her sister had tied the knot? Sarah and Junie made their announcement that same weekend she graduated from high school. In retrospect, she should have known something was up by the way Sarah nervously pranced around the house, complimenting everyone and chattering endlessly about how nice it was to be home.

They had arrived in Brawley in Junie's black Mercury on a Friday afternoon the weekend Betsy graduated from high school. The car's sleek paint shimmered in the afternoon sun. The big, white-wall tires gave the illusion the car was floating over the road.

Sarah wore her Sunday best, a caramel-colored dress with a lace bonnet and sash. She draped her long, reddish-brown hair down her right shoulder. Junie was also dressed nicely, though his suit was ill-fitting. He carried a handful of yellow roses that had wilted from the long, hot drive down from L.A. They gathered themselves on the porch. Sarah nodded at Junie, and he nodded back to her before knocking loudly on the door. She shouted, "Where is everybody?"

Momma Knight did not recognize the voice and wondered why someone was banging that hard on her door. She was prepared to give the person a piece of her mind until she saw her daughter standing there.

"Sarah! Is that you?"

"Yes, it is Momma."

"Well, Lord Jesus. Come on in here and get out of this heat."

Momma Knight looked her up and down, shaking her head. "It's so wonderful to see you. It's been too long."

"Yes, it has," Sarah answered. "Momma, I want you to meet someone special." She motioned toward Junie, who had been standing quietly next to her.

Momma's face almost fell off when she saw the big-jawed, thick-muscled, black man standing on her porch.

"This is Albert, Momma, but everyone calls him Junie. He's the man I wanted you all to meet."

"Hello, ma'am. These are for you," Junie declared, nervously presenting the roses to her.

"How nice," she replied, noticing their sad state of the flowers.

"They need a little water," he added.

"I can see that," Momma smiled. "Well, come on in and have a seat. I'll put these in a vase."

Just then, Pappy and Betsy came into the parlor.

"Is that who I think it is?" Pappy asked. He was smiling from ear to ear.

"Yes, it is!" Sarah replied.

"Hey!" he shouted, pulling her close. "My goodness, look at you."

"Pappy, this is my friend, Albert. We call him Junie."

"Nice to meet you, sir," Junie held out his big hand.

"Nice to meet you as well," Pappy answered, giving him the once over.

Sarah turned to her sister. "Well, well, the graduation girl!"

"That's me!" Betsy affirmed.

"We were just planning her celebration." Momma Knight added.

Pappy and Junie shared an awkward moment of silence as the women hugged.

"Congratulations! I know you worked very hard to get that diploma."

Betsy could see that Sarah was nervous. She was also shocked to see Junie there.

"Hi, Junie," Betsy whispered.

"Hello, Betsy. Congratulations." He gave her a gentle hug.

"You two have met before?" Pappy asked.

"Yes, Pappy. We all had dinner one night when I was visiting Sarah."

"Oh. You never mentioned that." Pappy seemed surprised.

"I'm sure I did," Betsy replied.

"Well, come on, sit down, and rest. That was a long ride," Momma imparted.

They sat at the kitchen table and chatted about all sorts of things while Momma poured them some cold lemonade. Junie and Pappy sat mostly silent except for the occasional chuckle. Now and then, Sarah would nudge Junie to get him to remember one thing or another.

"Ain't that right, Junie?" she laughed, elbowing him in the ribs. He shook his head in agreement.

Later that evening, they all had dinner together as Betsy served the food.

"Mrs. Knight, that cornbread smells heavenly."

"Thank you, Junie. I hope you like the rest of my cooking."

"I'm sure I will."

"Junie, what's your full name?" Pappy asked sardonically.

"Albert Ross, Junior. Junie is my nickname."

"I see. And your people from Louisiana?"

"Yes, that be correct. How'd you figure that?"

"Oh, we got a few folks here from New Orleans."

"We do speak a little different to folks outside Louisiana."

"Yes. You do," Pappy stated. He was not happy that Sarah brought someone home unannounced as she did. He was unimpressed with this lug of a man who talked with his mouth full of food and chugged down his good whiskey instead of slowly savoring it. To Pappy, it was a sign of how he treated his daughter.

Sarah stood up after dinner and announced, "I'd like to propose a toast."

"Yes," Junie agreed. The liquor had soothed his nerves a bit more.

"To my dear sister. Congratulations on a job well done."

"Thank you, Sarah." Betsy smiled.

"Here, here," they all toasted.

Betsy wondered what to say in response, but then Junie stood up, glass extended. "I would also like to add to the celebration," he said nervously. "I've known your daughter for some time, and I apologize for not coming here before now."

Pappy glanced over at Sarah.

"I've enjoyed meeting you all very much and sharing this meal. Mrs. Knight, your cooking was real fancy. And to Mr. Knight, thank you for sharing your good hooch."

Sarah nudged his leg under the table.

"Uh. I am very fond of your daughter, as you can see, and I want your blessing. Uh. What I'm trying to say is, I want to marry your daughter and would like your blessing. Very much."

Momma Knight exhaled deeply.

"Well, this is sudden, wouldn't you say?" Pappy asked, his voice several pitches higher.

"Pappy, I know this might not be the best time and all, but I love Junie. He is a good man, and he comes from a good family."

"I have no doubt, but I barely know him. No offense to you, Albert."

"None taken sir," he returned.

"Pappy, I'm twenty-one years old. I want what you and Momma have. I don't want to wait."

"Sarah, I wish I knew more about the man and had time to see what he thinks and believes. You understand, Albert?"

Sarah started in again, but Junie cut her off. "Sir, I mean no disrespect here. I'm not the prettiest, most sophisticated man. Nor the most learned man, but I love your daughter. I'd do anything for her. I do not take this lightly. It would be an honor for me to join your family."

Pappy sighed and sat back in his chair for a moment. All eyes were on him. He nodded. "Then I won't stand in your way. You have my blessing." He stood up, glass extended. "To Albert and Sarah."

"Thank you, Mr. Knight," Junie drawled, relieved as they tapped glasses.

Betsy sighed. Her celebration would have to wait.

A month later, the Knights had a small ceremony in Brawley. Momma Knight worked tirelessly, getting Sarah's dress ready. Reverend Drew officiated, and Betsy was the maid of honor. They had a small reception at home.

"Sorry. We spoiled your graduation party, didn't we?" Sarah questioned as Junie packed their luggage into the car.

"This was much better," Betsy answered, not wanting to disagree with her. "I got to be the maid of honor."

"We have a place for you in Los Angeles, whenever you're ready to come."

"Are you sure about that?"

"Sure as sunshine, sister," she laughed. "Say that three times fast!"

She hugged Sarah tightly, whispering in her ear. "Look for me then."

"The sooner, the better, you're wasting away down here," Sarah replied.

Betsy held onto her sister just a little bit longer before Sarah got in the car. Betsy did not know the exact date, but she would leave this place, this town in the middle of nowhere. For the time being, this would still be home.

DESTINY – SEPTEMBER 1950

As the previous year was one of success, 1950 was a tumultuous one for the All-Stars and James in particular. Many of the team's best players, including Samuel, went on to other teams or home. Most were weary from the road, but also James' heavy-handedness. The replacements James cobbled together were not ready for the level of play he demanded. After some bitter defeats, James looked to Mexico to season his young talent for next year's tournaments.

Gladys saw how much losing was taking out of him. She did not dare mention Samuel's success after leaving the team. He was doing well playing minor league ball in Minnesota. Gladys kept that to herself. She spoke to James the night before he departed for Baja, California.

"Why don't you stay here? My father could get you another coaching job. Better players, better pay."

"Yeah, that all sounds good, Gladys, but I have to do this."

"Do what? Be your own boss? Is that more important than being happy?"

"Just one more year to get it right, you know."

"What's back in the States for you, James? I don't understand. People are staying home more, and the talent isn't there. I don't know how you do it."

"These boys are good. They just haven't had the time to put it together."

"Well, if anyone can turn it around, it's you, James."

"I want to come back and win this thing. One last time."

"Just think about what I said, okay?" She added.

"I will," he hesitated, looking away from her eyes.

He was too tired to debate it further. He knew Gladys was right, but his pride stood in the way. The same bull-headedness that drove Samuel and the other players to leave. James wanted to prove to them that he could put together a championship quality team without them. He had come to another fork in the road, and it beckoned him once more.

The next morning as the bus readied to pull away, he kissed Gladys on the cheek.

"You know where to find me," she conceded.

Buckey put the bus in gear, and they pulled off, leaving Canada in their rearview mirror. The team set out across the Midwest, turning south toward California. Two days later, after they passed through the desert towns of Coachella and Westmoreland on their way south to Mexicali, a border town on the Mexican side, Buckey stopped at a filling station in Brawley and let the boys stretch their legs.

They slowly walked off the bus, worn down from the long ride. The sun was high and hot. It reminded James of the desert heat at Fort Huachuca. Parked on the other side of the filling bay was a black DeSoto, where James noticed a woman sitting in the passenger seat, her arm resting on the windowsill. Her red-checked shirt was neatly rolled up to her elbow, exposing her smooth, brown skin. He glanced down at her as he went to speak with the attendant. She looked up at him, meeting his gaze. He tipped his cap, and she nodded back.

James spoke briefly with Edgar Knight, the gentleman driving the car. He'd lived in Brawley for over twenty-five years. Edgar seemed very interested in the team and invited them all over for dinner. It was rare for someone like James to come through the valley. At the Knight's home, the team members met Edgar's wife Ellen, and their daughter Betsy. She had been in the car that day at the gas station.

While Momma Knight served some of the players, Edgar invited James into the parlor.

"James, you want some whiskey?" he asked.

"Yes, Edgar, very much."

"Please call me Pappy, everybody else does," he said, pouring James a glass filled about two fingers high with whiskey.

"Now that is wonderful," James agreed after taking a sip.

"Isn't it?" Pappy smiled, pouring himself a glass.

He was quite pleased to see a black man who had been outside the country. James shared stories of his many travels that had taken him across the Great Plains up to Canada. During the war, he spent time in Australia and fighting in the Pacific Islands. Betsy stood by the doorway, listening in as well.

James, his tales and his adventurous life, fascinated her. He was otherworldly, charming and confident, exuding a strength that some thought arrogant.

They spoke at length about whatever James could recollect. He loved her smile, and his eyes traced every curve and nuance of her face and lips. She was full of life and curiosity. Her voice and laugh mesmerized him.

"I hope I'm not bothering you with all my questions," she asked.

"You aren't, you just so damn pretty. I forget where I am."

He stunned her. No one had spoken to her like that. Most men in town were polite and kind. She knew most of their families.

"I'm sorry. Did I offend you?"

"Not at all," she said, composing herself.

"I don't want to be too forward. I'm sure you hear that all the time."

"I don't. Ever," Betsy admitted.

"Well, that's a shame."

"Thank you," she whispered.

They couldn't keep their eyes off each other for the rest of the night.

Unfortunately, for James and the All-Stars, the tournaments in Mexico were not what they expected. The last-minute changes for game locations and reduced prize money bothered James to no end. Two weeks in and he had had enough. He finally had grown tired of wanting to win more than his players did. He did not want to admit it, but he needed Samuel, needed his old team. They knew how to play and win. But the real truth was that he had not been himself since the stopover in Brawley.

The players were shell-shocked when he announced he was disbanding the team at breakfast that morning. Some argued that they were finally coming together, but James did not see it that way. He drove them to a railroad junction in Yuma, put a few dollars in their pockets, and bought them each a train ticket.

"We had a good run, didn't we?" Buckey mourned. He tried to smile, to be happy at that moment.

James answered. "We sure did."

"What you gonna do now, James?"

"Not sure. I'm thinking about heading to Brawley for a spell."

"Brawley? What you got going on down there?"

"It's gotta be a woman!" One of the players shouted.

James smiled broadly. "That might have something to do with it."

The men laughed, slapping each other on the back.

"Well, friend," Buckey smiled, "You know where to find us. We'll be right there in Hondo."

James nodded at them and chuckled.

Buckey held out his hand. "I want to thank you, James Atkins," he stammered. "For giving a cripple a chance."

James felt a tug in his heart. "You earned your place."

"Thank you just the same."

James did not know what to say. They paused for a moment as the sadness sunk in.

"All right, all right. Enough of this shit! You all going soft on me," James protested.

They had one final goodbye before boarding the eastbound train. James hitched a ride over to Brawley after selling the team bus to a local transportation company. He spent some of the money on a little flophouse near the railroad tracks on the east side of town. A few days later, James got a job as a mechanic working with Manny Valdivia, one of the war veterans James had met in town. He then quietly settled into life in Brawley.

The next Saturday, James drove over to the Knights' home. Pappy was surprised to see him. James explained what had transpired, and they spoke for some time before Pappy had to excuse himself. He had to pick up Betsy from the Holly Sugar plant.

"Tell her I said hello if you don't mind."

"Sure thing. Betsy enjoyed your stories. All she talked about for days on end."

James took the bold step of calling on Betsy at her job, and she agreed to a date. James showed up on the appointed day in a new suit, clean-shaven, his hair neatly trimmed. Pappy answered the door and stepped outside to speak with him in private.

"James, I like you very much, so please don't take this the wrong way, but I have concerns about you seeing my daughter."

"Mr. Knight, I understand how you feel. I want the best for her, as well. No disrespect to you or your family."

"I can appreciate that, but Betsy is young. She hasn't been out in the world as you have."

"Sir, with all due respect, she's a grown woman. I think you should trust her choices."

Little did they know that Betsy was standing in the parlor and listening in on their conversation. She could not believe her ears. No one, not even her father, saw her in the way James had just described.

"Fair enough, but don't be fooled. If something happens to my child, there will be hell to pay. You get my meaning?"

"Loud and clear, sir."

"Come on in. I think she's ready."

James' breath caught in his throat when Betsy appeared. Her black sequined dress hugged the curves of her body just so, and she let her hair down, curling it behind her ears.

Pappy couldn't believe what he was seeing. She had grown into a lovely woman right before his eyes.

"You look like one of them Hollywood movie stars!" James said, finally finding his voice.

"Thank you, James. You look nice too."

"You ready to go?"

"Never more." Her voice was filled with excitement.

James turned to Pappy and replied. "I will have her back by eleven o'clock." Pappy eyed him cautiously. Things were moving much too fast for him.

The couple went to the Asia Café just across the railroad tracks on the Northside of Main Street, just behind the newly built fire station. The food was good, and the booths comfortable. It was a busy night, but the couple was seated promptly. As the food arrived, they made small talk. James asked her about her job, but the conversation quickly changed.

"So you've been on a ship to Australia?" she asked.

"Yes, I have. I've spent almost a year recovering there. Got shot in the back. Left side," James remarked, motioning to the area.

"That had to be a terrifying time."

"Scariest day of my life. But that's a boring story. I want to know about you."

"Talk about boring?" She said, pointing at herself. "The only place I've been that was exciting was Los Angeles."

"Los Angeles. I hear it's nice." James pronounced it "Loss-An-ga-les."

"It is, but there are so many other places I'd like to see."

"Like where?" he quizzed.

"Paris for one. I'm gonna get there soon."

"You're not afraid to fly or be in a strange place by yourself?"

"I live in Brawley. Can it be any stranger?" Betsy replied.

"I guess not," he chuckled.

They enjoyed the rest of their meal. Later, as the couple sat in James' car outside her house, Betsy asked, "Can you keep a secret, James?"

"Who could I tell in this town?" he questioned.

"One day, I'll be out of here. As soon as I've saved up enough money to pay for college."

"Really?"

"Yes."

"You'll need someone to carry your bags, you know," James added.

She laughed. "You looking for a job?"

"With you?" he answered. "I'd do it for free."

Betsy smiled. "I accept."

James walked Betsy to the door, lifted her hand to his lips, and kissed it. They stared at each other for a moment longer before she thanked him again for a wonderful evening. Over the next few weeks, they became inseparable. They picnicked together in the Longfellow Park, underneath the tall, water tower. Some days they would take long drives to the Glamis dunes or to the base of the mountains near Ocotillo, where they would spend hours gazing at the stars.

He began to pick Betsy up from work, much to Pappy's chagrin. That was his time with her, and now James was taking that too. Fridays, they'd be back at the Asia Café, sitting in a booth near the door, holding hands.

And when they looked across the table at each other, they saw something beautiful despite their obvious differences. James was not educated and was almost ten years Betsy's senior. She was soft and naive, still the idealist in her parents' eyes. Betsy had not experienced the world as James did. Her mother had someone else in mind when she thought of an appropriate suitor for her daughter. But Betsy was falling in love, and there was nothing in the world to keep her away.

They ended up back at his apartment after one of those many dinners at the Asia Café. He kissed her softly and slowly unbuttoned her blouse, staring longingly into her eyes. She sighed when he caressed her shoulders with his calloused hands. He was gentle with his touch and patient, never wavering from his intense gaze. Her breathing quickened, and they both knew it was right. She kissed him, allowing herself to get lost in the sensation of their lips and naked bodies touching. She pulled at his hair as he entered her, closing her eyes tightly as the pain slowly faded to ecstasy.

One day after work, as James made his way down the walkway to his apartment, the mail carrier called out to him.

"You, James Atkins?"

"Yes, that's me."

"I got something for you," he handed him a letter marked General Delivery.

He knew who it was from the moment he saw the Canadian postmark. He opened it and read it slowly.

> *Dear James,*
>
> *I trust you are well. It has been some time since we last spoke. I learned of your whereabouts from Mr. Kline, the booking agent. I'm sorry to hear about the team busting up, but that's probably for the best.*
>
> *Samuel and Matilde got married last week. He wanted to invite you, but no one knew how to reach you. It was a wonderful ceremony. He*

is playing for the Montreal Royals, the same team as Jackie Robinson. Pretty exciting.

I am hoping, frankly, that you find your way back to Saskatchewan, and I'll be with you soon. I miss you very much, James. If you feel something for me, please say so. We could have a beautiful life together. Just tell me honestly how you feel. I can handle a broken heart, but not being ignored. I think of you always.

Yours truly,
Gladys

Once inside, James folded the letter and placed it on the table. Canada seemed like another lifetime ago.

A SPECIAL DELIVERY – 1951

Betsy seemed preoccupied when James picked her up from work that day. They drove silently to his apartment. He let her in, apologizing for the mess. Betsy did not seem to mind; she had something much more important to talk about and did not know how to break the news. After a few failed attempts at small talk, she finally blurted out.

"James, I'm pregnant,"

He looked as if she had slapped him across the face.

"How far along?"

"Nine weeks," she trembled.

He sighed heavily.

"What are we going to do? What am I going to tell my father?" The tears began to well up in her eyes. James pulled her close.

"We're going to do what's right," he assured her.

"What are you saying, James?"

"I'll come by tonight and speak to your mother and father. It's going to be okay, honey."

Betsy still had her doubts.

"Let me get you some tissue. I can't have you going outside with your eyes all red." He said as he went looking.

As he stepped away, Betsy noticed the envelope from Canada on the table. Curiosity got the best of her, and she unfolded the letter, skimming it before James came back.

"I'll be by your house around six o'clock?" he promised, handing her a tissue.

She nodded. "I'll tell them to expect you."

James arrived promptly at six. Whatever nervousness he felt was quickly replaced by an overwhelming sense of duty. James hadn't thought about having children or starting a family, but he did not want to give Betsy a bad reputation about the town. He knew old man Knight expected as much of him. James calmed himself, taking a deep breath as he got out of his car. James straightened his necktie and brushed off his trousers. He tapped the front door three times, and Betsy opened it slowly.

"Can I come in?" he asked, taking off his hat.

"Yes. Yes. Sorry," Betsy apologized, stepping aside.

Her parents sat in the parlor; both looked ready for blood. Pappy set his glass of whiskey down as James entered.

James greeted them but was met with silence. The tension was heavy in the air.

"I guess you all are wondering why I'm here interrupting your supper."

"We already had our supper," Momma Knight cut in.

"Then let me get on with it."

"That'd be nice," she added, sensing something was amiss.

"I've been seeing Betsy for some time now and I love her. With your permission, of course, I'd like to marry her."

"You all in love, you say?" Momma Knight stated sarcastically. "How could that be? You've only known each other for a short time."

"Let him finish," Pappy insisted, he was too calm, and it unnerved James.

"I have a job. It's not much, but it pays well, and I'm good at it. I have a small place, but with time I will get us a proper home right here in Brawley."

He looked over at Betsy for support, but she kept her eyes fixed on the floor.

"Where's all this coming from?" Momma Knight asked, ignoring her husband.

Pappy adjusted himself in his chair as James fiddled with his hat until he finally spilled the beans. "Betsy is going to have a baby, and I want to do right by her."

The words came out of his mouth, but he couldn't believe he was saying them.

"What?" Momma shouted. She struggled to get to her feet. She pointed at James. "You've soiled my child and ruined my family's good name?"

Pappy commanded. "Sit down, Ellen!" She did not budge. Pappy repeated calmly. "Sit down, Momma. Please."

Betsy covered her eyes. She had to face the music now, and she had no idea what her father was going to say or do.

"Betsy, how did this happen?" Pappy asked. The weight of the disappointment in his voice was enough to sink the Titanic all over again. Before she could respond, he uttered, "Don't answer that. I already know." He wanted better for her and not be the subject of gossip and rumors.

"And Betsy, this is what you want, too?" He queried, looking up at her.

"Well, we hadn't discussed it. I'm sorry, Pappy."

"Child, it's too late for sorry," Momma Knight advanced. "You should've thought of this before you went and lay with that man."

Pappy asked. "So, what are your plans, James?"

"Well, to start." He turned to Betsy, producing a small box from his jacket pocket, "It ain't much."

"Ain't that the truth," Momma muttered, rolling her eyes at him.

He opened the case and revealed a small engagement ring, not more than half a carat. He'd bought it after Betsy told him she was carrying his child. Betsy caught her breath when James got down on one knee.

"Will you marry me, Betsy Knight?"

"James." She paused for a moment. The whole world seemed to be falling in around her. She then opened her arms and shouted, "Yes, I'll marry you."

Momma's mouth dropped. "Oh, God in heaven."

James slowly placed the ring on her finger. "A perfect fit."

She lifted her hand and smiled. "It is." A tear pooled in her eye.

"Do y'all have a date in mind so we can plan a proper wedding?" Pappy asked. He was resigned to the fact that this was going to happen, despite the misgivings he had.

"No, sir. Like Betsy answered, we haven't discussed it much."

"Let me sit down with Momma, and we can decide on a good day," Betsy offered.

"Now, you want my advice?" Momma cut in.

Pappy snapped. "What's done is done."

"That might be—"

"You want our grandchild not to have a father?"

"No. I do not."

"Like it or not, it is her life now," he maintained, eyeing both Betsy and James.

James tried to explain further, but Momma Knight walked away before he could get the words out of his mouth. Later in bed, she cried, wondering what kind of future was in store for her daughter.

"He is so much older than her, Pappy. And we don't know much about him."

"That may be the man's way. He isn't from these parts, Momma."

"Who does he think he is, King James? He stood there, mocking us tonight."

Pappy wondered when it happened. When had James tricked their daughter into falling for him?

"She can't live in that flophouse!" Momma continued, wiping the tears from her eyes. "He's an arrogant man, and believe me; he's not ready to be responsible for a family. Mark my words."

Momma Knight was determined to see her daughter off in style, and a wedding fit for her daughter. Word circulated town of the coming nuptials. The family secured the church and minister. People in town offered their congratulations when they saw the couple out.

As the big day approached, James' nerves became more and more frayed. He was withdrawn and reflective. They were having a baby, bringing a life into this world. A life that depended on him that needed him in ways that he had no idea how to give.

Betsy came up to the job each day to have lunch. Their small talk was a source of tension and relief, all wrapped in the same tight knot. One day, Betsy mustered the courage to tell him how she felt.

"Momma is worrying me to death about these invitations!"

"Have you mailed them yet?" James asked.

"No. Not yet."

"Don't then," he contended.

"What are you talking about? We have to—"

"No, we don't."

She looked at him, confused. "What are you saying?'

"I'm saying let's get married right now. Why do we need this big ole ceremony?'

"Because that's what my parents want."

"What do you want?"

"Well."

"We could use all that money they're planning to spend and buy us a nice place for you and Junior."

She laughed. "You don't know if it's a boy."

"Oh, I know it's a boy!" James took her about the waist with his greasy hands.

"You're going to get my dress dirty, James," she burst out.

"So what? I'll get you a new one. Come here," he beseeched, kissing her on the cheek and neck. "You so damn pretty."

"James. Not here!"

She tried to pull away from him, but he only held onto her tighter, so tight she felt faint. He kissed her on the lips; she imagined that this must be what it is like to fly. When she met James, she had never been with a man, had never been kissed before. Her mother always told her, "Keep your legs closed, and your mind open." Each time she looked at her belly, she couldn't help but think of those fast girls, as her mother called them, who got pregnant in high school. She did not want to be known as one of those girls, but his heat, his passion overwhelmed her. The truth was she wanted him just as badly, and when she lay down with him, her reputation was the last thing on her mind.

"So, what do you say?"

"Momma's not going to be happy."

"What's new?" He laughed.

"Okay," she hesitated, trying to catch her breath. "But you're gonna tell my parents!" She knew there would be hell to pay.

"When do we do it?"

"Right now."

"What? James...I..."

"Baby, there's no time like today. We can have a small ceremony at our house when it's finished. How does that sound?'

"I like that."

He winked at her and told her to wait while he went and let the boss know he was leaving. James cleaned up and drove them to El Centro, the county seat. A judge had the couple recite their vows, and they were officially married on September 29, 1951.

Pappy was angry, but Momma Knight was downright furious. She threw a fit that rivaled the summer storms back in Georgia. James tried to explain why they did what they did, but it did not matter to Betsy's family. She was their daughter, their youngest child. They lived in this town, and he had just arrived.

"This is nonsense! Why do you insult us every chance you get?" Momma Knight asked.

Finally, James had had enough of the browbeating and put his foot down. He looked squarely at them. "Well, you can holler all you want. She's my wife, and we are here to get her things. We'll get us a fine house for our baby. Might take us a little longer than I want."

Betsy's mother and Pappy stood by, flabbergasted.

"Betsy! Let's go," James called.

Betsy entered the parlor, her bags in tow. She loved how James took charge and stood up to her parents when most people she knew did the exact opposite. It amazed her how her mother's criticisms bounced right off him. James was never shy about what he wanted or what he was going to do. He was like an exotic warrior, and Betsy was falling deeply in love with him despite her unease. It was happening all too fast, but she followed James anyway. He grabbed her suitcases, and they walked out the door as man and wife.

Momma shouted at Pappy. "Is that all you're gonna do?'

"What did you want me to do? She's a grown woman."

"She is *not* grown!"

Pappy shook his head and swallowed hard. "You don't see it, but she is." Pappy blamed himself for bringing James into their world.

"We've been here thirty damn years! He showed up practically yesterday, and we have to accept him and his ways?" Momma Knight was outraged.

"It's her choice," Pappy repeated. "Betsy will have to lay in the bed she made," Pappy replied.

"It ain't right. What am I gonna tell the minister?" she sobbed on his shoulder.

"Aw, hell. I'll talk to Drew tomorrow. He'll understand."

"And what if he doesn't?'

"Ain't our problem."

A few weeks later, after cooler heads prevailed, the Knights hosted a small reception at their home. The calm was temporary, as James soon found out. Momma Knight and Pappy had soured on him, and James' actions only reinforced Momma's bitterness towards him. Still, they did not want their first grandchild to grow up in some little shack as Momma called it. They grudgingly accepted James and loaned him the money to build a nice home on the lot they owned next door. This way, they could keep an eye on things and be close to Betsy and her baby.

James began working right away. The house went up slowly, and with the help of friends, Betsy and James would soon have their tiny slice of freedom.

THE BUILD – 1952

A little more than a year after James had seen Betsy Knight at the Texaco gas station on Main Street, they were married and expecting not one child but two. They were having twins. Momma Knight was beside herself with joy, buying double of everything. Pappy warned her not to go off the deep end, being they didn't know the sex of the babies. She fawned over Betsy and made sure she was comfortable at all times. The couple had been staying with her parents, while James built their home on the lot next door.

Friends gathered from around the neighborhood to pitch in, working some days from sun up to sundown, first mixing cement and laying the foundation, next framing each room. Pappy and Momma Knight sawed planks and hammered them in place. Betsy served lemonade and sandwiches during breaks as the house slowly took shape. By the end of the sixth week, they placed the first shingles on the roof. James was thankful for the help. Betsy noticed him grimacing from time to time and massaging his lower back. It was not a job he could have done alone.

James wiped some dust from Betsy's face, kissing her on the lips. "We're almost done, baby." She smiled at him, her belly full and round, pushing at the edges of her blouse.

"Well, this is it, James," Pappy said after he screwed the door hinges in place. "Rounding the corner."

James nodded to him. "A few more coats of paint."

One of the neighbors slathered canary yellow paint on the front wall as James and Pappy set a brick pathway from the gate to the front door. After weeks of hard work, the Atkins home was complete. James stood a silly grin across his face, reveling in accomplishment. He grabbed Betsy's hand and opened the front door.

"Hold on. Hold on," Pappy noted. "We need to bless this home."

"Yes, we do," Momma Knight agreed. "Bow your heads."

"Heavenly Father, bless this home. Bless all who enter and dwell here, in the name of Jesus Christ. Amen."

"Amen!" they all repeated.

James produced a bottle of sake he had in a big metal trunk and poured some into several plastic cups that Betsy served. He raised his drink to the sky.

"To our home," he shouted, proudly and in earshot of Betsy's parents.

Momma Knight whispered under her breath. "Hmm. Built on our land." Pappy hushed her, and she snapped at him. James knew what he was doing. He enjoyed antagonizing Betsy's mother each chance he got. There was an uneasy truce between Betsy's family and James. He had lost favor with them. In Momma Knight's eyes, he was nothing more than a bully and opportunist.

A few months after the home was finished, the family held a formal celebration. Momma Knight prepared a feast for the workers: black-eyed peas, cornbread with lots of butter, and cabbage. Pappy set up several large tables and metal chairs in his yard. Some of the neighbors from down South Eastern Avenue, a few Filipinos he worked with came by to celebrate and welcome James to the neighborhood.

Not long after they had settled into their home, Betsy's water broke. James drove her to the hospital. Pappy and Momma Knight following right behind. The doctor appeared after several hours of labor. He approached the awaiting family with a worried look on his face.

"Is everything alright?" James asked.

"Mother and child are fine." He began. "But the second baby." He paused briefly to exhale. "Was stillborn."

"What?" Momma Knight began.

"Can I see her, my wife?" James said.

"Yes, yes. Please." The doctor motioned to the room.

James knocked gently on the door and stepped inside. Betsy held the child to her chest, stroking his soft skin and little tufts of curly hair. His eyes never opened, never got to see daylight. He lay on her bosom, motionless and cold. James sat at the foot of her bed, not knowing what to say, refusing at first, to hold the baby, not wanting to recall the chill of death. In the end, James curled him under his arm. James touched his fingers as sadness filled his heart.

"He's perfect," James whispered.

The Atkins came home with their son, James Jr., a few days later. Though happy with Junior, James struggled with the idea that his other son was not with them. The birth was compounded for Betsy, who had carried the child in her womb. She often cried to herself, remembering James down on one knee, speaking to her tummy in the early part of her pregnancy when they learned they were having twins.

"I got my catcher and my pitcher!" he boasted. "A couple of home run hitters, maybe?" His smile was big and happy. He hadn't always been so keen on starting a family. He hid his ambivalence from Betsy when she first told him she was with child. They had plans that couldn't wait and didn't have space for children. She convinced James somehow that this was a good thing. She caressed his face and gave him the assurance he was lacking.

Later that week, they buried a little pine box deep into the earth next to their new home. James told her this is how they did things in his family. Their son, their other little boy, was close to them in spirit and body and never far from their memories. James poured his anguish into making improvements around the property, putting the loss of his child into his work, occasionally glancing at the cross that marked the grave.

James began this new life with a vigor he had not experienced since his days playing baseball. He put his heart and soul into the home, and it became a sanctuary to him. It was a place where the world and his troubled heart could maybe find peace. He put that desire for the road and the need to stay one step ahead of his demons, aside for the time being.

He built a small chicken coop, filled it with birds, and planted a small garden with okra, beans, and tomatoes along the fence line he shared with his in-laws, fertilizing the plants with his mix of cattle and horse droppings.

Another son, Leroy, was born a few years later in 1955. And as the children grew, they worked around the house just as their father had. They'd feather, gut, and clean the chickens when James killed one for dinner. Momma Knight stood over them, pointing out which pieces to save, smiling happily when James Jr. brought her a bowl with the gizzards and neck bones she wanted.

In the evenings, James and Betsy sat on the porch and greeted their passing neighbors while Junior played with his brother. Betsy enjoyed these moments the most, and James was more relaxed after a good dinner and a cold beer.

"So there I was pushing the cart with one hand and holding my britches together with the other."

"Oh, I bet that was a sight!" Betsy chuckled as her husband continued.

"Well, I'd split them down to the knee. Don't ask me how I did it."

Betsy laughed harder now, unable to contain herself.

"The best part was when I went to pay for the groceries. I just hoped my underpants were clean!"

"James!" she shouted, gasping for air after laughing.

"Ruined a good pair of khakis."

James loved her laugh. Loved how she understood him. He sat back and took another sip of beer. He paused for a moment, the silence now deafening.

"What?" she asked.

"Did I ruin your life?"

"Why would you ask such a thing?" she replied. Her brow furrowed. There were times when James' melancholy would spoil the moment.

"I know you wanted to get away from here. And look at us now."

"We will, James. One day, we will."

He nodded, but deep inside; he saw that window closing on that promise he had made to her at the Asia Café. A promise he wanted to keep as much for her as for himself. He had regaled her with stories of his travels, the adventures of the Atkins All-Stars, as Betsy leaned forward in her seat, enthralled.

"Those were good times. Good times. Now and then, I'd take the wheel and watch the road open up. We'd come around a bend, and just off the road, there'd be a lake or stream or a wild animal run across the highway. Saw a bear once up in Minnesota."

Betsy hung on his every word. "I can't imagine."

"Good times. Not a care in the world, you know. I didn't have to think about anything when I was on the baseball diamond. As long as we had enough gas to get us to the next town."

"You're so lucky. You've seen so much. I always wanted to travel."

"Well, you should. You should see it all."

"Would you drive me around the countryside like that?"

James smiled at her. "Of course. Let's go." James said, getting up from his chair.

"Huh? Now?" Betsy asked.

"Why not?"

"Promise?"

"Yes. I promise."

"I'm serious," she insisted.

"So am I."

"Shake on it?" She told him.

He took hold of her hand firmly and shook it. She leaned across the table and kissed him on the lips. She never knew how serious he was about following through with this idea. He dreamed about it often, a carefree life where getting old and losing, never crossed his mind. Worry would pass them by and float away.

AN EYE FOR AN EYE – 1955

Three-year-old Junior pranced around in Momma Knight's shoes as she got herself ready for Easter service at the Baptist church a few blocks from their home. The heels made a loud, clunking noise as he walked across the wood floor while Betsy nursed her newborn son, Leroy. James knocked on the door to the Knight's home and peered inside.

"Y'all ready to go?" His anxiousness had no explanation. Maybe it was the guilt of only showing up to church twice a year for Christmas and Easter.

"No, Momma's still getting ready," Pappy called out. "Momma, James is here."

"Just one more minute," came a voice from the rear of the house.

Junior scurried off as James took a seat next to Betsy.

"Why is he running around in those shoes?" he asked Betsy.

"What shoes?"

"*Those* shoes!"

Betsy shook her head. "Now what, James?"

James tracked the boy down, yanking the shoes off Junior's feet and sending him into a crying fit.

"Did you have to do that?" Momma Knight asked, emerging from the bathroom.

"I don't want my boy wearing women's shoes."

"Stop all that crying now. It's okay," Momma Knight pleaded, wiping away his tears as James stared angrily. It was Easter Sunday, and he felt compelled to go despite the fact that Reverend Drew preached too long, and the church was hot and stifling. James wanted to resist, but he went anyway.

After the services, on the ride home, James complained. "This is why I don't come on Sundays."

"Oh, I'm sure you've got a good reason." Momma Knight said sarcastically.

James ignored her and continued with his rant. "Why does Miss Annabelle have to have a solo? That right there cut ten, fifteen minutes!"

"Why do you come when you don't like it?" Betsy asked, exasperated.

James looked at her in the rearview mirror. "I don't know. I don't believe most of what they're preaching."

"Really?" Betsy asked, indignantly. "You don't believe in God?"

"Oh, I believe in God and all, but what they preach is what confuses me."

"How so?" Momma Knight asked.

"Well, in the Bible, it says an eye for an eye, and then in another passage, it say to turn the other cheek. Well, which one is it?"

"James, you shouldn't confess things with your mouth. That's in the Bible too," Momma Knight stressed.

"Why?" James asked.

"You're speaking sin. That's why."

"What's the difference if I think it or say it?"

Betsy shook her head. "God is not something you believe in, like Santa Claus, James. God is real, and I want to know God."

James replied coldly, "That's the problem. Nobody knows what God is."

"That's why it is called faith."

"It's all nonsense. If God knows all, then why go to church? Huh? They pull at your heart with that organ music then pass the collection plate! You ever ask yourself, how many people practice what Reverend Drew preach?"

"You're missing the point. People come to God at their time. So you never know when he'll touch your heart," Pappy assured.

"At least I ain't lying to myself."

"I'm sure when you were off fighting, you prayed to God," Pappy continued.

James snapped, "No! What I saw was people killed for God. And killing for God. Now tell me, what does God have to do with who wins a war? Shoot, this country hates a black man just as much as them Japs shooting at us did. No, I never prayed once during the war," he held up his finger. "And you know what? Everyone I knew who did got killed. I ain't about being right with God or Santa Claus because I've already seen hell."

"If that's how you see it." Pappy snapped back.

"Pretty much."

Betsy readied to fire back when Momma Knight touched her leg, beckoning her to let it go. They continued home in silence. James dropped them off in front of the Knight's home but stayed in the car.

"You coming in for lunch?" Betsy asked.

"No, I'm going over to Family Liquor for a spell," he answered.

As James drove away, Pappy held the gate open for her. Betsy had learned to give James his space. She knew he was battling demons she could never comprehend. Betsy tried in the beginning, that first year together, but not now. She stood there, two children and her aging parents by her side, watching the car roll down the road out of sight.

He'd come home later, smelling of beer and sweat, in a playful and apologetic mood, wanting sex as he usually did when he went to town. Betsy wondered if he'd drive away one day and not come back. Sometimes she wished he would.

"Can't tame a wild animal," Momma Knight voiced, walking into the house with a sleeping Junior slumped over her shoulder.

"Ain't that the truth," Pappy agreed.

After stopping at Family Liquor, James pulled off the road at the edge of town next to the road sign that read: Los Angeles 198 Miles. He kept the engine running and thought back to the many times he and Betsy spoke of starting on their own. Now here he was with two children, a house, and waning hope that it would ever happen. James felt every bit of his thirty-seven years, and his chances slipping away. He gripped the steering wheel a little tighter with one hand while reaching for his can of beer with the other. It was not the first time James thought of leaving. The few times he did, he found the will to turn back toward town. But, *'One day,'* James said to himself. One day he'd muster the courage and drive away with or without her. Over the next two years, this conviction would only deepen.

SAD NEWS – 1957

James was headlong into the morning newspaper reading that integration had come to schools across the South. He didn't believe Jim Crow was dying, but something profound was happening. That sea change had little impact on life in Brawley, where the Atkins boys were more concerned about playing with their toy guns and plastic army men.

Glimpses of this changing world were all around, from the music on the radio to the styles of dress. These changes excited Betsy. They reminded her of the summer she spent in Los Angeles with all the bright lights and fancy clubs. There was an energy, anticipation of all things possible that was missing in bucolic Brawley. Sure, she could drive across the border to Mexicali, but when in Los Angeles, she could be with people who looked like her, spoke her language, and wanted the same things she did. She loved the idea of being closer to her sister, but that life was further away than she wanted to admit.

James had no stomach for what he called the fast life of Los Angeles. Sure, a taste of it now and then was fine, but not as a lifestyle. Vacations were simple and, to Betsy, the same drudgery. They'd pack the car and drive to San Diego or up to the mountains near San Bernardino, sleeping in roadside motels. One summer, they went as far as the Grand Canyon. James relished being out on the open road, and the children enjoyed camping. While the rest of the family enjoyed the break, it fell short of what was in Betsy's heart.

Betsy planned visits with Sarah, hoping James would change his mind about moving away, but he remained skeptical. He did go on one trip to the city that started wonderfully. Junie was a big baseball fan, and the two men hit it off, sharing their love of whiskey and raunchy tales. After a late lunch, they went to a Dodgers game and had dinner in one of the popular diners on the south side, where Junie told him about all the colored movie stars that frequented the place. Later, they went dancing.

"Come on, James. Let's dance," Betsy beckoned, grabbing his arm as she headed to the floor.

"You go on. I'm fine."

She then turned to Junie. "Care to dance, kind sir?"

Junie hesitated for a moment, looking over at James, who only shrugged. He took her hand, and Sarah followed. The three of them cut up the rug. Betsy was happy. It had been a long time since she enjoyed herself like that.

The next morning as they sat down for breakfast recounting the night's events, there was a pause in the laughter when the phone rang. Sarah answered the call.

"Yes, he is here. May I ask who calling?" Sarah put the receiver down and called James. "Do you know a Bob Kline?"

James looked startled as he took the phone from Sarah. Kline was his old booking agent from his baseball days.

"Bob. How you doing?"

"I'm good, James. Been trying to find you for almost two days now. I wish I had some good news."

"What's the matter?"

James listened closely, then thanked the man for calling and hung up the phone.

The change in James' voice alerted Betsy. She sensed something was amiss.

"Honey, what's going on?" Betsy asked.

"It's my brother."

"He okay?" Junie asked.

"He's dead. Car accident."

"My Lord!" Sarah gasped, placing her hand on his shoulder.

"I need to get to Minnesota."

"Minnesota! When will you be leaving?" Sarah asked.

"Today. His body is in the morgue."

"I'll pack our bags," Betsy said.

"You can't go, Betsy. The boys need someone here with them."

"James, you shouldn't go alone," Junie fretted.

"There is nothing I can do for him now, Junie. And no sense in bothering anyone else."

"You got any family back in Texas that can help you out?" Junie asked.

"No. They're all gone."

"James. I'll go with you. We can split the drive."

"I can't ask you to do that, Junie," James hesitated.

"I think that is a great idea," Betsy added. "You should leave here. It'll be faster than from Brawley."

"And how'll you get home?"

"I can take a bus back," Betsy answered.

"She's got a point there, James," Junie cajoled.

"We got a long drive."

"I'll make you some sandwiches for the road," Sarah added. "Won't take but a minute."

James' reaction to the news left Betsy a little baffled. He became quiet and determined. They went outside and got Junie's car started.

"Are you okay?" Betsy asked James as he put his suitcase in the car and shut it with a heavy thud.

"I'll be all right," he supposed.

"James, that's not what I'm asking you."

"Please, Betsy. I don't know what to say to you. It's my brother."

She paused for a moment then backed away. "Call me when you get there."

James nodded and waved goodbye as they started on their trip. In no time, they were heading east toward Nevada, taking route sixty-six to Gallup, New Mexico, and later, Abilene, Texas. Some six hundred miles later, they came to highway thirty-five near Springfield, Missouri, and went north. It was a highway James was very familiar with, having traveled it many times with his baseball team.

James felt a certain kind of freedom being out on the road again despite the circumstances. Seeing the distant lights and open spaces bought back many memories, but also some peace of mind. These places were still familiar to him, while others were brand new, each one with a story to tell.

"You done drove all up and down through here. That must have been some time," Junie asked.

"Yes, it was," James mumbled.

"Lots of fine ladies for a pretty boy like you. All that good hair. I know you had a stable full."

James chuckled but did not respond.

"You never talked about your brother before. Were you all close?"

"As close as brothers can be, I guess. We had our differences."

"Sounds about right. Man, my brother Tommie used to beat the stuffing out of me growing up. That boy wasn't afraid of nothing. Not even snakes. You scared of snakes?"

"Not particularly."

"Well, I am. Don't bring them near me!" Junie roared with laughter. "So, where was I? Oh yeah, so Tommie's two years older than me, but I whipped him one day right there in the yard. My daddy just laughed. Told the rest of them they better watch out!"

James yawned, but Junie continued.

"That was some fight too. We get to wrestling, and I got around Tommie somehow and smashed him down on his side. Broke the fool's arm. Boy, was he mad! You ever fight with your brother like that?"

"Sure, when we were younger, we'd throw a few punches."

"Sounds like you liked your brother!" he laughed.

"We had our moments," James paused, remembering the times he and Samuel fought as kids. James hit him across the face, and Samuel, as small as he was, rushed him. They wrestled until Sissy came and broke them up.

"Better not hit him again," she commanded, before punching James hard in the face and busting his lip. He remembered that day vividly. It was the first time he'd seen his own blood.

"I hated them bastards in my family. That's why I come to Los Angeles. Then this fool Tommie gonna move out to Santa Ana wanting me to get him a job. All the shit he did to me," Junie disclosed.

"He made you tough, though? Got you ready," James responded.

"Never thought of it like that, but it makes sense. I see why you get along with Betsy. She's smart as a whip, that girl. Take a special kind of man to catch her eyes."

"Hmm." James leaned back in his seat. He looked out the side window to some nearby mountains. The last of the sun's light spilled over the crest. It had been fifteen years since he last saw his brother, fifteen long years ago, that tournament day in Canada. James couldn't forget the harsh words they'd shouted to each other. He could not blame Samuel for accepting an invitation to play against the Big Leaguers in Chicago. James let his anger and jealousy get the best of him. He believed he would do it differently if it happened today. Samuel's last words to him had so much hurt in them.

"You're off the team," James said to Samuel.

"Why are you doing this?" Samuel pleaded with his brother.

"Don't do this, James." Gladys cried.

"Hand in your uniform to Buckey." James' voice echoed in his mind.

James' eyes got heavier with each mile they put behind them. As he fell into a restless sleep, he tried to imagine happier times, imagining how that last evening with his brother should have gone.

James opened his eyes slowly and sat up in his seat.

"Bad dream?" Junie asked

"Huh?"

"You been mumbling for a while," Junie said, looking ahead. "Whatever the trouble, the Lord will carry you through it."

"There ain't a God. Not in the way you think," James alleged, looking away from him to the night sky.

"That's terrible."

"Just telling you the truth."

Junie was unmoved. "The Lord has got me through a lot in my life, and I'm grateful."

"My brother was killed along with his wife. Is that how God works? Or was it bad luck?" James replied.

"It was their time, and one day, it'll be our time. I don't question it."

"Hogwash! That might be good for you, but ain't for me," James stated.

"I'm a simple man. I don't try to make it harder."

"They are all gone now, except for me," James grieved, the words surprising him.

"You ain't alone, James. You got family."

"Ain't the same."

"Life don't come how you want it. It come the way you need it," Junie reasoned.

"People that knew me from knee-high to now are gone, Junie," James felt a lump in his throat grow larger. A tear slid down his cheek, out of Junie's sight. James kept his face turned to the window away from the driver. Junie finally went silent as they drove into the night.

They arrived in the quiet town of Stillwater, Minnesota, after another full day on the road. James got them a room at a lodge, and they rested a bit before going to the morgue. As Junie slept, James' mind went back to his Atkins All-Stars days, the many fantastic pitches Samuel threw that amazed not only him but also the fans and players alike. It would have broken his mother's heart to know they had not spoken in years, as close as they had been growing up.

When Junie woke, he and James took the short drive to the municipal center. There they met the coroner, who brought James to the freezer while Junie waited down the hall. The coroner's small talk only made James more anxious, but he was suddenly quiet when he stopped in front of one of the lockers.

"You ready?" he asked solemnly.

James nodded.

The coroner then slid the gurney out carefully. There was a body covered by a black bag. James shuddered at the sight of the lifeless shape as the coroner carefully unzipped the bag.

James' breath quickened almost to panic, making him dizzy.

"I know this is hard, sir. Take your time."

James tried his best to hold it in, but his emotions overwhelmed him. He let out a pained howl.

"Samuel," he whispered, touching his brother's cold face.

"They're all here, you know. Your brother, his wife, and their child."

James looked at him, confused, "Child?"

"Yes, she's over here, your niece?" he answered. "Do you want to see her?"

"Yes, please," James said, shutting his eyes. He had no idea there was a child involved.

The coroner pulled out another gurney, and there she was, a little girl of six, her cheeks frozen hard. She had long, black hair like her mother, but her features—her lips, nose, and the shape of her face were all Samuel.

"What was her name?"

"It's right here. Jamie Marie Atkins."

"Jamie?"

"Seems they named her after you."

James folded over, putting his hand on his knees and sighed deeply, suddenly feeling nauseous.

"Are you okay, sir?"

"Just give me a minute," he whispered, the words coming out slowly.

"Did you want to see his wife—?"

"No, sir," James replied before the man could finish his sentence. "This is too much already."

"Okay. See me when you are ready. I'll need you to sign some papers."

The coroner looked back over his shoulder as James slumped over the child's body, and started to sob.

James now stood silently over his brother's body. Driving across the plains, James could not imagine him gone. His death did not register, but seeing him here brought it to finality. James composed himself, chocking down his grief. He wiped his eyes, but they remained as red as an apple when he walked out into the hallway. Junie waved him over.

"James! These are Matilde's people."

"I know who you are," an elderly man said to James. It was Matilde's father, Pierre. He spoke with a heavy French accent. "Samuel spoke about you all the time."

James put his hand out, but the man leaped into his arms, hugging him tightly.

"We lost them, James," he wept.

"Yes, we did." James agreed.

"We want to take him back to Saskatoon if you don't have a problem. It is where they belong."

James did not object.

"Will you please come back with us? We will have a service for them there."

"I don't know. My friend here has to get back to Los Angeles."

"No, I don't," Junie shared. "May never get another chance to see Canada."

"It's settled then," Pierre agreed.

They signed some papers and drove the four hundred or so miles across the border. James had not been back in these parts in so many years that he hardly recognized the streets and buildings.

They had grown up on the road, these black brothers from Hondo, Texas. It all came together for them here, their greatest triumph and most significant loss. They lost each other during what should have been their happiest moment. Now Samuel was gone forever. No chance to reconcile, no time to say sorry.

The family's final resting place was a hillside cemetery overlooking the city. As James addressed the gathered family and friends, he recognized a familiar face. It was Gladys.

"I'm honored to be here amongst so many people who loved my brother. Samuel was a good man. He was the best in my family, a much better man than I'll ever be. You all have been so gracious and kind. Thank you for coming."

James felt the urge to call out for his brother as the caskets were lowered into the ground. He fought with his emotions, struggling to make sense of why he had to endure one painful event after another. It seemed that every knock on this door left him with a sense of foreboding.

At the repast, James sat alone. He watched Junie talk, laughing and joking with his newfound friends. An unexpected sense of loneliness began to weigh on him when suddenly someone touched him on the shoulder.

"Hello, James," Gladys said softly.

James rubbed his eyes and smiled. "Hello, Gladys. How are you?"

"As well as can be. I lost my best friends."

"Yes, me too."

"I'm sorry," she replied.

"Thank you. What's new?"

"Got married three years ago to a wonderful man. I have a daughter who is the light of my life."

"That's wonderful."

"And you?"

"Been married five years now. I have two boys, five and three."

"I guess that explains why I never heard back from you."

"I'm sorry about that, Gladys."

"Life goes on. Right, James? It worked out for us both in the end."

Pierre interrupted their conversation.

"Sorry, but we must speak about some things," Pierre began.

Gladys graciously said goodbye. "I've got to get going, James. Nice to see you."

"Nice seeing you, too," James answered.

"Your brother had some money and clothes." Pierre continued.

James shrugged. "There's nothing I want of his."

"No, no. There must be something you want to remember your brother?"

Just then, Pierre's wife spoke up. "Papa," she looked to her husband, "the valise with the pictures."

"Ah, yes. Come with me."

Pierre pointed on top of some boxes was Samuel's old suitcase, the one their father had given to him.

James shook his head. "I'll be damned."

Pierre pulled it from a pile and placed it on a nearby desk, running his hands across the rawhide surface, then springing the latches. Inside were newspaper clippings of the All-Stars going back to 1947. Mixed in were photos of the players, people from the road, and the old team bus.

James sifted through a few of them: the team picture after winning the first Indian Head tournament and several of a much younger James out with Gladys, Matilde, and Samuel. His heart stopped when he came across the last picture. It was a recent one of Samuel, Matilde, and Jamie. James swallowed hard, choking back his anguish.

Pierre confirmed, "This was taken maybe a month or two ago."

"Yes. I'll take this with me," James remarked, shutting the case.

The next morning, Junie warmed the car. He'd filled the tank, checked the oil, and packed the trunk. It was time to go. It had been bittersweet, this return to Canada. The place had given James his first real taste of life unencumbered by Jim Crow.

James knew he was seeing it for the last time as they crossed the border a few hours later. Two days on, they were back in California. Leroy, his youngest son, ran out to greet his father when he parked the car out front. James lifted him, giving him a big hug and a kiss on the forehead while Betsy and Junior stood at the door and waited for him.

There was relative peace in the home for a few weeks after James returned. He was more subdued and spoke softer. Betsy knew the loss of his brother weighed on him more than he let on, but she liked the tranquility. He had been ill-tempered with the boys before them leaving for Los Angeles, and it had become a cause of disagreement with Betsy. They had argued about his harsh treatment of the children. Once, when some tools came up missing, he was especially brutal. He had them stand at attention, hands at their sides while he interrogated them.

"I'm going to ask you both one more time," he glowered, while he menacingly wrapped a thick leather belt around the palm his hand.

Junior could not contain himself; the tears rolled down his face as he pleaded with his father. James scowled as Leroy shook his head "no" when his father had questioned him.

He asked Junior again, "Where are my tools?"

"I don't know, Daddy," he begged between gasps of air. His heart pounded in his chest. His feet felt heavy as bricks. James raised his arm high, belt in hand, and let loose a stinging strike across the back of the boy's legs. Junior shrieked in pain as James calmly stepped over to Leroy and asked him again. The boy tilted his head back and shook his head, "no." His father struck him across his legs, repeatedly.

"One of you is lying, and I'm going to get to the bottom of it!" He went back to Junior, now more terrified than before. "No, Daddy, no." But his pleas did not sway James as he swung the belt with impunity. The leather tore into his skin. He tried to block the blows with his hand, but that only made James angrier. If he could not strike him on his hind parts, he hit him across his back and neck. He grabbed the collar on Junior's shirt when he tried to run away. The belt caught the soft skin just below his buttocks. He struck him so hard he knocked the boy off his feet.

"Stand up!" James yelled at him. "Stand up, I said!" He yanked his arm and beat him across his shoulder and chest. The boy fell in a heap on the floor, sobbing loudly. The blows burned like fire on his body.

James started in on Leroy, gritting his teeth as he hit the boy all over his legs and torso. James did not seem to care where or how he struck the boy, but Leroy was able to break free and run away.

"Come back here, you little bastard!" James shouted, but the boy kept running. He screamed out in terror as his father pursued him through the kitchen toward the front door. James caught him, jerking him to the ground. The strap came up high and made a thwacking sound as the leather burned into his legs and ribs. James was in a fury.

Just then, Betsy came in the front door, groceries in hand. "James!" She shouted, dropping her bags and breaking a jar of mayonnaise in the process. She stepped between him and Leroy. James turned, raising the belt high again.

"Get out of the way, Betsy!" he shouted, his chest heaving.

"What the hell are you doing?" she screamed, draping herself over her son. "What did this boy do to deserve a whipping?"

"They were playing in my toolbox again. I've told them boys to stay out of there!"

On one side, she heard Junior sobbing. "James!" She carried Leroy over to his brother. She found him curled in a ball on the floor, crying. He screamed when she touched him.

"Baby, its Momma. It's Momma." She marched back to confront James. He was putting the spilled items back in the bags.

"You broke the mayonnaise jar," he mocked, without looking at her.

"I don't give a damn about that jar. What the hell's gotten into you?"

"Nothing's got into me."

"Look at me!" she cried out.

James stood up quickly and turned to face her. "Woman, don't raise your voice to me like that."

"Or what?" she said. "You gonna beat me too?"

"I just might."

"No, you will not!" she snapped, defying him.

"Those boys need to be taught a lesson."

"There won't be any more lessons taught today or ever like this again!" Betsy declared.

"Or what!" he yelled. Betsy screamed, raising her arm to protect herself.

He dropped his hand to his side. "I bet they stay away from those tools from now on."

Their mother gritted her teeth, her limbs trembling with anger, wanting to gouge his eyes out. A few days later, Pappy came over and returned the missing tools.

"Hey, James borrowed a few things from your toolbox," he chuckled. "I hope that you didn't need them."

"Any time," James smiled, but he was angry. Angry that Pappy had gone through his things again without his permission. He was mad at himself, embarrassed that he took his frustrations out on his children. He had no harsh words for Pappy nor an apology for his children. Leroy limped about for almost a week from the beating. Momma Knight was not happy when she saw the welts and bruises on the children's legs and back.

"What kind of a man disciplines a child like this?" she asked, looking at Betsy with disgust.

"Ellen, not for you to tell the man how to raise his children," Pappy said from behind his newspaper.

"Raise his kids?" If he doesn't kill 'em first."

"Spare the rod, spoil the child," he added.

"Spare me that shit!" she snapped. Momma Knight rarely cursed. Pappy lowered the paper and glared at his wife.

"I'd have never let you put your hands on my children like this," she continued.

"Those boys will be fine," he snarled, dismissing her complaint. "That's how I was raised."

"If he puts his hand on them again, I swear, I'll kill him."

Pappy shook his head and went back to reading.

None of them knew what was going on with James. They didn't know the many times he parked by the road sign at the Brawley city limits sipping on a beer, imagining another life he could have had. And with each sip, his frustrations dimmed just a little bit more. He remembered his days strapped to a plow, the dark earth turning over, and Samuel tossing fresh seed into the ground. Then there was Mr.

Ney, long since dead, telling him that he could be a major league ballplayer. A few centimeters to the left, and James would have a completely different life, not the one that filled him with regrets. He couldn't abandon his family, not like he did with his brother. James couldn't fathom getting another phone call telling him someone close to him had died. He had to stay no matter how much it ate away at him.

The severe punishment continued, which to the children was arbitrary and capricious. With Betsy and the boys, the home was a happy, joyous place, until James walked in. The air in the room suddenly disappeared as they tried to anticipate his temperament. Would he be smiling and jovial, or after a bad day, be grouchy and sullen? Betsy ran these questions through her mind each time she heard the car door shut as did her children.

They waited in terror when the door swung open, not knowing if a monster or a jolly giant was entering. When he was happy, there was laughter, and he'd tell a story or two, kissing Betsy on the cheek and asking the boys how their day went at school. When James fell into one of his moods, it was pure hell.

For a few weeks, after he returned from Canada, he was a different person. He was attentive and kind. Betsy could tell he was despondent over the loss of his brother. But she wondered when he was going to erupt, especially when the sadness and anguish over the loss finally tracked him down. She feared for their children. Would he lose his inhibition to strike her too? The family did their best to adjust.

The boys' personalities could not be more different. Junior was sensitive, a good student, and earned excellent grades. He mostly stayed to himself and loved being around his mother and grandmother. It did not matter what they were doing; Junior wanted to be a part of it. He sang along when his mother played her favorite Tom Jones or Temptations record on the old phonograph Pappy had given her. She pulled Junior up from his chair and danced with him many times. They bonded over her musical tastes.

Leroy was quite the opposite. He was a popular and funny boy, better at recess games than getting his schoolwork done. Leroy was scrappy and loved the way paper money smelled. He loved to play with his toy soldiers in the soft dirt near his grandmother's garden. Momma Knight watched Leroy playing from the kitchen window one day while Betsy sat at the table.

"Don't know why you had to quit school. Boys are old enough for you to go back."

"It's been so long, Momma. At the end of the day, I'm exhausted."

"Exhausted? I worked two jobs, took care of my husband and children, and I never missed putting a meal on the table. Did I Edgar?"

"No, you didn't, Ellen."

"Momma, that's you. I am trying my best to keep a house."

"You'll have to try to harder because I want you to go to college."

"Why is that so important to you?"

Momma Knight looked at her sternly. "Do I need to answer that for you? You should already know why it's important. Set a good example for your children too."

Betsy shook her head. It seemed there was no winning in either home.

"That Leroy is something else."

"What's he doing?" Betsy asked.

"Throwing rocks at the Sosa boy from up the street." Momma Knight pushed the latch on the window and opened it. "Leroy! Leroy! You hear me, boy?"

Leroy turned to see who was calling him.

"Stop throwing them rocks before you break a window! Stop..." she suddenly felt light-headed, and everything went dark. Her knees buckled, and she collapsed onto the floor.

"Momma!" Betsy screamed and rushed to her side, but she was unconscious.

They arrived at the hospital as quickly as they could, but the prognosis was not good. Momma Knight had an aneurysm caused by a massive tumor in her brain and fell into a coma. The family was naturally devastated. They sat quietly on the little couch in the waiting area in silence. Betsy put her head on her father's shoulder and wept.

Sarah arrived the next afternoon and helped support their father. Betsy hated that the last thing she and her mother did was fight. Sarah stroked her mother's hair, while Betsy rested her head in her lap, caressing her hand. She whispered how sorry she was many times. She prayed that her mother would be all right, that they'd go home, and she'd be back to her old self. But Momma Knight remained unconscious for days.

Betsy refused to leave her side, praying for her recovery. Thursday morning, Sarah came by with a change of clothes. As she chatted with her sister, Betsy felt a slight twitch; her mother's hand jerked. She went silent and looked at her mother's face, but her eyes remained closed.

"What's happening?" Sarah asked.

"Nothing," Betsy replied, resting her head again. Suddenly, there it was again.

"Momma," Betsy whispered.

Momma Knight opened her eyes slowly about a quarter of the way. "Why are you praying so hard? Don't think I'm going to heaven?"

Betsy covered her mouth with her hand and laughed. "No, Momma, I just can't lose you," she said, her eyes welling with tears.

"There's never a good time, baby, but I'm still here."

"Amen to that," Sarah agreed. She then called Pappy. Momma Knight smiled meekly as Pappy held her had.

"Take care of my garden," she whispered.

"Yes," Pappy's voice trailed off.

"And take care of the family… promise me that, Pappy."

"I promise, Momma. I promise."

Momma Knight died a few hours later with her family by her side. When she closed her eyes and went limp, Pappy kissed her, mumbling "Wait for me" under his breath. Sarah stood over the bed, her clenched fist covering her quivering lips, her eyes rimmed in red. "I'm sorry," the station nurse whispered as she unplugged the monitors.

James was the picture-perfect husband over the next few days. So much so, that he stunned Betsy with his compassion. James was sweet to the boys, helping them get dressed. He then set up the tables and chairs for the repast. James caressed Betsy's shoulders and provided tissue to dry her eyes, telling her about the time his mother died with this far off look in his eyes.

"We were on the road and couldn't get back to be at her funeral. She's buried in the yard with Sissy and my father."

"Are they gonna put Grandma in the ground too?" Leroy asked.

"Yes, son, so we can visit with her all the time and never forget her," Betsy answered.

"But she's an angel now. She's going to heaven, ain't she?"

Betsy smiled, "Yes, son, her soul is in heaven."

"What's a soul? Is that what we put in the ground?"

"No, Leroy. Her soul is that thing inside Momma that made her special," she answered. "Her body is what protected her soul. When God calls you home, you won't need this body anymore." She touched his shoulders gently.

"In heaven?" he asked, a tear forming in his eyes.

"Yes, in heaven. She's with the angels now. Her body is here, so we visit with her any time we want."

"Will I be an angel when I die?"

Betsy looked at James before answering. "Yes, son. If we were good people on Earth, we will go to heaven and be together forever."

"Why, Momma? Why can't we be *here* forever?"

"Leroy, we all have to die, and one day you can ask God for yourself. That day won't come for a long, long time. So don't you worry about it, okay?" She kissed him on the top of his head.

At the funeral hall, many people had already arrived. Betsy and Sarah sat with their father, holding his hands and leaning on him when they felt overwhelmed. James sat with Leroy while Junior sat alone. He was not taking his Grandmother's death very well. They had been close his whole life, and it pained his heart that he did not get to say goodbye to her. At the end of the service, Pappy addressed the mourners.

"I want to say a few words. First, thank you all for coming and seeing my wife off to her homecoming with the Lord."

A few members whispered, "Amen."

"I want to thank my two sons-in-law for all their help during these tough, tough times. I want to thank my old friend Frank Tamayo, who comforted me these last few days. I could not have made it this far without my lovely daughters, Sarah and Betsy, to lean on. Thank you." He bit down hard on his lip. The lump in his throat was so large it was painful.

"Take your time, brother Edgar," someone shouted.

He steadied himself. "Please join us at our home for the repast. Thank you all again."

Betsy and Sarah took him into their arms as the processional began. After everyone said their final goodbyes, the family walked over to the casket. Momma

Knight looked content in her favorite necklace and dress, her arms folded across her waist.

"They'll be closing the casket shortly," Reverend Drew disclosed. "Let us pray one last time.

"Goodbye, my darling," Pappy whispered.

Several townsfolk gathered in the Knight's home and enjoyed good food and memories. Pappy was gracious and patient with those who had come, but deep down, he was destroyed. He could not imagine being in his home alone. She was the pioneering woman who convinced him to come out to California. He never believed the end would come like this.

"You know, I almost turned around and went back to Georgia when we arrived in Yuma," he revealed to Sarah. "There was nothing but sand and a few bushes. And hot! Good lord, it was hot." Pappy's eyes swelled with tears. "Momma worked so hard for the Mitchell family all those years till Betsy was born. She saved everything she earned. No new dresses or a hat for church. We were able to build a house and buy the lot next door."

Sarah tried to lighten the mood, wanting to celebrate her mother's life and not have it feel like such a sad affair, but she quickly had a change of heart when Tamayo's daughter Isabel walked in.

"Hi, Sarah."

"Isabel!"

"I loved your mother," Isabel said, tears sliding down her face.

Sarah tried to hold back her tears as Isabel spoke.

"I'm sorry for your loss."

Sarah hugged her, but it was all too much for her. She needed a moment alone. She pushed through the crowd to the back door and outside, where she found Leroy and Junior.

"What are you all doing here by yourselves?" Sarah asked, wiping her tears away.

"Nothing," Junior replied.

She pulled out a cigarette and lit it. "Hold this," she directed, handing her drink to Junior. He stared into the glass and sniffed it.

"You want to try some?" she asked.

Junior looked at her, surprised.

"Go ahead. Take a sip. You know what a sip is?"

He tilted the cup to his mouth. The liquor burned his tongue and tasted nothing like what he expected. He coughed a little and wiped his mouth with his sleeve. Sarah chuckled as she blew smoke from her nostrils.

"You want to try, boy?" she asked Leroy. He set his sights on the cigarette in her hand.

"Here," she said, holding it out to him. "Just suck on end a little bit, then blow it out." Sarah believed that if they tried adult things like drinking and smoking with family first, they were less likely to try it with strangers.

Leroy followed her instructions and took a toke on the cigarette, blowing the smoke out.

Right then, James came around the corner. He looked at Sarah, then at Junior with the glass of whiskey in his hand, then over to Leroy, with a burning cigarette between his lips.

"Leroy!" he shouted. "Get that outta your mouth!"

"Yes, Daddy," he obeyed, dropping the cigarette on the ground.

"Junior, what you got there?"

"He was holding my drink for me," Sarah assured.

"And I suppose Leroy was just holding your cigarette?"

"Don't make it into a crime, James. Better they learn these things around family than on the streets."

"How about they don't learn these things till they're old enough?"

Sarah waved him off.

"Come on inside, right now!" James grumbled to the boys.

Junior handed Sarah her glass and walked to his father.

"I don't ever want to catch you doing that again. You all are too young."

"Yes, Daddy," Leroy replied.

"That woman's a damn fool!" James barked loud enough for Sarah to hear him.

"No, a damn fool could see his children are growing up," Sarah shouted back.

"What do you know about raising a child?" James asked.

"A lot more than you know. I don't have my head stuck up my ass as you do!" Sarah shouted back at him. "So go on. Get away from here!"

PART TWO

1960 — 1970

UNEARTHING THE PAST

CHRYSALIS – BRAWLEY 1960

As the years passed in Brawley, James and Betsy each endured the pain of losing a loved one. For Betsy, there were reminders of her mother all around. Momma Knight's grapevine in their yard was one of the constant ones. Betsy made time to tend to it, spending hours in this part of the garden as she did when she was a young child. She and the boys stood near it as butterflies floated in the air, some landing on her head and shoulders. Junior shied away, frightened of the insects.

"Son, they don't bite. Here, put your finger out," she offered. She slowly lowered the butterfly toward him, its yellow wings flapping up and down. It crawled right over to his hand.

"It tickles!" he giggled.

"You aren't scared of bugs, Momma?" Leroy asked her.

"No, son," she answered. "Nothing to fear from butterflies. They're like little angels. See these worms here?" She pointed to some caterpillars. "They turn into butterflies. So you gotta protect them. See how they make you smile?"

"Yeah," he giggled.

"Yes, little angels," she smiled, suddenly thinking this might be the reason she was unafraid of bugs and insects. She remembered the time when a caterpillar crawled over her hand.

"Momma, is that true?" Junior asked. "These ugly worms turn into butterflies?"

"It sure is, son." But Betsy only told them part of the story, the part that hid her sadness from them. "You see, these little worms crawl around, eating leaves and getting fat for a big trip they'll take."

"A big trip?" he asked.

"Yes. A wonderful trip. The worms build a cocoon to prepare."

"What's a cocoon?" Junior queried.

"It's like a shell that grows around them. Let's see." She carefully parted the leaves around the grapevine until she found one to show him.

"See here," she pointed to the tiny, brown sack that hung from one of the branches.

"That's nasty!" Leroy squealed, making a face.

"No, son. It's not nasty. Look here. See, inside, there's the caterpillar."

"What's he doing?" Junior asked.

"Preparing for his journey," she answered. "Over the next few days, that little caterpillar will change into a beautiful butterfly. It's called a chrysalis. That's a big word, huh?"

"Yeah, Momma!" Leroy cried out, trying to pronounce it.

"Remember; all the butterflies started as little worms. Now, look at them." She turned around to the garden, filled with hundreds of them floating through the air.

Junior smiled at the thought. "Chrysalis," he repeated.

"That's it. You got it, son," Betsy smiled.

THE BLACK CABINET

It was a late Friday afternoon in Brawley. Gusts of hot, dusty air blew from the east across the entire Valley, but the field hands, gin workers, welders, and mechanics still gathered at their favorite spots across the town. Black men parked their cars along Ninth next to the Family Liquor store, while the Mexicans made their way to the cantinas on Main. The streets were alive. People were working and had money to spend.

Unlike his older brother, Leroy loved his father's big, booming voice. His face lit up like a hundred birthday candles when he came home from work regardless of his father's mood. As Leroy grew, he and his father were inseparable, driving around town and hanging at the liquor store where James chatted with some of the locals he befriended. The men were often leery of speaking openly around Leroy, but James assured them it was fine. The boy often sat quietly by his father while the men talked.

Today, James was in town without Leroy drinking with his friends on the shady side of Family Liquor. They called themselves the Black Cabinet in a mocking reference to President Roosevelt's Negro advisors. Their conversations had little to do with high-minded matters of state and mostly covered the latest sporting news, with a bit of town gossip thrown in. The men had much in common. They all left their homes in the South for a new start in the West. Most of them were former soldiers, but not career military men.

Frank Barnes was a member of the Cabinet. He spoke with a mix of Southern gentility and bayou slang, but also with a terrible stutter. He answered to L.A., which was short for Lower Alabama since his people were from Mobile. James was impressed with L.A. because he never borrowed money from anyone.

Benjamin Cook, who was nicknamed Chef for obvious reasons, had round pink lips and a face with mottled brown spots.

"I knew you'd be right here!" Chef shouted. "As soon as I came 'round the corner and saw that piece of shit you call a vehicle parked out front!" he thundered.

L.A. laughed. "Look, man, I ain't selling you my truck no matter how much you beg."

"Beg hell!"

"She never lets me down, and that's more than I can say for your wife!"

At that, Gold let out a loud laugh and slapped the palm of his hand on his knee. Ernest "Gold" Robinson got his nickname because of all his gold teeth.

Desotos, Cadillacs, and flatbed trucks crowded the street. The men, still dusty and dirty from the long day at work, had arrived in droves after the cotton gin let out. They greeted one another and shared a story, while others watched the ebb and flow of people. A crowd gathered around the Black Cabinet as L.A., Gold, James, Chef, and Jerome White, discussed the hot topic of that day. Jerome's people were from Arkansas. He was a tall, lanky man with thin, pointy fingers and a long, tired face. His clothing was old, but not ragged. The worn heels of his shoes matched the sad look on Jerome's face.

"Nixon has this election sewn up. They ain't gonna elect that Catholic boy," Jerome shouted to a chorus of boos. "Besides, Republicans got all the money."

"No, no," L.A. started in with his heavy drawl. "I like that Kennedy boy. He's a veteran."

"That don't make you a good President," Jerome countered.

"Yes, it does. Eisenhower was one of the best."

"Eisenhower? Are you plum crazy? I wouldn't let him shine my shoes!" The men around him began to hiss, but Jerome was playing to the crowd.

"All right. You best be careful now."

Chef cut in, "Jerome getting uppity, y'all."

"Yes, he is," Gold added.

"Jerome gonna end up like that fool on the train from Phoenix to Tucson," James started.

The men looked at each other confused. Finally, L.A. asked, "James, who are you talking about?"

"I was on that train a while back," he began.

"See, you lying right there! Ain't been on a train in twenty years!" laughed Gold. His front teeth shimmered in the sunlight.

"I said a while back!" James chuckled.

"Let the man finish!" L.A. shouted.

Gold quieted down.

"Go ahead, James. Finish what you was saying."

"So I was on the train headed for Tucson, and this boy gets on in Phoenix with a big, red hat, wool vest, jacket, pressed shirt with them broad cuffs."

"Was he one of them dandy boys?" L.A. inquired.

"Hell if I know!" James chuckled. "I wasn't trying to get to know the fella." The men around him howled with laughter.

"That fool was probably sweatin' up the whole train," Chef added.

"But he was right fancy," James continued.

"Oh yeah, know plenty of them type of fools," L.A. glanced at Jerome.

"So as the train pulls into the station in Tucson, this boy gonna run over to the conductor and ask 'Is this Too-Soon?' Well, the conductor was a big ole peckerwood, Irish boy. He grabs his Billy club and says, 'Naw nigger you are right on time!' and goes to whacking this fool upside his head!"

Gold laughed so hard he almost fell off the tomato crate.

"James, you are the damn fool!" Jerome proffered, shaking his head.

L.A. laughed so hard it bought tears to his eyes.

"What's crackin' everybody up?" Champ asked from the back of the crowd. Silence followed after Champ Fountaine spoke. He had a narrow face and smile that made women blush. His gentle way of speaking was in stark contrast to most of the gruff men in Brawley. Champ's wavy hair, a pencil-thin mustache, and high cheekbones gave him an aristocratic visage. Champ had gone to high school with Betsy, and they remained good friends. That is how James wanted to keep it.

Fountaine's family had arrived in the Valley around the same time as the Knights and opened several small businesses. James had a strong dislike for the man that started when he heard him tell people his name meant "fountain" in French.

"Nobody gives a shit about that," James said to his cabinet friends one day. "That nigger got a slave name just like everyone else. Yellow piece of shit!"

"You got some nerve there, James. The only thing black on you is your belt!" L.A. scoffed.

White tried to reason with James. "Your name is everything, James. You know that."

James knew there was more to his disdain for Champ than his last name.

Gold finally answered Fountaine, "James just telling us one of his tall Texas tales."

As usual, Fountaine was dressed impeccably in a starched, white shirt and black slacks. His nails were clean and neatly trimmed. Champ knew many of the men had contempt for the success of his family businesses, for his looks and his name, but what they did not realize was that he had nowhere else to go, and he wished he could tell them so.

Though the white people in town appreciated his charm, he was not one of them. He had made good friends and associates, but there was still a divide, just as the railroad tracks that ran through the middle of town, divided it in two, between east and west, Blacks and Mexicans on one side and white people on the other.

Champ had quit trying to prove himself to these black folks a long time ago, joining them on occasion to listen, laugh, and spend a little time with the few unthreatened Negroes. It never occurred to him to pick up and start anew. His family had already made those sacrifices to come to the Imperial Valley.

"What you say, James? Can you tell it again?" Fountaine asked.

James bristled at the request as Fountaine approached, shaking hands with people in the gathered crowd. James hesitated when he held out his hand, giving it a quick squeeze.

Chef cut in, "No, boy, you had to be here the first time."

"Oh, come on now," Fountaine insisted.

James turned away from him again and began to speak with Gold, ignoring him altogether. Champ stood there until Jerome White took pity on him and told him the story. He laughed when White got to the punch line.

"That was funny, James," Fountaine interjected. James waved at him and moved on to some new topic that was brewing. L.A.'s wayward teenage son was giving him problems. Fountaine stepped a little closer to hear what the men were saying.

"I'm trying to teach him something about life, you know, and he won't listen to a damn thing I say," L.A. lamented.

"I got two at home that don't listen. One worse than the other," James mused.

"I wish they didn't have to learn the lessons we already learned. Can you imagine how much further along they'd be?" Gold added.

"Better they don't know all that until they get a little older, don't you think?" Chef countered.

"What you saying, Chef?" Gold asked.

"You talking about education, learning a skill, making a living. I'm talking about life, the ugly side. Children don't need to know all that," Chef responded.

"My momma, God rest her soul, never hid nothing from us. No matter how young we were," Gold added.

"Shit! I don't care what your momma told you. That's probably why you such a damn fool now," Chef continued, upset. "Be nice to let children be children is all I am saying, fellas."

"Alright, man. Don't you talk about my momma like that, or I'll bust you in your goddamn mouth," Gold shouted, angrily jumping to his feet.

"Best sit your old black ass back down. Ain't nobody studdin' you," Chef yelled, also standing.

"Is that bastard talking to me?" Gold responded. The drink and heat were finally getting to the men.

"Cool down Gold," L.A. cautioned.

"Children have to learn the ways of the world, Chef. They got to know their place in it." James contended.

Chef tried to reason with them. "I do not disagree with that. I am saying there be ways to do that. Like the prodigal son in the Bible."

"Oh, hell, now he's gonna preach!" L.A. said sarcastically.

Gold laughed. "We already got a preacher in town."

"The prodigal son would have been the dead son in my house!" James joked. The men laughed again. "Never woulda got to prodigal. My ass!"

"That's what I am saying!" L.A. claimed. "Put a whip to them little bastards quick, and you never have to worry about nothing!"

Chef shook his head. James had a way of ruining some good discussions, especially when he had a point to make. He took a sip of beer as L.A. slapped him on the back.

"James, you have very nice children. I can't imagine they're a problem." Fountaine remarked.

James looked at Fountaine. "What the hell you know about my boys?" he snapped.

"Met them once when I dropped off some dry cleaning to Mrs. Knight."

James finished his beer and threw the empty can into a pile of garbage. He waved to his friends, and, just like that, the men began to disperse. He brushed past Fountaine without glancing his way.

L.A. stared at Fountaine for a moment and then replied. "You know, you talk too much."

A short time later, James pulled up to the curb at home. His anger rose with each step he took on the brick path to the doorway. All he could see was Fountaine's face, smiling at his kids, his wife. James knew the Knights thought highly of Champ and that only made things worse. He flung the door open.

"Daddy!" Leroy shouted happily, running over to his father, but James pushed him aside, making his way into the kitchen where Junior stood next to Betsy. She was making stew for dinner.

"Hi, James. You hungry?" she asked.

"You keep that bastard, Champ Fountaine, away from my boys," he said.

"What are you talking about?"

"You heard what I said!" He moved closer to Betsy, towering over both his son and wife.

Junior closed his eyes and began to tremble when his father shouted.

"Daddy, why are you mad at Momma?" Leroy asked.

"Shut up! I'm not talkin' to you!" The anger in his voice made the boy cry.

"Do you have to take this out on the child?" Betsy yelled at James. "Come here, Leroy." As he started toward his mother, James blocked his path. "I'm speaking to you, woman."

"James, what is wrong with you? You are scaring everyone in this house. For what?"

"If I see Fountaine around my house, there's gonna be a problem. *That's* what I'm talking about."

Betsy shook her head as James stepped aside and let Leroy pass. She held him close. "Don't cry, son."

James stood there, veins throbbing in his neck. He wondered, sometimes, where such a rage came from, but then he saw in his mind Fountaine laughing it up with Betsy and his sons. James looked at Betsy and Leroy, then to Junior. The boy stared at his father, scornfully.

"What are you looking at, boy?"

Junior did not answer but did not look away either.

"I'm speaking to you!"

Junior went to hug his mother, but James grabbed him roughly by his arm and yanked him back.

"You look at me when I am speaking to you. I asked you a question!"

Tears rolled down Junior's face; he trembled and sobbed uncontrollably, which only seemed to anger James more. He shook him again and shouted even louder. "I asked you a question!"

"Leave him alone! Are you crazy, James? He's a child!" Betsy screamed.

"You shouting at me?" James snarled. He raised his open hand in the air as the boys screamed in fear. That was when he noticed a small, but growing puddle around Junior's feet.

"Look what you did! Come here, baby. Let's get you out of these clothes." Betsy wrenched her son away from him. "They're just little boys. They don't know any better."

"Well, they better learn," James uttered sharply.

Betsy knelt and placed her arms around the frightened children. They heard the front door slam. At that moment, Betsy didn't care where James went.

"I'm...I'm sorry, Momma," Junior cried.

"No, son. It's okay. I don't know what's gotten into your father."

They held each other tightly, and she cried on their shoulders.

James started the car's engine but turned off the ignition. He sat back and took a deep breath to calm himself down. James looked up at the night sky. He hated himself for the things he did to his family. If he were man enough, he thought, he'd ask his sons to forgive him for his selfish ways and tell them how sorry he was for bringing them into this world. James lamented over the fact that their birth also meant their death. Something he learned at a very young age. It was something he feared they'd also have to figure out.

To James, it was insulting when the pastor's answers to life's mysteries were always the same old 'that's where your faith comes in.' James, on rare occasions, opened himself up to talk about things dear to his heart. He often questioned his own beliefs and those of others. He wanted to stand and shout back at these religious folk, "But why did God leave it to faith, to chance? Why have any doubts? And more importantly, why was it wrong for him to want to know?"

His feelings were further conflicted every time he lost someone he loved. These same questions arose when he looked at his family. He often pictured where he would be when his children died. He didn't know why he thought such things, but he couldn't seem to help himself. He hoped he'd long be gone when that time came. It was too painful to contemplate. Each time he did, his heart hardened just a little bit more.

He sat there for a long time before going back into the house. The boys were in bed, and Betsy was washing dishes.

"There's some stew in the oven," she spoke without turning around.

He took a seat at the table, and Betsy placed a piece of cornbread on his plate.

"Thank you," he whispered. Then he reached out and gently brushed Betsy's hand.

"You're welcome," she whispered back.

"Betsy, I'm sorry." James started. "I just wanted more for us. I've never felt closer to anyone than you."

"You don't act it."

"I know, I know." He said, rubbing his eyes.

"Then why, James? Why do you do this?"

"I don't know. The thought of losing you, it's just too much. Maybe that is why I push you away. I don't mean to hurt you or the children, but it's all I know."

"This is not the way to keep us."

"But what about us, Betsy?"

"Us? Can't you see all that I'm doing?"

James sighed. "What about us seeing the world and doing all those things we planned? It wasn't that long ago, was it?"

"You don't think I want that as well?" Betsy said, her voice rising. "These are the cards we have. Its where we have to be right now. I thought you were in this with me when you asked me to marry you."

"I am. Not all sunshine and rainbows for me either. I've stayed because I love you."

"So why do you lashing out at us? You can't have it every which way, James. What more do you want of me?"

He let go of her hand. "Nothing," he demurred. "Just nothing." It was at that moment James made up his mind. He knew he had to find a way to leave, with or without her. It was all fading away, and it was clear to him now that she was not going to keep her promise to him. They would not see the world together.

A few days later, while sitting down at breakfast, long after his father had gone to work, Junior told his mother earnestly. "I'm not gonna cry no more."

Leroy stared at his brother, confused.

"Junior, what do you mean?" Betsy asked.

"When Daddy yells at me, I'm not gonna cry no more. I'm not gonna be scared."

"Son, he may not always show it, but your daddy loves you."

"Not the way he shows it," Junior shook his head. "I don't want to be afraid no more."

Betsy gently cupped his chin. "It's okay to be afraid. And it's okay to cry."

His words broke her heart. She could not imagine what was going on inside his eight-year-old head.

THE PAST RETURNS — 1964

James paused at the open doorway, watching Betsy and the boys decorate a small Christmas tree. He remembered those first few Christmases were happy affairs. He and Betsy wrapped presents as the boys waited anxiously nearby. She somehow convinced them that she was negotiating with Santa.

"He's going to ask if you've been naughty or nice," she told Junior.

"Will you tell him I've been good, Momma?"

"I sure will," she smiled.

Just then, they heard a thumping on the rooftop. It sounded like footsteps.

"Santa's here!" Leroy screamed.

"Yes, Santa's here," Betsy laughed. "Better stay put 'til we come for you. Santa will throw sand in your eyes if you come out."

"I'm going to stay right here," Leroy declared, his eyes as big as saucers.

James quietly opened the door. Betsy had already begun wrapping the presents. She smiled when he walked in.

"Did they go for it?"

"They sure did." She kissed him on the lips. "They'll never forget this Christmas."

His children were older now, and holidays were a hard time for James, as memories of Texas would drift into his subconscious. His grandfather would get him and Samuel's new clothes. Most kids would have been disappointed not getting a toy, but not James. He was grateful to get out of the rags he wore to church on Sunday. He knew his grandfather had sacrificed much to buy them. That was not the only reason for his sadness. Each season, around this time of year, he'd visit his son's gravesite in the backyard and tie a red ribbon around the cross that marked his plot. His little boy never got to know the joys of Christmas.

Leroy made his way over to the empty lot where his father had set up a makeshift garage. Three cars were parked at odd angles, two of them with their hoods up. He traversed the brick steps leading out to the gate and street, noticing the tiny tracks of a pocket gopher that meandered toward the Chinaberry tree on one end of the yard.

As Leroy walked along the side of the car, he saw his father's thick forearms covered in dirt and grease buried in the chassis of an old Studebaker. He enjoyed sitting on the hood, watching his father work. Before he could announce himself, James hollered for Leroy to hand him a crescent wrench.

Junior had no interest in learning auto repairs, or in spending time with his father. He was off having his adventures along the canal bank across the street from his grandparents' house. It was a narrow, dirt canal. An assortment of shrubs and weeds covered its banks that grew out of the shallow water. With a running start, Junior could leap from one side to the other. He had first walked along this path when he was nine years old.

He made his way through the brush to a blackberry tree growing out over the canal. A large, wrought iron gate fenced in the tree. Inside the gate, several horses roamed freely in the vast field that led up to a little adobe structure. Junior pulled up some of the grass growing along the canal and waved it through an opening in the gate, beckoning the horses to come.

A gray, female Appaloosa walked to Junior taking long, lazy steps. She greedily ate the grass, tugging it right out of his hand. His heart pounded as he petted the horse's mane. The Appaloosa nudge him gently, and Junior pulled up some more grass, enamored with the towering creature. He loved looking into the horses' big, dark eyes as much as their scent. Junior rubbed his face against the horse's long jaw completely lost in the moment when someone from the yard shouted to him.

"Junior! Is that you?"

He was frightened at first. He did not know who lived in the home, but a girl with thick black, shoulder-length hair approached. He recognized her from school.

"Daisy?"

"What are you doing back here?" She asked.

"Nothing. You live here?"

She nodded and then pointed to the horses. "These are my dad's. The Appaloosa's named Concha, and that one is Vieja because she's old. This one is Loco."

"I like Concha."

"Yes, she's very friendly, but not Loco. He is not very friendly at all."

"Wow. It must be nice to have so many horses."

"Yeah, but my dad makes me take care of them. My sister never has to do anything on account she's so little." Daisy climbed up on the top bar of the fence. "Where do you live?"

Junior pointed to the other end of the canal. "Just over there on South Eastern. It's not far."

"You come here a lot?" she asked.

"After I finish my chores, I sit in the tree and eat the berries, but only if they're ripe. One time, I saw a momma bird bring food for the little chick, but it fell out and died."

"Oh! That's sad."

Another little girl appeared by the side of the house. She was much smaller, and her skin was milky white.

"Daisy!" she yelled. "Momma wants you right now!"

"I gotta go." She jumped off the fence and waved goodbye.

Junior waved too. "See you later."

He watched her go inside, never looking back, but this became their meeting place.

That Christmas evening, Leroy set up battle lines on the floor with the plastic army men he got as a present.

"Does this remind you of anything, Dad?" he asked. Leroy was an inquisitive child and questioned his father all the time.

"No, son. It doesn't," he replied.

"Doesn't it remind you of the army?"

"We weren't plastic men. Our blood was real!" he said.

"I'm sorry, Daddy," Leroy apologized, his eyes welling with tears.

His father didn't respond. He returned to the newspaper he was reading.

The next morning as James made repairs on the Studebaker, Leroy meandered down the pathway over to where James was working. James saw him before he passed the gate and decided to let him ask whatever he wanted after him snapping at his son the night before. James was careful not to sound annoyed or angry when he answered. It wasn't long before he peppered his father with questions.

"Where were you born, Daddy?"

"Hondo, Texas."

"Do you miss Texas?"

"Not so much."

"Why?" the boy continued.

"Texas ain't my home."

"Why not? You were born there?"

"Yes, I was, but that don't mean it's my home."

"Well, where is home, Daddy?"

"I guess where you feel most welcome, son. Where you fit in," he postulated, looking up from the engine.

"Isn't that Texas?"

James chuckled. "Yes and no, son. Hondo was where I lived for a long time, but I wouldn't call it home," he stuck his head back into the engine, but his mind wasn't solely on the job at hand. James tried to think of a better answer to his son's question.

"Where's home then, Daddy?"

"Oh, if I had to guess, I'd say on the baseball diamond. Closest I have ever come to that feeling, son."

James remembered the many miles he had traveled, the smell of freshly cut grass and the chalk lines, the smooth dirt on the pitcher's mound. The memory made him smile.

"I'd like to see these places one day, where you played baseball. Why don't we go to Texas?"

"One day, you'll have the opportunity to travel wherever you want. I hope you go far away from here. And you know, wherever you go, you'll take a little piece of me with you."

"How's that, Daddy?"

Across the road, a dirt devil whipped up some topsoil and trash. They stopped to watch it spin through the cornfield and disappear. James and Leroy were so engrossed in the tiny tempest; they did not notice Mr. Tamayo walking up from the street.

"Señor Jaime," he called out, tapping the rooftop.

"Señor Tamale," James responded.

"Tamayo. My name is Ta-MY-Yo," he spoke slowly, his speech heavily accented. "Why can't you remember that? It's easy."

"I don't know. I love tamales, and that's *easy* for me to remember," James retorted, mocking his neighbor's heavy Spanish accent.

Tamayo laughed. "Señor Jaime, you crazy! What are you working on here?"

"Same thing. Car won't turn over. Don't know what could be wrong with it. Checking off my list."

"That's one way to do it," Tamayo began.

James rolled his eyes. He hated it when Tamayo used that phrase.

Tamayo continued, "Or you know, depending on what the car does, you start there. You have to know your cars."

"Well, that's one way to do it." James shot back.

"That's true. Very true." Tamayo missed James' subtle jab, but the man knew his repairs. "Mind if I take a look?"

James shrugged. "Suit yourself."

He fiddled with it for a short time when the engine finally sputtered to life.

Tamayo asserted. "It's working fine now."

"Looks that way," James agreed, grudgingly.

"Well, I gotta go," Tamayo said. "My mother made me breakfast – *chorizo y pappas.*"

James perked up. "She makes some good *chorizo,* huh?"

"Yes, the best."

Leroy laughed at his father whenever he tried to speak Spanish. He sounded so strange to him.

"Maybe I bring you some tacos later," Tamayo offered.

"I'll be home. Come by any time, Tamale!"

"Senor Jaime! I bring you nothing until you get my name right."

"You bring me some of that *chorizo,* and I'll get it right!"

The men laughed and shook hands. Tamayo waved from the street. He had been spending a lot of time at his mother's since his wife passed away.

"One down, two to go," Leroy stated, surveying the lot.

"Yeah, son," James agreed, wiping his brow. "Let's take a break and get out of this sun." He took Leroy's hand, and they walked into the house.

A short time later, there was a knock on the front door. James opened it with a big smile on his face, thinking Tamayo had returned with the promised tacos, but standing there was someone he'd never dreamed he'd see again. His wrinkled clothes smelled of three-day-old sweat.

"Major?"

"It ain't Dorothy L'Amour!" Major grinned as he held out his hand.

"I'll be goddamned," James proclaimed, shaking his hand briskly. "What brings you to these parts?"

"Can I get out the sun first?"

"Yes, yes. Come on in. I'll get the wife to fix you something. I know you're hungry."

"Starving!"

Major stepped inside, and James introduced him to Leroy and Betsy. Major washed his hands and face and then fell in a seat at the table in a heap. Though James was happy to see a familiar face, he had mixed emotions. It had been almost twenty years since they had seen each other.

Major filled them in on what he had been up to since the war ended. He had worked a few odd jobs in Kansas City, then Lincoln, Nebraska. That's where he heard about this baseball team, the Atkins All-Stars, and remembered that James played baseball. He asked around, and someone told him that James had settled in some small town in California.

"Boy, I thought you were a goner the way you were bleeding out there on Buna."

"Yeah, me too!" James nodded. He tried to shake the shock of seeing Major again. It brought back too many disturbing memories. His whole body felt heavy and tired.

"The look on your face when we put you up on that stretcher. Fear of God!"

"Daddy, you were hurt in the war?" Leroy asked.

Before he could answer, Major cut in. "Yes, indeed, Sonny. Your father got shot in the back. I had to put my finger right in the hole to keep the blood from gushing out," Major put his stubby finger on the boy's forehead.

Betsy found the conversation unpleasant. She sent Leroy to get his brother. He briefly objected but went on after his father gave him a stern look.

"Those were dangerous days," Major ended, solemnly shaking his head.

"Yes, they were," James agreed.

"You know we lost a few more fellas after you. Fats Wiggins lost a leg. Emmitt Haskins got killed. Head blown right off."

"I'm sorry, Mr. Major, but could you please talk about this another time?" Betsy interrupted.

"Oh, I'm sorry, ma'am. Didn't mean to upset you."

"I understand, but not in front of the children. They don't need to hear about people killed and such."

"Yes, ma'am, it was terrible. I won't say another word about it again."

"I appreciate that, Mr. Major."

"Just Major, ma'am."

Betsy pushed back from the table and got up. "Nice to meet you, Mr. Major."

Though James did not say it, he disagreed with Betsy. He believed everyone should know about war and all its horrors. Major was someone who had been there with him and understood the ordeal, but he brought with him many bad memories.

A few minutes later, Junior and Leroy entered the house. Major shifted in his chair, eyeing him up and down before holding out his hand.

"We have a guest, Junior," James added.

"Nice to meet you," Major murmured to Junior.

"Mr. Major and I served in the war." His father continued.

Junior walked over and shook his sweaty hand. When he tried to pull away, Major clung to it. "You have a handsome boy here, James," he admired. "Fine family."

"Thank you," James chimed in, rising from his seat. "Let's head into town and get a drink. I'll introduce you to some folk."

"That'll be nice," he answered, still looking at Junior.

"Take Mr. Major's things to your room. You and Leroy can sleep on the couch."

"No need to put them out."

"No, no. You're a guest in my home."

"If you insist," he said, smiling at James.

"Go on now. Take Mr. Major's things."

James took his war friend around to Family Liquor, where they had a beer and talked more freely with some of the men who were out that afternoon. Major sat back and listened, sipping his beer slowly, which surprised James. The Major he knew was in the middle of everything. That was twenty years ago, James reminded himself. A lot could change about a man in that time.

"So this big peckerwood gonna jump up and tell me that they know how to deal with someone like Martin King - with a tall tree and a strong rope," L.A. angrily intimated. "I wanted to bash that bastard right in the mouth."

"They scared of that King boy. Bobby Kennedy, too," Chef added.

"Hell, you see what happened to the folks in Birmingham?" L.A. continued. "And what did slavery do for the poor white man, huh? You all know what I'm saying? What kinda job could they get with a slave working for nothing? They just as bad off as the colored man, but you cain't tell them that. No sir."

Major spoke up, "White people bring their troubles everywhere they go. My grand momma, she told me when I was just a little boy, she say, before the war we did all the work, and the white folks did all the worry. Now the war over, we do all the work and the worry too."

"Boy, ain't that the truth," Chef agreed.

"Look what they doing in Vietnam. Starting a new war, but these young folks out here ain't buying it. Kids in New York burned their draft cards. Right there on the street," L.A. revealed.

"A colored man can't do that and not get put in jail," James stressed.

"Sho 'nuf," L.A. agreed.

The conversation turned on that somber note, and the men decided to talk about something less political. They drifted over to baseball and the new heavyweight champion, Cassius Clay. Clay had beaten Sonny Liston a few months earlier.

"Ole Cassius is something ain't he?" L.A. smiled.

"What they calling him now?" Cook asked. "Mohammed something."

"Ali, Ali." L.A. stammered.

"That boy runs his mouth too much," James interjected.

"That's what I like about him." Cook added. "he don't care what them white folks got to say 'bout him."

Major smiled, remaining silent. James glanced over at him regarding his worn skin and thin, dry lips. He remembered that odd, toothy grin from so many days ago.

James recalled one evening as he walked back to the barracks at Fort Huachuca when he saw some figures in the shadows wrestling near the latrine. He rushed over to find Major taking a beating from Chicago and another brute of a man nicknamed Paiute.

"All right, boys, break it up!" James called out.

"Stay back, James," Paiute yelled.

"Thirty days in the stockade when the M.P.s catch ya," James warned.

"Don't you mind Atkins. I'mma enjoy them thirty after I get done with this fool," Chicago added.

Major spat a wad of blood from his mouth. "Don't worry, James; I got these sons of bitches right where I want them."

Paiute snidely answered, "Yeah, where is that, kicking your ass?"

The men stepped forward to finish Major off, but James got between them.

"If y'all gonna fight, it's gonna be fair. Man to man. Not this shit."

"Who are you to be giving orders?" Paiute leered, stepping forward into James' face.

"I ain't. If you two want to take him down, do it man to man. Not like some yellow belly."

"You'd fight for this bastard, James?" Chicago asked.

"If you want him, go at him like a man!"

Paiute turned to James and touted. "Ain't no, never mind. I'm gonna whoop his ass; then I'll be looking for you too."

"I ain't going nowhere," James replied, confidently.

The men squared off. Paiute was a few inches taller and stronger looking. He caught Major with a shot to the ribs then hit him twice in the face with straight right hands. Major threw a wild punch that Paiute sidestepped. He then kicked Major and laughed as he tumbled to the ground.

"This fool's head is as hard as a rock!" he laughed. "But, I'm gonna crack it."

"Finish that motherfucker!" Chicago shouted.

Major surprise Paiute with a wild punch, catching him across the chin. Major tackled him to the ground, then slipping a knife out of his sock. He raised it high over Paiute's face, but James pushed him off before he could do any damage.

"Get off me!" Major screamed as he scrambled to his feet, still clutching his knife.

"You want to get hung?"

"If it means this bastard's dead, then yes."

Paiute staggered to his feet, still dazed. "I'm going to kill you for sure now."

"You ain't gonna do a goddamn thing except head back to your barracks."

"Your rank doesn't mean shit here, Atkins," Paiute shouted.

"I just saved your worthless ass and you still barking? If you come back at him, you gonna deal with me too."

"You taking sides now?" Chicago questioned James.

"Looks that way," James answered.

"You gonna regret this, Atkins!" Paiute said.

James intervening for Major did not sit well with some of the men, but he didn't care. Major was grateful to have one ally in camp. Deep down, James admired some things about him. Major was as persistent as a stinkbug, but a stinkbug nonetheless. James didn't want him around, but how could he turn the man away, a fellow brother in arms, especially one who had saved his life on the battlefield.

The drive back home was a quiet one until Major broke the silence.

"I get the feeling you don't want me here."

"Ain't that," James answered quickly, "Things have changed. I got a family now."

"I understand. I had a family once."

"Only knew about your father. Didn't he kill himself?"

"No. That's cause I lied to you."

"You what?" James shouted as they pulled up to the driveway in front of his home. "You lied about what?"

"Why I joined the Army. You see, I told you it was on account some people taking land from my pa. And see, that ain't what happened exactly."

"Well, what *exactly* happened?"

"You ever see a man lynched? See his eyes when they put the noose around his neck, and he knows he gonna die? You ever saw something like that?"

"Thank goodness. No."

Major continued, talking over James' answer. "He cain't fight, there four, five of 'em holding him down. Sure enough, he starts getting his mind set to die. That don't mean he ain't hoping for a miracle. Can you imagine what a fella might feel at that moment?"

"Hell no! I done told you that."

Major spoke dispassionately. "Well, I have. I was only fourteen when it happened. Could barely lift a sack of potatoes. Some white boys rode to the house one night after supper and dragged my daddy outside as Momma, and I watched. She was screaming and crying the whole time. They claimed he stole from one of the neighbors. We all knew it was a lie, but how are you gonna stop 'em? They the law, the judge and jury. They threw a rope over the big oak in our front yard. Took three of them suckers to pull him up. He kicked and jerked around for a bit. He fought 'em, James. Then one of them crackers say, 'sure is taking this nigger a long time to die.' So he pulls out his pistol and shot daddy dead in the chest. He didn't move after that."

James looked at Major, stunned.

"Then they gonna tell us to be out that house by morning. So yeah, I killed those people I told you 'bout. I burned their house to the ground and asked God to forgive me. You know what forgiveness is, James?"

Major didn't wait for an answer. "It's asking God to plow your sins into the earth so you can get a fresh start. I asked for forgiveness because they didn't have nothing to do with my daddy getting killed. They just happened to be the first white people I came across the day after those men killed my pa. Now that is the truth, James. I wanted to kill everyone and everything. I still do sometimes. That's why I ran off and joined the Army. There it is, the truth. And I know you feel the same way about it too."

"Seems like you kept a lot of them old habits."

Major grinned at James. "That's why we friends James. You see my insides like I see yours."

"No, Major. You don't."

"You lyin'," he grunted. The words came out slowly. "I see your anger. You hate something so deep, so bad. You ain't ready, to tell the truth to yourself."

James opened walked inside. Major's words unnerved him, but he didn't know what to believe. Was he letting a murderer in his home, or was Major just embellishing his reputation? People never really bothered to understand Major, but he did, and that made James uncomfortable because he knew he truly was a dangerous man.

A few minutes later, he heard Major shut off the light and go to bed.

Over the next few weeks, Major did odd jobs around the house and yard, but James had to send Junior to finish up after him most times. One thing that had not changed was Major's poor work ethic. He sat back and watched Junior work, complimenting him, which made the boy increasingly uncomfortable. Major knew it, but that didn't prevent anything. He got bolder as time passed.

"You got a pretty mouth, boy," Major told him once.

Junior tried to ignore him. He was afraid to complain to his father, who would chastise him for the smallest thing. Junior felt trapped by his elders, whose rules made him feel powerless. He recounted the number of times he'd heard that children were to be seen and not heard.

One day, as they were moving two by fours into the back yard, Major became more fearless. Junior could smell the liquor on his breath and decided right there and then get the task done as quickly as possible. He detested being alone with Major.

"You got yourself a girlfriend, boy?" he questioned, slurring half the words.

"No."

"You like girls, don't you?"

"What?"

"I asked you like girls, don't you?"

"Yes, I do."

"But you don't have a girlfriend?"

"I told you no."

"Well, that's good. They all just bitches and whores."

Junior did not respond.

"You know what a whore is, don't you?"

"No, and I don't want to know."

"Well, someone ought to teach you. How old are you now?"

"Twelve."

"That's a good age."

"If you say so."

"Oh, I say so."

Junior tried to focus on the job.

"You know, if you were a girl, I'd give you all my money."

Junior did not understand what he meant but knew it was something disgusting. Major laughed when he saw the look on Junior's face and how his hands shook.

That night he asked his mother how long Major was going to be staying with them. He could not bring himself to tell her about the things he was saying. He feared the trouble it might cause for himself.

"I don't know, son. It's up to your father."

Major was, as always, very cunning. He spoke kindly to James, took his money and handouts, making empty promises about his work. But that began to wear thin. James came home one day and discovered that the few things he asked him to do that morning had not been done. And Major was nowhere to be found.

"Junior, go out back and feed the chickens. Bring them eggs in too."

"But Daddy, isn't that what you asked Mr. Major to do?"

"Boy, what did I say? Now do it! I'll deal with Mr. Major." he shouted. Junior stomped off to the backyard. The sun was setting, and it would be dark soon, and Junior still had homework to finish. He entered the coop, shaking a small bowl filled with seed on the ground as the chickens squawked and flocked.

As he turned to retrieve some fresh water, he saw Major standing in the doorway.

"You doing my chores again?"

"Yes. *Again!*" Junior replied angrily.

"I guess I'll have to give you a cut of my pay."

"I don't want it."

"You don't like money?"

"Just do what my father asked you to do," he called out, trying to walk past him. "Hand me that bowl you got there. I'll fetch the water."

"No, I'll do it. I don't want my father waking me up tonight because it didn't get done."

"You got some fire in you, don't you, boy? Now give me that water bowl like I asked," Major said sternly.

Junior would not comply. He could tell Major had been drinking by the smell of alcohol on his breath. Major stepped inside and closed the door. He then pushed the teenager backward, pinning him against the wall. Major was too strong for him to get around, and the man chuckled as Junior struggled against him. He then reached slowly across his waist to get the bowl in his hand. Major touched him on his chest, then raised his hand to his face and touched his cheek with the back of his hand. Junior turned away from him.

"Leave me alone."

"Oh, you don't want that. I don't believe you."

Junior looked at him angrily, but Major was undeterred.

"You sure are a pretty boy," he whispered as he slid his hand down to Junior's waist.

"Stop touching me," Junior shouted.

"Don't you raise your voice at me!" Major shouted him down.

He then grabbed at Junior's belt buckle and began to undo it. Junior tried to scream for help, but nothing came out of his mouth. Tears welled up in his eyes and slid down his face.

"I ain't gonna hurt you, boy," he whispered, a devilish glint in his eye. He reached between Junior's legs, cupping his scrotum in his hand. Junior struggled to get free. He could not fathom what was happening to him. Major had a devilish glint in his eye.

Just then, the door flew open. "What the hell you doing?" James shouted.

"Nothing. I had to reprimand the boy for talking back," Major shuddered stepping away from Junior.

"What kind of reprimanding you call this?" James looked over at his son, his belt unbuckled, and then back to Major. "I asked you what the hell were you doing?"

"Now James, I asked the boy for the water bowl, and he shouted at me," Major beseeched.

"That why his pants undone?"

"I don't know. Ask him."

"I'm asking you!"

Before Major could say another word, James grabbed him by the throat and lifted him off his feet, then pressing him against the wall. Junior stood by, tears flowing from his eyes.

Major tried to speak, but James held him too tightly. He grabbed at his father's arms, clawing at them in a feeble attempt to stop him. James then punched Major in the stomach with the full force of his body weight.

"You nasty son of a bitch. What you do to my boy?"

Junior stammered, "Nothing, Daddy. He didn't do anything!"

"Go on in the house!" James shouted.

James placed his other hand on Major's throat and began to choke him. Major struggled to break free, but he was no match for James' strength or fury.

"Daddy, please stop!" Junior shouted.

Blood flowed out of Major's mouth.

"Daddy, stop it!" Desperate, Junior pushed James with all his might, until he released Major, who slid to the ground unconscious.

"What you do that for?"

"You were gonna kill him, Daddy."

"That was my intention, boy," James was irate. "Go in the house and fetch his bags. You meet me out front and don't say nothing to your mother."

James dragged Major to the car, sliding his listless body in the backseat of his car. Junior appeared with Major's duffle a few minutes later.

"Get in!" James shouted.

"Why?"

"Boy, do as I say!"

Junior tossed the bag in the backseat and got in the car. He was afraid of what his father had in mind to do. James drove west past Westmorland, pulling over a few miles outside of town. He opened the door, jerked the dazed man out of the backseat, and threw him on the ground. He then grabbed the bags and tossed them next to Major as he staggered to his feet, his face a bloody mess.

James stared at the man.

"You saved my life once, and my son just saved yours. So we are even, but If I ever see you again, I'll kill you."

Major sat in the road and watched as the lights of the car faded from sight as James drove away. He gingerly touched his swollen lip, then spat out a mouthful of blood. He produced his blade from his boot and smiled.

"That son of a bitch lucky I couldn't reach my knife," he bellowed. He then laughed, wiping his face with the bottom of his shirt.

"You ain't so smart, James. I see right through you." He pointed at the fading taillights of the car. "Thy iniquity! I see right through you."

He then gathered his bags and started walking down the road toward Indio as if nothing had happened.

On the drive home, James admonished his son.

"What the hell happened back there?"

"I don't know, Daddy. He's been bothering me ever since he came."

"How could you let him affront you like that?"

"I didn't let him."

"Well, what do you call what you did? Why didn't you knock him on his ass?"

"He was too strong. I couldn't get away."

"Then why didn't you holler? I was in the house."

"I don't know. I got…frozen."

"Frozen? Well, you had better learn how to get unfrozen. And don't you ever push me like that again."

Junior just looked down at the floor, unable to respond.

"Don't say a word about this to your mother. Do you hear me? It will just upset her."

"Yes, sir."

When they walked in, Betsy looked alarmed. Splattered blood covered James' shirt and face. Junior was silent.

"Don't ask," James roared, storming passed her and Leroy. As he washed his arms and hands, he grew even angrier. As much as it pained him, James knew he had to wait. How could he possibly leave with his children so vulnerable, so unsure of themselves? He had to know they were capable of fighting back, even if that meant taking a life. Least they be lambs to the slaughter. Delay did not sit well with James. He splashed some cold water on his face and stared into the mirror. No, waiting did not sit well with him at all.

RAGE – APRIL 1968

The sky in the valley was a peaceful shade of blue that belied the tension in the air. The boys went out to play after breakfast, and James made an urgent stop at Family Liquor. Everyone in town was quite anxious after the news of Martin Luther King's assassination spread across the country. The interrupted TV programs showed scenes of the horrible destruction in Louisville, Chicago, and Washington, D.C., with the patrolling National Guard troops' guns at the ready. Betsy was sure it was a hot topic for everyone, especially the Negro men in town.

She visited Pappy after washing the dishes. She had tried her best to get him out of the house in the years following her mother's passing, but her father had become a recluse. So it came as a surprise to her to find Champ Fountaine sitting next to Pappy when she walked in. They were discussing the chaos.

"Just a new way to lynch us," Pappy fumed.

"No doubt about it," Fountaine agreed.

Betsy greeted them.

"Hi, Pappy, Champ."

"Hey, Betsy," Fountaine smiled.

Pappy waved to Betsy then returned to his conversation with Fountaine. "What's this world coming to?" he asked, sighing loudly.

"Reverend Drew preached this is a sign of the end of times," Fountaine added.

"Oh, I believe it," Pappy replied.

Fountaine paused for a moment, looking over at Betsy, who waited patiently by the door. "Well, I'm going to get going, Mr. Knight. Gotta close the shop."

"Okay, Champ. See you next week?"

"Yes, sir."

Betsy stepped aside, her hand still on the door handle.

"You sure do look nice today, Betsy," Fountaine intimated. "I put you some flowers in the kitchen for you."

"Oh. Thank you," Betsy said. She blushed at the compliment.

As he passed her, his hand touched hers. It was the slightest caress, but it startled her. Their eyes met briefly.

"I'm sorry!" she exclaimed, quickly moving her hand from the doorknob.

"Don't be." He lingered a moment longer, looking her way warmly. He glanced at her once more before leaving.

Betsy took a deep breath. Though unexpected, it was nice he had noticed.

"Pappy, come on outside with me. Let's work in the garden."

"No. Not today. I don't feel up to it."

"You've got to get out, Pappy. It isn't good for you, staying locked up in here."

He scratched his neck and replied, "I get out. You ain't around to see it."

Betsy shrugged. "Have it your way. I'll bring you over some dinner later."

"Thank you, daughter," he answered.

The mood when the Black Cabinet met that day was subdued. There was palpable anxiety within the gathered crowd.

"I can't believe it. What they expect folks to do after they gun King down like that," Chef angrily paced back and forth.

"Won't surprise me if they never catch who did it. If they do, that killer won't serve any time," Gold asked.

"What you think, boy?" L.A. answered. "You know as well as I do what's gonna happen."

"I'm sick of this shit," James added. "This got to end!"

"What you gonna do, James? Get out here and riot?" Chef asked, but before James said another thing, Chef continued. "If they killed Dr. King, a man on the news and such, a man of the church, a reverend. If they didn't fear killin' him, then what you think they would do about you or me?"

"That's not what I am saying," James began, clearly agitated.

Chef was having none of it. "Ain't nothing gonna change. All he wanted was for colored folk to be treated like any other human being. And they shot him down like a dog. Like a dog." He took a long drink from his whiskey bottle and wiped his face on his shirtsleeve. Chef threw the empty bottle on a pile of trash and walked away silently to his car.

James had never seen his friends so grim as today. James parked his car and slammed his fist on the dashboard when he arrived home.

Betsy could hear James shouting at Junior through the door when she returned from her visit with Pappy. It turned her stomach into a knot. She did not know how much more she could endure. The fear they all lived with continued, unabated. She was sick of putting her children through all this turmoil and not being able to defend them.

"Where you been?" James asked when he heard her come in.

"I was next door," she snapped. "Why are you shouting at Junior now?" Disgust lingered on each word.

"Playing that damn Juju music again. Today is not the day for that. Show some respect."

"It's called Jazz, and you wouldn't understand it even if you tried," Junior scoffed. At sixteen, he was already two inches taller than his father was, lanky and sinewy, and defiant.

"You saying I'm stupid?" James asked, his face flushed with anger.

"That's not what he's saying, James."

"Let him speak!" James glared at her. "I asked him a question."

Leroy started to breathe heavily. He muttered something that no one heard.

"Shut up, Leroy. No one is doing a thing to you," James yelled, training his ire back on Junior. "Now, answer my question, tough guy."

"If you think you are, then you are," Junior replied.

"You smart mouth, little bastard," James raised his hand.

"Stop it!" Betsy pleaded, but before she could finish her sentence, James slapped Junior across the face, knocking him onto the phonograph, crushing it under his weight. Blood trickled from the corner of his mouth. James balled his hand into a fist this time, but his son cowered, retreating from his father. He rushed passed them, locking himself in his room. He didn't come to dinner despite his mother's pleas. Betsy had finally reached her limit.

DREAMS DEFERRED – SPRING 1968

Mr. Tamayo exited the gate to Pappy's house just as Betsy arrived. He came by from time to time to share a story or two with her father. They'd watch a little TV or listen to the radio and, occasionally, Tamayo's son helped Pappy with some legal work. Fountaine also came by, but Pappy wasn't his old self. He was more withdrawn, and Betsy could see defeat in his eyes. She too felt the loss of her mother deeply. Not a day went by that Betsy didn't wish to hear her voice. She made a promise to keep up Momma Knight's garden, and that is what Betsy did.

Winter had lingered well into May, but Betsy worked in the yard unworried. The ground was still cool even after a few hours in the midday sun. Though she was not feeling well, Betsy dug up the earth around the base of the many plants while Junior and Leroy played with bugs and worms. She had chronic aches and joint pains that she ignored. Sarah urged her to go to a doctor, but Betsy put it off. When would there be time for that when she was caring for her father and children? As she rationalized to Sarah, it was probably her being sad and depressed that made her ill. Betsy truly believed that.

Pappy sat on the porch reading the newspaper, yelling instructions as Betsy worked in the yard. It was times like these, peaceful times with James away at Family Liquor, where she could lose herself in her dreams and escape these bottled up frustrations. Betsy's life became that of caretaker for her husband, children, and aging father, but never her own. The boys were older and clung to her less and less, and still, her dreams were the ones pushed aside.

It did not help when Pappy reminded her of all the missed opportunities, her deferred dreams. He wished she would go back to school. It only made her condition worse. So in these carefree moments, she fantasized of other places she would rather be—on a drive to the Grand Canyon or walking the streets of Paris. Dreams she had shared with James when they first met.

Fountaine pulled up in his car. He was picking up some of Momma Knight's old things for a charity in Mexicali. He waved to Pappy, who, without saying a word, went inside to get the donated items. Fountaine stood at the gate unnoticed and watched Betsy water the plants and bushes along the fence line. Three hummingbirds hovered around her, darting back and forth, just out of her sight. He let his eyes drift all over her body, appreciating her still attractive figure.

"Pappy, I'm going to make some lunch, you hungry?" she asked, wiping her hands on her pant leg. No one answered. "Pappy?" she called again, turning toward the porch only to find Champ staring at her with a mile-wide grin.

She blushed. "Champ! When did you get here?"

"Just now. Your father stepped inside."

"Oh. Okay."

Champ tried hard to compose himself, especially with the children present. He felt a tug at his heart whenever he spoke to her, but he sensed she was afraid of something.

Betsy found him very handsome, his smile, the flakes of gray in his hair. It was a style that suited him well. She couldn't get her husband to dress up for anything other than funerals. She remembered when she and James first met. He would bring her fresh cut flowers. They'd sit and talk at Asia Café for hours until the owner put them out. Now he stumbled home, belly full of beer, smelling of sweat. These days he barely touched her. Although the lack of intimacy left her feeling unfulfilled, she thanked her lucky stars that she did not have more children.

"How are your parents?" she asked Champ.

"They're doing well. Slowing down."

"Yeah, aren't we all?"

"Speaking of slowing down, are you going to our reunion? It's not far off."

"Twenty years. Has it been that long?" Betsy asked, stepping closer to the fence.

"You going?"

"I doubt it. I didn't go to the ten-year either."

"You didn't miss much."

His eyes greedily took in every detail of her face. Her eyelashes seemed as big as daisy petals. Her dreamy smile lit up the darkness in his heart.

Just then, Pappy appeared. "Champ, I got your boxes here."

"I'll let the folks over at the Mission know that this came from you."

"That's not necessary. I'll have a few more for you next week."

"Okay, Mr. Knight. I'll come by next Saturday to pick them up?"

"That'll be fine."

"See you, Betsy. Have a nice day."

"You too, Champ," she waved to him. She was happy to see her father was willing to let go of some of her mother's old things. Maybe that would bring him out of his funk.

"He's one of us, you know," Pappy pointed out after Champ had departed. She knew exactly what he meant.

Fountaine began stopping by regularly on Saturdays and spoke with her father whether he had things to donate or not. Most visits coincided when Betsy was over too. Pappy enjoyed their company. One day as Fountaine pulled away from Pappy's house, he paused to speak to Betsy.

"I left you some flowers. You don't have to take them home."

"That's very thoughtful of you."

"Pretty flowers for a pretty woman."

"Thank you," she hesitated.

"You rather I didn't?" He asked.

"No, it's not that, I don't want any trouble for you."

"It's no trouble."

"You know what I mean."

Though she enjoyed the idea of James being jealous, she knew he was a prideful man and a dangerous one too.

"I'll be careful."

"Please do." The longer he lingered, the more anxious she became. The last thing she wanted was for James to come driving by and see them. It did not matter how innocent their interactions; she believed her husband was capable of anything. She rightfully feared for Fountaine's life.

Betsy leaned over the vase of flowers and took in a deep breath of the roses once he was gone. She caught herself smiling and thinking about him, and when he came close, she did all she could to catch a whiff of his cologne. She liked the way his cheeks dimpled when he smiled. Betsy kept these feelings hidden deep inside. She couldn't afford to let herself dream about him, but she wanted to. There was something unexplained that excited her about him. It was more than the attention he gave or the way he looked at her. She not only felt his passion and his desire for her. Somewhere underneath that smooth exterior was a gentle soul that she connected with as well. Slowly, she began to believe those things about him. Then there was James, that promise unfulfilled and the empty spaces between them. That space exhausted her. All she felt day in and day out was ache. She took another deep breath of the flowers and smiled.

This morning was the first time all spring Betsy was able to coax Pappy off the porch to help in the garden. Betsy smiled as she watched him trim the dead branches off the rose bushes and cutting some fresh bulbs for a vase he had set in the parlor.

"We planted that red one when Sarah was born and these yellow ones when you came along."

"I didn't know that, Pappy."

"And I *planted* these bushes, not your Momma. These are *my* roses!" he bragged.

Fountaine pulled his car up to the curb and reached across the seat to roll the window down.

"Hey, y'all."

"Hello, Champ," they replied.

"Getting some yard work done?"

"Yes, sir," Pappy noted. He gathered up some freshly cut roses and took them into the house.

Fountaine got out quickly as Pappy went inside. Betsy avoided his glances but smiled shyly when their eyes met.

"I've got to tell you something." He stared her way intently.

"Yes," she answered, nervously removing her gloves.

"I know you aren't happy."

"Champ, please."

"Wait. Let me finish."

Her heart raced. She was afraid of what Fountaine was going to say next.

"I know you aren't happy, and I want to help."

"You can't help me, Champ."

"Yes, I can. I can help you can get out of here. Give you and the boys a new start."

"What?" She replied.

"I have a little money set aside."

Betsy shook her head. "I can't…I can't take that Champ."

"Before you say no."

"Even if I did, I don't know when I could pay you back."

"I'm not worried about the money. I'm worried about you staying here."

"Why are you being so kind?"

He shook his head. "You don't get it do you, Betsy Knight? This is my second chance. I'm not going to miss out again."

Betsy sighed. "I didn't know you had these feelings for me."

"I don't know how you could've missed them!"

"Champ. What about my father? I can't leave Pappy here alone."

"He won't be alone. I'd be here."

She searched her mind for all the things that could go wrong.

"Why didn't you ever marry, Champ?"

"The woman I loved got married before I could ask." He reached over the fence and touched her hand. Betsy closed her eyes. She had forgotten how a simple touch could be so electric and intimate. She allowed herself this moment to see the future she always wanted.

"I would have married you."

Fountaine paused, squeezing her hand gently. "It's not too late."

"Champ. Not here." She was worried, but each time she looked in his eyes, the seeds of doubt subsided. Could she love him or anyone ever again? Could she do the unthinkable and leave? She had loved James, but the pain of being together was too much. She wondered if there was anything she could salvage.

"Once you get settled in Los Angeles, I will come up and join you after I get some things here in order."

"It's so much and all at once. Let me think about this."

"Of course. I understand."

Later that afternoon, Betsy called Sarah.

"He said all that?" Sarah sounded incredulous.

"Yes, and he's serious too."

"I always thought he was corny. What are you gonna do?"

"I have to do it, Sarah. School is almost out for summer. That's the best time to go."

"Junie can come down and get you."

"No. No. I'll have Pappy take us to Calipatria. We'd catch the bus there."

"Better. No prying eyes over there."

"Yes."

"Be careful," Sarah warned.

"I will. I have to have to hang on for a few more weeks."

"The boys will love it up here."

"So will I."

Betsy went home and put clothes and other belongings aside, so when it came time to make a getaway, she'd be ready. She prepared dinner and tried to contain her happiness. She seemed lighter, and she laughed with the boys as they sat down to eat. Her day was coming. She was finally going to live out some of her dreams. Finally, she would have something genuine in her life.

The next day she met with Fountaine at his dry cleaning shop. He turned over the sign in the window from "OPEN" to "CLOSED."

"Are you okay?" He asked her.

"Yes. I'm going to take you up on your offer," Betsy shared.

Fountaine smiled. "Betsy, that's the best news I've heard in a long time."

"For me too."

Fountaine took hold of her hands and pulled her close until his lips touched hers. They embraced for a moment until Betsy broke away. "I'm sorry, Champ. I just can't. Not now."

"Its fine, Betsy. I understand."

"Thank you. Let's get something to eat, okay?"

"That sounds perfect," he answered.

They exited the back of his store and walked across the alleyway toward the Asia Café. Betsy was all smiles. She couldn't help but let that happiness spring forth. Something she had held in for so long. Little did Betsy know that James was waiting at the traffic signal and saw them walking together. He felt his chest tighten, which each step they took to the restaurant. A fire began to rage in him.

That night, James was stirring a pot filled with chili beans when Betsy returned home from Pappy's place. She was surprised to see him.

"What are you doing home so early?"

"We had a light load today," James answered, lifting a spoon of beans to his lips.

"What are you cooking?"

"Some chili and cornbread."

"Smells wonderful," she said happily, placing her purse and the mail on the table.

James placed the top back on the pot and wrapped his arms around her waist. He kissed her gently on her neck, inhaling long and deep.

"James, wait," she implored, but he would not be denied, kissing her ears and back of her neck. His hands groped at her breasts and neck. "James!" Betsy shouted again as he spun her around, forcing his lips onto hers. Before she could say or do anything, he yanked at her skirt, pulling it up over her hips.

After loosening his trousers, he lifted her with ease and laid her on the kitchen table. She exhaled nervously when he entered her. He placed his hand on her throat and began to thrash around, forcing himself inside her harder and harder. He groaned and shook for a moment, then released her. He then buttoned up his pants and checked on the cooking pot of beans as though nothing had happened.

Betsy barely slept that night. Tears rolled over the bridge of her nose, dampening her pillow. She and James had not been intimate in a very long while, but she also didn't want to raise any suspicions. Maybe letting him have his way would quiet him for the time she needed. And a moment was all she would need. Fountaine had the bus tickets in hand. A few more days for him to get the money and her escape was set. This coming Wednesday, she'd be gone far away.

Betsy wiped her mouth before speaking. James stood in the doorway as she tried to exit.

"I heard you in there."

"I'm okay. I think it was that egg foo young from last night."

James exhaled. "You've been sick for almost two weeks. You think I haven't noticed?"

"It's nothing. I haven't been feeling well for some time."

"All the more reason to get it checked out," James added matter-of-factly.

"Not today James. I've got all this laundry, and I need to take Pappy to get groceries."

"All that can wait. Come on. Car is already running."

"James," she started.

"Come on. I insist. Called the doctor this morning. He's waiting for us."

"Okay, but you're going to see it's nothing," Betsy replied. She tried her best to hide her anxiety. She'd missed her period for the second month. It was something she had not shared with her husband. It only complicated her departing, only two days away.

"Well, Mrs. Atkins, I got some wonderful news. It seems you're pregnant!" Doctor Sanchez smiled. Betsy placed her hand over mouth in shock and held back the sadness growing in her throat.

"Are you okay, Mrs. Atkins? I thought you'd be happy...."

"I am. I am. It's just a shock."

James starred at her oddly, not comprehending her reaction. He, too, hid his ambivalence at having another child but didn't let on.

The next day Betsy called Sarah to give her the news.

"I can't have another child with him," she began. A flood of emotion rose in her voice. Betsy fought hard to keep it all in.

"I know, sis. We'll deal with it when you get here."

"I'm sorry, Sarah. I can't do it. I can't do this all on my own."

"You aren't alone. I'll be here for you."

It finally broke her, this overwhelming grief, and tears rolled out of her eyes. "I just can't."

That morning she put away a few more things in the boys' suitcases and placed them under their beds. When the time came, there wouldn't be a moment to waste, and the day finally arrived. It was on Wednesday. The day she'd escape. The day she'd get to live her life. She spoke with Pappy, chatting away nervously, hoping Champ would come by as planned.

"Should I call him? We need to get to Calipat soon, baby." Pappy asked.

"No, Pappy. He'll be here."

She knew her father was not happy with her leaving, but understood why. But the hours passed, and Fountaine never showed Disappointed, she went back home and prepared dinner for the evening.

The boys came home from school and changed clothes. Now all she could do was watch the wall clock as it ticked down each second until James arrived home. Another day they would have to endure. When the door opened and shut with a thud, she took a deep breath. James' heavy steps approached the kitchen.

"I made some..." Betsy started.

He stood there with a nasty smile on his face. His shirt stained in blood.

"What happened to you?" Betsy asked. Her brow furrowed.

"Nothing happened to me. Can't say the same for Champ. I know this; he won't be coming around here no more."

"What did you do, James? What did you do to him?"

"I taught him a lesson 'bout disrespecting me. And it's your fault."

The boys stared nervously at their father.

"You think I wanted this life?" he shouted.

"I gave you my life, James! You're not the only one who wanted different, like living in Canada with Gladys, whatever her name was."

James looked perplexed.

"I know the whole story. Did you see her when you went there with Junie? Is that why you came back so happy, you bastard!" she cried.

"Do you know what I gave up for you, Betsy? For these kids? Now, you gonna cry over Champ? I saw you two at the Asia Café. Of all the places!" He grabbed her wrists tightly, twisting them. Pain shot through her shoulders. "With another man?"

"You're hurting me, James."

"I'm gonna do more than that!"

"Stop it," she screamed.

"Leave her alone!" Junior shouted, taking ahold of his father's arm.

"Daddy! Please," Leroy cried, lodging himself between his father and mother.

"Take your hand off me, boy," James shouted, but Junior did not comply, not this time.

James swung the back of his hand at the boy, hitting him across the face. Junior fell to one side as James turned back to Betsy and balled his fists. Junior got to his feet and locked his arm with his father's, pulling him back with all the strength he could muster. James stared at him angrily but could not break the grip. He lowered his hand slowly and walked away. His son was becoming a man.

As James approached his car, his temples throbbed in pain with each beat of his heart. It wasn't the first time he felt this way. He gathered himself, taking a few deep breaths before driving to the edge of town. James stayed away from home until the next morning.

FOR BETTER OR WORSE

"I am glad you came back in. I was concerned about this tenderness you had during your last visit."

"It's been bothering me for a while now," Betsy told Dr. Suarez as he examined her back and right side.

"Did you fall or strain yourself?"

"I...I don't think so."

The doctor looked over at the nurse. "I want to consult with Dr. Adams. Can you wait here for a little while?"

"Why? What aren't you telling me?"

"I don't want to alarm you, Mrs. Atkins," he paused for a moment. "It's probably nothing, but let's make sure. Is that okay?"

"I guess so," she replied.

Betsy heard from one of the nurses, a family friend, that Champ had spent time hospitalized. He had taken an awful beating. Betsy felt sick. She had brought this upon them both. His life in this town would never be the same.

Pappy came by that morning to take the boys to school and then drive Betsy to the hospital.

"Is my little brother going to be okay?" Leroy asked, pointing to her stomach.

"Yes, son." She smiled. "Your momma is going to be fine too."

"Good! I can't wait to have a brother. I promise Mommy to help you with everything. Even changing his diapers."

Pappy laughed as he drove. "Be careful what you wish for young man. You might get it!"

"Well, son, what if it's a girl? Would you still play with her?" Betsy quizzed.

"Yes!" he answered.

Junior was strangely silent. He looked out the window, feeling anxious. He did not eat that morning. It didn't matter that Betsy told them not to worry and to focus on their studies. He mumbled a goodbye when Pappy dropped him off.

That day, the doctors poked and prodded Betsy. Later, she had a biopsy while Pappy waited. He was there when the doctors came in with her test results. Their conversation ended abruptly when Dr. Suarez appeared at the door.

"Can I come in?" he asked.

"Yes, please," Betsy replied.

"We got your results back," he began, taking in a deep breath.

Pappy asked. "Should I wait outside?"

"No, please stay," Betsy chocked up, taking his hand.

Suarez took a deep breath before he began. "Well, there is no way to say this but to say it. You have hepatocellular carcinoma. Liver cancer. It's very advanced," he said, letting his words linger a moment before continuing. "We need to get you into treatment as soon as possible at the medical center in San Diego."

Betsy took a deep breath. "Liver cancer…" she repeated. "Are you saying it's too far gone to treat?"

"It is advanced, and this type of cancer is challenging to treat, but you're young, and that will help. There is another option called chemotherapy. Drugs target the malignant cells and, I won't sugar coat this, it's risky, but there has been some success in treating lymphoma."

"Oh, Lord," she placed her hand on her heart. Pappy closed his eyes.

"I'm so very sorry to have to tell you this, but there is very little chance the fetus will survive either treatment."

"And if I don't have the treatment, how long can I expect to live?"

"Anywhere from two weeks to three months. It all depends."

Pappy exhaled loudly. "Lord, no."

"I'll give you my phone number in case you have any more questions."

Pappy and Betsy drove home in silence, both shell-shocked, far away in their thoughts. As they came to a stop in front of her house, Betsy sighed deeply. "Pappy, I don't want to be home alone. Can I stay with you for a little bit?"

"Of course, Betsy."

Pappy took her hand and helped her up from the seat. He thought about his daughter, who almost died at birth, now facing another challenge. They walked slowly up the steps to the front door. It was a warm, sunny day, a day when they would usually be in the garden. But the sun felt like a fireball today, draining her strength with each unsteady step she took from Pappy's car to his house.

As soon as they were inside, Betsy threw her arms around her father, clawing at him in desperation. For a moment, he wanted to tell her to be strong, but those were empty words. Instead, Pappy held her tightly as she slowly melted to the floor. He felt helpless, crushed. The more she cried, the harder it became for him to hold it in.

"Pappy, what am I gonna do?" she choked on her tears.

"We're gonna fight this together."

Hot streams of tears rolled down his face. Betsy was his miracle child. He wanted to believe there would be another one for her.

Later that day, Betsy called Sarah.

"Betsy, what's wrong?" I can hear it in your voice. Did James do something to you? Something is wrong. Is Pappy okay?"

"Pappy is fine, Sarah."

"Then what is it?"

"Please let me speak. This is important. I went to the doctors."

"Betsy, what'd James do now?" Sarah's voice was angry.

"This is hard enough without you interrupting." Her throat pained her with each word.

"Okay. I'll be quiet."

Betsy sighed. "Sarah, I have cancer. Liver cancer."

"No. That can't be." Sarah said, skeptical of her hearing.

"I am going to San Diego for treatment in a few days."

"That serious?"

"Yes, sis. It is."

Betsy could sense Sarah was about to break down, but she needed to get this out. Despite what everyone believed, she knew different. It was that awful feeling in the pit of her stomach. She hated the idea of telling her children and breaking their little hearts. But it had to be done.

"I can't believe this is happening to you. What did I ever do to deserve this?" Sarah asked.

"I don't know anything anymore," Betsy revealed. "I need to think." She then hung up the phone without saying goodbye.

After Betsy collected herself, she hugged Pappy and went home to wait for her family. Junior arrived first. She hugged him, noticing how much he had matured in this last year. He was tall like his father, broad-shouldered, and with the same intense eyes.

Leroy came in right after him.

"Momma!" he shouted excitedly. He placed his lunchbox down on the kitchen table and ran to his mother's arms.

"When did you get home?" James asked as he closed the door. "I went by the hospital after work."

"Pappy was there when they discharged me," she explained. "He gave me a ride home."

"It would have been nice to get a call." The words were not angry but from deep concern.

"I'm sorry. There's so much to do."

James cautiously asked, "Any news?"

"Let's all sit down."

James sighed. "Okay."

"There is something I have to tell you all."

"What is it, Betsy?" James asked.

She reached out and held her boys' hands.

"What's wrong, Momma?" Junior asked.

She started slowly. "I have cancer. It's serious, and Momma needs to go to another hospital right away."

"What?" James asked.

"Momma, what's cancer?" Leroy asked.

"Baby, it is a bad, bad illness. Momma is very sick."

"Are you gonna be okay?" Junior asked, his eyes searching hers.

"I don't know, son. I don't know." She did not have the heart to tell him what she truly felt.

"What do you mean you don't know?" Junior asked.

"Son, I'm very, very sick." The sadness grew stronger as she tried to hold back her emotions, but a tear escaped her eye.

James sat back, trying to make sense of it all. He had no concept of cancer, no understanding of what they were facing.

"Momma, I'm scared," Leroy agonized.

"I'm sorry, son. I didn't want to upset you."

Junior leaned his head on his mother's shoulder as James sat, elbows on his knees, hands clasped. He looked around like a lost child, wondering what to do next.

"I'm gonna check the mail," he said and walked out.

Betsy watched him leave, but it did not upset her. She was more concerned about her children.

"Listen to me, Leroy. If something happens to Mommy, you are going to have to be strong for your father and your brother. You are going to have to get along with them and not fight, you hear me?"

"Yes, Momma," he agreed. He covered his face with one hand, trying to stem the flow of his tears.

"Momma, why are you talking like this? Are you gonna die?" Junior exclaimed.

"I don't want to die, son, but I don't ever want to lie to you."

"No, Momma!" he yelled. "This ain't right."

She took Junior's hand and insisted, "You have to keep an eye out for your little brother whether you like it or not. You have to help around the house. Take out the trash."

Junior shook his head, not wanting to hear what she was saying. But Betsy continued to set her expectations of them despite their objections.

"The same goes for you, Leroy. You hear me?"

She motioned for them to come close, opening her arms to them. She knew how overwhelmed they must have been feeling at that time.

Next door, Pappy sat in his chair with his hand resting on a shoebox in his lap. He opened it slowly, unfolding a checkered cloth, revealing a pistol wrapped inside. He remembered what his father had told him the day he gave it to him. The idea of taking another man's life was repugnant to him, but he rationalized its necessity. With all the lynchings and violence directed towards black people, it was a natural response. He could hear his father's words in his head.

"Might come down to their life or yours. I say, take a few of them with you if they dare. Aim steady and shoot to kill, son. Shoot to kill."

Those words reverberated in Pappy's mind as he came to his daughter's front door. The back of his neck was on fire. James stood outside, leaning against the fence that faced the Vasquez home across the empty lot.

"James," he called.

"What can I do for you, Pappy?"

"I got something to say."

"Okay. Say it."

"Champ is good people. He didn't deserve what you did."

James cut him off. "Well, he might be, but I warned him about coming around here when I wasn't home."

"That's all? Champ's been helping me on and off for months now!" Pappy shouted. "You didn't have to do him like that."

"Man should have shown some respect," James complained, stepping closer to Pappy.

Pappy touched the gun in his pocket, sliding his finger over the trigger, but he did not pull it out. He muttered. "I never wanted to hurt another soul until now."

"Sometimes you have to," James said, turning his back to Pappy. "I'd try to be in the other's man's shoes before I judged him if I was you."

Pappy tapped the gun once more then left as quietly as he came.

That night, as everyone slept, James stared at a crack in the wallpaper. He thought of the many repairs he needed to make around the house. With the boys out of school for the summer, James would have a couple of extra hands. He made a mental list of things to do until he came upon new lists, distracting himself as best he could.

His mind eventually drifted to visions of life without Betsy. They'd spent the past seventeen years together for better or for worse. He wondered what would have happened if he had just gone to Canada or back to Texas with the rest of the team that day in Yuma. He had some money and not a worry in the world. But he was lonely too. *What a price to pay,* he thought to himself. He tortured his mind until the morning sun peeked through the blinds.

Sunday, Betsy got the family ready for church. She was surprised yet pleased when she saw James shaving.

"You're coming with us today?" she asked.

"Figured it couldn't hurt."

"No, it wouldn't," she smiled.

As James turned, their eyes locked together briefly. In that instant, he recalled the first time he saw her. She was waiting in her father's car, her arm resting on the window frame. He had caught a glimpse of her profile as he passed the vehicle. He was smitten with her in the very first encounter.

Betsy looked away. "I better check the boys," she suggested

She had forgotten how James could give her chills just in the way he looked at her. Betsy was reminded of the years of unspoken intimacy between them, the many moments they had let pass, that was now lost. She could not pinpoint when she became the woman she now barely recognized. Betsy was a shell of her former self. The Betsy she knew had disappeared into her role as wife, mother, and caretaker.

The family piled into the car, and James turned toward J Street. Betsy saw her father standing outside as they came around.

"James, stop the car," Betsy said. She leaned over into James' lap and called out the window. "Daddy, you riding with us?"

"Oh, y'all go ahead. There's no room in there, no how."

"Nonsense. We got plenty," Betsy motioned for Junior to move over for his grandfather.

Pappy opened the door and sat behind James. They glared at each other through the rearview mirror.

James felt a bit silly being at church. Leroy was a child the last time he attended a service, but he believed he had to do something, especially now.

The congregation listened intently to the sermon, then sang "A Charge to Keep I Have," along with the choir. Later, Reverend Drew and several of the deacons stood at the doorway, greeting the parishioners after the service ended.

"James! It's been a long time," Reverend Drew exclaimed. Drew had a strength to him that reminded James of his grandfather Bernard.

"Yes, it has, I'm ashamed to say."

"Don't be. We're happy you came. Please come back soon, brother."

"Reverend," Junior inquired, "Can I ask you a question?"

"Sure, son," He began, taking Junior by the arm. "How can I help you?"

"It's my mother."

"Yes."

"Well, I...I remember in one of your sermons where Jesus healed the sick."

"Yes, son. The scripture is filled with miraculous healings."

"Well, my mother, she is sick, and I was wondering if you could say a special prayer for her"

"You were paying attention. Of course, I do you one better. Y'all come to the prayer room."

"Everyone?"

"Yes, everyone. You *ALL* need a blessing. The whole family!" Drew emphasized, motioning to James.

Junior recalled the many times he and his brother made fun of the church people who were touched by the spirit. The inspired would get up from their seats, swaying to the music, their eyes shut tightly, and trembling hands raised skyward. The boys would bet on who would fall under a spell on a particular Sunday service.

"Where are we going?" Leroy whispered to him.

"To get healed," Junior replied, not fully understanding what that all meant. He had his doubts, remembering his father criticizing past sermons, saying everyone wants to go to heaven, but no one wants to die to get there. Now he was hoping for some of what those touched people felt. The true spirit of God, he believed.

The intricacies of eternal life befuddled Junior, but his mother's illness was his main concern now. And around that reality, there was no confusion. So here he was, asking God for help. He vowed then if this worked, not to ever make fun of church again.

Much to the chagrin of his father, they marched back inside. Reverend Drew rolled out a small rug and placed it in front of a large cross that hung on the wall.

"Can you kneel, Betsy?"

"Yes, reverend."

"Your son informed me of your illness, and I wanted first to say that I will do whatever I can to help you through this most difficult time. The church is with you, Betsy."

"Thank you," she stammered.

"I also wanted to bless you and the entire family. We will pray for your healing, and I'll give you some information to help you all keep your spirits up."

"Thank you," Pappy added with conviction.

"May I ask your affliction?"

"I have cancer, Reverend."

He shut his eyes for a moment, then proclaimed, "Prayer is a powerful healer. Everyone join hands."

Reverend Drew placed his hands on Betsy and James' heads. "Lord, bless this family. Oh anointed one, show them your love and grace as they face this difficult time. Keep your servant, Betsy, safe, and strengthen her every day. In Jonah 2:2, it says, 'When I was in trouble, Lord, I prayed to you, and you listened to me. From deep in the world of the dead, I begged for your help, and you answered my prayer. We call upon you now to heal Betsy, heal her family. Turn this cancer away from her body."

"*Amen!*" Pappy and Junior said loudly.

"Lift it from her. Heal her Lord as only you can. Reveal yourself in the miracle of her health restored."

"Amen," Betsy whispered.

As Junior slowly opened his eyes, he noticed his father's hands were clasped together in prayer.

"Amen," the reverend added triumphantly. "Please rise."

The family stood together.

"Trust in the Lord. Lay your fears and anguish on his shoulders. Let him carry your burdens. Have faith in the Lord to deliver you."

"Thank you, Reverend," Pappy shook his hand tightly.

"Junior, I'll write down some verses to give you comfort."

"Thank you, sir," he replied.

"You're welcome. Go with God. Thank you for bringing this to my attention. That was a good thing. Keep the Lord's commandments and pray. Prayer heals, son."

Junior kept his word. He prayed before he went to bed each night as well as in the morning when he got up. Leroy joined him, and they recited the passages that Reverend Drew gave them. He repeated the verses he had memorized to his brother, telling him to read it aloud with him. "And in that same hour, he cured many of their infirmities and plagues and evil spirits, and unto many that were blind he gave them sight."

He talked to everyone who would listen about his newfound faith in God, including Daisy, on their walks home from school each day.

"I'll pray for you too," Junior shared with her.

"Why, do I look unhappy?"

"Everyone can use a prayer, Daisy, even you."

She laughed.

"You don't have to believe me. From now on, I'm going to pray for your soul every day whether you like it or not."

With each passing hour, he became confident his mother would beat this disease. He believed with all the fiber in his being that his prayers would have an impact.

The next morning James had coffee made and toast with scrambled eggs on the boys' plates before Betsy was out of bed. Uncertainty clung to all of them, each wondering about the days ahead. Betsy joined them for breakfast and tried her best to put on a happy face. She did not want her family to be so glum.

With only two weeks remaining in the school term, Pappy would take his grandsons to school, while James and Betsy were in San Diego.

"Okay, boys. Time to go." He called from outside. He peered in the doorway and repeated himself.

Leroy began to tremble. "No. I don't want to go to school. I want to go with Momma!"

"Oh, baby," she lamented.

"Son, Pappy is going to bring you up this Friday. It will go by quickly. I'm telling you," James assured.

"No, it won't."

Junior tugged at his shirt. "Come on, little brother. Remember what Reverend Drew told us? We should trust in Jesus and put our worries on his shoulders."

Leroy shook his head, "yes."

"That's what I did. You see, I'm not crying."

"You ain't?"

"No. I prayed this morning. And we can pray together next time. You'll feel better, I promise."

"Okay." Leroy murmured.

"We have to go to school. That's what we have to do. And Momma has to get to the hospital to get her medicine."

"I guess so."

"Come on, let's go to school," Junior comforted, throwing his arm around his brother's shoulders.

"Thank you, son," Betsy replied. She was proud of the way he handled that situation.

"Give Momma a hug before you go." She fought back the sadness in her heart. "Love you, Little Man."

"I love you too, Momma."

She looked at her eldest son, looking at every detail of his face. He stood five or six inches over her. "When did you get so big?"

Junior smiled shyly.

She touched his face once more.

"See you on Friday."

With that, they were all out the door. Soon after the boys departed, James and Betsy began the ride up to the San Diego highway, passing the turnoff near Ocotillo, where they had come to admire the night sky in the early days of their courtship.

"Remember that time we ran outta gas!" James said to her.

"Yes, I do," she smiled. "You were just trying to get me outta my clothes."

"Sure was," he laughed. "But, I didn't plan on walking six miles for gas!"

Betsy and James laughed for a minute, leaving them both to ponder why this hadn't happened sooner. They could be together so effortlessly. James patted her hand as they both went silent again. Betsy wondered where this side of him had gone all these years. He used to make her laugh all the time. It was just a glimmer of the man she fell in love with.

They continued through the valleys and canyons. The highway ran alongside huge terracotta-colored boulders, some as large as a school bus, that were stacked one on top of the other forming pathways that only a giant could follow. Black sage and chaparral grew between the rocks giving the landscape a stark, prehistoric look. There were no traces of civilization across the barren landscape once they passed the little gas station in Jacumba. It was not until they reached the higher elevations on the leeward side of the mountain that the environment became lush with pine and yucca trees in the cool, mountain air. The border of Mexico was on their left and ahead another sixty miles, was the city of San Diego.

Betsy remembered when she was almost free; when she had risked everything to strike out on her own. She wondered what happened to that bold person. Betsy was just a girl of sixteen when she defied her fears and made a break for herself. How quickly she had fallen back down to earth.

HARD DAYS AHEAD

James and Betsy sat quietly in the waiting area, holding hands for the first time in many years. Over the last few miles of the drive to the hospital in San Diego, they contemplated what news would come. The hospital's oncologist, Dr. Baker, launched almost immediately into his plan after inviting them into his office. His rosy cheeks and fiery, red hair added to the passion of his delivery.

"The standard treatment consists of two approaches— surgery and radiation. We do have a new treatment called chemotherapy that I think may help. You see, radiation affects a localized area, its concentrated, and has side effects like nausea and vomiting. Hair loss will occur. I won't beat around the bush here but you have advanced cancer, Mrs. Atkins. We are going to use two, possibly three, of these therapies. I want to prepare you. We are going to fight this thing together. I'm here to help in any way I can," he offered.

"Will you be treating my wife?' James asked.

"It's a team effort. You will meet the rest of the staff after you've settled in. We want to begin treatment right away."

Shocked, Betsy asked. "Today?"

"Yes, immediately." Dr. Baker said. "So I'll see you in about thirty minutes? The nurses will get you started."

Betsy changed into her gown as James sat in the only chair around. It was uncomfortably small for his large frame. Moments later, a nurse arrived pushing a wheelchair and took Betsy down the long corridor. James kept pace until they slowed at a set of double doors.

"This is the end of the ride for you," The nurse remarked to James. He looked startled.

"I can't go in here with her?"

"No. I'm sorry."

Betsy gripped his hand tight.

"I'll be right here," he whispered to her as the nurse wheeled her away.

Betsy cried when she returned an hour later. James tried to console her, but she curled up in a ball on the bed and turned away from him. A nurse came a few minutes later, lifted her gown, and cleaned up between her legs. James saw traces of blood on the wipes the nurse used.

Betsy's regimen of pills for the chemotherapy made her nauseous. The nurse reassured her it would pass. After that first round of treatment, she took a long nap. Later that evening, she ate sparingly, picking at the bland food, her stomach still unsettled.

"Nothing like some pork fried rice from Asia Café right now, huh?" James smiled.

Betsy tried to be upbeat. "I'm honestly not hungry."

"Hey, let me fix your hair."

"It's a mess, isn't it?" Betsy asked.

James didn't answer her. Instead, he began softly brushing it. Betsy closed her eyes, feeling suddenly emotional.

"How do I look?" she asked, tears welling up in her eyes.

James only smiled.

It became their routine for the next few days. James got maintenance to bring him a more comfortable chair, and he watched her day and night. The blinking lights of the various monitors became a form of solace. They produced a rhythm that became familiar and comforting. Nurses flowed in and out during the day, checking the drips and tubes stuck in her veins. Meals arrived at the appointed hours. Betsy took several rounds of chemotherapy each day, which became harder and harder to endure. Her food wouldn't stay down, and she was losing her beautiful figure. Morning bought new pain, new challenges, and new fears. Five days into her treatment, her hair started to fall out while James brushed it.

He looked at a clump of her hair in his hand and shuddered.

"Oh my god," Betsy shrieked, looking in the hand mirror. "The boys…" she whispered.

"Don't worry. I'll take care of it," James understood.

She was horrified by the sight of her lost hair, but this was just the beginning of her ordeal. Bone-heavy fatigue set in so much so that Betsy could barely lift her head to take her medication. The powerful drugs destroyed her body and will. This war was exacting an immense price. Her spirit, though strong, began to wane. Those supporting her could see the toll it was taking on her.

Sarah arrived late Friday evening with Junie and saw how run down her sister looked. Betsy's once youthful sparkle was flat and uninspired. Betsy was happy to see her. She tied a scarf over her head to hide her bald spots.

"Hey, sis. How are you?" Sarah tried to sound cheerful.

"I'm okay." Betsy's voice cracked as she hugged her. "But I'd rather know how you're doing?"

"Been better," Sarah cautioned, her face wrought with concern.

"Hi, Junie," Betsy smiled as he walked in.

"Hey, baby girl," Junie added, "Brought these for you." He sat a bouquet of red and orange roses on a table near her bed.

"Thank you. They're lovely."

The sisters chatted as James and Junie spoke quietly to themselves near the doorway.

Sarah sat on the edge of the bed and took Betsy's hand. "How are you?"

"Not good, Sarah. These treatments make me sick. I'm tired all the time and look at my hair!"

"I got something for that." Sarah produced a wig from her bag. "I am sick to my stomach over this."

"Keep your spirits up, Sarah."

"Here, I thought I was the problem child when it was you all along!" Sarah cackled, more to keep herself from crying.

"You got that, right!" Betsy's laugh turned into a cough. When she was able to breathe, she spoke up, "Pappy ever tell you I tried to run away?"

"What? When was this?"

Betsy chuckled. "You never heard about that? Senior year in high school. I packed my bag and walked over to the bus station."

"Where were you going?"

"Los Angeles. Where else would I go?"

"You could've ended up in New York City for all I know."

"How nice that would've been," Betsy lamented. "Pappy talked me out of it. Said he'd change."

"Did he?"

"Yes. Pappy did. He did indeed."

"He's good for that."

"We'll be right back," James announced. "Want anything from the cafeteria?"

The women both said no.

Betsy grabbed Sarah's arm tightly. "I need to tell you something."

"What's that, Betsy?"

"The baby," she whispered.

"God, no."

She nodded. "Eight weeks. It's gone now," she whispered as tears streamed from her eyes. "I had to abort my baby."

"This is awful, Betsy."

"Listen, I need a favor." Betsy grabbed her arm.

"Anything. Anything at all."

"I need you to be there for the boys."

"I am their Auntie, of course, I will be."

"No, I need you to spend time with them. Have the boys with you in Los Angeles for the summer and during Christmastime. Let them know they can count on you. I'm afraid to leave them alone with James, especially Junior."

"Why are you saying this?"

"I need you to do this one other thing for me." Betsy continued.

"Okay. Okay," Sarah fought back the tears.

"Give this letter to Junior when the time is right."

Sarah looked confused. "Why can't you give it to him yourself?"

Betsy shook her head defiantly. "Sarah, I'm not gonna leave here."

"Don't say that!"

"Shush. I need you to promise me. Promise me that."

Sarah finally broke down in tears. "You can't die. You're only 37 years old. What the hell is going on here?"

"I know. I'm terrified, too, but I got to make my peace with this."

Sarah rested her head on Betsy's shoulder, her voice trembling.

"I promise, Betsy." She took the letter and placed it in her purse.

"They'll appreciate seeing more of their Auntie and Uncle Junie."

Sarah nodded.

"You can take them to all the places I never got to see, just got stuck in that little town, and the best I got out of life was a trip to the hospital."

Sarah laughed. They laughed for a while until the reality of it all came back, and they grew quiet again. All the times, the sisters seemed to be at odds with each other had withered over the years. There was no one she trusted more than Sarah.

Pappy showed up with Leroy and Junior the next morning. James was in the cafeteria, getting breakfast with Junie and Sarah. They were staying in the same motel as James. Betsy was happy with the wig Sarah brought her. It was a nice fit, and though it didn't look anything like her natural hair, Betsy felt better when she looked in the mirror.

"Well, look who's here," Pappy rejoiced, walking in with the boys.

"If it isn't my handsome young men," Betsy declared.

Leroy and Junior ran to their mother.

"Hi, Momma," they cried out happily.

"Hello there," she smiled. "How was the ride up?"

"Okay. Pappy drives too slow," Junior complained. "We should have been here an hour ago."

"I heard that!" Pappy grumbled.

"Son, you got here when you were supposed to. Now kiss me."

Junior placed a gentle kiss on her cheek. She cupped his face in her hand, caressing his hair.

"I brought something for you," he said.

"You did?" she smiled.

"*We* brought something for you," Leroy corrected him.

It was a morning glory cut from the main vine and re-potted in a jar. It was growing fast, winding around a small stick set in the center of the pot.

"Look at that. You're taking good care of Momma's garden for me?"

"Yes, we are," Junior pointed out.

"Put it by the window for me so it can get some sun."

"What else you got for her, Leroy?" Pappy added.

"We got our grades. Here's mine."

Betsy opened it excitedly. "Leroy! How fantastic." He had made the honor roll for the first time in years. "I knew you could do it. I want to see many more too."

"You will, Momma. I'm going to high school next year."

"I know, son! You're getting so grown."

Junior handed his report card to her. "Messed up the final in History and got an A-minus."

Betsy shook her head when she saw he had high marks in all his classes.

"Oh, James, I'm so proud of you. Come here," she said, placing her hand over her mouth for a moment. She was so happy. "Keep this up. It's your ticket out of Brawley."

They sat and talked as a family for a good part of the day. Later they ate lunch together with Sarah, Junie, and James. They all watched a little television until the sun began to set in the distance.

"Okay, boys, let your mother rest," Pappy demanded. He could see that Leroy was about to protest. "We'll come back tomorrow."

"Where are you staying?" Betsy asked.

"The motel right up the hill," Pappy answered. "Same place as James."

She shook her head. "Better check with the doctors before you come tomorrow."

Sarah got up from the chair near the window and kissed her on the cheek. "I'll be back next weekend. Junie and I both have to work, but I requested time off after that."

"Don't wait too long, Sis," Betsy remarked. She hugged her tightly, and Sarah felt the lump beginning to grow in her throat. Betsy did not want to fall apart and worry her children, though a part of her did not care. Junior was last to say goodbye after Pappy and Junie. She nodded to him, and he let out a big sigh before leaving.

Betsy did not realize how much the visit had fatigued her. The treatments exacted a greater cost on her body and mind. Her skin turned a sallow gray, bags accumulated under her eyes, and she lost more of her beautiful hair. She hated seeing the rapid changes the disease imposed upon her, forcing her to see what she was and what she wasn't. She was still a proud and modest woman, and it was tough for her to remove her clothing or call for assistance whenever she soiled herself, but over time, she and the nurses became very accustomed to each other.

"After this is over, will you come and keep my home too?" she joked with Nurse Thomasina.

"If the pay is good!" Thomasina laughed.

Betsy learned that Junior was not taking any of this very well. He was upset that he could not stay longer with his mother after his last visit. Pappy found him on his hands and knees, praying with curtains open each morning at sunrise. He became more and more agitated when he couldn't visit at all.

"Why can't we go and see Momma today?'

Pappy answered gently, "Son, your Momma is very sick. They don't want you to see her that way."

"She won't care. We need to be with her and pray over her body."

"I'll call up to the hospital, maybe we can go later today," he acquiesced.

The boys spent the day trying to find something to occupy their time. The motel was a two-story building with about fifty units. The rooms were old, but quaint with lumpy beds. There was a cacophony of traffic noise night and day that came in from a nearby freeway.

The next morning Betsy looked even more disheveled, her gown wrinkled and buttoned in the wrong order. A thin layer of sweat covered her face and neck. She was in tears as the orderly wheeled the gurney down the hallway.

"Please make them stop, James," she pleaded, grasping his hand tightly.

"Hang in there, baby. It'll be over soon."

Tears rolled from her eyes. "It hurts so badly. Please, I am begging you. Make it stop, please."

James swallowed hard, not knowing how to answer. "I'll be right here when you come out. Right here!"

She laid back down as the gurney went through the doors of the treatment center, her lips trembling in quiet desperation. It ripped her husband's soul to shreds.

James walked back down the hall. With each step, it became more difficult for him to focus. When he got outside, he put his face in his hands began to cry uncontrollably, not caring about the people coming in and out of the hospital. He wanted her pain to end. He wanted her home. James felt the crushing weight of a lifetime of anguish and grief.

Back in her hospital bed, a piercing chill spread throughout Betsy's body. There was no way to know whether the treatment was working. Only time could tell, and that was a precious commodity. She hated doubt, it frightened and terrorized her nights, but in a way, she became stronger each time she was able to push it away.

She slowly made peace with her circumstances, with this disease that ravaged her flesh. She cried less and less. James saw it on her face, her quiet surrender, the hollowed out look in her eyes. After his visits, he, too, broke down alone in his car. He never wanted her to see his distress.

Betsy fought through nausea, vomiting so hard, her stomach muscles cramped, her throat burning from the acids. At times, she lost control of her bowels. It happened more often than she would have liked.

"I'm sorry," she relented as Thomasina cleaned her up.

"Don't worry, Betsy. That's what we are here for."

Every joint felt as if someone had hammered nails into her bones. She screamed out in pain when the nurses turned her over to wash her.

She looked at James one day and faltered, "I'm so tired."

"I know you are. Tomorrow's a new day, and the boys are coming."

She smiled. "They are?"

"Yes. Junior can't wait. Been bugging me since Sunday."

"I don't want them to see me like this."

"That's what I told him."

"Tomorrow will be better," she breathed.

"Yes, it will. Try to rest."

Dr. Baker waved to James from the hallway. "Can I have a word with you in my office?"

"Sure, Doc." James looked at him uneasily.

"I was just on my way to see Betsy, but I wanted to speak to you first. The treatment is not taking hold. There's no other way to say it, but to say it. Cancer has spread. It is just a matter of time now. We found it too late."

James stared at him in disbelief. "A matter of time? How long is that?"

"Any day now. Truthfully, you should get her affairs in order. We'll work on making her comfortable at this point, but there is no need to put her through any more treatments."

"There's nothing more you can do? You're giving up?" James criticized.

"I'm sorry, Mr. Atkins. I know this is terrible news."

"Please don't tell her now. Tell her another day. I'm bringing our children for a visit tomorrow."

"I don't know if I can do that Mr. Atkins. She has a right to know, and it's my duty to inform her. But I'll wait until the morning. It's the best I can do."

"I just want to be there," James fumed, rubbing his temples from another pounding headache.

Instead of leaving, James went back to Betsy's room. She was asleep, curled up on one side, a pillow tucked under her head and neck. Some nights she was so tired she could not sleep, but tonight she rested peacefully.

James told Pappy the sad news when they talked that evening. He spoke quietly, not wanting to wake the boys as they slept. There was silence on the other end, and Pappy hung up.

Pappy took a moment to compose himself, and then he called Sarah, Reverend Drew, and several relatives back in Georgia.

"It's not good, Sarah. You should come as soon as you can."

"I'll be there tomorrow," she confirmed.

"What is it, baby? Betsy, okay?" Junie asked when she hung up the phone.

She shook her head, no longer able to hold back the tears.

James was up early the next morning. He took a quick shower then shaved, trying to make as little noise as possible. There was a gnawing in his stomach. He had no idea what he faced this day. When he stepped from the bathroom, he saw Junior on his knees, hands folded in prayer. James stepped around him and sat on the edge of the bed to put his shoes on.

"Can I go with you, Dad?" Junior asked.

"Son, it is better if you come with Pappy. I don't want him driving alone."

"Leroy can go with him. Besides, the hospital is just a few blocks away," Junior protested.

"Junior, not this morning." He consoled.

James arrived at the hospital a short time later to find the doctor and nurses already there. Betsy smiled as he came in. She seemed rested and energetic.

"I can't wait to see my boys. Where are they?"

"They're coming with Pappy."

"Okay. I told the nurses we want pancakes today. They love pancakes. With lots of maple syrup."

James tried to smile, but the overwhelming grief gripped his mind. The doctor gave him a look, and James nodded to him.

"Betsy," the doctor began, "I've got some news about your treatment."

"Yes, doctor," she began to worry.

"I wish I had better news, but the treatment is not..." He paused for a moment. "The cancer has spread."

"What are you saying?" she asked as James took hold of her hand.

"There is nothing more we can do for you. We can't continue with the treatment."

"No...that can't be...," she wailed.

James tried to calm her.

"Lord Jesus." She began to weep.

"I'll leave you two alone." Dr. Baker said, looking down at the floor as he left the room.

"Reverend Drew will be here later today," James added.

"Does he know?"

James nodded.

"When did you find out?"

"Last night."

"Last night? Why did you keep this from me?"

"I didn't want you to be up all night worrying about it."

"I'll have plenty of time to rest when I'm dead!" she yelled. "You had no right to keep it from me."

"I'm sorry, Betsy. I'm so sorry."

Betsy seemed to deflate. All traces of her earlier energy was gone. "It's okay. You didn't do anything wrong, James," she reached out and touched his face. "Pappy and Sarah know too?"

"Yes, Sarah and Junie are coming down tonight."

"Can you leave? I need to be alone right now."

"Yes, baby."

After James closed the door, Betsy sobbed. Her mind wandered to depressing things like all the birthdays she'd miss. All the music and history she'd never experience. She imagined all the places she had dreamed of as a young girl. But more importantly, all the things Betsy would never be. She would never get to see her boys become men; never be a grandmother; never grow old.

How does anyone imagine his or her death or an eternity of non-existence? She cried for several minutes before steadying her nerves. She did not want this to be her children's last image of their mother. She wanted them to remember her smiling and happy.

Pappy and the boys arrived a short time later with several photobooks. James sat in his usual place in the chair across from the bed.

"Come in. Come in!" Betsy exclaimed. "How is my handsome man?"

"I'm fine, Momma. How are you?" Junior responded.

"Much better now that you are here. And where's my baby boy? Come here, Leroy, and give me some sugar."

Leroy giggled as she kissed him all over his face. She patted the bed, beckoning the boys to come and sit next to her. As she put her arms around them, Pappy took out a camera.

"Let me get this shot here." He snapped a few pictures.

"What have you got there, Daddy?" she asked, noticing the bag he had set down by her bedside.

"A little surprise for you." He pulled one of the albums out and placed one on her lap.

"You didn't."

"Why not?"

"Yes. Better times." She agreed.

She opened the album, slowly turning the pages. She sifted through each picture, recalling every detail for her children.

As she lay on the bed with her sons and all the promise they held, she wished she had her mother's resolve and grace. She was glad Momma Knight was not around to see her child wasting away.

They looked through a few more pictures until it was lunchtime, and James took them to the cafeteria. As they started the door, Reverend Drew came to the door.

"James Junior. How are you, son?" The Reverend asked.

"I'm fine."

"Praise be to God. And Leroy, how are you?"

"I'm okay. Thank you."

"Glad to hear that."

"I've been praying every day like you said to do. Momma is feeling better now."

"Jesus rewards the faithful son," he confided, casting a worried look at James. "Let me go say hello to your mother, boys."

The Reverend knocked gently on the door. "Hello, Betsy."

"Hi, Reverend."

"Good to see you," he replied.

"I ain't much to look at."

"You are perfect in the eyes of the Lord."

"That's kind of you."

"Just speaking the Lord's truth Betsy."

She swallowed hard, not wanting to have this conversation.

"How are you holding up?" he asked, taking her hand in his.

"Best, I can. Are you here for my last rites?"

The Reverend paused. "That's all that is asked of us, to trust in the Lord."

"Why?" she asked, her face wrought with anguish.

Reverend Drew squeezed her hand, "Because, through Him, you will live eternally."

"But I have to die to get there?" Echoing something James had said years before.

"Yes, you know well the wages of sin is death, but a physical death, not a spiritual one. The gift of God is eternal life in Christ, our Lord."

"Is this all there is to my life, Reverend? Is this where I end, buried in some cold ground. Is that all there is? I've barely even lived," she choked up.

Reverend Drew took out his handkerchief and offered it to her.

"Betsy. I believe with all my heart that the answer to your question is no. No, this is not all there is to you, to me, to anyone who believes in the Lord. Jesus' resurrection defeated death."

She was not comforted. "I'm scared," she whispered. "Terrified, actually."

"It's okay. You must find the courage to face death as we all must. Your trust in Jesus will strengthen you. As sad as this moment is, we should rejoice. You will meet our savior and sit at the feet of God forever."

She stared out the window as the tears welled in her eyes. "I hope I see my mother," she volunteered as Reverend Drew began to pray.

"Our Father who art in heaven hallowed be thy name. Thy kingdom come. Thy will be done on earth as it is in heaven…"

She held his hand tightly. His words reminded her of her baptism prayer when she was a young girl.

"Lord, I confess my sins and put all my trust in you. I believe Jesus died for our sins. I believe Jesus Christ is my Lord and Savior, Amen." The Reverend held her hands a little while longer as he continued to pray. "Oh anointed one, please deliver Sister Betsy from this earthly pain and suffering. Give her strength to face this moment and reveal your truth to her. We say this in the name of Jesus Christ. Amen."

When James, Pappy, and the boys returned, Betsy and the Reverend were saying their goodbyes.

"James, I'll speak to you soon." Reverend Drew said, passing him at the door.

"Thank you for coming," James replied.

Betsy sat up and smiled as the group came over to her bed. "How was your lunch?"

"It was okay. Kinda dry," Leroy frowned.

"I've been eating this food for almost a month now! How do you think I feel?" She laughed. "Pass me another photo album, please."

Junior handed one to her, and she told them as many stories about her life as she could remember. They laughed with each other for quite some time until she came across a picture that gave her pause. It was one of Betsy holding her great grandmother's rag doll. It was a coveted heirloom that she misplaced somewhere in the house.

"What's wrong, Momma?" Leroy asked.

"These pictures bring back many memories, and some of them are sad."

"Don't be sad, Momma."

"I'll try, son."

Pappy reached over to her and took her hand. "Tell Momma I will be coming soon."

A lone tear meandered down Betsy's face.

"I love you, sweet pea. Very much." Pappy chocked up.

"I love you too, Pappy. Forever."

Junior sensed something was amiss as he watched his mother. "What's wrong, Momma? Why are you and Pappy so sad?"

Pappy held in his emotions before answering. His eyes rimmed in red. "Just thinking about the past."

The harder he tried to suppress his emotions, the greater the need to release them became. He finally let go of his concern for appearances. Too much had already been lost. He and Betsy both knew these were their last memories together. Pappy wrapped his arms around her for several minutes while the tears fell freely from his eyes. Junior rushed over, wrapping his arms around them both. When they all seemed to gather themselves, Betsy smiled at her father and son.

"Pappy. Can you turn my bed around? I want to see the sunset."

"Sure, baby." He unlocked the wheels around the bed and moved it slowly. Junior carefully adjusted the IV bag, and Leroy opened the curtains. The sun slowly sinking behind the clouds was a remarkable sight. A line of golden light stretched from one end of the horizon to the other. From their vantage, they could see to the distant harbor with several large, navy ships in port. Betsy closed her eyes for a moment, letting the warmth of the sun wash over her hands and face.

"Where's Sarah?"

"I don't know. She should be here by now," Pappy articulated.

"I need to see her."

"I'm sure she's on her way."

Nurse Thomasina came in to check her medication. It was their sign that visiting hours were over.

"See you in the morning?" Pappy asked.

"Yes," Betsy nodded.

"Come on, Junior, Leroy. It's time for your mother to rest."

"Can't we stay a little longer, Pappy?" Junior protested.

"Your mother is tired. We'll come back first thing, I promise."

"You promise?"

"Yes," he finished.

"Momma. First thing tomorrow," Junior asked.

"Yes, baby. We'll have pancakes again."

She kissed Leroy and Junior and hugged them tightly. Betsy was worried about Sarah. It was not like her.

"Can I sit here with you?" James asked, standing over her bed.

"Of course," Betsy answered. She hadn't realized how long he had been standing there.

He held her hand in his and brought it to his lips, kissing it softly.

"Betsy."

"Yes, James."

"I'm sorry." He swallowed hard. He could feel a lump growing in his throat.

"For what?"

"Everything. Never taking you anywhere. I wanted to see the world with you."

"Me too." She reached up to touch his face.

"I don't know what we'll do without you."

"I'm scared, James."

"Me too, baby."

"I don't want to die."

James felt himself falling away, losing his breath. "I'm sorry, baby. I'm sorry I brought all this on you. Champ and all."

"Why did you do that to him? That was terrible."

"I don't know why. I couldn't stand it, seeing you with another man."

"I wasn't so innocent in all this, but nothing…nothing happened between Champ and me, James. I couldn't do that."

James' looked away as tears pooled in his eyes.

"Why didn't you trust me?" She asked.

"I wish I could answer that. I felt you slipping away from me. You had a history with him. He was taking my life away. I was fighting for that. All I did was make things worse."

"How could you think I didn't love you?"

"Betsy, I love you more than anything in the world. I love you, baby."

"But you made our lives insufferable, James."

"Yes, there's no going back from that. When I think of my own life, all I see is hurt. Just one thing after another. And God knows I'm not a religious man, but I can't help but feel like he done taken from me over and over." James choked up. "What price I gotta pay to stop him coming round me and mine? Just for once, I'd like to know."

"I can't answer that, James. I know you got a deep pain inside you and one day, you will have to let it go. For the sake of your children, you have to let it go."

James thought carefully and said "All I want is for you to forgive me." He then kissed her gently on the cheek. "From the day I saw you, I never wanted anyone else."

Betsy touched his face, and their eyes met once again. "Sorry, we won't get to see Paris together," she smiled. "But you should go. Go before your time comes."

"Why? Why go without you?"

"See it for me." She squeezed his hand tightly.

James shook his head, tears falling from his face.

He leaned over and kissed her on the lips, resting his head on her lap.

"I forgive you, James. Now forgive yourself," she whispered.

"I don't know how. Can you tell me how?" James pleaded.

She lay back on the pillows. There was nothing to be angry about, nothing more to fight. There was nothing more that she could change. Betsy lovingly stroked his hair before nodding off.

Later that morning, James felt Betsy stirring. She was breathing rapidly; her eyes shut tight. He thought to get the doctors but decided to remain by her side. When he touched her hand, it was ice cold. James whispered in her ear.

"I love you, Betsy Knight. Forever baby."

Betsy exhaled one last time.

It was 6:30 in the morning by the wall clock, and Sarah had not yet arrived. Betsy had waited as long as she could for her sister. The shift nurse came in and checked for a pulse.

"She's gone?"

The nurse nodded.

Dr. Baker came in a little while later. He shook James' hand. "I'm sorry for your loss, Mr. Atkins," he empathized.

James found a payphone and called the motel where Pappy and the boys were staying. Junior and Leroy were playing cards when the phone rang. Pappy answered it. Junior had a sinking feeling all night that something more was going on. Pappy glanced his way and lowered his voice.

"Momma died, huh?" Leroy asked Junior.

"Yeah," Junior replied. "I think so."

After hanging up the phone, James got in his car in the hospital parking lot, and sat there for a long time, struggling to catch his breath. His hands clutched the steering wheel tightly as he sobbed. "I'm sorry."

He wondered what this all meant. Was this his cross to bear? He pondered about the life that Betsy should have had. If he had just died on Buna that terrible day, her life might have turned out so differently. They'd both be free of all this pain if that bullet had killed him instead.

At the hotel, Pappy finished making his phone calls to family and began to pack his suitcase when Leroy walked in.

"Where's your brother?" Pappy asked.

"I don't know. He's outside somewhere."

"Go get him, please."

Leroy searched for Junior along the pathway leading to the lobby, out to the sidewalk to the entrance. No one was around. Then he heard a mix of sounds, someone's voice on the other side of a wall, but he couldn't make out. Leroy peered around the corner.

"You broke her down to nothing," he shook a fist to the sky. "You bastard!"

"Junior," Leroy called out, startling his brother. "Pappy wants you."

"Go away," Junior shouted, wiping the tears from his face, but Leroy kept walking toward him.

"Get away from me, Leroy. I mean it."

"Pappy wants you," Leroy shouted, coming closer. He extended his arms towards his brother. "Come on."

Junior continued to back away. He shoved him, but Leroy grabbed his arm and tried to pull him close.

"Get away from me, Leroy! Get away now!"

Leroy wouldn't. He did not understand why his brother was acting this way. This time Junior pushed back hard with both hands, knocking him to the ground. Before Leroy could get up, Junior was gone, running toward the street.

Pappy was on the phone with Junie when Leroy returned. Junie was letting Pappy know why he and Sarah had taken too long to arrive. The police pulled them over for speeding the night before. Sarah tried to explain to them that her sister was dying, and she went into a rage when they delayed them further. She yelled and swore, refusing their commands. One of the officers struck her with his baton, and Junie got into a fight with him. Sarah was injured and taken to the hospital, and police locked Junie up. They let him out that morning.

"Same old bullshit they have been doing to black folks for years!" Junie shouted.

"Is Sarah okay?"

"Yeah, she's okay. I'm gonna go see her now."

"What else could go wrong?" Pappy wailed.

"If I ever see those crackers again, I'm going to kill 'em. I swear before God."

Pappy covered the receiver when Leroy returned. "Where's Junior?"

"He pushed me down, Pappy!" The boy was in tears. "Then, he ran away."

"Let me call you back, Junie." Pappy hung up the receiver.

"Come here, Leroy. He didn't mean it." Pappy took him in his arms. "He's just grieving. You'll have to forgive your brother."

"I hate him, Pappy. I hate him!" Leroy sobbed.

HOMECOMING – JUNE 1969

Soul-stirring organ music filled the air as people took seats in the hall. The choir sang an old spiritual, "We Are Called," as Betsy's body lay at rest in a beautiful gold-colored casket. The program's cover photo was the one taken of Betsy with her sons that last day in the hospital. They were all smiles and happy. Betsy's high school and work friends filled the seats, along with her teachers from Junior College. Even Fountaine dared to come and pay his respects.

Sarah, with her still bruised face covered under thick sunglasses, took a seat next to Junior and on the other side of him sat Daisy. Betsy's passing filled Junior with anger. Sarah tried to comfort him, taking his hand in hers, but he let go of it. He dropped his head into his hands, trembling with sadness.

James and Leroy sat in the very first row, with Odelle, Momma Knight's sister. She had come from Georgia to be with her brother-in-law and was immediately taken with her grandnephews.

Reverend Drew began the eulogy. "Death makes life bittersweet. Does it not?" After a chorus of amen from the congregation, he continued. "All of our experiences, possessions, passions, love, gone in a moment. Just as it was for the departed, so shall it be for each and every one of us. Not the rich nor the poor can escape it. Not the baby. Not your mother or friends. We are all on the same path. Though it is painful, it is a beautiful circle that God has promised to us.

Our lives are shaped not only by the love received and given but also by the love and dreams unfulfilled. *Amen.* I speak of your faith in Jesus; through him, we will have everlasting life. Death of the flesh shall not be the last chapter of your life. Matthew 25:21 says, '*Well done, good and faithful servant. Come and share your master's happiness.*'"

He took a moment to wipe his brow. "And Betsy lived a full life in those thirty-seven years. Had two children, a loving husband. A graduate of Brawley Union High School, she attended Imperial Valley College. Betsy was a good and faithful servant, and her place in heaven is secure. She faced her passing with courage and put her trust in the Lord.

Come to Jesus and ask for forgiveness. His death and resurrection was God's promise to you, to all of us that, though our physical death is real, so is God's promise. In Romans 6:23, Paul says, '*For the wages of sin is death, but the gift of God is eternal life.*' Jesus died on the cross for each one of us so that we would know God's love and his promise to us.

"Though I walk through the valley of the shadow of death, I will fear no evil, for Thou art with me. Thy rod and staff, they comfort me. So let us mourn our sister Betsy Marie Atkins, but let us rejoice in the knowledge that she is free from pain and is sitting by the Father's side, there with her mother and all of her loved ones. God did not forsake her. Please rise and say the Lord's Prayer with me."

The congregation rose, heads bowed, and repeated the words many had known since childhood as the choir began singing "Going Home." Junior leaned on Daisy's shoulder. Sarah placed her hand on his shoulder. She placed her arm around his shoulder as she swayed to the rhythm and hummed the lyrics.

At the end of the eulogy, many friends made their way to say their last goodbyes, forming a line to speak with the family. James perfunctorily shook hands with the well-wishers, but he was in another world. He had no reserve of emotions to tap. Mr. Tamayo offered support, as some in the congregation cried aloud over Betsy's casket. Several were overcome with grief and were assisted by the funeral staff. Reverend Drew comforted those whom he could. Soon it was the family's turn to say so long. Junior touched his mother's face, moaning at how cold she felt.

"Why'd he take you, Momma?" Junior whispered.

"She's with the Lord. Betsy accepted Christ as her savior." The Reverend paused. "That is a blessing."

Junior shrugged in disagreement.

The cemetery sat on a bluff overlooking a river that flowed toward the Salton Sea. The ground was soft, and flowering bougainvillea formed a boundary along the gate. The narrow, unpaved roads crackled as the cars rolled over the gravel. Betsy's plot was not far from the edge and just a few yards from her mother's gravesite.

The pallbearers placed Betsy's casket on the green straps that extended across the grave, and after the family assembled, Reverend Drew once again asked for their attention.

"Let us pray. Lord, we come to say one final farewell to our dear friend, mother, and sister, Betsy Marie Atkins. We know that she will be by your side for all eternity, having been a faithful servant."

Junior began to rock back and forth in his seat. His arms folded as his face tightened into a scowl. He stared, fixated on his mother's casket.

"In sure and certain hope of the resurrection to eternal life through Jesus Christ, our Lord, we commend to Almighty God, our sister Betsy, and we commit her body to the earth. Ashes to ashes and dust to dust. The Lord will bless her, keep her, and shine his light upon her. He will be gracious unto her and give her peace and comfort. Amen."

With each word, the Reverend uttered, the more agitated Junior became. Reverend Drew gave the pallbearers a signal, and they began to lower the casket into the freshly dug earth. Junior looked away, his leg twitching uncontrollably. Suddenly, he jumped from the folded chair, rushed toward the coffin, and grabbed one of the handles. The pallbearers waited, as Pappy and Daisy pulled him away.

"No!" he shouted, struggling to get to the casket. "No, Momma! Don't go! Don't leave me."

People in the gathered crowd shook their heads sadly. Others wept. James only watched as Sarah joined Pappy in trying to calm him. Leroy leaned on his father, wiping away his tears with the back of his hand. He didn't know how to comfort his brother. The pallbearers lowered the casket once Junior calmed down.

"No, Momma," he sobbed inconsolably as the services continued.

Later, at the repast in the church hall, the boys sat silently with their father, their faces forlorn. James made small talk with L.A. and Chef, while their wives were off chatting with their friends and neighbors. It seemed like any other day at church except today they had buried their mother. It upset Junior to see people smiling and laughing while his heart hurt so badly. He searched his mind for a reason how anyone could be happy on such a solemn day. He reasoned that funerals were not about the departed, but for the living. The dead were just the reason people got together. He pushed the thought from his mind as quickly as it entered.

James finally had had enough. He tapped his sons on the shoulders, and they too rose to leave. He shook hands with a few friends, and as they walked out of the church, Sarah confronted James on their way to the car.

"I need to speak with you, James," she stressed, adjusting her purse.

"About what?"

"The children."

"What about 'em?"

"They need a proper home. I can give that to them. And you can go wander all about like you always planned," she contended, taking a deep drag from the cigarette in her mouth. "She was going to leave you. Did you know that? Just a few more days and she would have been free," her voice trembled.

James looked at her, not responding.

Pappy took Sarah gently about the arm and asked her to quiet down.

She cried out to him, "My sister is gone, Pappy! And you want me to do what?"

"I'm asking you to honor her memory, please," he pleaded. "This is not the time nor place for this talk."

She turned back to James and shouted, "Go on home, you miserable bastard."

"Sarah!" Pappy shouted.

"I didn't get to say goodbye!"

"Baby, I know. I'm so sorry," Pappy apologized. "The world is full of these evil people."

"White people are the devil!" Sarah hissed. Then she closed her eyes and fell into her father's arms.

Leroy and Junior had come to a standstill in the street, startled by the commotion, but they all piled into the car. Their father drove down South Eastern Avenue and parked on the road. Dusk was coming on. A few rays of sunshine filtered through the trees from the setting sun, but there was nothing but darkness around the home like a shadow. The air was heavy with humidity, sapping the life out of everything around. The leaves on the trees bent toward the earth. Even their dog seemed exhausted, shuffling up to greet them with his head down, slowly wagging his tail, as if he sensed their grief. Junior had found him wandering the streets a few years back. Someone had tied baling wire around his neck, and it had cut deep into the dog's skin. Betsy cleaned his wounds with mercurochrome and let Junior keep him. He named him Rex.

As they entered, a rush of familiar scents surrounded them. James placed his hat on the kitchen table and took a seat. Junior looked at the old phonograph, still damaged from the night his father had knocked him into it. He gazed sadly at the albums his mother loved to play—Sam Cooke, Etta James, and Tom Jones.

"Why were you acting a fool at the cemetery?" James asked. "In front of the whole damn town."

"You won't have to worry about me doing that at your funeral. I'll have the choir sing happy songs!"

James gave him a look that would put the fear of God into most people. He wanted to beat the hell out of him, but he had no fight left. Junior walked out, slamming the door as he headed to the only place he had ever found peace.

He leaned against the fence near the canal bank behind Daisy's house. Concha lumbered over to him, stuck her head through the iron bars of the gate, and nudged him with her muzzle. Junior rubbed her neck and mane.

"Just you and me, Concha," he sobbed, staring into the night sky. He wondered if there was a heaven out there. If so, was his mother looking down on him now, seeing how much he was hurting and missing her? Was she an angel, watching over him and protecting him? He hoped so.

That night, as James lay in bed, Sarah's words stung him again. *'She was going to leave you, you know?'* He wanted to tell her about his plans to leave. Tell her of the many times he had come to the edge of town, a tank full of gas and enough money to get him anywhere he wanted to go. All he had to do was to put the car in gear and head for the horizon. Or the plans that he and Betsy made when they first met. James, eyes closed, saw the picture in mind—the road winding around the bend, leading to wherever, Betsy smiling big and pretty, her hair blowing from the open car window. He had staked so much of his life on that dream. He squeezed his eyes shut, fighting back the sadness in his heart.

The next morning Junior wandered over to Pappy's, knocking on the door and peering inside when no one answered.

"Hello?" he called.

"Junior? Come on in," his Aunt Odelle responded.

She, Sarah, and Pappy were drinking coffee at the table. The smell of cigarettes and bacon permeated the air as he entered the kitchen. He looked out of the window and noticed two blue jays fighting over a small piece of bread.

"I know you have better manners than that!" Odelle chastised. "You come over here and give me a hug right now." When he did, her ample bosoms pressed against him.

"Now that's more like it," she replied.

"Where's your brother?" Pappy asked.

"Home, I guess."

"You guess?" Pappy questioned.

"Leave him be, Edgar," Odelle advised.

Pappy muttered into his mug.

"You hungry?" Odelle asked.

"Yes, ma'am," he answered.

"Go on and fix you a plate. Butter's in the fridge."

Junior dutifully pulled a plate out of the cabinet and spooned some eggs onto it.

"There are a few things I'd like to take back with me, if you don't mind," Odelle told Pappy.

"What things?" He sounded annoyed.

"There are some nice dresses and shoes that Betsy had, that someone could use and my mother's ring."

"No. I'm getting the ring, Odelle," Sarah cut in.

"Sarah, we spoke about this yesterday," Odelle protested.

"I don't recall agreeing to anything."

"Well, you did."

"And you just can't have everything of hers," Sarah shot back.

"Ain't that something?" Odelle snapped.

"I'm just letting you know, Auntie," Sarah added.

"I said it was fine, Sarah," Odelle spoke now in a more measured tone when she noticed Junior looking at them.

"We'll work this out like family," Pappy settled.

"Agreed," Odelle.

"You okay, Junior?" Sarah asked.

He shrugged.

"What do you think about your boys coming to live with me in Los Angeles? Do you think Leroy would like that? He's a lot closer to your father, you know."

Junior perked up. "I can't speak for him, but I would."

"Sarah, don't start no mess, you hear me?" Pappy warned.

"This is what Betsy wanted. She told me the last time I saw her. Someone has to look after them. You don't expect him to do it, do you?"

"I'm telling you now's not the time."

"There is no good time Pappy. Betsy's gone." Sarah choked up.

Junior was overjoyed when he broke the news to Daisy. She didn't understand and asked why he was so happy to go since he'd be leaving her too. Junior apologized but didn't tell her that he had already packed a suitcase, hiding it under his bed. He then began to count the days.

Odelle was not sold on the idea, and she pressed Sarah to think more about what she was doing. "Sarah, are you sure taking these boys from their father is such a good idea, especially after losing their mother?"

"Why would you ask such a thing?" Sarah answered. "You heard what Junior wanted. He'd leave today if he could."

"He ain't thinking right."

"He's old enough to decide, Auntie." She paused and put her hand on Odelle's arm. "Listen, I can't do this alone."

Odelle agreed. "James is a stubborn ole mule. I can see that."

214

"He'll do anything to spite my family," Sarah added.

Odelle shook her head. She had an awful feeling about the whole thing.

The day before Odelle was to leave for Georgia, she and Sarah went to speak to James. Junior had been waiting for what seemed an eternity for them to come. He smiled when he saw them at the door. They marched into the kitchen where he and James were sitting.

"Good morning James," Sarah spoke in as a civil tone as she could muster. Odelle stood by for support.

He nodded at them. "What can I do for you?"

Odelle spoke first. "If you don't mind, I'd like to look at some of Betsy's old things. Now, I don't want anything you're keeping."

He sighed. "No. I don't mind. Her things are hanging in the closet over there. Leroy, show your Aunt Odelle where to look."

Sarah made small talk with James as Junior listened, waiting for her to break the news to his father.

"How are you holding up?"

"I'm fine. Sarah," James had not forgotten the harsh words she had for him outside the church.

"Listen, James. I wanted to talk to you about the boys."

"What about them?"

Junior stood up from the table.

"I think its best they come to stay with me and Junie in Los Angeles."

The expression on James' face turned into a scowl. "What gave you that crazy notion?"

"They'd have a mother and father to provide for them. It was a promise I made to Betsy before she died! My sister wanted them—"

"They have a father, and they had a mother!" James yelled before she could finish.

"She wanted them to go to college," Sarah retorted, not backing down.

"And they will if that's what they want."

"We can provide better than you can. I've been to college, Pappy too."

"What kind of life can you provide them? Smoking and drinking and carrying on in the streets?"

"Now, you stop right there!" she shouted. Leroy returned to see what all the fuss was about, Odelle following alongside.

"That happened one time! I was showing them about life." She was undeterred by his temper.

"They're staying here," James shouted back at her. He stood up, towering over Sarah like an angry bear.

"That ain't what's right for them," Sarah motioned to Leroy and Junior.

"Neither one old enough to say."

"Junior IS old enough to decide for himself."

"He has one more year of high school, and then he can go anywhere he wants."

"So, he has to stay here with you another year before he can be on his own?"

"Not discussing this anymore. They're not leaving with you."

"It's what's best for them!" Sarah yelled. Then she turned to the boys. "Why don't you ask them? Junior already told me he wanted to come."

"Don't care. When Junior finishes school, he can go stay with you or anywhere else."

"You know, I don't like you very much, truth be told. I am sure you feel the same way about me, but I know this much. You never loved these children. You want them to be as miserable as you are. You're a hateful excuse for a man."

"You and Odelle can get the hell outta my house now and don't come back!"

"This ain't *your* house! Everything you have you got from *my* family," Sarah shot back. "You didn't know I knew that, did you? So this is *our* house. Not yours."

"Don't matter who paid for it. I'm living here now. You got what you came for, so leave." James took a step toward her.

"I ain't scared of you. I've seen the devil!" she shouted. "And I'll come back whenever I like. You will not keep me from seeing my nephews!" Sarah stared him straight in the eye. Neither of them wavered.

"There are some things of hers I want. Where's Momma's rings and jewelry?"

"In a box on the bureau." He turned to Leroy. "Go get them for your Auntie."

Leroy returned a few moments later with the jewelry box and handed it to Sarah. She stayed put, still itching for a fight.

"Got what you need, now leave us in peace."

Sarah looked at the box in her hand but didn't move. "This is all I want. What Betsy wanted me to take," she confessed, finally looking up at James. "I know what Betsy wanted for her boys, and it wasn't for them to stay with you."

"How would you know what Betsy wanted for these kids?"

"It was her dying wish. She made me promise. She didn't want you raising them."

"I don't believe that," James fired back.

"Why would I need to lie about that? You know, beating your children doesn't mean you love them. And how can you guide them, get them into college when you've never been beyond the eighth grade?"

"And it shows!" Odelle chimed in.

James exhaled. "You don't know anything about my feelings or my life. Not a damn thing. What has your education got you? All I see in front of me is a fool. Have some of your children to ruin,"

"When I have children is none of your concern."

"How are you gonna raise them when all you do is live it up? You were too busy partying to see her before she died. So now you're mad at me?" The look on Sarah's face let James know he'd struck her deeply.

"That's a goddamn lie! We drove all night to get to the hospital." Sarah swung a fist at James, but he quickly moved out of the way.

"Okay, fool. You gonna go too far." James chastised her.

"You watch your mouth! Spreading lies."

"Betsy died in my arms. Now you and Odelle here with this? Y'all want to hurt me all over again?" James sounded exhausted. "You weren't there when she died. I was."

Sarah broke down, wailing uncontrollably.

"I have promises to keep, too," James said to her.

Leroy stood there between his aunt and his father, mouth agape, confused. He didn't want to leave. He ran over to James and hugged him tightly, his tears staining his father's shirt. James tried to comfort his son, touching him gently on his neck and shoulder.

"See what you are doing to them?"

Meanwhile, Junior stood with his fists clenched, his eyes pleading with his aunt not to give up. But she did. Sarah shook her head sadly, wrapped her arms around

Odelle, and they walked out, leaving the door wide open. Junior looked on, unsure of what to do. He grabbed the suitcase, hurrying outside just as Sarah got in Pappy's car. Junior screamed as she shut the door. Pappy grabbed him as he reached for the handle.

"Take me with you," he pleaded.

Sarah rolled the window down. "Please, Junior. Be patient. It is only a year. It will fly by, and I'll be back to get you. I promise," Sarah reassured him, tears choking her words.

"I want to go with you now!"

"Don't make your auntie cry. Please, baby," Sarah bawled. "My heart's already broken."

"But that's what you're doin' to me," Junior sobbed, dropping his suitcase. "Now you're leaving me like Momma did."

"I'm sorry, baby. I am."

"Son, your brother needs you, and y'all have to stick together. Your time will come soon. Go on inside now," Pappy clutched him about the shoulders.

Junior shrugged, shaking off Pappy's hands. His grandfather paused for a moment; he then got in the car and drove them away, leaving his grandson where he stood. For Junior, they were ripping the scabs off the wounds in his heart all over again.

As he ran into the house, Junior slammed the door startling his father as he entered. James stared at him in disgust. His eyes followed him each step he took.

Junior paused at the doorway. "I hate your guts!" he yelled.

"Good!" James shouted back at him.

"The wrong person died!" Junior yelled again, running out of the back door.

James did not retaliate. Those words cut deeper than his son knew.

The solstice moon was but a small, opaque ball looming in the sky. Junior and Daisy lay under the mulberry tree on thick towels she had brought from her house. The sun descended beyond the mountains in the West, and the blue-green water of the nearby canal bubbled as it meandered by. Spiders floated on the current and dragonflies darted to and fro.

It had been almost a month since his mother's passing, and the pain was as sharp and deep as it ever was. Junior found a measure of comfort, letting his feelings show around Daisy. He lay on his back, a blade of grass in his mouth, a hat tilted over his eyes.

"I'm just sick of people laying their sadness on me each time I see them."

"Who?"

"Everyone! Especially my mother's friends. I cannot count how many times I've heard how she lived a full life. She married and had a family. *That's* a full life?"

"They're just trying to be nice, Junior."

"I guess that makes up for the terrible way she died then, right?"

Reliving the past only made Junior even more despondent. The sadness clung to him like moss to a stone.

"Have you ever dreamt of dying?" he asked.

"No, I don't ever want to think about that."

"I have. Many times." Tears welled up in his eyes, and the dull ache in his throat felt like he had swallowed an apple whole. He shook it off. It was so easy for him to get lost in reveries about his mother.

"You know they're landing on the moon today?" Daisy observed, changing the subject.

"That's right. The astronauts may be there now!" Junior agreed, looking up at the sky.

"I wonder if we could see the astronauts from here," Daisy asked.

Junior gave her a befuddled look. "Come on, Daisy. They're thousands of miles away."

"So! Don't make fun of me."

Junior laughed.

She punched him on the shoulder, surprising him with her strength.

Daisy continued. "You think you have it bad, James, and losing your mother *is* bad. But what if your mother didn't think much of you? You couldn't be anything more than someone's housewife."

"Who thinks that?"

"My mom," her voice crackled. "She told me *prietas* like me, dark-skinned girls, need to marry a white man. That way, at least my kids will have a better chance."

"What? No way."

"I got mad one day and told her that she gave me my color. I had nothing to do with it! So blame yourself."

"I had no idea she was like that. She's so nice to me."

"You think so? She's told me many times to leave that *Negrito* alone, that no one wanted black babies."

"What does that mean?"

"Means, little black boy. And she said a lot more and worse."

"More?"

"Yeah, but I told her I'm going to college, and I'll decide what I do with my life," she wiped the tears from her eyes.

"You told her all that?"

"You damn right I did."

Junior put his arms around Daisy and hugged her tightly.

A PAST REVEALED – JULY 1969

Where once there had been order, chaos grew. Newspapers, old tools, and opened mail cluttered any open space. James and Leroy's jackets straddled the back of the armchair, and books, clothes, and shoes littered the floor.

It was early morning, and Leroy was already up helping his father put away Betsy's things in the attic. James had not been up there in years. He had forgotten about all the items stored there, including his brother's old suitcase.

"What's this?" Leroy asked, inspecting the metal latches. It smelled of stale leather.

"That was my brother's suitcase."

"You had a brother?"

"Of course, I did. You've heard me talk about your Uncle Samuel haven't you?" Leroy shrugged his shoulders.

"I had a sister too," his father continued.

"You did? How come you never talk about them?"

"Didn't think anyone wanted to hear those stories."

"I do," he replied.

"I'll tell you one day, son."

"Can I look inside?"

"Let me put these boxes away first."

Leroy cleared a space on a small table as his father set it down. He smiled happily like he had found some buried treasure. It was so old and worn he worried it might fall apart before they got a chance to open it properly. James pressed the triggers on the latches, and they sprung open. He paused, looking back at his son and smiled. Leroy was getting to be so tall, growing like a weed, fourteen years old and all legs. He had the same bushy brown hair as his Uncle Samuel.

James lifted the cover gingerly, revealing bundles of old newspaper clippings, yellowed with age, and photos wrapped in rubber bands. He made himself comfortable, sitting down on a fold-up chair and undid the band around a set of pictures. He picked through them, handing each one to Leroy and filling in the back-story as best he could.

"This one here was in Minot, North Dakota. 1947 I believe."

"You went all the way up there just to play baseball?"

"Played a game here in Brawley too. Over at Beechey Field."

"Really, Daddy?"

"Pitched a few innings before my back gave out."

"Where else did you play?" the boy asked.

"Went to Canada. I played a few years in Saskatchewan. You know where that is?"

Leroy shook his head.

"Look here," he smiled, holding the receipt from the Indian Head tournament. "See that, twenty-five hundred dollars."

"Wow! You won all that money!"

"Sure did." James pictured in his mind the fresh-cut grass and the boys, all smiles, warming up in the infield. He heard the "pop" of the ball hitting their gloves and the commotion coming from the stands. Excitement filled the air. He let out a sigh when he turned to a picture of Samuel, Matilde, Gladys, and himself at a diner in Moose Jaw.

"Who are these people, Daddy?" Leroy asked.

"That's your Uncle Samuel right there and your Aunt Matilde sitting next to him. That is me and my friend Gladys." James answered, pointing to each person.

"That's you?"

"Yes, son. That's your old man."

"How old were you here?"

"Oh, thirty-something, I think."

"A long time ago, huh, Daddy?"

"Yes, it was. Before you were born."

"You look real young here!"

"Well, I should have. You know, I was a teenager once too. Just like you!" He tapped him softly on the stomach.

Leroy began reading some of the headlines.

"The Atkins All-Stars pull out 8-6 victory over DeLisle. Here's another one. "Atkins takes home top prize."

"Yup, your Uncle Samuel was a helluva pitcher."

"I wish I could've seen the games."

"Leroy, I want you to take care of this suitcase and everything in it."

"Me?"

"Why not? It's part of your family history. Somebody should have it."

"You don't have to worry. I'll take real good care of it, Dad."

"I know you will, son."

They continued sifting through the photos and clippings until James began to tire. They shut the suitcase, and James started dinner. He caught a glimpse of his reflection in a silver pot as he set it on the stove. He moved it closer, turning his head from side to side. The crow's feet around his brow surprised him, as did the gray strands on his temple, and his chin.

"Don't worry, Daddy," Leroy grinned at his father. "When you get old, I'll take care of you."

"You might have to start sooner than you think," James laughed. Where had the time gone, he wondered. It wasn't that long ago his baseball team was flying high and were playing in tournaments all over the Plains and in Canada. How his life changed once they crossed that border.

PART THREE

1970

SECRETS REVEALED

EVERYTHING CHANGES
– NOVEMBER 1970

James grabbed the mail out of the box, pulling the collar up on his old army jacket and rushed to the front door. A cold rain had been falling all day. "Pneumonia weather," his mother would have called it. He was surprised to see both Leroy and Junior home. Junior had been spending most of his time with Daisy and other friends in the neighborhood. He had stayed away for long periods and a good part of the summer. When he was home, James would find him sitting out on the porch with his friends. The two rarely spoke, preferring to keep an emotional as well as the physical distance between them. James shook his jacket out and placed the mail on the desk. He noticed a bucket on the floor, catching water from a leak in the ceiling. James could only grit his teeth.

He walked past his kids to the kitchen, staring at the bushy hair growing on Junior's head. The boys had made some chili beans and cornbread. James opened one of the pots and sniffed the contents.

"You make this, Junior?" he asked.

"I made it!" Leroy shouted before his brother could answer.

"We made it," Junior nodded. While his father's back was turned, he grabbed the stack of mail and shuffled through the correspondence.

"What you looking for?" James asked.

Junior almost jumped out of his skin. "Nothing. Just looking for my mail."

"Hand it over to me. All of it." James held out his hand.

Junior took a deep breath and passed the mail to his father. James sat down in his recliner and shuffled through it.

"Where's that letter from high school?"

"I got it. It's for me."

"Don't matter, hand it over. I want to see for myself."

Junior handed the letter to his father. James read the contents carefully.

"You want to explain this to me?"

"It's no big deal."

"No big deal? It says you may not graduate."

"So what?"

"Your mother wanted you to go to college. You won't get there with these marks."

"Nobody cares."

"Your graduating isn't for your mother or me. It doesn't put money in my pocket. That's for your future."

"What do you want me to do? Momma died," Junior shrugged.

"So, I guess you the only one sad or upset because your mother's gone?"

"No."

"I was married to her for seventeen years."

Junior folded his arms across his chest.

"You can do what you want. It's your life. But you best know you won't be lying around my house doing nothing."

"Who said I wanted to stay here?"

"No one. I'm just letting you know what the *big* deal is. You'll pay to stay here."

"Not gonna happen."

Leroy sat silently on the couch, his head pivoting back and forth between his father and brother. He hated the discord and the disrespect his brother showed their father. But he also disliked his father's stubbornness. Junior just added fuel to the fire. He seemed to enjoy disrupting the peace in the house.

"What should happen is me cutting that mop off your head. What do you call it - an Afro?"

"You ain't cutting my hair."

"My pa would have you straight. He'd take you out back and beat the tar off you. Beat you like the man you are pretending to be. That's what you need, a good ass-whoopin'."

"I don't need to know your pa because I am staring right at him. You don't act any different from him."

James muttered under his breath as Junior exited the home. "Yea, my daddy would set you straight."

He went into the kitchen, put some food on a plate, and ate his dinner in silence. His mind drifted back to the days on the farm. He tried to recall the little things he had forgotten, memories he had tamped down since his father had died. James did what Grandpa Bernard commanded him to do. He got on with his life. *'There will always be plenty of sadness in the world. No need to add to it,'* Grandpa would say, in his gruff baritone.

James, now having the benefit of hindsight and experience, agreed. He had played the good soldier and kept his promises, for the most part. He realized he was far from perfect, but he was raised this way. Though there were times, he felt he hadn't done enough for his family.

He put those memories away deep in the recesses of his mind. But like ocean waves, they came rushing back—the war, the baseball team, Sissy drowning, and now his wife. He looked at Leroy sitting on the couch reading a book and wondered if he was doing right by him and his brother. It wasn't that he hadn't considered Sarah's proposal. Maybe if she had asked him in a different way or at a different time, he could have gone with it. Now all he had was his spite and intransigence. He was adrift in this moment with nowhere to be, nowhere to go.

In the wee hours one morning, James awoke to find he had fallen asleep in his old chair. He stood up, staggering for a moment in the darkness, and walked to the bed. He could barely make out Leroy's outline under the covers. The boy had been sleeping in his bed since the new school term started, and James did not have the heart to make him go anywhere else. He tossed his shirt and trousers in the corner, and wearily laid on his side.

James reflected all those years ago to his childhood. He envisioned Grandpa Bernard calmly walking through the field of burning bushes and shrubs, oil can in one hand and a long machete in the other. James' father, Willie, looked so strong. The veins in his arms made one continuous line from the back of his hand up to his bicep as he hacked at a mesquite tree.

The family had so little, living off every scrap they could find, bartering for things they could not afford to buy. Momma Mabel did her best to keep their home and clothes. James tried hard to recall the sound of his mother's voice. She was calling them to supper, and he'd race Samuel, thin as a weed, to the front door. Sissy stood in the doorway, chastising them for running around with no shoes. She seemed to glow along with the candles burning behind her.

She'd say, "Y'all gonna step on a mesquite thorn. Get your foot infected, something awful!"

The boys paused for a moment and then pushed past her into the house. James felt the heat coming from the stove and the smell of stewed rabbit and cabbage his mother was cooking. Willie sat at the table, covered in dust as Mabel took a cool, wet rag and lovingly washed his neck and face. They smiled sweetly at each other. Willie took her hand and placed it on his lips, kissing it softly. So many things had escaped James over the years. He had never been happier than when he knew nothing about life. James yearned for that simpler time. It didn't seem that long afterward, all the joy dissipated.

Dew sparkled under the rising sun, and Rex snuggled in a moist dugout, his legs kicking intermittently. The neighborhood was silent; there were no birds chirping or cars humming on the road. Leroy lay sleeping peacefully, as James rose quietly. On his way to wash up, he passed Junior's neatly made bed; the corners tucked in just so. Nothing had changed in the two weeks that passed. His graduation was fast approaching. There was some doubt he'd make it through, but Junior had pulled his grades up enough to walk. Now there was a new anxiety that many of his classmates shared. The war in Vietnam was raging, and the new graduates lined up for the draft. Junior had been a shoo-in for college with the grades he had earned before his mother's death, but he had lost his way since. The last thing he wanted to be was in the military.

James washed his face and dressed. After eating a piece of toast with his coffee, he drove to the hardware store for some supplies to make some long-overdue repairs to the home. He was jealous of the upgrades his neighbors were making to their houses. He left a single-room shack in Hondo to live in a two-bedroom one in Brawley.

On his way to the car, he made a mental note of all the things that needed fixing— the chipped windowpanes and ragged curtains, bleached by the intense sunlight; the leaky roof that sagged in places; and his once bountiful garden overrun with weeds and desiccated plants. Divots filled the yard where the dog had burrowed. The latch on the chain-link fence was broken. It was all getting away from him. But today he planned to do something about it. He picked up a few cans of paint, canary yellow as before; two-by-fours; nails; and tar-based shingles from the hardware store.

As he pulled up to park, Richie, one of Frank Sosa's kids from down the street, and Junior were sitting on the porch, yakking it up. Junior's bare feet were propped up on a fold-up chair. James could hear the music all the way out on the street, and it only further soured his mood. James opened the gate and slammed it shut in anger.

"Can you turn that goddamn Juju music off?" He yelled at Junior.

"What?" he asked.

James walked over to the teenagers. "I said turn that Juju music off."

Junior just rolled his eyes but complied.

"Sounds like a bunch of monkeys banging on pans."

"This is good music, Mr. Atkins," Richie voiced.

"That ain't real music. You ever heard of the Harmony Kings? Trixie Smith? Now that was real music. I expect a gorilla to jump out a tree when I hear that mess you're playing."

Richie laughed.

James dropped the supplies by the doorway and called Leroy.

"I need you and Junior to help around the house today. There's a lot that needs fixin'."

"Okay, Daddy," Leroy agreed.

Junior was not happy with the idea of spending his Saturday doing chores.

"I'll see you later, Junior," Ritchie said as he stepped off the porch.

"You don't have to leave," James mocked.

The boy smiled and kept going.

James continued. "You afraid of a little work?"

"Must you always embarrass me in front of my friends?" Junior asked.

"You should be embarrassed to let your friends see how you live."

"What are we doing? Let's get this over with!" Junior replied exasperated.

They got to work. James cut back the trees in the yard, and then fixed the gate while Junior and Leroy painted the wall around the front door of the house.

The rising sun burned the back of James' neck. He paused for a moment to see how the boys were doing and nearly blew a fuse. Junior had lackadaisically slapped the paint on the wall. Just as James was about to lay into them, the Sosa boy came running over again, shouting to Junior as he approached.

"You won't believe what I just heard, man."

"What?" Junior asked.

"The Beatles broke up, man. Yeah. They just announced it."

"No way. I don't believe you."

"It's true. John Lennon left the band."

"Oh shit! That's terrible!"

James fumed, as now neither of his sons was doing what he asked. He watched as Junior chattered away, and Leroy, paint drying on his brush, listened in. James placed his bucket of tools down on the ground, deciding they had procrastinated enough. He was going to whip them all back into shape. He wanted some order—his garden to grow food for the table, and his home not to resemble a shack.

As he yanked the already rickety gate open and marched toward the unsuspecting boys still in conversation, Rex began to dig a bigger hole in the ground.

"Goddammit!" James shouted, grabbing the slack in the dog's chain in one hand, looping it around his other hand. He then began swinging the metal chain down hard on the animal's hind parts. Rex howled and tried to scamper away, but James tightened his grip on the chain and struck the animal once more. The dog jumped and howled again.

"Stop it!" Junior shrieked.

James was about to deliver another blow just as Junior grabbed one end of the chain.

"Let it go!" He screamed. "I'm sick of this damn dog digging up my yard!"

"Look around, man! What yard?" Junior shouted back.

"It was nice until you bought that mutt here. All that dog does is eat and shit everywhere."

James jerked at the chain again, but Junior held fast.

"What did Rex ever do to you?"

"You hard of hearing? He tore up my yard. Now let go of the goddamn chain!"

"I won't; you mean ole bastard!" Junior screamed, gritting his teeth.

James dropped the chain and slapped his son across the face with his open hand. Junior took the blow and balled his fist, facing down his father.

"Go ahead, boy. I know you want to," James shouted to him. His eyes were filled with rage.

Junior stared at him, his fists ready for a fight, but something held him from striking his father. Instead, he bent down and unhooked Rex from the chain.

"Don't hit my goddamn dog again."

"Then I'll beat your ass next time he digs a hole in my yard."

"Yeah, you do that."

"I'll do what I goddamn please."

Junior stopped in his tracks. "You aren't hitting my dog or me anymore."

"You think so?" James hissed. He lunged toward his son, swinging his fists at him. Junior blocked each one with ease, which only angered his father more. James caught his breath; his fist still held high.

Junior stared at him for a moment, then leashed the dog to the gate near the mulberry tree in Pappy's yard. After a few minutes, Junior and Richie took off down the canal bank.

"The army would do them fools some good. At least they'd get a haircut." James turned to Leroy. The boy looked away as his father approached, dipping his brush in the paint can, and going back to work. James knew he had upset him.

"Son, I know you think I'm hard on you all, especially your brother, but you see he ain't worth a damn. Look what he did here," James said, pointing at the wall. "Painting like he don't care. Now, look at how you did it."

Leroy stepped back, eyeing his part of the frame, then back to where his father stood.

"Look at this mess," James grumbled, gathering a brush from the bucket and slathering more paint on the wall.

Later that afternoon, James and Leroy went back to the hardware store and ran into Chef. They had not seen each other since Betsy's funeral.

"L.A. had what?" James asked.

"Had a stroke, man," Chef replied.

"He ain't that old."

"What you know, James? He old as Methuselah," Chef smiled, trying to keep the conversation light.

"I didn't know. I'll go see him after I get this work done on the house."

"That sure would lift his spirits. He okay, but weak, I hear."

James just shook his head in disbelief.

"Come by sometime. We don't see you no more." Chef said.

"Yeah. Trying to get the house in order, you know."

James sighed when they got back to the car. The news was quite disconcerting. They had been friends for a long time. L.A. was only fifty-nine, seven years older than James was. He had reason to worry. His persistent headaches gave him cause for concern.

"Is Mr. L.A. okay, Dad?" Leroy asked.

"I don't know, son," he answered. "I don't know.'

Back at the house, as James and Leroy emptied the car, Mr. Tamayo walked down the road with a noticeable limp.

"Cow step on your foot?" James joked.

Tamayo laughed. "No, no. Señor Jaime. Don't be silly. I am going now to get some medicine for it."

"You want a ride?"

"No, just going to J Street." He pointed down the road.

James frowned. "What doctor lives over there?'

"I didn't say I was going to a doctor," he answered. "I'm going to the *curandera*."

"The what?"

"*Curandera*. Señor Jaime, you know, the healer?"

"Never heard of such a thing."

"Well, you should. You never know when you will need one," Tamayo continued on his way.

THE PRICE OF GROWING OLD – SEPTEMBER 1971

"But the hour cometh and now is when the true worshipers shall worship the Father in spirit and in truth: for the Father seeketh such to worship him. God is a Spirit: and they that worship him must worship him in spirit and in truth." John 4:23-24

James read the passage as he waited patiently in his doctor's office. The quotation was taped to a filing cabinet near the desk of Maria DeGloria, a raven-haired Mexican woman. She spoke Spanish into the phone while James waited with Leroy.

The doctor's office was neat and well organized. The dark blue carpet complimented the sky blue walls. Mundane pieces of artwork—a small sailboat and another with children playing in a park, decorated the walls. Leather chairs and tables with neatly stacked magazines furnished the waiting area, which was in stark contrast to the chaos on the receptionist's desk. Trinkets littered every open space, from praying porcelain hands to a paperweight in the shape of a cross.

"Hello. How may I help you?" The receptionist asked, hanging up the phone.

Leroy spoke before his father could answer. "My dad is here for his follow-up visit with Dr. Suarez." Leroy was glad he had come. He finally convinced his father to see a doctor after experiencing shortness of breath that summer. The doctor who treated him at the emergency room found he had an enlarged heart, which was why he was also having regular headaches. James had come dangerously close to having a heart attack. He did not take the doctor's warning lightly. In the beginning, he dutifully took his medications and changed his diet.

But James was not prepared when the doctor told him he would have to retire. His arthritic hands and limbs were getting worse by the day, and his back was a constant source of pain.

"You need to take it easy. Relax and enjoy life while you still can," the doctor told him.

"But doc, I've always had a job. You know, money is tight. I use that to pay for these pills you prescribing me."

"Money's always going to be tight. Can your sons help you?"

It was the same argument they had each time he came into the office. James felt the doctor did not understand how difficult a transition this was going to be.

After his exam, Suarez wrote out a new prescription, and Leroy confirmed his next appointment. As they departed, the receptionist handed him a pocket-sized pamphlet. On the cover was a picture of a white Jesus in a semi-circle of gold. He handed it over to his father once they got in the car. James took one look and tossed it out of the window.

Not long after they arrived home, Pappy showed up at the front door with a bottle of whiskey. He looked worn out and haggard. The silver strands of hair on his head glistened in the sunlight.

"Your father here?" he asked Leroy.

"Yes, Pappy. Come on in."

Pappy stepped inside and greeted James.

"What's new?" James asked, looking at the bottles from his prescription.

"A whole lot right now."

James put down the bottles. "What's the word?" His gut told him it was not good.

"I got some bad news and more bad news. Have a drink with me?"

"Leroy, bring us some glasses." James requested.

Leroy looked at his father then over to his pills. The doctor had specific instructions about not drinking with his medication. That meant no alcohol, but he got them anyway and lingered in the kitchen out of sight.

Pappy cleared some old papers from a chair and sat down. He took a big swallow then refilled the glass.

"Got a call from Junie this morning. Sarah is in a mental hospital."

"What for?" James asked, sitting up straight.

"She's just not herself. It seems she never got over, you know, Betsy dying and all. And especially her not being able to see her before she passed."

Leroy listened secretly from the kitchen.

"That and the beating she took from those damn police. Junie told me she refuses to leave the house, and when they do, she yells at white folks on the street. Some days she has crying spells for hours on end."

"Terrible," James shook his head.

"Spoke to Junior. He's driving me up there in a few weeks."

"Don't worry about a thing. Leroy and I will keep a watch on your house."

Pappy gave him a surprised look. "Can't lose her too, James. Already too much to bear. First, their momma, then Betsy. You know what I'm saying?"

James agreed. "Yes, I do."

Leroy slowly slipped away, out to the backdoor.

"How's Leroy taking all this?" Pappy asked.

"He holds a lot inside."

"They both do."

James took another hit of the whiskey, and Pappy refilled his glass.

"You know Tamayo's sick?"

"I figured as much from the last time I saw him," James commented.

"Diabetes done got him."

"That what he's got?"

"Yep. Going to San Diego for the surgery. Losing his leg."

"What you say now?" James was shocked when he heard that. He'd seen Tamayo a few weeks back.

"Thing got so bad he couldn't stand no more."

Pappy paused for a moment and took a deep breath. James could tell something was weighing on him. "You know, when my wife died, it hurt so bad, like a mule kicked me. Then Betsy. The world just stopped." He squeezed his glass tightly.

"Took a lot out of us, too," James confessed.

"I thank God each and every morning that he saw fit to give me another day," Pappy said, and as James began to respond, Pappy waved him off. "I'm not complaining. I've had a good life, James. Raised a family, had a beautiful wife and children, a good home. I never had to borrow from anyone. Treated people the way I wanted to be treated."

James nodded.

"But everything that made me happy is gone. The good Lord knows it. No one but me in that house," he paused, closing his eyes slowly. He then smiled, clearly feeling the effects of the alcohol and conceded, "Except them ghosts."

"Ghosts?"

"You know what I'm talking about."

James took another sip and looked around: the places that still had Betsy's touch. She had made their house a home. There was order, but now there were papers stacked in piles and scattered all around, and clothing was strewn across the old couch. The linoleum on the floors was worn to the foundation.

James and Pappy sat and drank some more in silence, both living in the past, with their ghosts, recognizing their presence and the reminders of life long passed--children playing in the yard, their wives smiling at them. That sunny, wonderful life, lost in a dream of what should have been. It was the price of growing old.

FOOL'S TALK – 1972

As the year went, James saw less and less of his eldest son. One morning, Junior packed some clothes, walked out, and didn't come back for a week. James didn't ask him where he was going or where he was staying. The house was a lonelier place without his presence, and it wasn't getting better.

Despite their best efforts, the house kept falling apart piece by piece. Abundant leaks in the roof forced Leroy to place buckets around the house to catch the water when it rained. Then two or three more sprung open. They dealt with it as they did everything else. They were already miserable, but eventually, everything was going to give way. The news only got worse.

A man from the city rode by one day, right as James and Leroy were walking out.

"Are you Mr. James Atkins?"

"Yes, I am. May I know whose asking?"

"My name is Carl Davis. I work for the city of Brawley. Can I have a moment of your time?"

James nodded.

"I was out here a few days ago. You weren't available, but I inspected your home. You have some serious structural issues that need resolution."

"I know that. Money's tight, but we'll get to it as soon as we can."

"I wish it were that simple, Mr. Atkins. You see, these are violations of the building code. Your roof is about to collapse, and that could injure someone or worse. And these windows—"

James cut him off, "I know everything that's wrong with this house. Like I said, I'm gonna get them all repaired as soon as I can."

Davis shook his head, then handed James a piece of paper. "I'm going to give you sixty days, Mr. Atkins, to bring your home up to code. That's the best I can do."

"And after that?"

"If it's not repaired, we will have to condemn the property. It's all explained in the letter there."

James looked at the paper, not understanding what the man was getting at. As Davis walked away, James turned to Leroy, "That's fool's talk. Nothings gonna fall in on nobody."

Leroy worried about losing his home as much as his father, but he didn't agree with him on everything he said.

James thought hard about where he could get the money for the repairs. He already had trouble putting food on the table after the cotton gin closed down. James was only bringing in half of what he did a few months back. The food ran out shortly after the money did. James was too proud to ask Pappy for help but managed to get word to some of his Black Cabinet friends.

Leroy got one meal a day at his school, but he dreaded the weekend when faced with an empty refrigerator and pantry. He'd walk to Pappy's around dinnertime, in the hopes that he'd invite him in to eat. Leroy also earned a few dollars doing odd jobs for the neighbors.

James put a dollar's worth of gas in the car and spent the rest on a sack of potatoes and beans, two onions, and a loaf of bread. He cooked a big pot for them that lasted almost a week. When that ran out, they sat quietly, not knowing where they would get their next meal. Suffering was not new to James. Coming up during the Great Depression had prepared him for these hard times, but he felt shame when he looked at his son, knowing he could not provide for his family.

The next day, he sold one of his guns and some rusted metal for a few dollars. He seemed to be going from one crisis point to the next. James looked for extra work anywhere he could, but it hardly covered the bills that came due.

One evening, Jerome White came to the door. It was late. Leroy had already gone to bed.

"Jerome. How are you doing?"

"Oh, I'm doing fair. How y'all holding up?" He asked as he handed James a bucket of chicken from one of the local fast-food joints.

"What's all this?" James asked.

"Leftovers from what they don't sell. They have some from time to time. My boy Tommy worked there and brings some home now and again."

"Well, thank you. We sure are hungry."

"I'll see what else I can do."

"I appreciate that."

James couldn't thank Jerome enough. James woke Leroy up, and they sat down to eat. Fried chicken never tasted so good. They ate down to the marrow in the bones. White came back a few days later with several grocery bags full of canned vegetables and spam. The dates on them had expired, but that didn't concern James at all. The food was still good.

"They usually throw these out, but I know a girl at the store, and she collected them for me. She gave me some bread too. I got it in the car."

"Jerome. I wish I could give you something for all this?"

"I know you'd do the same for me," White replied. It was an unspoken acknowledgment. They were all prideful men but would not turn away help, especially during tough times.

On his son's graduation night, James sat in his car along the canal bank on the side of the baseball field, waiting to hear his son's name called. He heard a smattering of clapping when they called Junior's name. He was the first Atkins to graduate high school. He had somehow pulled it together in time to earn his diploma.

Later that evening, Junior opened the front door and stepped about halfway in. He stood there in his dark suit, collared shirt, and one of his father's ties. James and Leroy turned away from the television.

"See you got through," his father said, breaking the silence.

"Still have to go to summer school, but I got to walk today," Junior answered nervously.

"Well, let me see it," James motioned to his diploma.

Junior handed it to him, stepping back to the doorway.

"You celebrating tonight?" James asked, handing it back to him.

"Yeah, a little later."

"Okay," James replied, returning to his television show. Junior shrugged at his brother, but as he turned to leave, his father called out. "Some pork chops and green beans on the stove, if you're hungry. Leroy made the cornbread."

Junior cautiously opened the door a little wider. "I could eat."

The odd absence of tension that night was palpable. It always seemed to be there between them all like a second skin. Leroy looked at his brother and smiled. He was happy he was staying. Junior sat beside him with his plate full. James earned a few extra dollars fixing cars, and there was food in the house. For how long, no one knew, and none of them cared. They had survived another rough patch. Another was bound to come, but for the moment, they enjoyed their good fortune. A comforting peace-filled each of them with a calm that reminded Junior of his mother.

Junior nudged Leroy. "This is good cornbread."

His brother smiled back at him. "I know."

MAKE IT RIGHT – JUNE 1972

James turned the key in the ignition, and the engine sputtered to life. A small eternity had passed since he had driven the car. He tapped the gas pedal gently once more before putting the car in gear and setting off down the street. The car's velocity overwhelmed him at first. It felt as though a mule team was dragging him around. He rambled down the road, slowly passing the familiar houses of his neighbors. He noticed a man sitting under a shade tree. It was Tamayo. He waved, and James pulled over to the curb, nudging it slightly with the front tires. James hadn't seen him since his surgery.

Tamayo shouted hello as he wheeled his chair over to the gate.

"Well, well. How are you, Tamale?" James asked through the open car window.

Tamayo laughed. "I am good, my friend."

James got out and walked to the gate. He looked down at the stump that once was Tamayo's left leg.

"No more chasing women, Señor Jaime."

"More for me!" James laughed.

"That *pinche* doctor say they were gonna cut off the other one if I don't take my *pinche* medicine and eat better. You know what this *eating better* is? It means you eat shit."

"Nothing wrong with you, Tamayo, just one leg is shorter than the other."

Tamayo shrugged. "You in a hurry?"

"No, just wanted to get out of the house."

243

"Nice day for a drive."

"Any day I can see the road is a good day to drive!"

"Oh *sí*," Tamayo answered. "Come on. You want a beer?"

"That damn piss water you drink? No, thank you."

"You insult the man who offers you a drink?" Tamayo complained. "And Coors is not piss water, amigo!"

"You ain't supposed to be drinking anyhow, Tamayo. You know better."

"Yeah, and what about you and all your medicines? Pappy told me he drank whiskey with you many times."

"That's true, but I ain't had my leg cut off."

"Señor Jaime, but you gotta problem with your heart. No?"

"Ain't nothing I can't handle."

"You aren't young anymore, my friend. You better take it easy."

"Yeah. How are your kids doing?" James changed the subject.

"They doing great. Hector is a lawyer. Do you remember my daughter Isabel? She went to school with Sarah. She's married."

"I wish mine stuck around your kids. Maybe they'd have done better in school."

"You got good kids. So polite. Your son, Junior, helps me sometimes with my groceries. What is he doing now after graduation?"

James was surprised to hear that about his son. "He got a little job and going to the college out there in Imperial."

"You see, he's getting an education. That's good."

James nodded.

"You know they are selling this land," Tamayo pointed across the street.

"What, over there?"

"Yes. To build some houses."

"You don't say."

"I just heard the other day. Richards is too old. And his boys don't want to farm anymore. It's too hard."

"Wasn't too hard for us."

"No. It wasn't. I was up every morning at four o'clock," Tamayo remembered.

"Same here. Slopping pigs, feeding the chickens and cattle, then off to school. Walked two miles to get there."

"Good for you. You went to school. We just followed the crops — first, the onions, then grapes, and strawberries. I was born in a field near Coachella. They tell me my mother cleaned me, fed me, and then went back to work," he laughed.

"I can believe it. You had to work hard to survive those days."

"Kids got it too easy today, James. Too easy."

"Yes, they do." James agreed.

"Long hair! That crazy music. What is that?" Tamayo added.

"I tell them all the time. I'll put that boy in the army! That will straighten them out."

"No, no, James. So he can be killed in Vietnam?"

"Living is hell, Tamayo. Maybe they'll take it seriously if their life depended on it."

"Okay, but my kids are not going to fight that war." Tamayo leaned to one side in the wheelchair and pulled out an old leather wallet from his back pocket. "Let me show you my grandchildren."

"This is my son Hector and his wife. He is the lawyer. They have two girls. Look at that. Just like my son, huh?"

"I see. Yes," James looked at each picture carefully. He paused at a striking black and white photo.

"This your wife?"

"Yes, my beautiful Izel. She died before you moved here. She was the best wife I could ever have." Tamayo stared at the picture. "This was 1945, 46. You know she had five sisters and oh man, were they beautiful. Her mother wanted me to marry the oldest girl, Hortensia?"

"Hortensia?"

"*Si.* And let me tell you, she was beeeaauutifil," he emphasized, kissing his index and middle fingers. Tamayo paused again, staring at the picture. "But to me, Izel was the prettiest of them all. We met in the camps near Salinas, working in the strawberries." Tamayo's eyes got a little misty. "Don't you miss your wife?"

James stammered. "Of course I do."

"Because I miss my Izel," Tamayo grieved. "You know what I miss the most?"

James shook his head.

"The way her hair smelled. She had beautiful hair too." A tear slid down the side of his face. "Why did they die first, James, when we need them the most? I'm not even a man anymore."

"Okay, Tamayo," James patted him on his shoulder.

"You know James; I remember when Betsy was a child. Izel watched her and Sarah. Just like family. Then that *pinche* cancer took her from me. Why did they die first?"

James could not look him in the eye nor answer his question. He put these things out of his mind long ago and did not want to relive them again. As he fought to hold his emotions in check, the sliding glass door opened, and Tamayo's nephew appeared.

"*Tio, estas bien*?" he asked, seeing the tears on his face.

James nodded. "He's okay. Just give him a minute."

A short time later, James got in the car and took off down the road. How he ended up at Family Liquor, he could not recall. He found a space around the block to park, bought a beer and some cheap whiskey, and then made his way over to the silos, searching the crowd for a familiar face. But not one of the Black Cabinet was around. He did recognize some of them, children of people he knew, now grown men themselves. It was an odd feeling being a foreigner on familiar ground.

These men sported big, bushy afros and pork chop sideburns. The bright-colored clothing with huge collars and mismatched patterns, dashikis, black berets, and gold chains were off-putting enough. Then came the cars with big white-wall tires and loud music blaring from inside. They had taken over this part of town for themselves. They were youthful-looking, carefree, and energetic. It was their turn, their world, and for a brief moment, James envied them, but he knew better. Yes, he could tell them a thing or two about life. He wished he could impart that knowledge as they walked past him, their hair shimmering in the sunshine, but they were too self-involved and too much in a hurry to listen to an old man.

"Hey son, you ever hear of Satchel Paige?" James asked a teenager with a headband and tasseled leather vest.

He shook his head.

"He was one of the greatest baseball players ever to wear a uniform."

"I don't like baseball. Basketball, now that's my sport," the young man smiled at his friend. They laughed loudly, slapping each other's hands like some game of patty-cake.

James tried again, tugging at the young man's shirt. "What about Rube Foster?"

The man shook his head, returning to his conversation with his friends.

"Jackie Robinson?"

"Sorry, old-timer. I don't know any of your friends."

"They ain't my friends. They're ballplayers. You never heard of the Negro Leagues?"

"No, sir."

James could not believe his ears. How could he not know about Jackie Robinson? '*What the hell are they teaching you in school*?' He thought.

James took one swig after another from his beer, chasing it down with whiskey. He did so until the big grain silos cast shadows over the road. Across the street, the café he used to frequent looked abandoned. The wood frame around the door had warped. The alcohol played in his head, and he lamented those halcyon days when he and the Black Cabinet held court in this arena. They were top dogs no more. Those days were gone for good.

Someone tapped him on his shoulder, and, as he looked up from his stupor, he finally saw a person he recognized. Leroy grabbed his father under the arm and helped him to his feet.

"Hey, boy!" James smiled, happy to see a familiar face. "Wanna beer?"

"No, Daddy. Let's go home."

"So soon? Just getting cool."

"Give me the keys, Dad."

"Okay," he agreed, tossing the empty bottle in a pile of trash as he staggered to his feet. He began to happy dance through the crowd, the whiskey playing a tune in his mind. Leroy kept a firm grip on his arm as they walked back to the car and started the drive home. James stared out the window at the houses and people sitting on their porches, enjoying the cool evening; the grass neatly cut and green as clover. In the air were children's laughter and the sweet scent of lemon blossoms.

As they came around the corner, James stared toward a silhouette in the fading sunlight. His home resembled a lifeless shell. The broken fence, faded curtains, and his dirt yard added to the ragged feel of the place. As they walked the brick path, James noticed a red piece of paper stapled to the door. When they got close enough to read the note, James gasped.

"This ain't right!" he shouted as Leroy. "How they gonna take a man's home? They can't do this, can they?"

Leroy shrugged. He did not have the heart to tell his father what he believed to be accurate. He held the door open and let his father inside. James took one last look at the notice. Stamped in big, bold letters was the word CONDEMNED, followed by 30 Days to Vacate.

"I just need a little time. I done told that man," he agonized, staring at the sagging roof. "I know its falling apart, son, but this is my home. I built this place. No one got the right to make me get out! No one!"

"Come on, Pop. Let's get you tucked in." His father rested his head on the row of pillows as Leroy lifted his feet and turned his long frame onto the bed.

"There's no plan, son. No rhyme or reason to this life. We just got this brain that can't think past our bellies being full."

"I know, Dad. I know," he answered, untying his shoelaces.

"Don't be a fool. There's no plan. We just spinning around on this big ole rock."

Leroy took off the other shoe, half-listening to his father's rant. James closed his eyes, imagining the time when his kids played in the yard. It was beautiful, covered in thick, green grass with blossoms everywhere. He remembered sitting on the porch with his young bride. Betsy had brought him a cold drink, and she sat in his lap while they watched their boys run around. The memories only brought him pain.

"Let 'em have this place," James muttered. "This is my new start!"

He closed his eyes and let his mind drift away. He saw himself and Leroy packing their bags. Later, they would fill the tank of his old Desoto and set their sights on somewhere far away from Brawley. This time when James came to the old road sign at the edge of town, he'd hit the gas pedal that much harder, kicking up dust as he cut out of town.

"Ain't dying here! No sir! Got better places to die than Brawley, California. That's for sure."

He would never leave without his youngest son. It was time to make that last run at freedom. He smiled. He was on the road with Leroy. A full tank of gas to take them to some distant horizon where the demons couldn't find him. He sensed that they were close now, very close. He turned around, and sure enough, there was Sissy, her hand covering her mouth as if she was laughing at him. He looked away from her, but on the other side of him was his father. He still had that smile on his face from the day he died, as if he had seen an angel. Then the spirit of Grandpa Bernard reached out to him, grabbing his hands tightly.

Suddenly, James sat up. He grabbed Leroy around his arms and asked, "Why we got to suffer so?" Leroy tried to avoid his eyes.

"I don't know, Daddy. I wish I did."

Tears slid from his eyes when he remembered his other son, Junior's twin, buried in the backyard, deep in the earth. What would happen to his grave if they lost the house? What about his soul? Would he be angry, thinking his father had abandoned him?

"There ain't no reason to be here other than to suffer. For what? What did I do that was so wrong? Maybe I…I deserve it?"

"No. You don't, Daddy. No one does."

"I've lived ten lifetimes out there on the road. Just playing baseball. Only other home I knew besides this one. And now they taking it too."

All the sweat and tears they had put into building the house was something James derived a lot of pride. Betsy smiled happily, his hands touching her swollen belly with their twins. He was brash back then, full of confidence. Where was that man? Where did he go?

The city inspector was not swayed with James' promises. He swore up and down he'd make good on all the repairs needed to keep his home, but the decision to condemn the property stood. With not much time to move, the boys cobbled together whatever they could in old boxes and bags, leaving much behind in their haste. Leroy made sure he took his uncle's old suitcase. Junior even left Rex with Pappy until they could figure out what to do with him. At least here, he'd have a yard to play in, and it gave Junior another reason to check on his grandfather.

They stayed on the east side of town, moving into a small apartment not far from Family Liquor and close to where their father first stayed in Brawley. After they settled into their new digs, James kept returning to the old house and staying for hours, staring at the walls.

One day Leroy found him there sitting in his beat-up loveseat, a bottle of whiskey at his feet. His old baseball glove was next to that.

"Dad, it's not safe for you to be here like this," Leroy told his father.

"Leave me, son," James pleaded, reaching for the bottle and taking a long swig. Leroy sighed deeply. "I'll check on you tomorrow."

"Mmm-hmm," came the reply.

James watched his son leave, and then he took another sip. His throat burned with each swallow of the liquor, but it got more comfortable the more he drank. The heat of day lingered in the home, and sweat trickled down the side of his head, his drunken stupor complete. It was another hot summer night. He had opened a few windows earlier in the day, but there was no breeze to cool the air. The house was devoid of the life that had filled it at one time, much like the farmhouse in Hondo after James' father died. He then recollected the biscuits his mother made and fighting Samuel over the last one. But thinking of his brother caused a searing pain in his heart. He blamed himself again, punching his leg with his fist, but that did nothing to alleviate the ache he felt.

He took another swig as tears slid down his cheeks. He brushed them away, angrily with the back of his hand.

"So much sadness, so much death," he mumbled. "Why am I still here?" he sobbed. "Why am I here and not Betsy?" He took another long drink. "Why take her and not me? Why take my infant son and not me?"

His eyes clouded with tears, and he struggled to put the empty bottle on the ground. When he did, his hand touched an old baseball glove. He had found it amidst the chaos in the house. A few of the laces had broken away, and the leather was bone dry and stiff in places, but he was able to get his fingers in the right places. The glove felt heavy to his hand; it had been over twenty years since he last put one on. He imagined he was on the pitcher's mound, a batter in the box awaiting the pitch. He rolled a ball in his hand, looking at that imaginary batter he planned to dominate. There was no doubt in his mind. His body was strong. No one could hit his fastball.

The burning sensation in his back returned as a reminder of what was taken away on Buna Island. As that invisible stranger rolled him on his side and slipped a gurney underneath him, he whispered, "I can't feel my legs."

James slowly came back to the present, to the nearly empty room and his bitterness.

"I had my whole life ahead of me. So much promise..." It was all gone. He'd never be whole again.

He slammed his fist into the glove as his eyes again filled with tears.

"What are you crying for?" He shouted to no one.

James sank deeper into his chair, his heart heavy, and his mind troubled. He heard a door slam and saw Pappy leave his house. James pushed himself, unsteadily out of his chair and stumbled into Pappy's house to steal a bottle of whiskey from his liquor cabinet.

He sat in the shade of the porch as the neighborhood children played. Their laughter haunted him. He thought about all the times he yelled at Leroy. James did not mean to be so hard on the boy, but his words hurt more than his hand or fist.

'He was just a boy. Hell, I was just one too!' He took a big swallow from the bottle. The visions tortured him.

'Couldn't let it go.' His head was spinning. When he tried to set the bottle down, it slipped from his fingers, spilling the remaining contents over the floor.

Suddenly, James heard footsteps approaching. He turned wearily around and saw his father standing there. He blinked twice, rubbing his eyes in disbelief.

"Hey, boy," Willie called out. "Let me show you something." He waved him over. Willie had mesquite branches burning on a fire. The flames glowed in the dimming light of dusk. His father passed his open palm through them. "Not nair a burn!" he smiled. "You try it. Come on."

James smiled, passing his hand back and forth through the fire, mesmerized by the dancing flames.

When James turned to face his father, he met Willie's angry eyes, "Sissy died cuz of you." He told James.

The joy of the moment subsided as quickly as it came. "But I didn't mean for her to fall in. I was just a boy."

"Don't matter. Ain't never gonna forgive you. No matter what."

"That's not right," James groaned, backing away from the blaze and his father.

"You can't forgive yo'self, why should I?" Willie pressed on.

"That's not fair, Papa." James pleaded.

"Life ain't fair. Ain't you learned nothing?" Willie's voice trailed off. "Make it right."

He put his hands to his ears, trying to block out his father's words.

"I don't know what the hell you want from me!" James shouted to the sky. "The one time I asked for your help. The one time I needed you, you let me down, and you let her down too. Will I ever be forgiven?"

James woke, breathing heavily and sweating. He realized he'd been dreaming, but his pounding head and sick stomach forced him to lay down.

In the early morning sun, James came to understand that death was savage and cold. Death was angry, not peaceful. Death did not care for your age or how you were loved. Dying was final, inevitable. And he had been avoiding that inevitability all his life. Betsy, his child, his brother, his parents, Sissy, were all gone, forever. It made sense to him now. There was nothing more for him in that old house.

THY SIN IS PURGED

On a dimly lit street, a man hidden by the tall stalks of corn stared across the narrow road at a vacant, wood-framed dwelling. The way ran the length of the long block and dead-ended at a canal bordering the many farms in this unincorporated part of town. A few moments later, he hurriedly crossed over to the metal gate at the front of the house. He paused to catch his breath and then continued down a brick pathway that led to the front door. There was no sign it was occupied. A notice stapled to the door with the word CONDEMNED in bold letters fluttered in the breeze. The man looked around and then pushed open the unlocked door. He took slow and deliberate steps, drawing a deep breath of the thick, musty air.

Within the dark depths of the room, the man maneuvered about the house. He grabbed a handful of old newspaper from the floor and twisted it into a long roll. With his silhouette illuminated by the flicker of a burning match, he turned the paper toward the flame. His hands shook as it caught fire.

A short time later, he made his way outside, returning to the field across the road into the shadows and waited. In the windows, a bright light radiated as the blaze spread quickly. Blood pulsed in the man's neck and wrists as beads of perspiration ran down his face. Burning embers floated peacefully upward into the night's canopy, resembling a hoard of fireflies.

The fire inside the home consumed everything in its path. It swept across the floorboards, and up the walls to the ceiling. Flames ate through the windows to the rooftop spewing a noxious scent of burning plastic, wood, and metal. The heat then exploded outward, cracking a windowpane. Shards of glass fell in a thunderous succession.

As the fire roared higher, the man's heart pumped faster. He retreated further into the field as the blaze engulfed the home, flames rising into the sky.

The man stepped aside in the bush, sweat now rolling down his face. Some of the smoke had drifted into the field and burned his eyes. He whispered as people ran about frantically.

"Thy sin is purged."

THE LONG DRIVE – AUGUST 1972

Junior readied the car for the long drive to Los Angeles. He thought to honk the horn, but he knew Pappy was already feeling anxious enough, and there was no need to agitate him further. Pappy appeared in the doorway, a small bag in hand. From where the car was parked, Junior couldn't help but notice the charred remains of his old home that had burned to the ground just a few weeks before. Pappy told him not to tell Sarah. She already had enough burdens to carry.

The pair drove down the lonely stretch of road past Westmoreland, thirty miles north to Indio, catching the main highway west to Los Angeles. Pappy eyed the gauges as Junior drove the car. Despite Junior's assurances, Pappy remained cautious, reminding his grandson of the speed limit. Junior figured his nervousness had little to do with his abilities and more about seeing his daughter. Sarah's doctor disclosed that her therapy was going well though she still had bouts of anxiety. It was going to take some time for her to recover.

They arrived at the hospital early that Saturday morning around ten-thirty, making good time in the light traffic. Junior parked on the street across from the pleasant-looking building. Bright green yucca and other succulents planted around the lawn highlighted the brick exterior. Roses and purple salvia filled a patio area and garden in the rear. Along the high walls in the garden area were tall bamboo shoots that grew in thick bunches.

Pappy and Junior entered through a set of dark, glass double doors and waited at the reception desk.

255

"May I help you?" The woman sitting there asked kindly. To her right was a secured door.

"Yes, we have an appointment to see Sarah Ross. I'm her father, Edgar Knight."

"Can you please sign in here?" She handed him a clipboard. "I'll call for someone to escort you."

Pappy filled out the form, and afterward, a tall man with a gentle disposition came to the security station and let them in. The group walked down a long hallway that smelled of cleaning solution. They saw Sarah, sitting alone reading a magazine with her back to the door.

"Sarah," the man called. "Your father is here."

She turned around and smiled. "Pappy, you made it!" She hugged him tightly. "And who is this handsome young man?"

Junior smiled shyly. "Hi, Auntie."

"Hey baby," she replied, taking him into her arms. "So good to see you both." Her voice was raspy, probably from too many cigarettes.

Pappy noticed the dark circles under her eyes. She was thinner than he remembered, too.

"Sit down. Tell me what's going on in the big city!" she laughed. Her voice cracked a bit.

"You know, Brawley. Ain't much to tell. Hot as Hades," Pappy replied.

"I bet it is. Nothing like August in the Valley," Sarah nodded. "And Junior, what are you up to these days?"

"Taking classes at the college."

"That's wonderful. Your mother would be very proud of you. I'm proud of you."

"Thanks, Auntie."

There was a moment of silence. Sarah looked down at the table.

"This seems like a nice place. How are you making out?" Pappy asked.

"It is. And I have an excellent doctor. It's helping a lot, Pappy." Her eyes yearned for something unknown to them.

"You all hungry?"

"Yes!" Pappy answered. "I barely had a cup of coffee this morning."

"Come on. The cafeteria here is decent."

They dined together. Sarah explained all the good food choices and what to avoid. Later, she took them on a short tour of the grounds. They sat near a small babbling water feature surrounded by colorful flowers and bamboo trees.

Sarah started. "Isn't it peaceful?"

"Sure is," Pappy remarked.

"Reminds me of Momma's garden."

Pappy nodded.

"Junie loves this place. Right here. Told me he's putting a fountain like this in our house."

"That sounds real nice," Pappy added.

"He's working a double shift this weekend. His union insurance pays for most of this."

"I'm sorry we won't get to see him on this trip, but there will be others, now that my chauffeur has his license," Pappy elbowed Junior.

"So, I get paid to drive you?" Junior laughed. Sarah laughed with them too.

"I'm getting better, Pappy. Don't worry about me," she blurted out, suddenly serious.

"Baby, I will always worry about you."

"In this place, I'm not afraid."

Pappy swallowed hard, wanting to believe her.

"And if I can be here and not be afraid, then I can be out there and do the same."

"That's the spirit. We're all pulling for you." Pappy assured.

"Doctor told me I have to learn to forgive myself. That's the hardest part," she shrugged, covering her eyes.

Pappy clutched her hands, rubbing them gently as Sarah continued.

"It's a good thing to cry and not hold it all in. My doctor said this is the grieving process," she chuckled. "We know plenty about that, don't we?"

Pappy agreed.

An orderly informed them that visiting time was ending. They thanked him and started back toward the reception area.

"You drive safely," Sarah continued, putting her arms around Junior. "Take care of my Pappy, you hear?"

"I will, Auntie."

"He stops by all the time, but mostly to see that Garcia girl," Pappy teased.

"You have a girlfriend?"

"Yes. Her name's Daisy. She's going to San Diego State."

"A smart girl!"

Junior chuckled.

"It was good to see you both."

"You too, honey," Pappy kissed her on the cheek.

"Pappy."

"Yes."

"I meant what I said earlier. About getting better."

"I know you did, Baby."

"I promise you. I'm getting better."

He nodded at her. "I love you." He knew she was still very sick.

"I love you too, Daddy."

They hugged one last time, then made their way through the security doors and into the reception area where Pappy signed them out. Suddenly, they heard someone shouting. It was Sarah.

"Wait!" she cried, hurrying toward them.

The security guard opened the door, and she stepped out into the reception area.

"I almost forgot," she shared, looking over at Junior. "Your mother told me to give this to you a while ago. I'm sorry it's taken me this long to remember, but here it is." She handed him a sealed envelope.

"For me?" Junior asked. Sarah cupped his hands in hers, nodding to her nephew. He handed the letter to Pappy once they got inside the car.

"Can you read it to me?" he asked nervously.

"Son, it's for you from your mother. Don't you want to read it in private?"

"No," he requested. "I want you to read it."

Pappy put his glasses on, and read it aloud.

Dearest James Jr.,

Son, the day I welcomed you into this world was one of the happiest moments of my life. You have been a blessing to me ever since. When the nurse placed you in my arms, I thanked God for you. I've watched you grow into a handsome young man with an amazing spirit. Don't ever change that about yourself.

You know, people struggle to have some purpose in their lives. You have to keep moving on, son. Live each day doing your best. Do not get stuck living someone else's life. Find your happiness and keep the faith.

You are so smart and talented. Do something good with your life. Forgive. You will lose yourself if you hang onto anger and hate. And please watch out for your brother. He tries not to show it, but he looks up to you.

I love you always.
Your mother,
Betsy

"She was a brave woman, huh?" Junior offered as Pappy put the letter back in the envelope.

"Yes, she was, son," he agreed, the words choked him up. "You keep her in your heart, son. She'll always be with you that way."

"I will Pappy," Junior confided, tears streaming down his face. "I miss her."

"I do too. You and Leroy are all I have of her." He reached over and grabbed Junior's hands, holding them tightly.

"It still hurts so much," Junior told him.

"I know. I know."

"Why do people have to die?"

His grandfather shook his head. "I wish I knew."

"Does the pain ever go away?"

Pappy swallowed hard. "No. It doesn't."

JACKIE ROBINSON · 1972

By 1972, Brawley had grown into a thriving farming community of nine thousand people. Most whites lived on the west side, and black folks and Mexicans occupied the east. Each group had staked out a place of their own to gather.

On Eighth Street, several establishments served the growing community of Mexican and Filipino farmworkers. The bars served cheap food and cold beer. Women with garish makeup and low-cut dresses, came in the evening to mingle. They danced for a nickel and hoped to meet someone to marry. And it happened often.

The music was raucous, loud Spanish corridas with their singsong beat. Harmonious guitars and accordions filled the air along with cigarette smoke and laughter from Thursday to Saturday night when this stretch of town came alive.

In the back parlors of these bars, hidden behind secret doors, Filipino men gambled. They were a small community of World War II vets that blended in with the Mexicans. James often ate at one of the more popular cantinas—the Monte Carlo— with its colorful, neon sign hanging in the window.

Many black families frequented these places for the food, but the majority of the men congregated a block away on Ninth and Main Streets next to the liquor store. They sat on makeshift benches made from produce crates. The drinking and carousing started early, especially when the conversation got thick. There always seemed to be something going on. The Black Cabinet usually led the charge.

James recalled the last time they were together before everyone got too old and age crippled their bodies further. It wasn't the same without L.A. there. He was the first of the Black Cabinet to be afflicted. A stroke left him severely impaired.

"Rich people stay with rich people. Ain't no way a regular man gonna marry into them families," Jerome White began.

"Not even folk from good, white families," Chef added.

"Why you worried about white folks' business?" Gold asked. "Y'all ain't never gonna be good enough for them!"

"James, I heard them Walker boys were the ones that set fire to your place," Jerome White stammered.

"Where you hear that?" Gold cut in before White finished his sentence.

"What you talking 'bout, man?" Chef asked.

"Well, I heard that too," Ernest pointed out, coming to White's defense. "Them boys been bragging about it for quite some time."

"It's what folks are saying. You should talk to his ole man. He's there now," White added.

"Nah. I'mma find out who did it," James replied.

"What you saying, James?" Cook shouted. "Cain't let this stand."

"What I want to know," White started, "Is why you don't seem to care?"

"Jerome, leave it be," James barked.

White shook this head in disgust. He wanted justice for James, and he didn't understand his reluctance to talk about it. He had witnessed the Klan burn too many families off their property.

James could not bring himself to tell them what the fire marshal had told him—that fire was suspicious and the person or persons who started it could be facing jail time.

"You having one of them *mid-life crisis* people going on about? You know, where folks scared of dying!" Chef asked sarcastically.

"Who said I wanted to stay here in the first place, much less long enough to die here?" James snapped.

"This town is as good as any to die in. Where's better?" Gold asked.

"Next to my momma would be nice," James answered.

"So why'd you leave Texas then?" Gold continued.

"I don't know. Believed there'd be something better out in the world to see. I was wrong. Everywhere's the same. People living in boxes. Nothing new here."

"Well, I don't believe that for one minute."

"And I don't give a goddamn what you believe," James scoffed angrily.

Everyone grew silent. The men knew all too well, James' temperament, and age hadn't softened it.

"Heard Tom Brown sellin' that old Cadillac," Gold chimed in.

"One with the big fins?" Cook asked.

"Shoot, he ain't getting nothing for that piece of junk!" Jerome laughed, breaking the tense air. James took another swig of beer from the can he had wrapped in a paper sack.

Just then, a police car rounded the corner and slowed. The men stiffened, turning their heads to the street and hiding their drinks. They did not trust the law. Most viewed the badge as an extension of Jim Crow oppression, but in Brawley, there was an unspoken truce between the authorities and the folks at this corner. They didn't act on their bigotry like most southern whites.

The cops, both white, stared at the men as the patrol car headed south. The officer on the passenger side tipped his hat, acknowledging the men, and they nodded back, never taking their eyes off the car while it was in sight. Just as the calm was returning to the street, the car backfired and startled everyone.

The loud and sudden noise sounded like a shot fired from a gun. It shook James more profoundly than he let on, taking him back to the war. He wanted to believe the years had put some distance between him and those ugly memories, but they hadn't faded as much as he believed. James remembered one particularly horrible day on Buna Island almost thirty years ago when they were holed up for three days surrounded by the enemy.

James was lost in that memory, the last time his friends were together on that corner of town, when he was startled back to reality by screaming children. He had fallen asleep in the waiting area of Dr. Suarez's office. To James, children were annoying accidents waiting to happen. He watched, observing the little brats crawling over and under everything. They ran from one side of the room to the other, screaming at the top of their lungs, ignoring the admonishing glares of the patients and parents alike.

The receptionist, Maria DeGloria, was happily proselytizing another patient as he filled out some forms. She spoke with sincere devotion and love for the gospel. Each time James came in to see Dr. Suarez, it was the same scene, the same questions. For some reason, her saying 'have a blessed day' irritated James to no end.

He questioned what she knew about life, assuming that she had never been out of this safe, little town far removed from the dangers of the world. Christianity was all she knew. What could she know about evil, here in this quiet, backwater place? It burned him to hear her talk about this loving, benevolent entity when the Bible was full of violence that God had commanded.

Still, his annoyance was not enough to keep him from chatting with her during his visits. It started with small talk at first with basic greetings, and when the office was not quite so busy, they discussed their families. She was fascinated by his stories, and James enjoyed that someone listened and had an interest it what he shared.

"My son's in college now."

"You sound very proud of him."

"He needs a kick in the butt, but I guess he is getting on with it."

"You know, I'm a grandmother." She pointed to the framed picture on her desk. "This is my granddaughter, Patricia."

"She's beautiful."

James' breathing troubles over the last few days caused this new visit. Leroy finally convinced him to see Suarez and deal with the lecture he would receive from the doctor.

James grabbed a magazine, anything to take his mind off the unruly children. As he thumbed through some of the pictures, he heard his name called. It took him a moment to lift himself out of the chair, and a few more for his back to loosen up.

The nurse escorted him to one of the examination rooms. In one corner was a poster of the human body. Next to him was a full-length mirror. He caught a glimpse of his reflection, recognizing some familiar traits, but not the person in it—this white-haired man with sagging skin and a rooster neck. He ran his worn and callused hand down his face, touching the bristled hair on his chin. He was only fifty-three years old but felt much older.

Dr. Suarez came in and checked his blood pressure.

"I know when you aren't eating properly," Suarez continued. "Because you end up in here. You do not take your medication and do everything I tell you not to. And I hear you're still drinking." He admonished James like a child. "Mr. Atkins. You're playing with fire. You are."

James curled up his lips and nodded to the doctor.

"I'll have another talk with your son about this, but in the end, it's your health."

Chef was waiting in his car for James. They were going to the convalescent home where L.A. was staying since suffering a stroke. James and Chef took the short walk down the narrow hallway and stopped at L.A.'s door. It was wide open. Just inside, L.A. sat in his wheelchair, his head sagging to one side and his eyes hidden behind thick, black-framed glasses.

"What's new, L.A.?" James asked.

L.A. lifted his head and smiled when he recognized them. "Nothing much," he slurred. The aphasia affected his speech, and he had trouble completing his sentences. James and Chef tried their best to fill in the awkward silence. It was hard to speak anyhow with the television blaring in the background. L.A. smiled along with them, but he was not his usual self. He had lost his sharp wit. James had not realized he was so bad off.

"What the hell is going on with these young people these days?" James asked rhetorically. "I was up by Family a while ago. Damn shame what's going on there."

Chef added, "I don't go up there no more. Someone's gonna get killed. Watch and see."

"Who...burn..." L.A. labored to say. "Yo...house?"

A few months had passed since the fire that destroyed James' home.

"Huh? What you say, L.A.?" James asked.

"Guess he wants to know about your house, the fire and all," Chef beckoned. "They ever figured out who did it?"

"Do you...care?" L.A. stammered.

"Of course, I care. I spoke with the fire marshal about it the day after. He has some leads, I think."

"Who does he thinks did it?" Chef asked. "Them Walker boys?"

"No," James shrugged. "I'm sure he'll let me know in due time."

"Sure does seem strange," Chef pressed. "I can't imagine why someone would burn your house down."

"Must've been an accident," James put forth. "Had to have been."

"Didn't the—"

"Shh!" James cut him off when a special announcement came on the TV. The reporter spoke. "Jackie Robinson, star of the Brooklyn Dodgers and first Negro to play in the major leagues, died today," James did not hear another word. His jaw nearly hit the floor.

"What the hell!" Chef shouted.

James waved at him to keep quiet. He wanted to hear what else the man had to say. One could not underestimate what Robinson meant to his generation. He was an inspirational hero to many black people and redefined Negro manhood. James felt a deep sense of pride when Jackie broke that color barrier. He was more than a baseball player to him. Many folks staked their entire identity on this lone figure. He exemplified what they too struggled through each day—Jackie showed them how to stand tall, and he was beloved for it.

"I can't believe he's gone," Chef faltered after the broadcast ended. "Lord, have mercy on his soul." Chef pulled out a handkerchief and dabbed at his eyelids.

L.A. looked over at James and squeezed his arm with his good hand. It was a sad end to an already miserable day.

THE WORLD AIN'T
CHANGED AT ALL – 1973

The Atkins men settled into their new home. A year had passed since the fire destroyed their old house. The local fire department declared it was arson, but they still had no leads or suspects. The rumor mill was in full swing. But James didn't care and retreated further from the public eye. Leroy found him spending most days going through Samuel's old suitcase, reminiscing about the good old days. He would stare at an old picture for hours on end, searching for something he lost out there on the Plains.

"Dad, I need to ask you something," Leroy said, knocking on the door.

Leroy was in his last year of high school and had no idea what he was going to do once he graduated.

"What is it, son?" His father asked, putting the picture aside.

"I was thinking of joining the military after high school."

James shook his head. "Son, you don't belong there. This Vietnam mess," he paused. "It's just a waste of life. No boy, think of something else. Get a job at the post office or Holly Sugar."

"I don't want to work there."

"You too good for work?"

"No, I just want something better."

"Ain't nothing wrong with an honest day's pay. Don't you forget that."

"I didn't mean it like that."

"Army's not what I want for you, Leroy."

"But you were in the military."

"I was drafted, son. Big difference. And it took a lot from me. More than you'll ever know."

"But Dad, I'd be serving my country. Isn't that a good thing?"

"A good thing? You ain't even equal in this country."

"That's not true. Times are changing."

"Said the same thing a hundred years ago when they freed the slaves, and we just now got the right to vote."

'If he only knew,' James pondered, *'even a quarter of what I have been through.'*

James recalled one day in Texas City, TX, when the team bus broke down. A man at the local filling station let them borrow a jack to fix the blown tire. Unbeknown to him, one of his players put the jack under the seat in the back row, thinking it belonged to James.

As Buckey drove out of town, they ran into a roadblock just before the entrance to the highway. Standing there with their guns drawn were the police and several locals. James got off the bus after Buckey stopped on the roadside. Some big-eared sheriff checked the bus, and after a quick search, he found the source for all the ire.

"Officer, this was an honest mistake."

"Your people can't be trusted."

"I'm a veteran. I fought for this country."

"Don't mean you can't be a thief," the sheriff mocked as he put James in handcuffs. He spent the night in jail and could've lost his life all for a tire jack that cost a few dollars. James had never been more humiliated. His service meant nothing to this man.

"The world ain't changed at all," he groaned.

Leroy shrugged. He didn't understand why his father was always so negative.

REUNION – SPRING 1974

Leroy dropped his father at the doctor's office once again and told him he'd pick him up in an hour. James' visits were getting routine. He'd come by every three or four months complaining of the same symptoms. Dr. Suarez chastised him for a few minutes, and James would do right for a little while, but he always seemed to be back in the doctor's office for something. Suarez had now installed a small television in the waiting area, and James intently watched the news of Hammering Hank Aaron breaking Babe Ruth's home run record. James giggled each time Aaron rounded the bases on that historic night.

A Mexican man sat across from him with a thin, graying hair and a thick mustache. James had seen him there before, looking lost and tired. His daughter had dropped him off. Now he sat alone on the other side of the waiting area. Whenever their eyes met, James quickly looked away. Something about him unnerved James. He felt pity, but couldn't say why.

Dr. Suarez appeared and waved James in. He pushed himself up gently, standing for a moment to gather himself. Suddenly, James rocked to one side after taking an unsteady step, then fell face-first to the floor and was knocked unconscious.

When James came to, he was lying in a hospital bed, his face bruised. Maria DeGloria was sat in the room, reading her Bible. She heard him ruffling and came to his bedside.

"Where am I?" He asked.

"You're at Pioneers Hospital. Do you remember what happened?"

"No."

"You collapsed in the doctor's office and hit your head pretty hard on the floor. Your son will be here soon." She touched his hand. "I'm so happy you're okay. I've been praying for you."

"Thank you, but I need more than prayers."

"Don't doubt the power of prayers," she smiled.

"Hmm," he smirked.

"You are a good man, Mr. Atkins. I can see that. You should try and make peace with whatever is eating at your soul."

James looked away, not meeting her eyes.

"You should make peace with whatever is in your heart that's weighing you down. You can only keep it inside for so long."

"What do you know about me?" James asked.

"I know a lot more than you think I do. I see you have more than physical pain. You have lived a good life. You have great children and been halfway around the world."

"More to life than just what you got."

"Yes, that is true. But if all you see is the dying part, how can you live?"

"Never saw it like that," James answered.

"You have to come to terms with death, Mr. Atkins. We will all die. I chose to believe that death is not the end, but you have to figure this out for yourself."

"How?" he asked. "That's a hard thing to accept when you think about it."

"Then live. Live without all these regrets."

Her words touched a nerve deep inside him.

"If I could, Mr. Atkins, I'd take away all your pain. I know you are a good man, and you've had a very hard life. I can see that. Let it out. Let it all out. You will see everything will be better. And I am here with you." She held his hands even tighter. He closed his eyes as tears rolled off his cheeks.

"You know, my wife was with child before she died."

"I'm so sorry to hear that," Maria whispered.

He shook his head. "Didn't deserve to have another child. I couldn't provide for the ones I had."

"Mr. Atkins, all this anger is just you destroying yourself. Don't you see that?"

"And I destroyed them too. You know why? Cause it hurts too much to care."

"You can't change the past, only what is in front of you."

"You know I've been to war, seen people die. I've never been afraid of anything in my life, but I am now. I don't want to die."

"Dying isn't the end. You have to believe that. Our lives have more meaning than we can ever comprehend."

"Then why are we here? Can you tell me?"

"Simply to love and worship God. I don't believe it's any more complicated than that. As a Christian, I believe the only way back to that purpose is through Jesus Christ. What he did on the cross reconciles us with God. That's what I believe, but I'm not telling you anything new." Maria replied. "This was all in those little pamphlets you and your son would throw away when you left the office. Don't think I didn't see." She smiled.

"What if there ain't no heaven?" James asked, ignoring her attempt at humor.

"I have my doubts sometimes, like everyone. I want to believe there is more to living. And that is where my faith comes in. Life, Mr. Atkins, is worth every moment. The good and the bad."

"I feel like I am just waiting for the end, you know. Like I've got nothing to offer anyone."

"What about the truth? You have to ask yourself, what has being mad at God gotten you?"

"Where'd you get that idea from?"

"I see how you look at me when I offer the booklets to you. How your lip curls if I read from the Bible."

James chuckled. "You're pretty smart there, Ms. Maria."

"I'd like to think so too!" She smiled.

"Yes, I do have to make this right. That's true."

"The time is now. Can I pray with you?"

Before he could answer, she began.

"Lord Jesus, please lay your healing hands upon your servant James Atkins. Lord, help him see your undying love and forgive his sins, Lord."

James suddenly felt a rush of emotions. Most times, these words did not affect him, but today, they were impactful. After she finished, James wiped his face with his gown. Maria clutched his hands even tighter and whispered, "Amen. Amen." She then took out a tissue and offered it to him.

"You know, I've been a fool most of my life," James confessed. "I'm so tired of running."

"Give your burdens to Jesus. Aren't you tired of being tired?" Maria pleaded.

"Yes," he whispered.

James felt conflicted – both relieved and ashamed. All this time he had believed he had done right, that when needed he had stood up to be counted, but in reality, he had been living afraid. He now understood and pondered if this was what the spirits had been trying to warn him against and maybe what his own mother had tried to get him to realize about his crippled heart? The unease of his conflict was of one awakening from a deep slumber, but in a strange place. James wasn't sure why.

"I have so much to set right. I gotta get out here." He looked around, panic on his face as he sat up in his bed.

Just then, Leroy appeared at the door. "Dad, are you all right?"

Startled, he answered. "Hey, boy. Yes, I'm okay. I fell and hit my noggin. This thick skull was good for something."

"The doctors said they are keeping you here overnight," Leroy added. "You got a nasty bruise."

"Yes, for observation," Maria added. "They are going to run a few tests tomorrow."

"I'm going to stay here with you. I brought my homework with me."

"Son, you don't have to do that. I'll be okay."

"No, Daddy. I have to be here," Leroy smiled at him. "Let me get my things. I'll be right back."

Maria stood up to leave. "You are always welcome in my church. I will come by and see how you are doing tomorrow."

"Thank you."

"God bless you, Mr. Atkins," she testified.

"God bless you, too," he replied.

Leroy returned a short time later.

"Son, I've made a lot of mistakes in this life." James began.

"Okay, Daddy. We all have."

"I know this might not make sense to you, but I gotta chance to fix this. Not have you crippled like me." He tapped Leroy's hand. "I'm going to make it up to you, son."

"Okay, Daddy," Leroy felt a lump in his throat.

"You know, we all got to die someday, son. My grandpa told me that one day, and I'll never forget how sad it made me feel," he conceded, turning over to one side. "He took whatever little bit of child I had left in me and killed it. Yes, he did."

Leroy nodded at his father that he understood.

"And I never wanted you and your brother to have to face that. I wanted things to be different for you, but I failed you because I was afraid. I took that out on you all. Your mother, too."

"No, Daddy. You did the best you knew how."

"No, son. I didn't," he paused. "That's why I need you to forgive me."

"For what?"

"Everything, son. *Everything.* Just say you forgive me."

"Daddy, you are everything to me. Of course, I forgive you."

"Thank you, son," he sniffled. "All I wanted for you all was to have a place in this world."

Leroy squeezed his father's hand.

"Dodgers playing, you wanna watch the game?"

"You like baseball?" James was surprised.

"Are you kidding? I just finished a term paper on Satchel Paige and Hank Aaron."

"What you know about Satchel Paige?"

He turned to his father, confused. "A lot! You talk about him all the time. All the old stars from the Negro Leagues."

"Well, I am…" James chuckled. He had never been more proud.

Leroy turned on the TV set, and they watched it until his father fell asleep. He admired his old man peacefully at rest. Here was his hero, his pillar of strength, now broken and worn down. But his admiration for him remained strong.

Leroy climbed under the covers with him, throwing his arm around his father's waist as he had as a boy. When he woke the next morning, he was careful not to wake him. He silently gathered his books and went home to shower before school.

272

Not long after Leroy went away, James woke from his slumber. He felt as if someone was standing over him, that same feeling he'd get when the spirits were nearby. He turned slowly and saw what looked like someone in the shadows.

"Who's there?" James called out.

"It's me," Samuel replied, smiling and stepping into the light. "I've come to get you."

James blinked again, not believing his eyes or ears. He tried to wipe the fog out of his eyes. But sure enough, it was his brother Samuel speaking to him.

"What you doing here?"

"C'mon, you gonna miss the game," Samuel said, ignoring his question.

"What game?"

"If you don't know, I ain't going to tell you," Samuel chuckled.

"Why are you fooling around, Samuel?"

"Are you still mad at me, James?"

"Why didn't you tell me you had a wife and child?"

"Would you like to meet them?"

James looked at him strangely.

"Come on, brother. There's nothing to fear". He motioned with his hand.

"I ain't afraid."

"Yes, you are."

James turned to him quickly. "What do you know?"

"You're afraid to care, brother. Hurts more to care. Don't it?"

James looked away from him.

"So you coming or what?"

"What's the point if I go?"

"Sorry, you feel that way. I'll leave you be then."

"See, that's your problem. Always in a hurry," James replied. "Let me get my clothes."

"You don't need 'em. Stop stalling!" Samuel yelled.

"What? Are you crazy? " As James peeled back the bed covers, he discovered that sure enough, he was wearing his old Black Spiders uniform, pressed and clean.

His glove and hat were on the nightstand next to the bed. He hadn't noticed them being there before. He sat up, letting his feet touch the floor, looking at his hand in shock. They were no longer gnarled and arthritic. He felt no pain anywhere whatsoever. James was confused, even more so now. He walked over to the sink and looked in the mirror. James could not believe what he saw. His face was unlined, his skin clear, and his eyes bright. He looked to be about thirty years old. He turned to Samuel.

"Am I dreaming?"

"Nope," Samuel grinned.

"My mind is playing a joke."

"I wish it were so, James," Samuel shrugged.

"But wait! I still have things to do," he protested. "I just…"

Before he could finish, Samuel cut in, "Ran out of time? We all did. Everyone runs out of time."

James turned to Samuel. "What about my boys?"

"They'll be fine." Samuel turned suddenly serious. "Trust me. They'll make their own way."

"How do you know?"

"Cuz you and I did when Momma and Papa passed on. Come on now. It's time to go."

"Where we going?" James inquired, pulling back the curtains to the window.

"You can't go back, James. That life is over."

James sat on the edge of the bed, took a deep breath.

"I've got so much to do. I'm not ready to go."

"No one ever is, James," his brother answered him. "But we had our time in sun brother."

"Yes, we did, didn't we?" James replied. He paused for a moment longer, staring at the wall. "I'm scared, Samuel," he confided, his lips trembling.

"I was too, big brother, but everything's gonna be all right. That's why we all came to be with you."

"Who's here?" He was surprised to see his mother, Mabel, his father, Willie, and Sissy. Matilde, with her daughter Jaime smiled at him. Even Grandpa Bernard was there with his corncob pipe in his mouth. But nothing could match the shock when he saw Betsy. She beckoned to him, and James delayed no longer.

Leroy heard the phone ringing down the hall. He hurried out of the shower, annoyed that his brother didn't answer it. By the time Leroy reached the receiver, whoever had called had hung up. He set it back down and then, and the phone rang again.

"Hello."

"Can I speak with Leroy or James Junior?"

"This is Leroy."

"Leroy, this is Dr. Vincent over at Pioneers. I'm sorry to tell you this, but your father passed away this morning. I need you or your brother to come over today."

"But I was just there, and he was fine." Leroy could barely get the words out.

"He went into cardiac arrest about an hour ago. I'm sorry."

"That can't be! I was just there."

"I'm very sorry for your loss, son."

Leroy thanked the doctor and hung up the phone in a daze. *'But I was just there,'* he wondered. Leroy closed his eyes for a moment, then called for his brother.

"Junior," he yelled.

His brother answered sleepy-eyed. "What are you screaming about, Leroy?"

"Daddy's gone."

"What?"

"He died this morning. I just got the call from the hospital."

Junior shook his head. "That old bastard got out easy."

"What?" Leroy was aghast, tears falling on his face.

"You don't see the irony in all this?"

"Irony? The only irony I see is expecting you to give a damn that our father is dead. But you hated him when he was alive, so of course you'd hate him dead," he shouted.

"You're so damn stupid. Momma suffered a terrible death, and she never hurt anyone in her life, but he dies peacefully in his sleep! Yes, Leroy, that's ironic! You know what that means, right?"

"Daddy lived through a lot. He was in the war."

"Stop making excuses for him," Junior disagreed.

"It's not an excuse. I talked to the man."

"You were always his favorite little soldier boy, and I was his favorite whipping boy."

"Nothing he did was ever good enough for you!"

"He was no saint, and I have the scars to prove it," Junior shouted back.

"No, Junior, he tried to do right by us, Momma too. But you can't see that."

"I guess you forgot all those whippings!"

"No, I didn't, but I forgave him."

"Well, I didn't. Not for all the stuff Dad did to me, to all of us."

"I feel sorry for you, Junior. You don't see that he cared about you just like he did me?"

"He didn't love me, Leroy. Never showed me love. Ever!"

"Maybe he didn't know how to show you?"

Junior paused. "You and I will never agree on this. So let's leave it where it is."

"Funny thing Junior, you're the same ugly person you accuse him of being," Leroy exacted, raising a finger to his brother's face. He was taller than his older sibling was but thinner.

"You have no idea what that man was capable of," Junior shook his head.

"He told me you weren't worth a damn, but I didn't want to believe him. But yea, I see it now."

Junior stepped closer to Leroy, barely a foot from his face, but his brother stood his ground.

"He's dead, and you're mad because I'm not as upset as you are?" Junior whined in disbelief. "Could you be any dumber?"

"Dumb is wanting to dance on his grave like you do."

"Go to hell, bastard!" Junior shouted angrily.

"Something I'm curious about, did you burn the house down?" Leroy spat at him.

Junior paused, shocked by the question. "What? Are you crazy?" Junior replied. "Why would I do that?"

"Just feels like something you'd do." Leroy poked him in his chest with his finger.

"What a stupid question," Junior raged, slapping his hand away.

"Yeah, you did it. That's the truth."

"You better get the hell outta my face, Leroy."

"Or what?"

"I'll beat the shit—"

"But you're nothing like Daddy, huh?"

They stared at each other for a moment. "You can't handle what I know." Junior mumbled, "It would break your heart." Then he slammed the bedroom door shut.

The next day, Pappy went with Leroy to the mortuary. He stood over the lifeless body of his father, regretting not being there to say goodbye.

"Oh, Daddy..." he whispered.

Pappy pulled him close. "It's okay, Leroy."

Leroy felt lost. He was weeks away from his high school graduation, and now was planning his father's funeral. Afterward, he spoke to the mortuary director and decided on cremation. Pappy was not pleased.

"Son, you need to think about this some more."

"No disrespect, Grandpa, but I know what I'm doing."

"Shouldn't you talk about this with your brother? Maybe bury him here in Brawley?"

"He'd be okay with this. Trust me. He wouldn't want that."

"You still need to talk this over with your brother. You all need to agree."

"I'll do it for you, but it's not gonna go well."

The next day Junior showed up at Pappy's house to discuss the arrangements. He arrived late and unapologetic. Leroy wanted the discussion to be short. He had no desire to entertain his brother's ideas about the funeral. He was doing this simply out of respect for his grandfather. They all sat down at the kitchen table without saying a word.

"You all need to come to some agreement," Pappy started.

"Well," Leroy insisted. "I'll take care of the funeral service for Daddy with Pappy's help. Junior can do everything else."

"What are you planning to do for the funeral? Have you picked out a casket?" Junior asked.

"No need for a casket, he's being cremated."

"Why would you do that?" he asked.

"Why do you care, Junior? You laughed when I told you he'd died."

"I didn't laugh, idiot!"

"Well, he's being cremated. That's that."

"Pappy," Junior pleaded. "Who put him in charge?"

Leroy stood up. "I'm the one who cared about him, that's why I'm in charge."

"You don't know shit about my feelings," Junior shouted, standing up, his chest heaving.

"You're right, I don't care what you feel," Leroy shot back.

"I'm sick of you, man."

"It's mutual," Leroy yelled, stepping closer to his brother.

The anger boiled over to a frenzy. Junior lunged at Leroy, tackling him to the ground. They tumbled to the floor, knocking over Pappy's favorite chair. Junior punched and clawed at his brother even as Pappy tried to get between them, but wasn't strong enough to separate them. He grabbed the only thing in sight, one of his favorite bottles of scotch, and threw it against the wall next to them. The noise of the shattering glass stunned the combatants.

"Simmer down now, the both of you! Goddammit, your folks raised you better than this." Pappy screamed. "You will respect me in my own house!" he yelled, looking from one to the other. "You'll both work on your daddy's service, or I'll do it myself," he finished angrily.

Leroy pointed at Junior, declaring, "This ain't over."

His brother agreed.

A week later, a large crowd of people gathered to pay their respects to James. His best friends, the Black Cabinet, were all there. Bent and aged, walking with hunched shoulders and canes, still they came to say their goodbyes. They took a seat in the front row. Mrs. DeGloria smiled and waved to Leroy as she sat down with her family. Even Junie and Sarah made the trip to Brawley to support their nephews. Sarah looked so much better than the last time Junior saw her. Leroy found an old picture of his father smiling in a dugout with his Atkins All-Stars uniform circa 1948 and used it for the cover of the funeral program entitled "A Life Well Lived." Junior was not happy with his younger brother making all the decisions, but out of respect for Pappy, he went along without argument.

Mourners gathered in their Sunday finest. A large photo of James greeted them with flower stands on either side. An urn held his ashes. Reverend Drew, now frail and elderly himself, began the service with an opening prayer followed by a spiritual, then some of the townsfolk spoke to the family.

They praised James, calling him a good man and father, but Junior was tired of it all. He knew a different man, one he had grown up fearing and even hating. He never got the chance to confront his father about so many things.

When he did finally cry, it was not for the man or his passing, but the memories it dredged up. He remembered a time when he had liked his father, the Christmases and birthdays. He saw the love his parents had once shared. He wondered where that love had gone. There was not a day that passed when he didn't think of his mother, now buried so many years. After everyone had their say, Leroy got up, finally able to address the mourners.

"My father could make me laugh like no one else. The stories that man would tell. You all know," Leroy turned to the Black Cabinet, sitting near each other in the pews. They smiled and nodded. "There were so many things I wanted to know about him. I don't know now if I ever will."

"Amen," came a chorus from the crowd.

"My father was a good man. I cannot imagine the strength it took for him to get this far in life. He had ways and reasons for doing things that many of us, including myself, will never understand, but he was my father. He was the greatest man I've ever known." Leroy fought back his grief.

"My only hope is that one day, one day, I'll see you again."

"Go ahead, son," Reverend Drew shouted.

"So, on behalf of my family, I want to thank each of you for coming here to celebrate my father's life and homecoming. We appreciate the prayers, cards, and all of you speaking here today. It gives us great joy and comfort to know that he was loved and respected in his community." Leroy turned to the picture of his father at the front of the church and continued. "Daddy, I will never forget you."

After the eulogy, Reverend Drew made his way over to Junior.

"Haven't seen you in church for quite some time."

"I've got a busy schedule with work and school."

"Too busy for Jesus?"

Junior hesitated to answer.

"I remember that teenaged boy, so devout. Had the fire of Christ in his heart."

"I'm not that teenager anymore," Junior replied.

"I see. But you must understand that your prayers were useful as they were fruitful."

"If so, why did mother die?"

"Son, you cannot bargain with God. You can't say I will believe you if you do this for me."

Junior shrugged. "It didn't matter anyway."

"Your prayers were answered. God will not forsake you, Junior. And he didn't forsake your mother."

Junior quietly stepped away from Reverend Drew.

Later that afternoon, Leroy parked the car at Beechey Field, where his father had played the last game of his career. Alone, he carried a container through the gate and onto the field, pausing on the pitcher's mound for a moment, before whispering these words.

"I'm gonna miss you something awful. I was so ready to make that drive with you. I promise you, I will. And when I do, you'll be with me."

He then tilted the urn, spreading some of the ashes on the ground. He continued, walking to the outfield, shaking the contents from the urn as he went. He rounded the diamond, ending at home plate where he spread a little more of the ashes.

"You're home now, Daddy," he wept.

FAMILY SECRETS – JUNE 1974

A month to the day of his father's funeral, Junior drove his father's old car to the east side of town. He was on his way to see Tamayo's lawyer son to get some papers signed. The lot where his old home used to be was still vacant, but some of the neighborhood kids had set up a baseball diamond and were playing a game when he turned onto South Eastern Avenue. Junior stopped the car, and as he watched them, he remembered playing fetch with his dog, his mother drinking iced tea, and smiling from the porch. Then he recalled the beatings, the fear he felt every time his father came home.

Being back on this block bought back memories of the night their house burned to the ground. The images were vivid and unsettling, as if they happened yesterday and not two years ago. Junior saw himself walking through the house, a burning match in hand setting the fire. He admired the flames racing up the walls, consuming everything in its path—the toys from his childhood, clothing, letters and old mail, furniture. How he wished the painful memories burned up like the many pieces of paper scattered on the floor. Seeing the fire raging through the house gave him a measure of satisfaction. Junior hit the gas pedal gently and continued on his way.

That is how he imagined it would have been, had he done it. For Junior, setting that fire would have been a stab at the God who took his mother and the same for his father, but could not claim another's deed. That honor belonged to someone else.

The truth of that night replayed in his mind. Junior decided to make a stop at Pappy's after visiting with Daisy. It was late, but many times, Pappy slept in his chair, the television still on. Junior had come in countless times to put him to bed and clean up a bit before going home. This night, Pappy was already asleep. Junior stumbled through the dark toward the kitchen and poured himself a glass of water.

He stood over the sink at the faucet when he saw a light coming from his old house. Junior couldn't believe his eyes at first, as the glow got bigger and brighter. Soon he realized it was a fire. As the ragged curtains burned away, he saw the man clearly as he passed through each room, torch in hand, setting more fires. The man moved briskly for the front gate and disappeared into the tall rows of corn in the nearby field. Junior recognized his walk and frame. His features came clear in the sporadic flashes of the fire. It was a face he knew very well. It was his father, James.

Junior couldn't believe what he was seeing, but as the blaze engulfed the mulberry tree and came closer to Pappy's home, he decided to call the fire department. He heard his dog, Rex barking loudly, still chained to the fence near the tree. Junior rushed outside to rescue him, grabbing a water hose as he unhooked the dog from the chain. The flames now had engulfed the fence, and Grandma Knight's grapevine as well as some of the branches stretching over to Pappy's home. He turned the hose on full blast and began spraying the flames as a crowd of concerned neighbors gathered.

"Junior, where's your father? Is he in the house?" Someone shouted to him. It was Tamayo, hobbling on one crutch with his son, Hector. They knew James had been staying in the old house after they moved to the new apartment.

"I don't think so," Junior lied, not knowing why.

Tamayo stepped closer to the flame, frantically calling out for James.

"Get back!" Junior shouted, but Tamayo didn't hear him. Suddenly, window glass cracked loose and crashed to the ground below. Tamayo took another step towards the fire, calling for James before Hector pulled him away. The red lights of the fire truck circled as it approached.

Junior had lived with the secret for two years, not telling a soul, not his brother, not Pappy, not Daisy, and not even his father. The longer he held onto it, the easier it was to carry. His father going to jail for arson was not the answer. He still had to live in Brawley. Secrets were hard to keep in this small town, so telling anyone was out of the question. The whispers had already begun around town, and he would not fan those flames. The thought of taunting his father with this knowledge, blurting out a hint at inappropriate times, had crossed his mind. *'What a fitting punishment that would have been,'* he smiled. But Junior knew better. He realized this would only make him more like his father—vengeful and cruel. That was something Junior never wanted. Deep down, Junior did have some sense of respect for his name, for his father, and he protected it.

On his way back from Tamayo's, Junior spied Pappy working in the yard trimming tree branches.

"About time you cleaned this up!" He laughed.

"Wouldn't have to if you took care of it," Pappy replied.

"How are you doing, Grandpa?"

"I'm fine. How's Hector? You get all the papers signed?"

"Yes. All done." He answered dryly.

He followed his grandfather around the yard, stopping in front of the charred grapevine. Seeing the burnt limbs from the fire made him sad.

"What you looking at?" Pappy asked as Junior inspected it further.

"Some buds are growing here." Junior pointed to an emerald green spud breaking through the blackened branches.

"You don't say. Look at that. That's a tough ole vine."

"I thought it was dead, Pappy."

A caterpillar crawled over Junior's shoe, surprising him a bit. He scooped it up with his hand and let it crawl over his arm.

"Chrysalis," Junior whispered.

"Your mother loved playing with them bugs too," Pappy laughed.

"Yeah, I remember," Junior answered.

A few weeks later, Junior walked into the county clerk's office and paid the back taxes owed on the property. He filed for a building permit, using the money from his father's benefits to buy the supplies, and with the help of his neighbors, started rebuilding the home. Junior began right away though he didn't know a thing about construction. He enlisted his friend, Ritchie Sosa, who worked in that industry, to help.

He had a simple design with spacious rooms and a kitchen: a large porch overlooking the garden and the street. The house began to take shape with each passing day and week until completion.

Pappy was ecstatic about Junior's progress. "You did it, boy," Pappy beamed with pride. "Just lay on a few coats of paint."

"Could use some grass too," Junior laughed, looking back at the bare earth in the yard.

"One thing at a time!" Pappy replied.

That Saturday, Junior and his friends started painting. A neighbor supplied them with an ice chest full of beer and sodas. Someone plugged in a stereo and turned up the music so loud they could barely hear each other speak. People honked their horns as they passed by on the street, happy to see him back in the neighborhood.

Pappy had a touch of déjà vu as he slathered on the paint. It was almost twenty-five years ago that he was standing in that same place, doing the same thing for his daughter. He smiled at his dumb luck.

Suddenly, someone shouted at Junior.

"Look at the mess you made. Just wasting paint."

"What are you doing here?" Junior asked.

"It's obvious you need my help," Leroy explained.

Junior shook his head and smile, placing his bucket down and extending his hand. Leroy gripped it tightly.

"You're here to work, right?" he asked in mock seriousness.

Leroy poured some more paint into the bucket and got to work. "This is how it should be done."

A rush of emotions filled Pappy's heart as he watched the two young men speaking to one another. It was a miracle in his mind. "I'll be damned," he whispered to himself.

HEADED EAST – 1975

Pappy and Junior watched as Leroy loaded a suitcase into the trunk of the car.

"Where are you going first?" Junior asked.

"I don't know," Leroy shrugged. "I've always wanted to see Mount Rushmore."

Junior pressed his lips together. "Well, you know you've always got a home here if you want."

Leroy recollected a conversation he had with his father about how he defined home. It made him smile. "I don't know if I'll be back, to be honest."

"You will," Junior answered quickly. "I'm getting married next June. You have to come back for that."

"Did you invite Daisy's mom? You know she doesn't like you *Negritos*!" Leroy joked.

"Shut up!" Junior laughed. "She's planning the whole thing. Aunt Sarah and Junie are coming. She's out of the hospital now."

"For real? That's good news."

"So, just say you're coming."

Leroy chuckled and looked over at his car. "I better get going before it's too hot to cross that desert."

Junior nodded at him.

"You be careful, Leroy," Pappy added, touching his grandson's arm.

"I will," he replied, giving him a big hug. He then turned to his brother and held out his hand which Junior promptly ignored, throwing his arms around his younger brother. Junior held Leroy tightly for several moments before letting go.

Pappy looked on at the two of them. He hadn't trusted they'd ever reconcile, given the vitriol that surrounded them when they buried their father. But they had come a long way. *'Forgiveness can do that,'* he thought to himself. He was happy for Leroy, remembering the wanderlust he felt leaving Georgia. The excitement of seeing the Mississippi and the open ranges of the West were memories he'd always treasure. He wished he could go too, but Pappy knew the boy had something to find, and he had to discover it for himself. He wouldn't burden Leroy with caring for another old man. Pappy knew better. For some reason, he did not fear for his grandson's safety. Gone were the apprehensions that informed his early years. A shift had occurred in his view of the world, or maybe his grandson was ready for manhood.

Leroy exhaled, nodding to them both before getting into the car. He adjusted his seat one last time, and then picked up the small black, rectangular-shaped urn that held his father's ashes. Leroy placed it in the passenger seat and secured it with the safety belt. He then unfolded a piece of paper that lay on the dashboard and checked it once more before folding it back up again. On it were places his father had found glory and happiness, locations he gleaned from the newspaper clippings in his uncle's old suitcase.

Etched in Leroy's brain were the names—Saskatoon, Minot, Sioux City, Muskogee, and Wichita along with many others. He hoped being there and seeing them through new eyes would help him make sense of this world and his place in it. Maybe he would find someplace he too could call home. Now was the right time to go. Leroy took that small part of his father with him. He planned to leave bits of his ashes wherever he traveled. His father's legacy was now secure. Leroy waved at his brother and grandfather one last time as he put the car in gear and started up the road.

A short time later, Leroy made the turn onto Highway 78 heading east toward the edge of town. His first stop was Hondo, Texas, and to the old family farm where his father grew up. To his right, the Brawley city limits sign came into view. His father had come to this obstacle many times – a barrier that he could never breach. But not his son. Leroy pressed on the gas pedal, leaving Brawley and that road sign in his wake. He sped off down the highway and into the rising sun.

ACKNOWLEDGMENTS

I want to thank all those involved in getting my first novel published, no matter how small the contribution—you are not forgotten. I also want to thank a few special people whose energy, honesty, wisdom, and time helped me get to this point—Reverend Doris Davis and Denise "Tboz" Boswell. A special thanks to Carol Taylor, Dan McAdoo, Heather Kowalski, and Karen Sibert, for getting me across the finish line. Thank you all very much. I could not have done it without you.

Printed in the United States
by Baker & Taylor Publisher Services